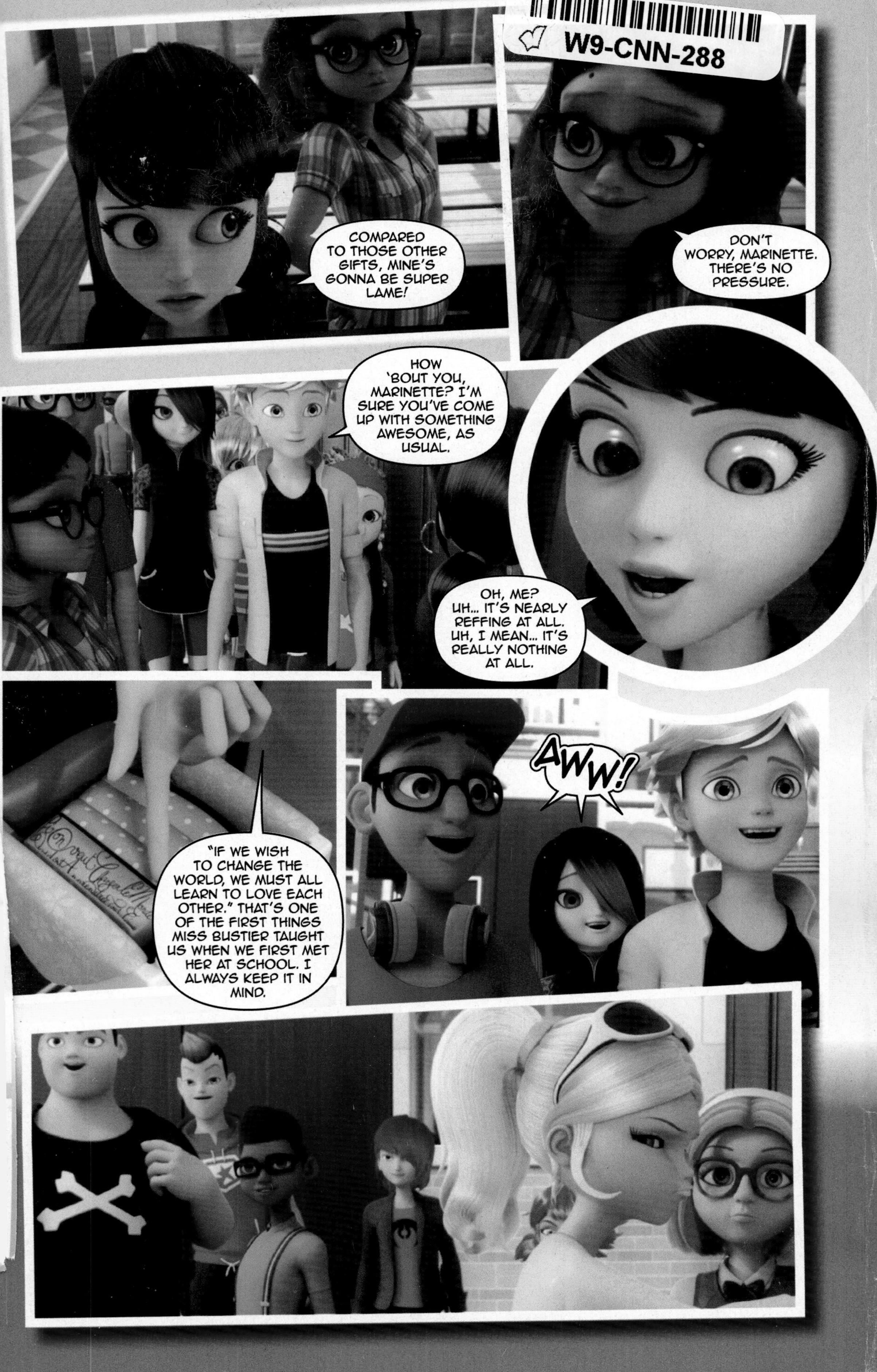
COMPARED TO THOSE OTHER GIFTS, MINE'S GONNA BE SUPER LAME!
DON'T WORRY, MARINETTE. THERE'S NO PRESSURE.
HOW 'BOUT YOU, MARINETTE? I'M SURE YOU'VE COME UP WITH SOMETHING AWESOME, AS USUAL.
OH, ME? UH... IT'S NEARLY REFFING AT ALL. UH, I MEAN... IT'S REALLY NOTHING AT ALL.
"IF WE WISH TO CHANGE THE WORLD, WE MUST ALL LEARN TO LOVE EACH OTHER." THAT'S ONE OF THE FIRST THINGS MISS BUSTIER TAUGHT US WHEN WE FIRST MET HER AT SCHOOL. I ALWAYS KEEP IT IN MIND.
AWW!

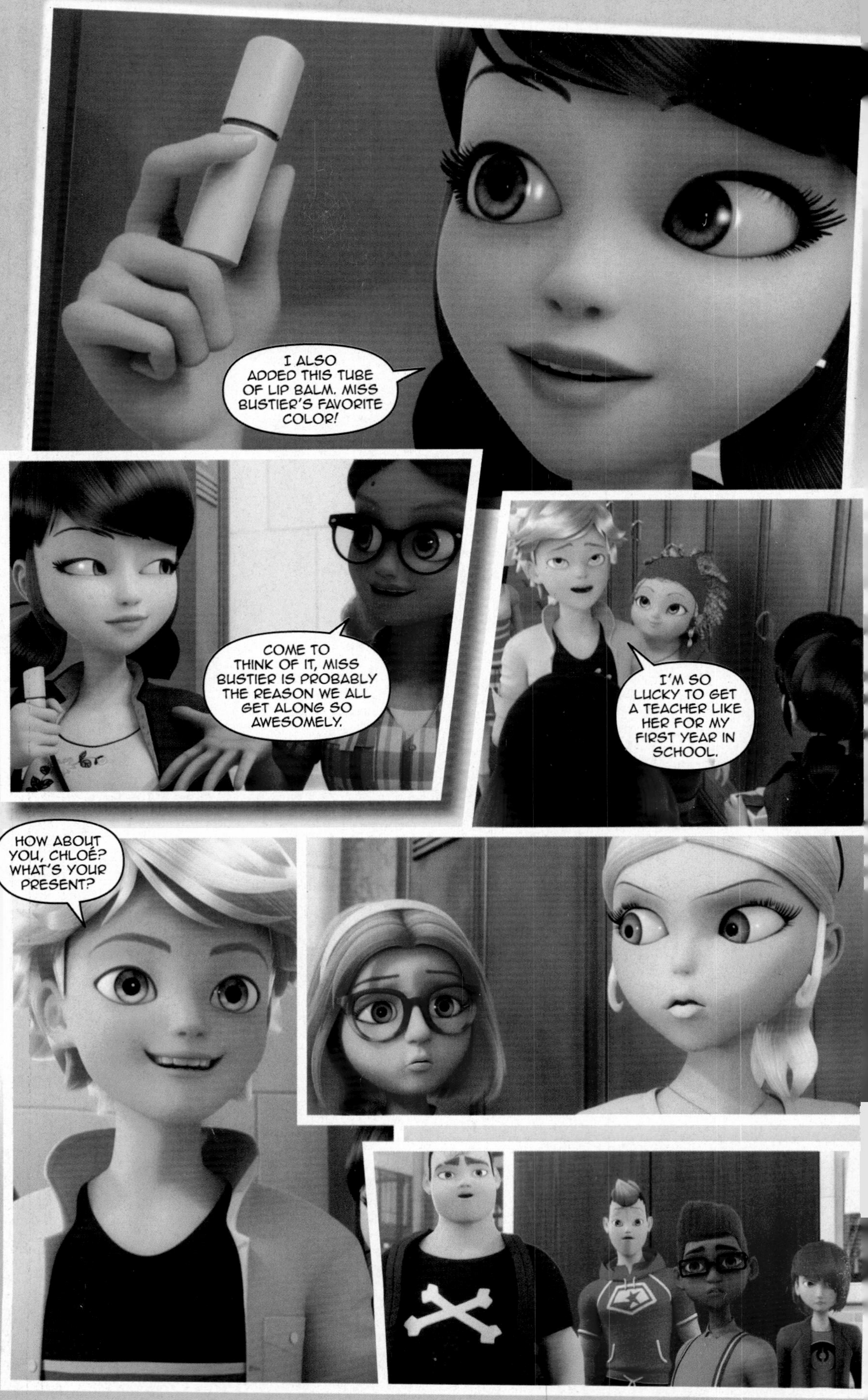
I ALSO ADDED THIS TUBE OF LIP BALM. MISS BUSTIER'S FAVORITE COLOR!
COME TO THINK OF IT, MISS BUSTIER IS PROBABLY THE REASON WE ALL GET ALONG SO AWESOMELY.
I'M SO LUCKY TO GET A TEACHER LIKE HER FOR MY FIRST YEAR IN SCHOOL.
HOW ABOUT YOU, CHLOÉ? WHAT'S YOUR PRESENT?

Zombizou

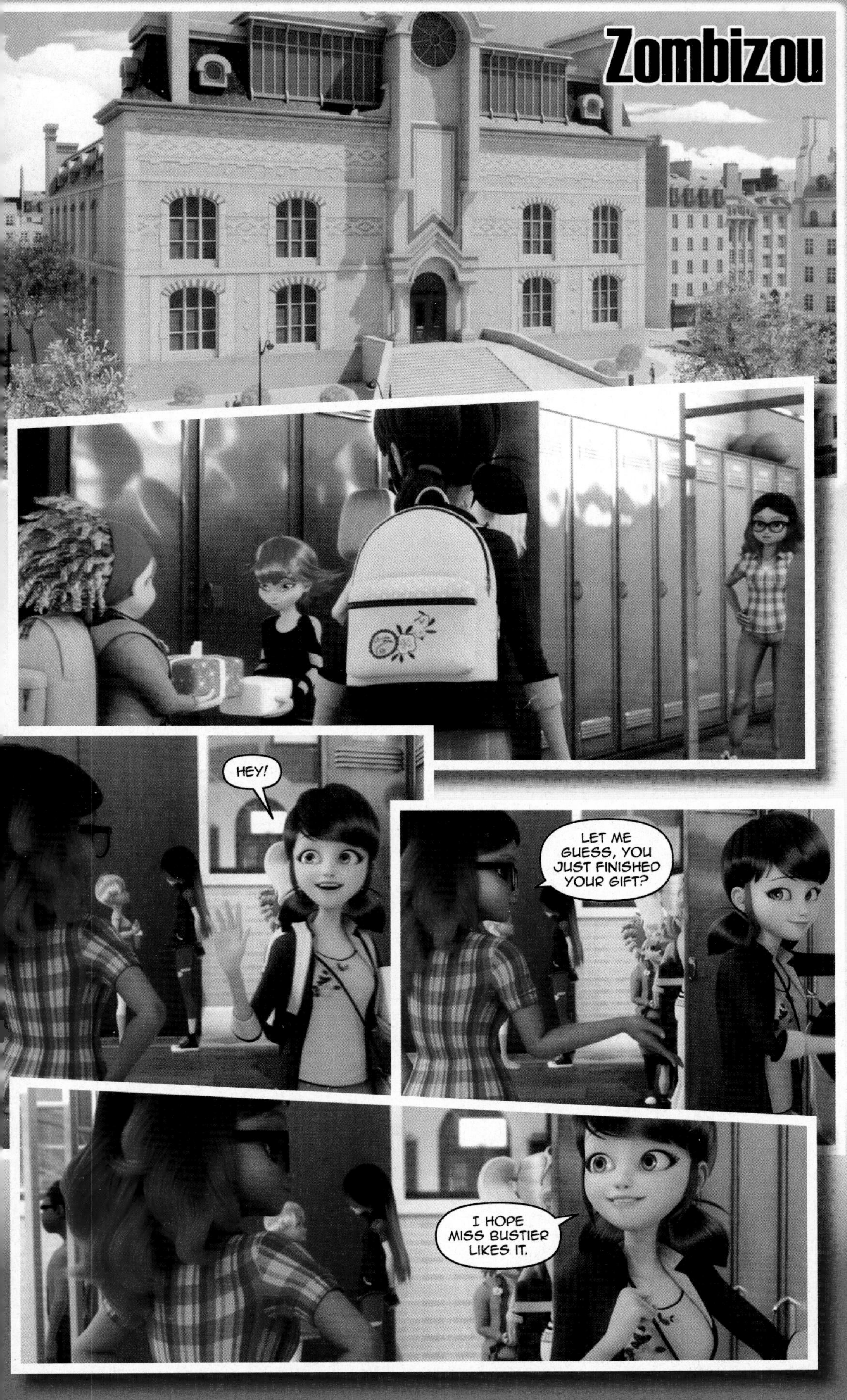
HEY!
LET ME GUESS, YOU JUST FINISHED YOUR GIFT?
I HOPE MISS BUSTIER LIKES IT.

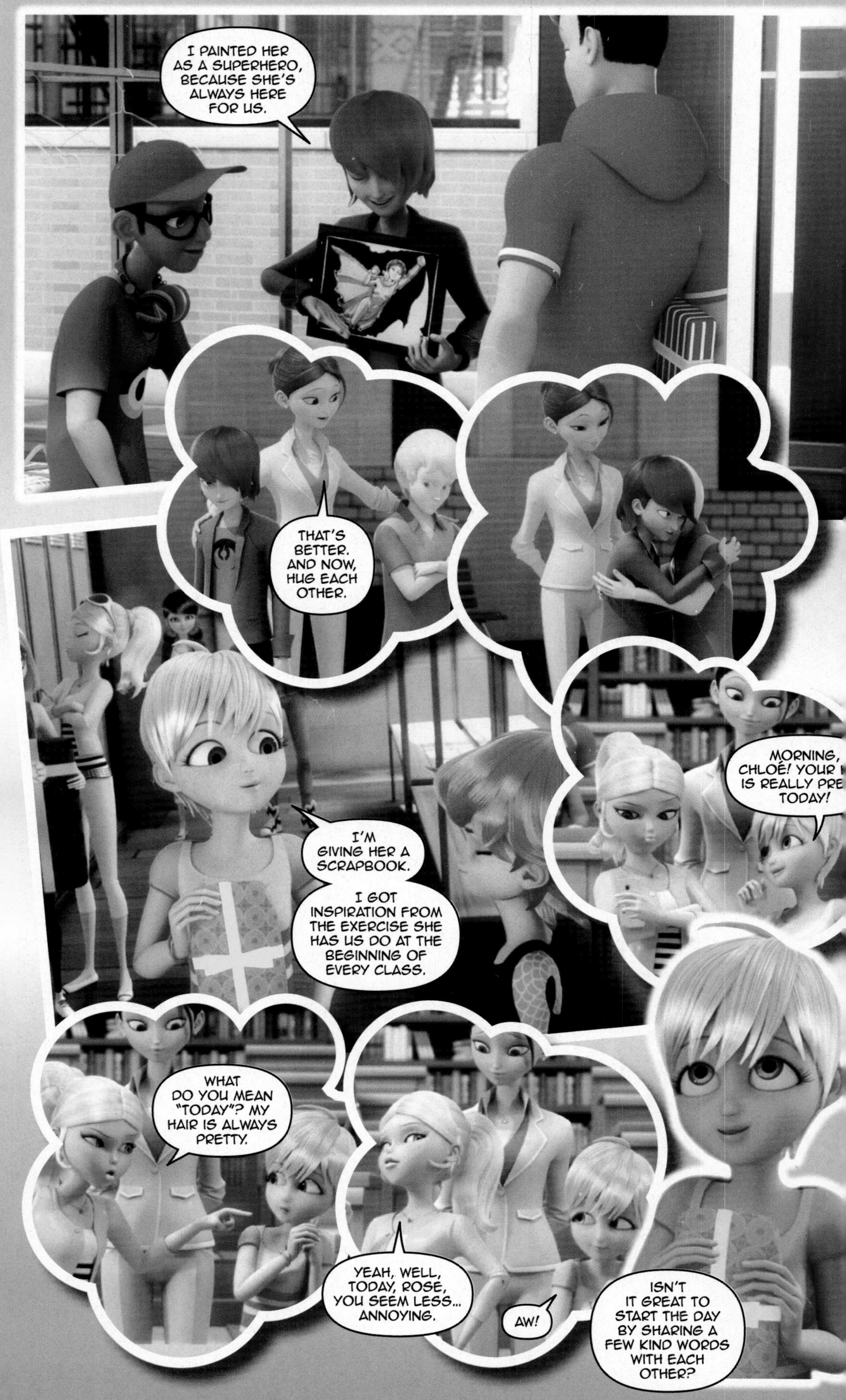
I PAINTED HER AS A SUPERHERO, BECAUSE SHE'S ALWAYS HERE FOR US.
THAT'S BETTER. AND NOW, HUG EACH OTHER.
I'M GIVING HER A SCRAPBOOK.
I GOT INSPIRATION FROM THE EXERCISE SHE HAS US DO AT THE BEGINNING OF EVERY CLASS.
MORNING, CHLOÉ! YOUR IS REALLY PRE TODAY!
WHAT DO YOU MEAN "TODAY"? MY HAIR IS ALWAYS PRETTY.
YEAH, WELL, TODAY, ROSE, YOU SEEM LESS... ANNOYING.
AW!
ISN'T IT GREAT TO START THE DAY BY SHARING A FEW KIND WORDS WITH EACH OTHER?

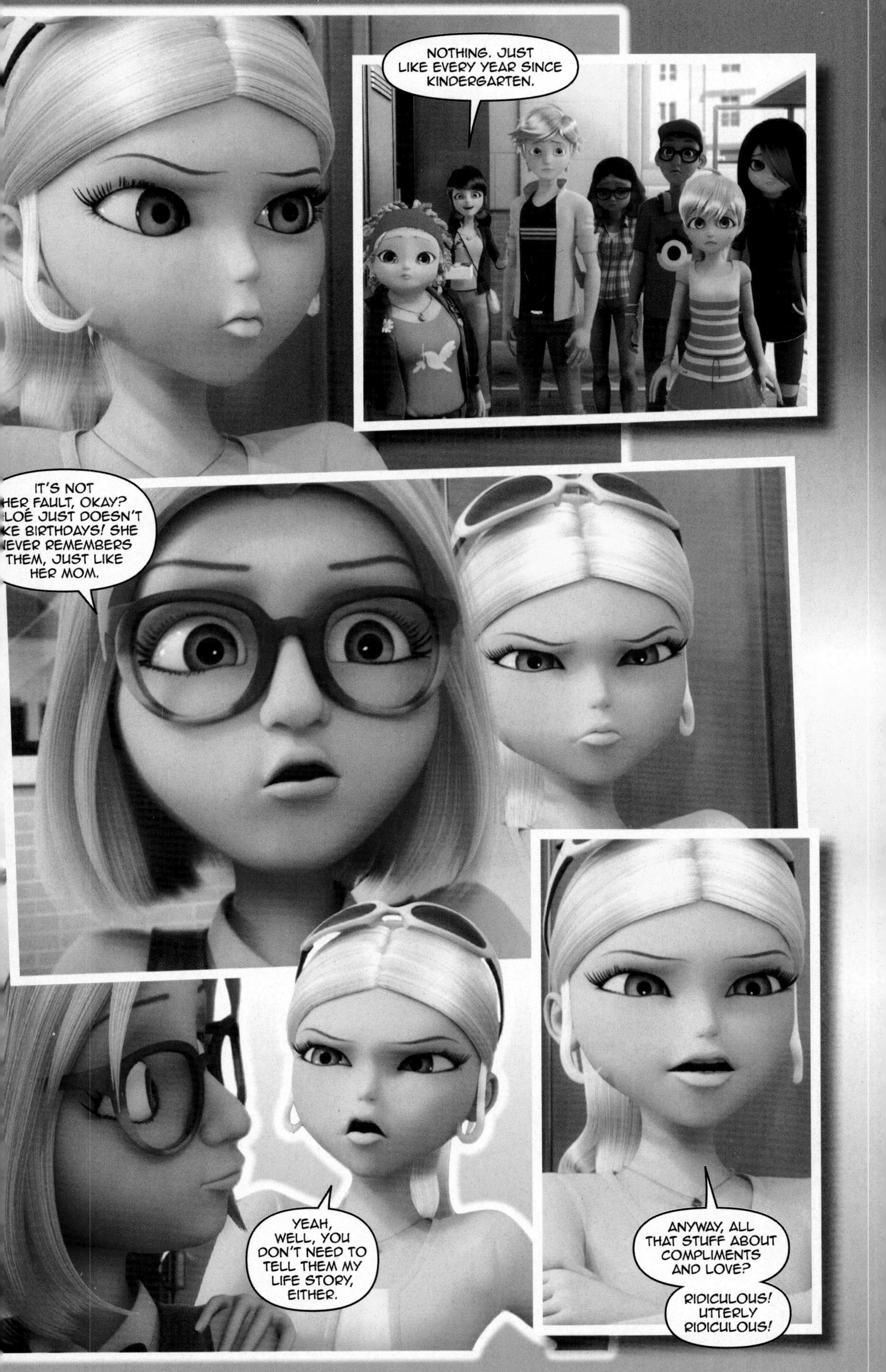
NOTHING. JUST LIKE EVERY YEAR SINCE KINDERGARTEN.
IT'S NOT HER FAULT, OKAY? LOÉ JUST DOESN'T KE BIRTHDAYS! SHE NEVER REMEMBERS THEM, JUST LIKE HER MOM.
YEAH, WELL, YOU DON'T NEED TO TELL THEM MY LIFE STORY, EITHER.
ANYWAY, ALL THAT STUFF ABOUT COMPLIMENTS AND LOVE?
RIDICULOUS! UTTERLY RIDICULOUS!

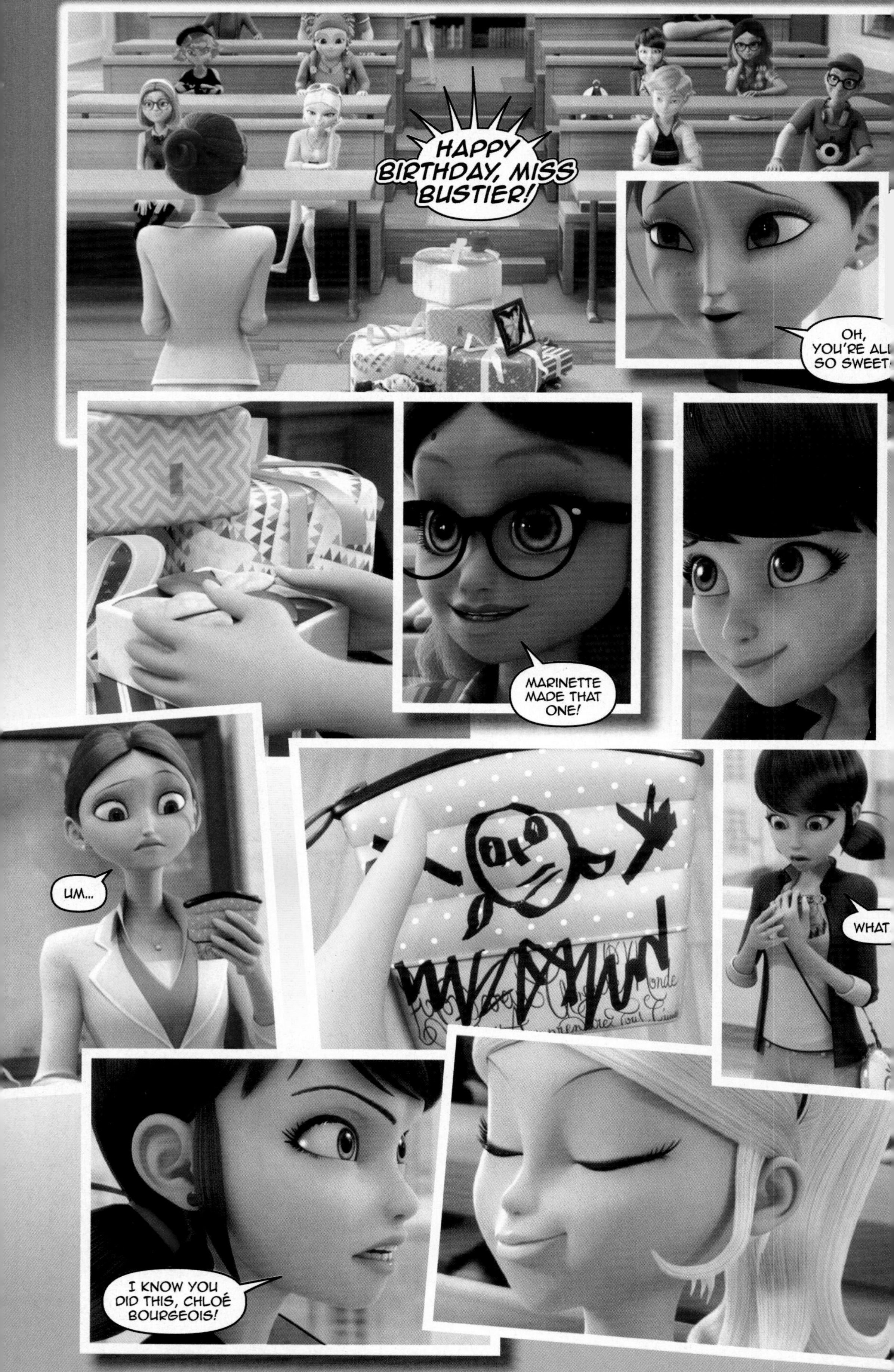
HAPPY BIRTHDAY, MISS BUSTIER!
OH, YOU'RE ALL SO SWEET
MARINETTE MADE THAT ONE!
UM...
WHAT
I KNOW YOU DID THIS, CHLOÉ BOURGEOIS!

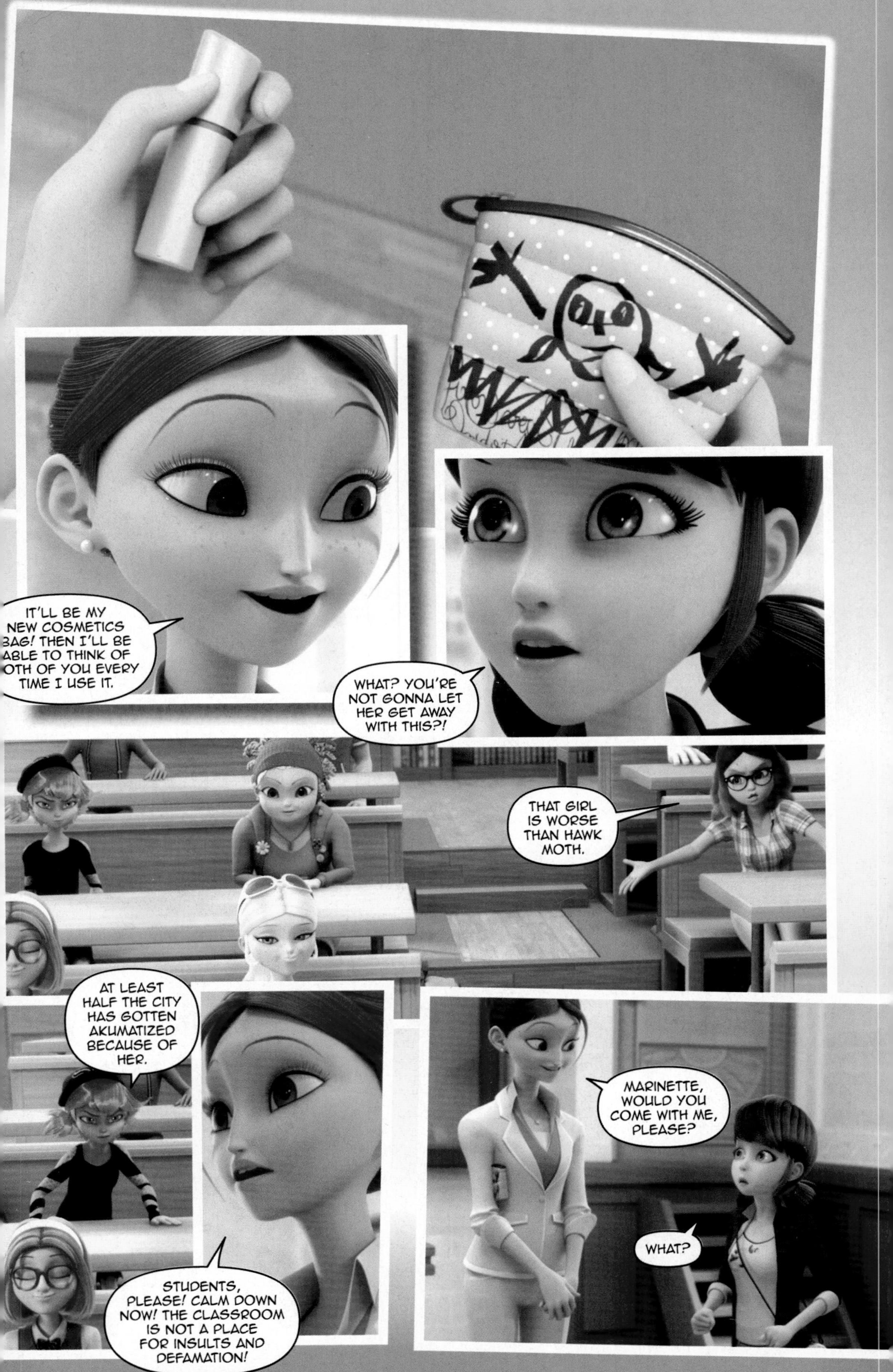
IT'LL BE MY NEW COSMETICS BAG! THEN I'LL BE ABLE TO THINK OF BOTH OF YOU EVERY TIME I USE IT.
WHAT? YOU'RE NOT GONNA LET HER GET AWAY WITH THIS?!
THAT GIRL IS WORSE THAN HAWK MOTH.
AT LEAST HALF THE CITY HAS GOTTEN AKUMATIZED BECAUSE OF HER.
STUDENTS, PLEASE! CALM DOWN NOW! THE CLASSROOM IS NOT A PLACE FOR INSULTS AND DEFAMATION!
MARINETTE, WOULD YOU COME WITH ME, PLEASE?
WHAT?

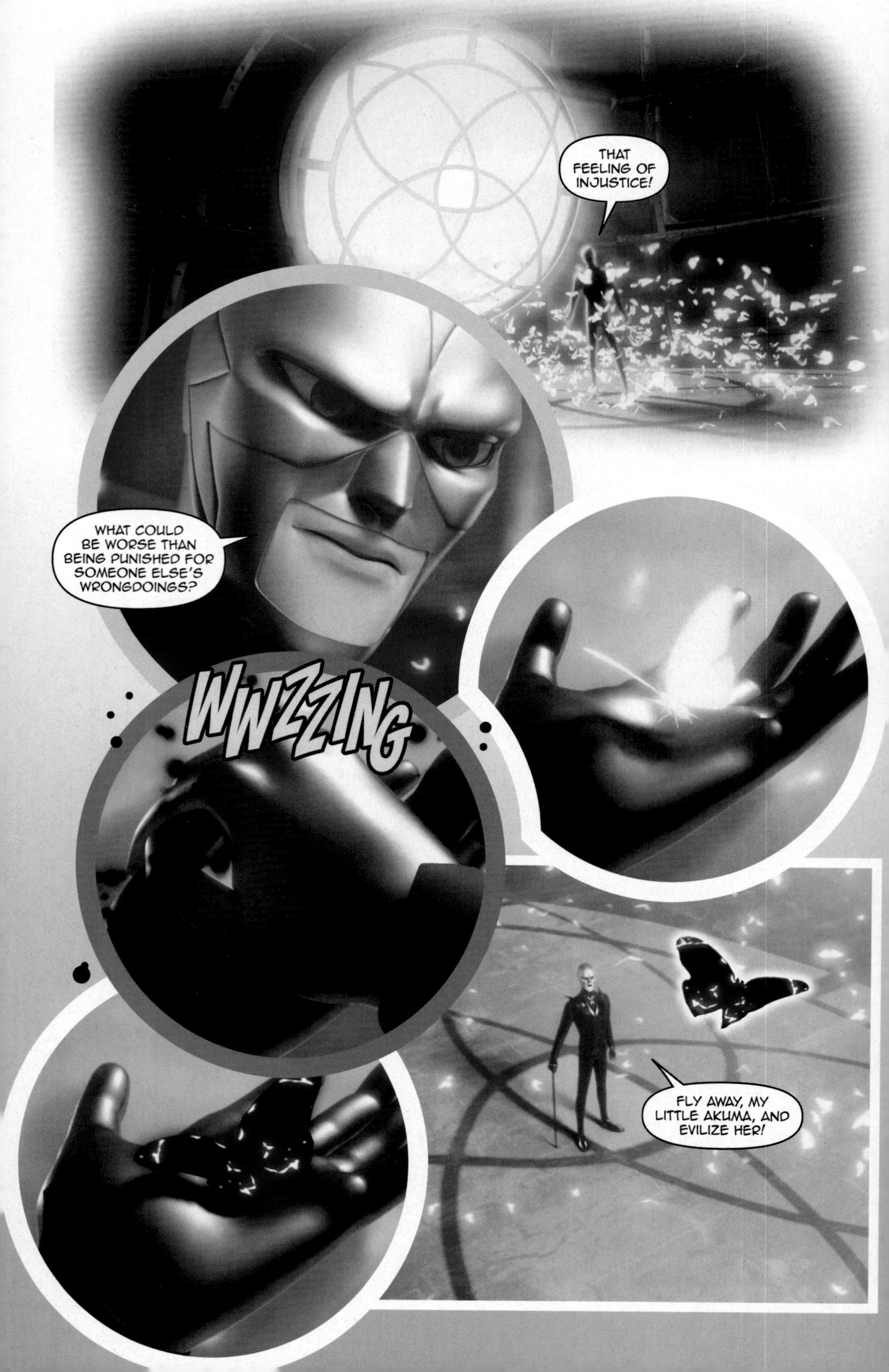
THAT FEELING OF INJUSTICE!
WHAT COULD BE WORSE THAN BEING PUNISHED FOR SOMEONE ELSE'S WRONGDOINGS?
WWZZING
FLY AWAY, MY LITTLE AKUMA, AND EVILIZE HER!

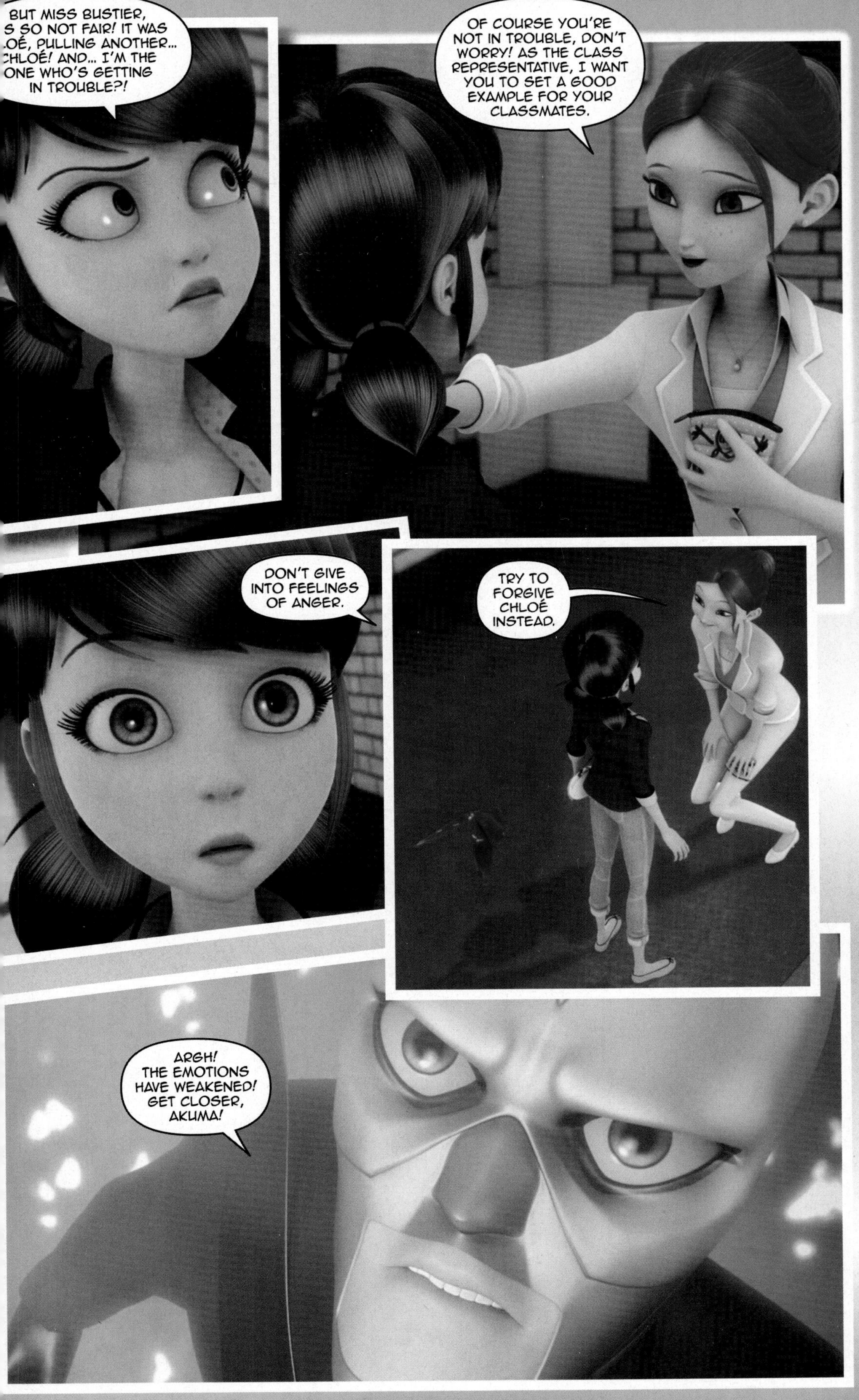

BUT MISS BUSTIER, S SO NOT FAIR! IT WAS LOÉ, PULLING ANOTHER... CHLOÉ! AND... I'M THE ONE WHO'S GETTING IN TROUBLE?!
OF COURSE YOU'RE NOT IN TROUBLE, DON'T WORRY! AS THE CLASS REPRESENTATIVE, I WANT YOU TO SET A GOOD EXAMPLE FOR YOUR CLASSMATES.
DON'T GIVE INTO FEELINGS OF ANGER.
TRY TO FORGIVE CHLOÉ INSTEAD.
ARGH! THE EMOTIONS HAVE WEAKENED! GET CLOSER, AKUMA!

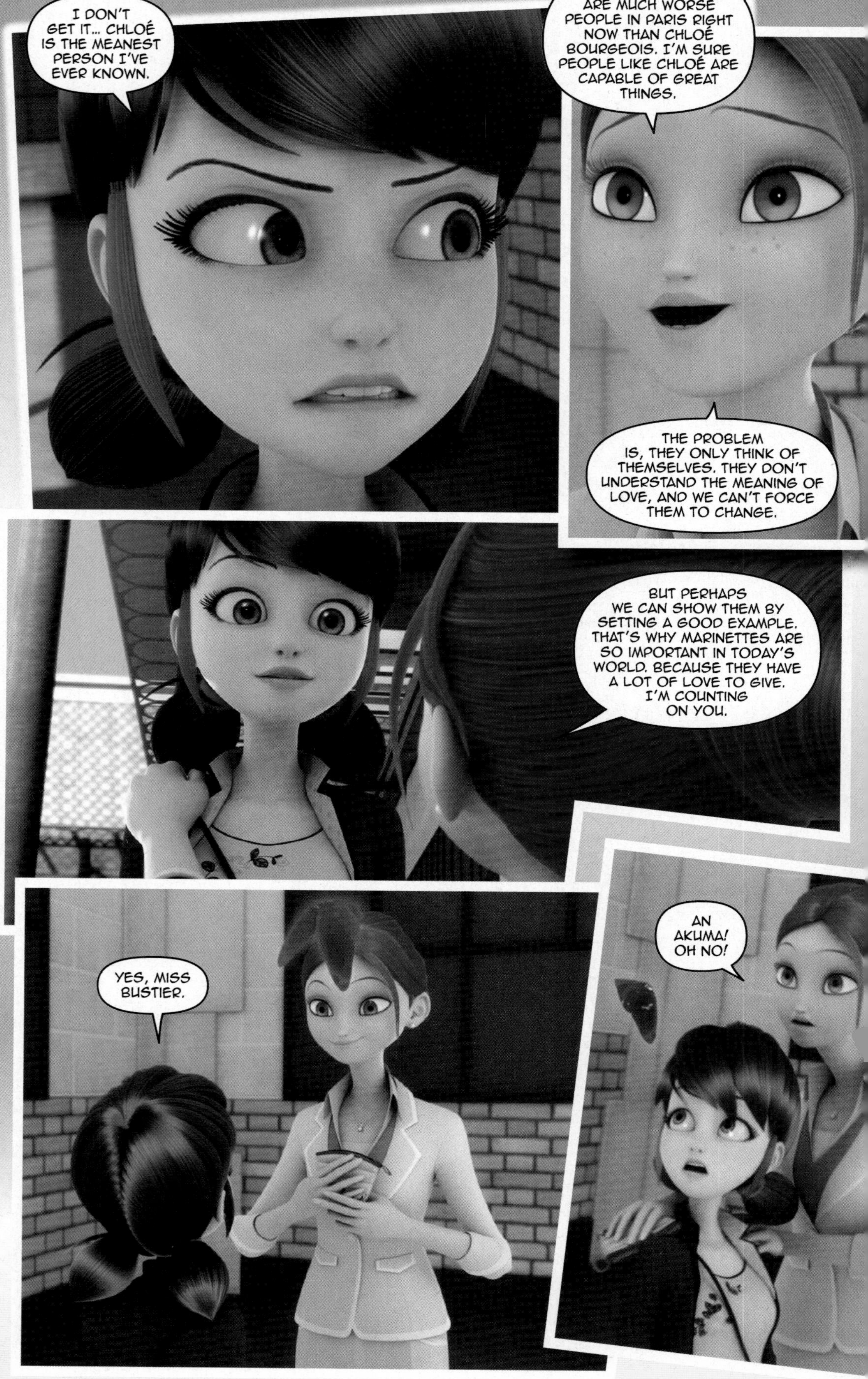
I DON'T GET IT... CHLOÉ IS THE MEANEST PERSON I'VE EVER KNOWN.
COME ON... THERE ARE MUCH WORSE PEOPLE IN PARIS RIGHT NOW THAN CHLOÉ BOURGEOIS. I'M SURE PEOPLE LIKE CHLOÉ ARE CAPABLE OF GREAT THINGS.
THE PROBLEM IS, THEY ONLY THINK OF THEMSELVES. THEY DON'T UNDERSTAND THE MEANING OF LOVE, AND WE CAN'T FORCE THEM TO CHANGE.
BUT PERHAPS WE CAN SHOW THEM BY SETTING A GOOD EXAMPLE. THAT'S WHY MARINETTES ARE SO IMPORTANT IN TODAY'S WORLD. BECAUSE THEY HAVE A LOT OF LOVE TO GIVE. I'M COUNTING ON YOU.
YES, MISS BUSTIER.
AN AKUMA! OH NO!

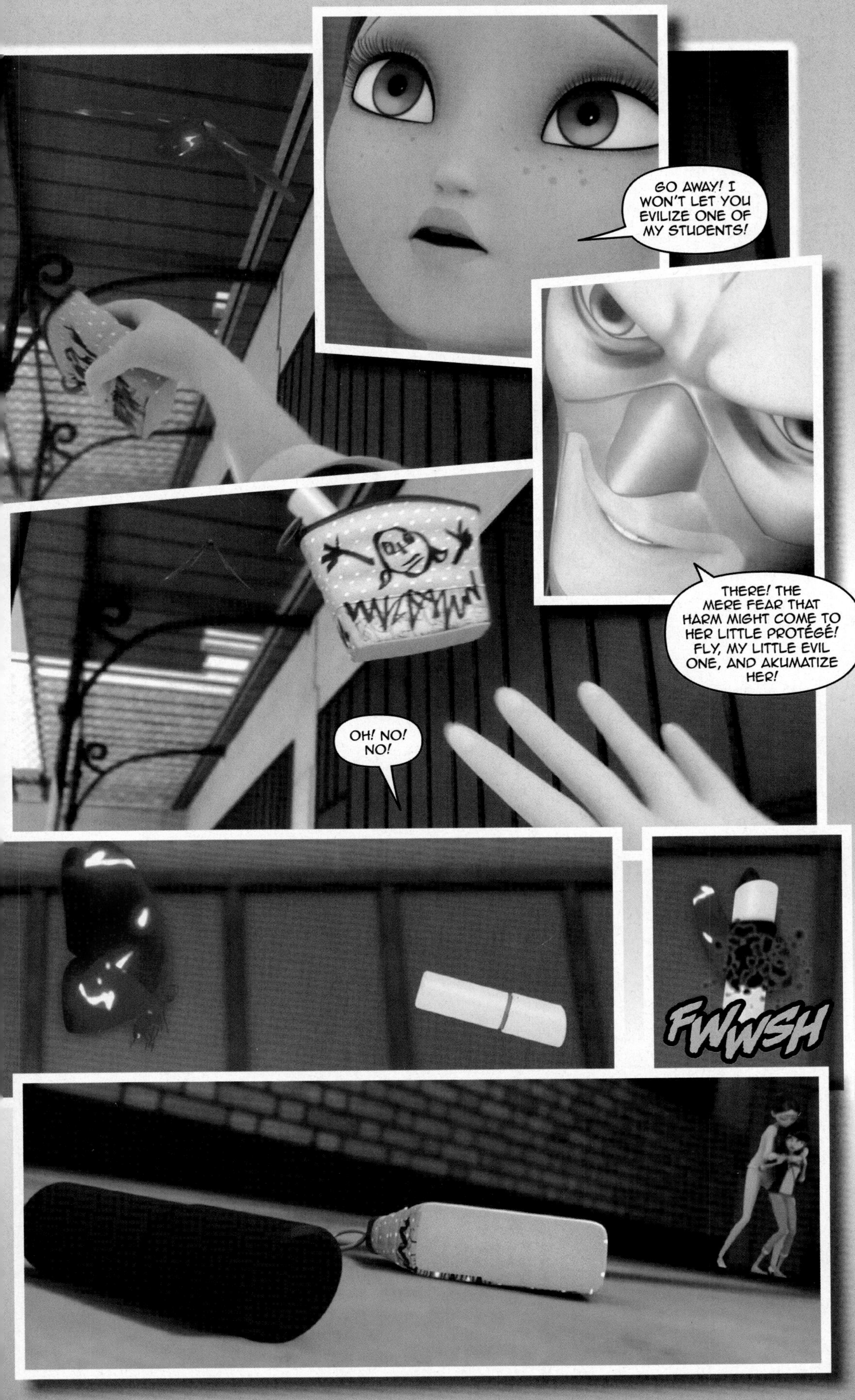
GO AWAY! I WON'T LET YOU EVILIZE ONE OF MY STUDENTS!
THERE! THE MERE FEAR THAT HARM MIGHT COME TO HER LITTLE PROTÉGÉ! FLY, MY LITTLE EVIL ONE, AND AKUMATIZE HER!
OH! NO! NO!
FWWSH

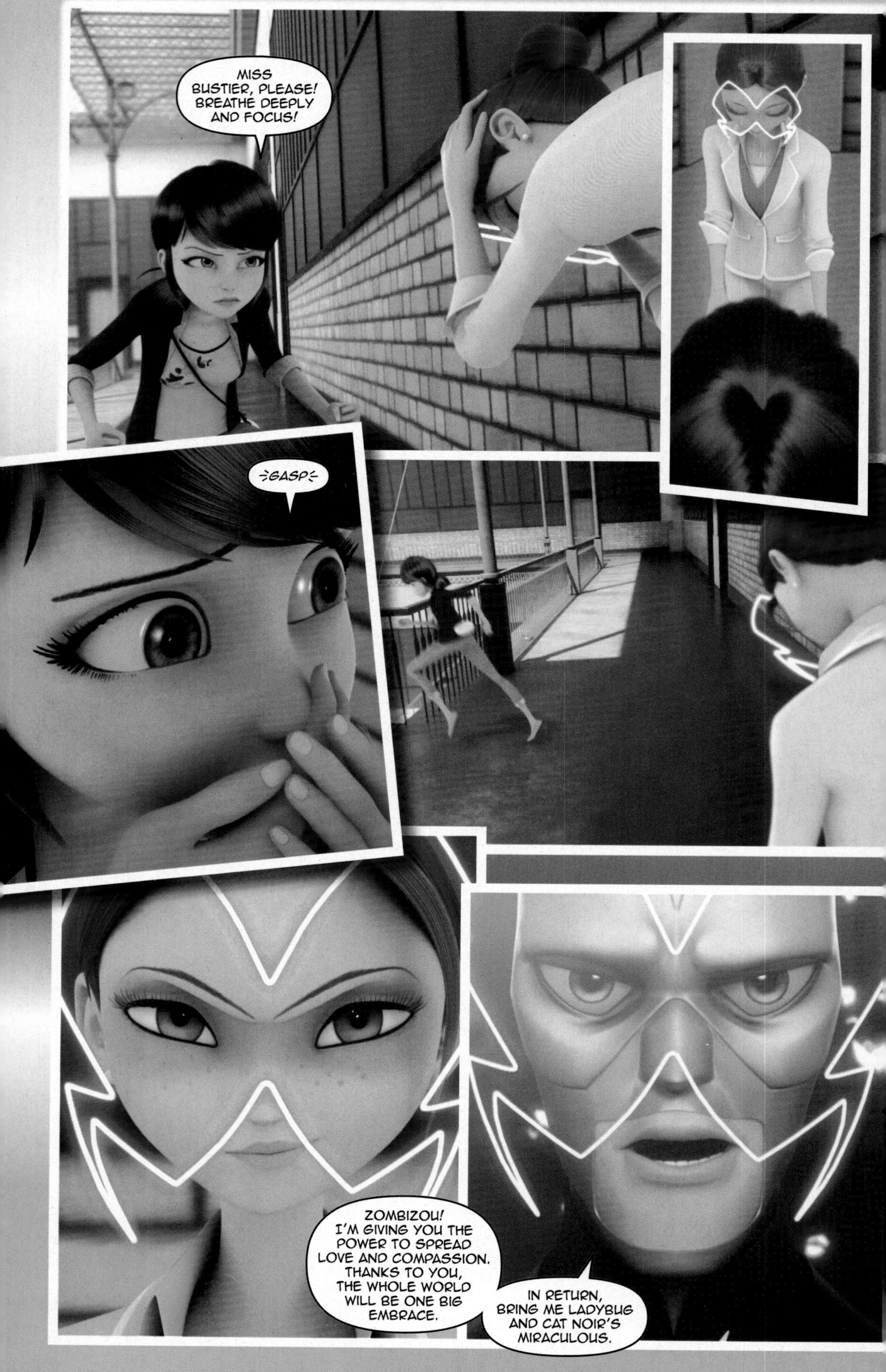
MISS BUSTIER, PLEASE! BREATHE DEEPLY AND FOCUS!
GASP
ZOMBIZOU! I'M GIVING YOU THE POWER TO SPREAD LOVE AND COMPASSION. THANKS TO YOU, THE WHOLE WORLD WILL BE ONE BIG EMBRACE.
IN RETURN, BRING ME LADYBUG AND CAT NOIR'S MIRACULOUS.

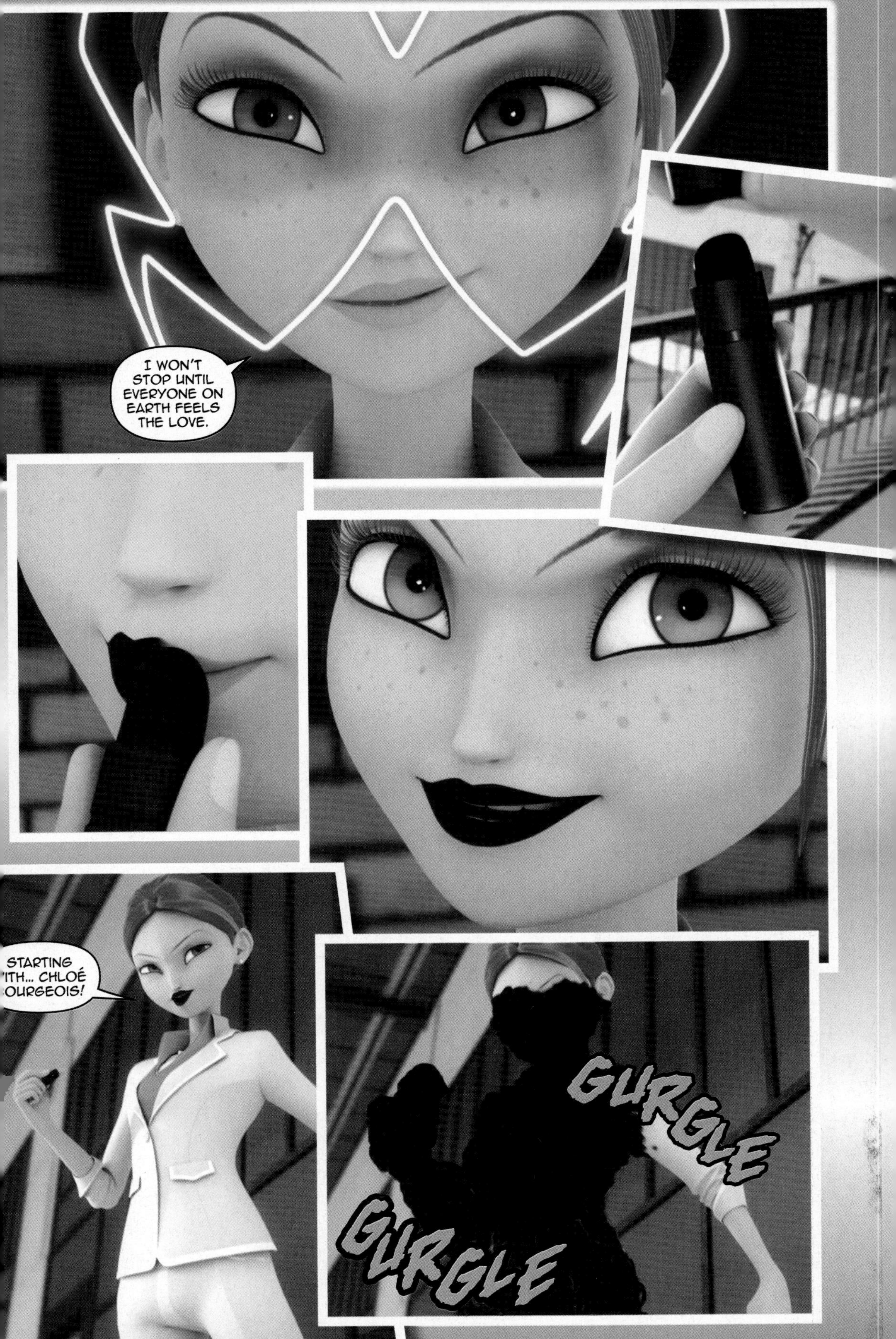
I WON'T STOP UNTIL EVERYONE ON EARTH FEELS THE LOVE.
STARTING 'ITH... CHLOÉ OURGEOIS!
GURGLE
GURGLE

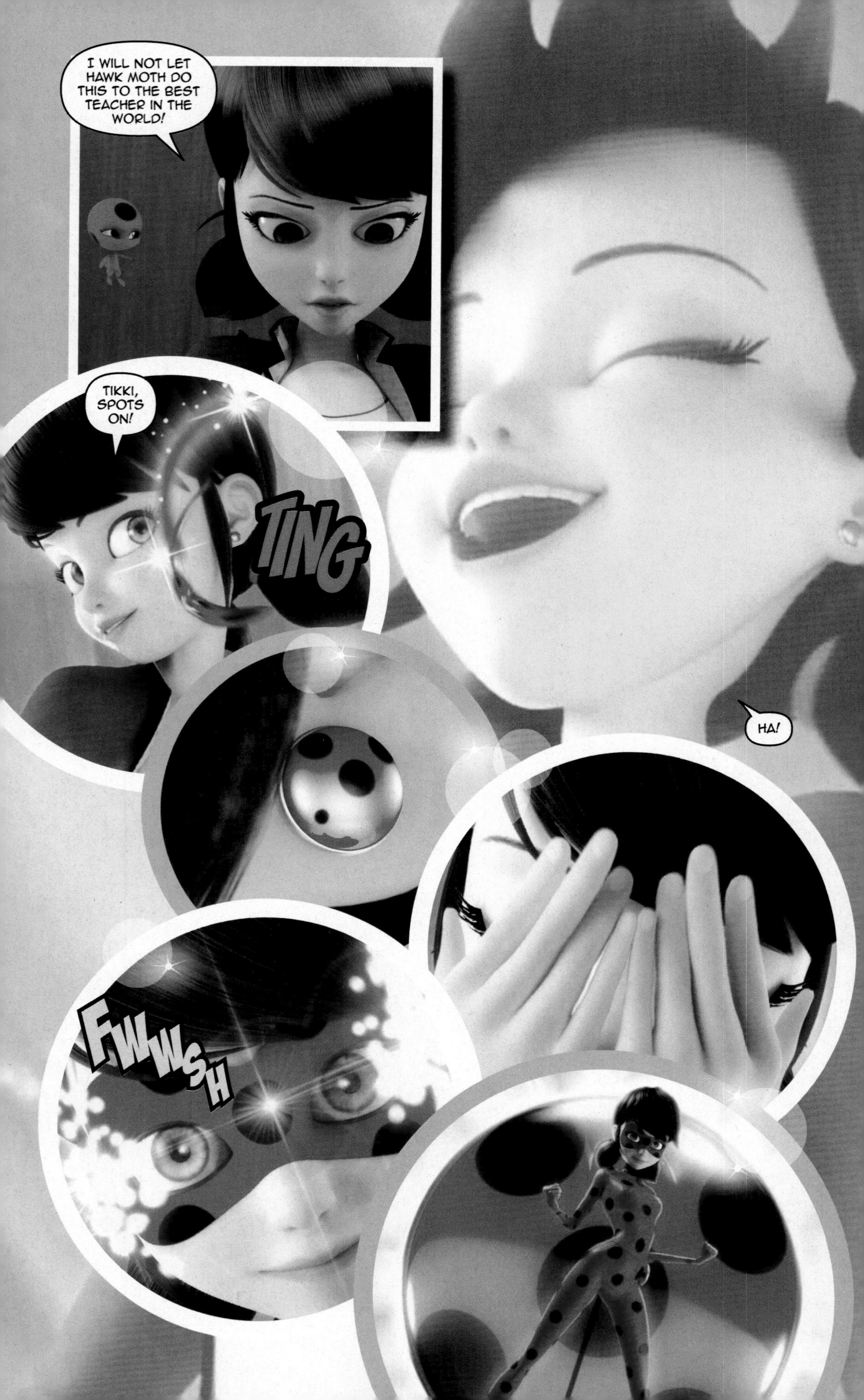
I WILL NOT LET HAWK MOTH DO THIS TO THE BEST TEACHER IN THE WORLD!
TIKKI, SPOTS ON!
TING
HA!
FWWSH

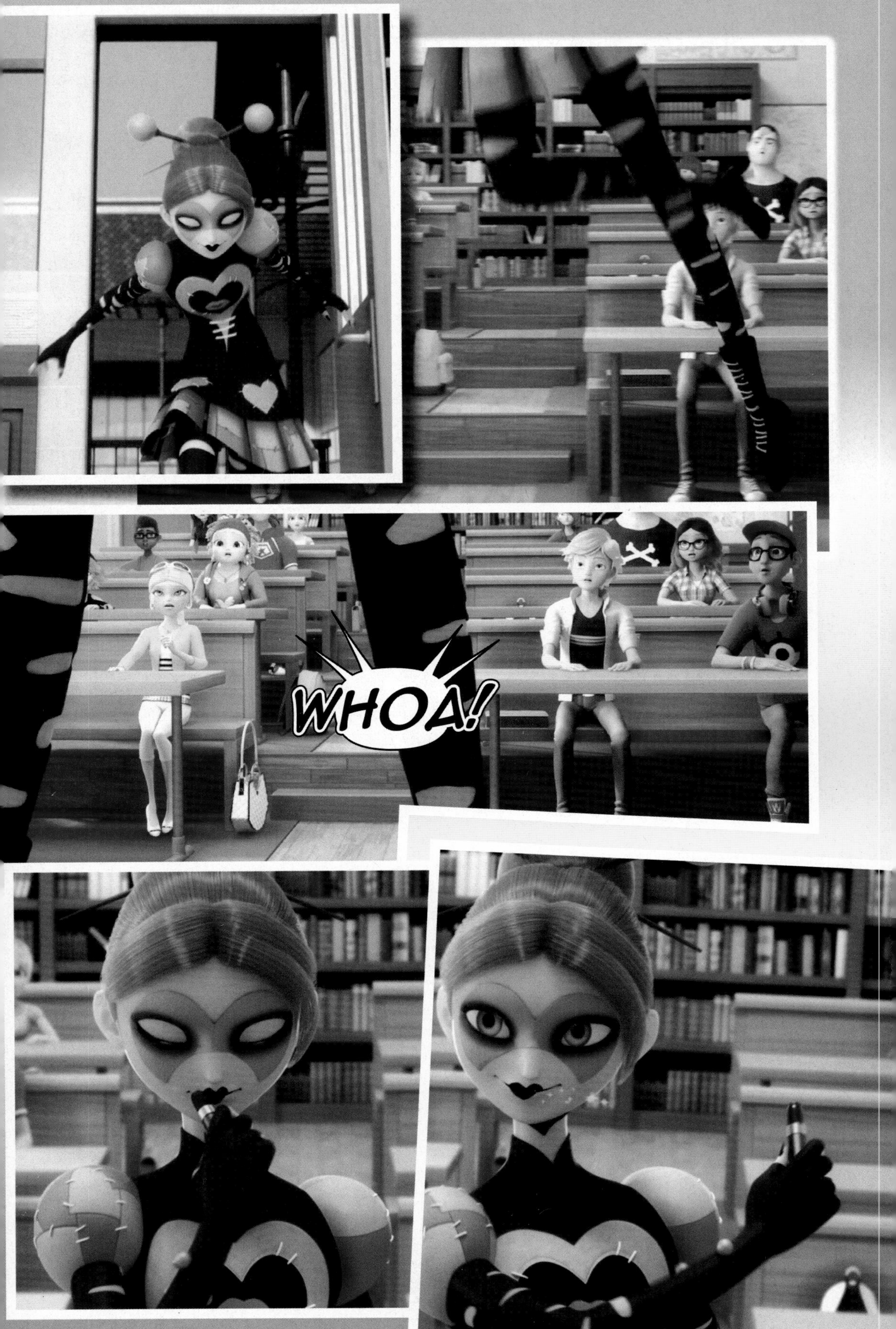
WHOA!

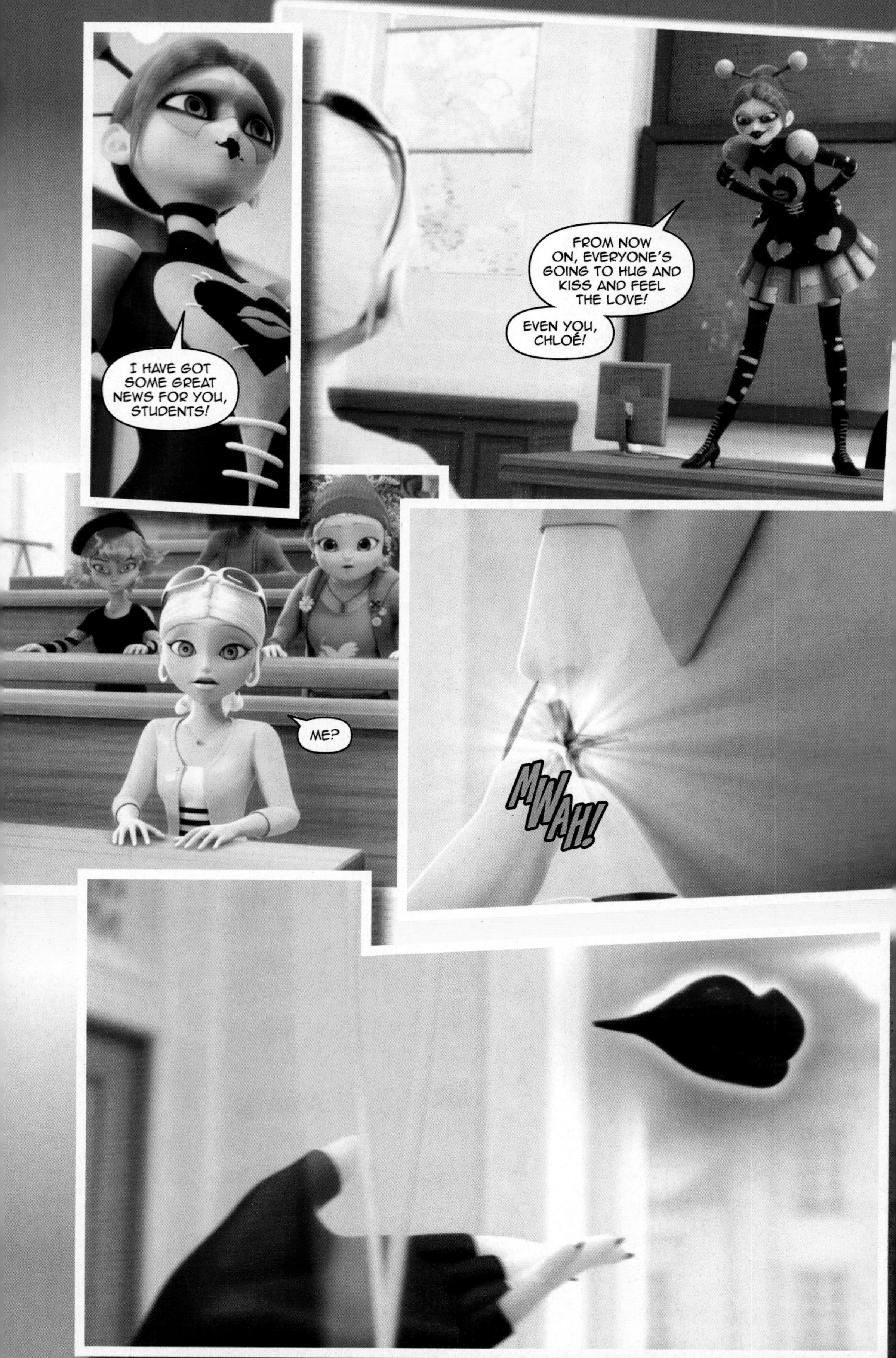
I HAVE GOT SOME GREAT NEWS FOR YOU, STUDENTS!
FROM NOW ON, EVERYONE'S GOING TO HUG AND KISS AND FEEL THE LOVE!
EVEN YOU, CHLOÉ!
ME?
MWAH!

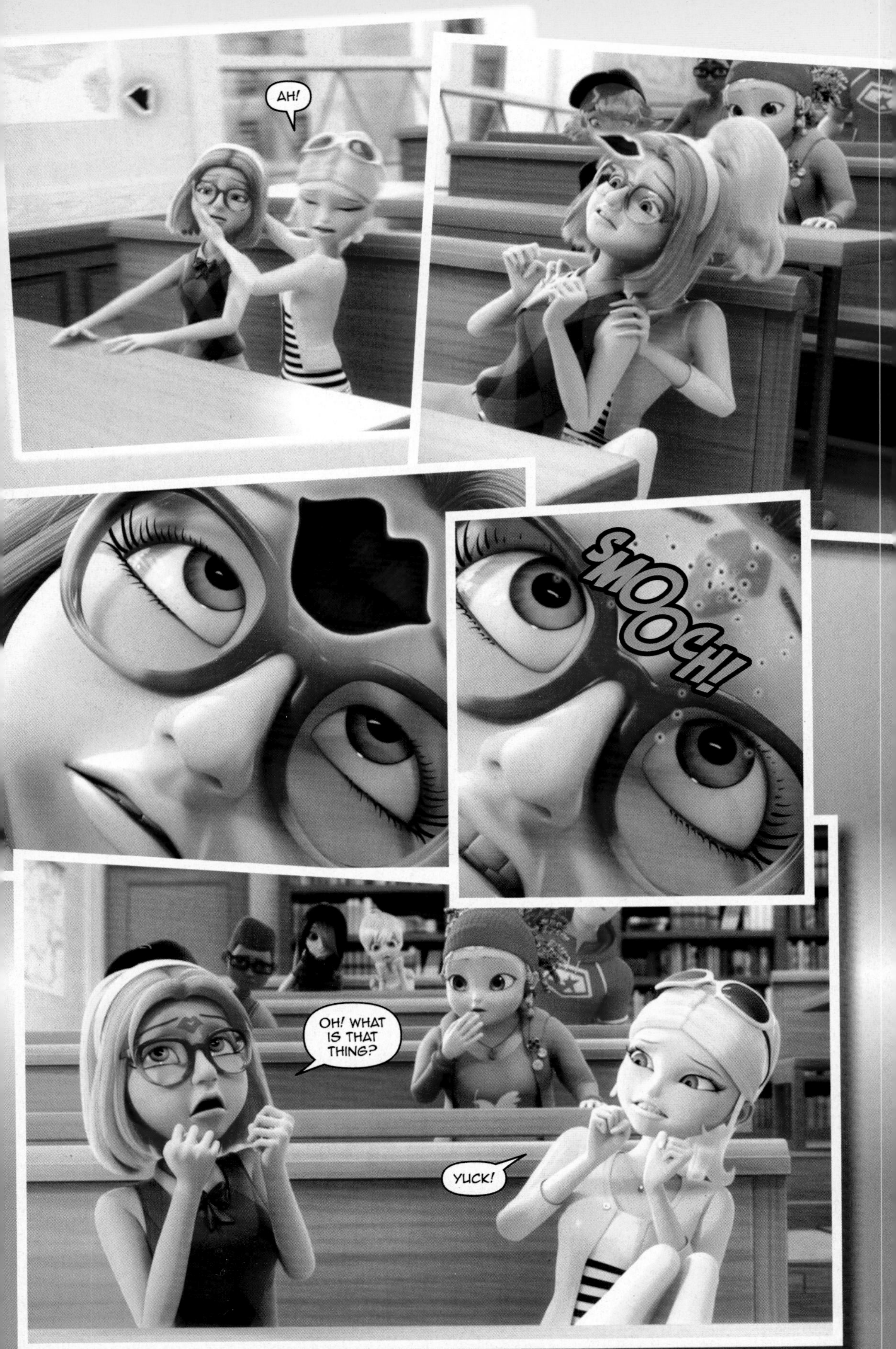
AH!
SMOOCH!
OH! WHAT IS THAT THING?
YUCK!

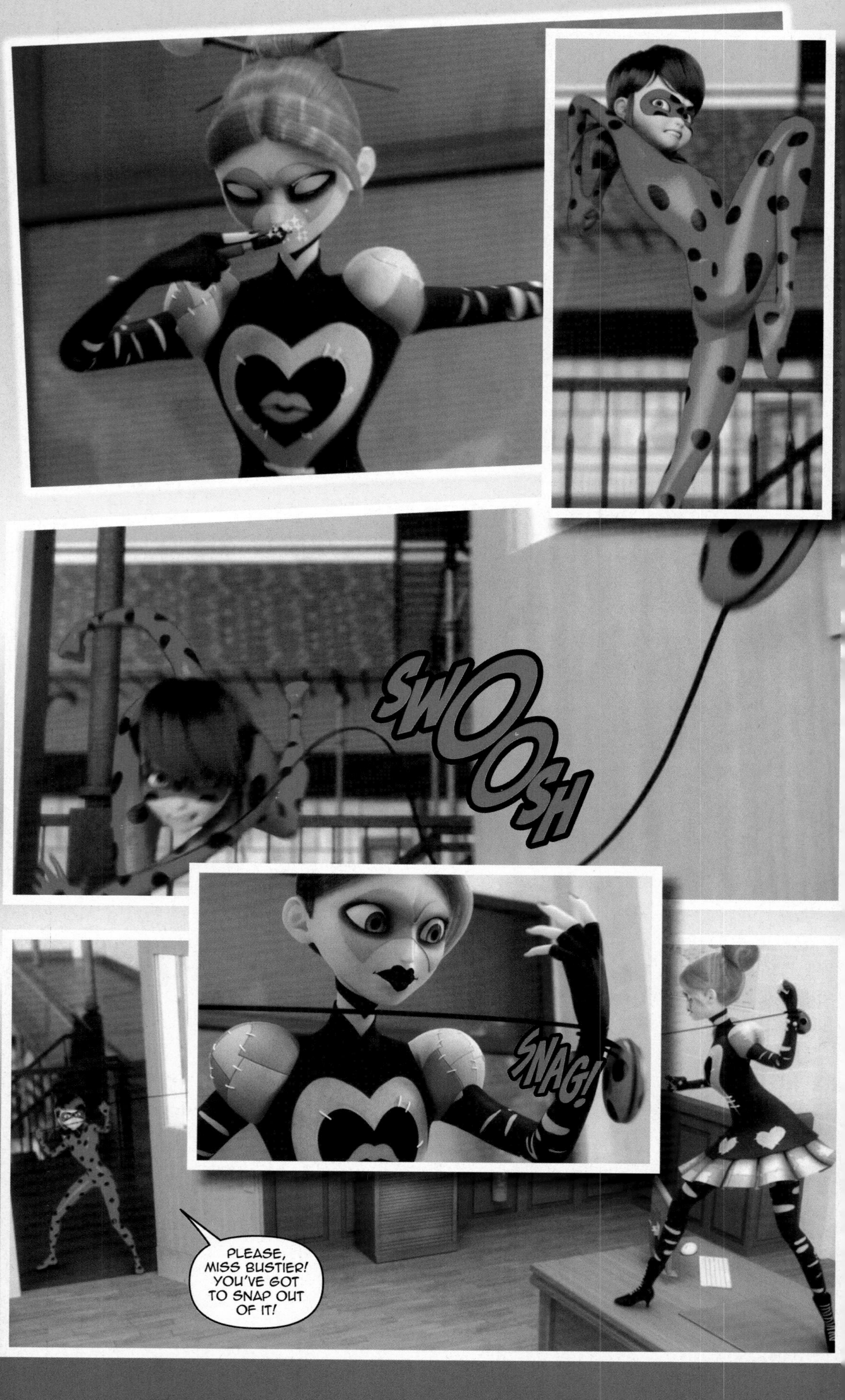
SWOOSH
SNAG!
PLEASE, MISS BUSTIER! YOU'VE GOT TO SNAP OUT OF IT!

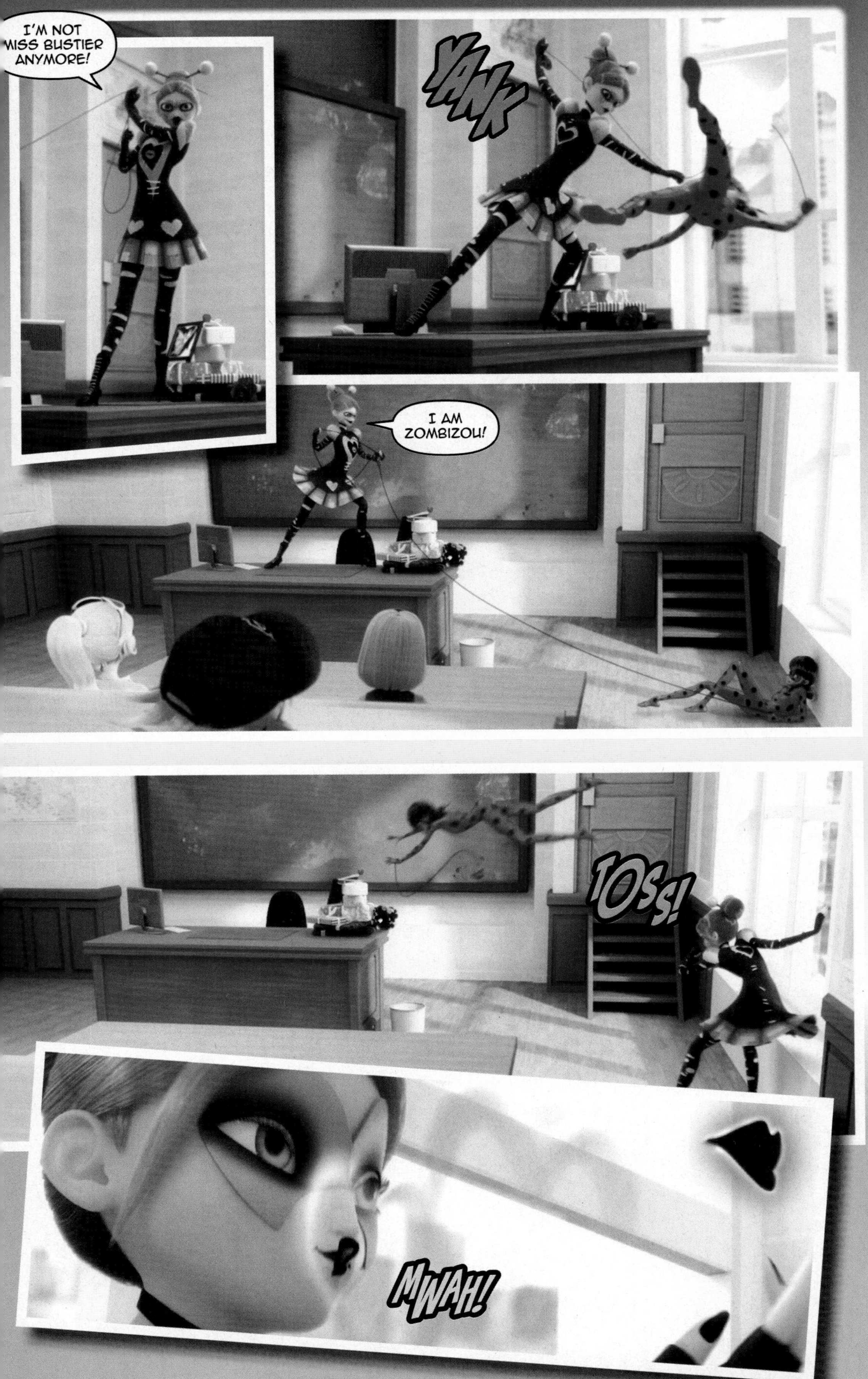
I'M NOT MISS BUSTIER ANYMORE!
YANK
I AM ZOMBIZOU!
TOSS!
MWAH!

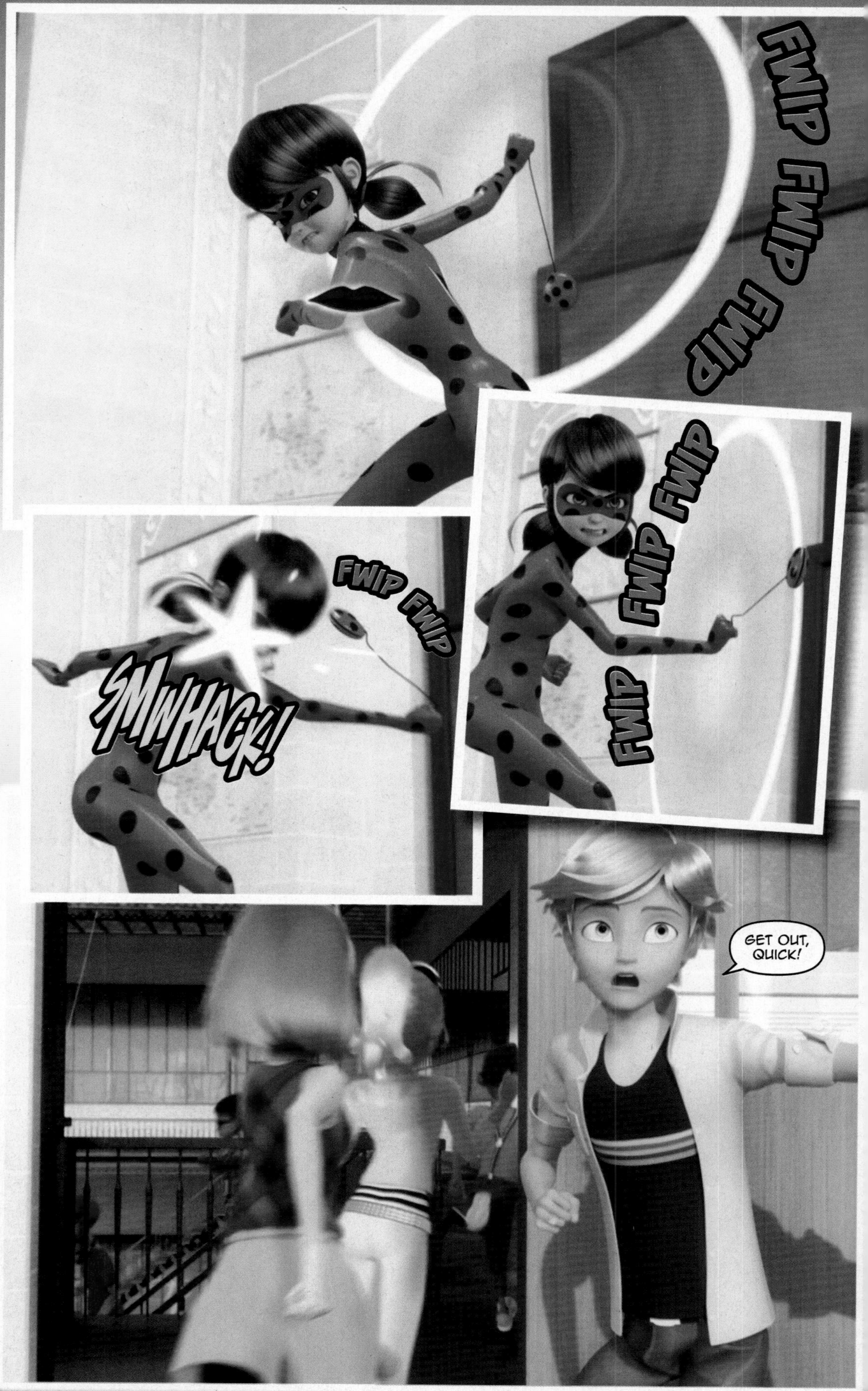

FWIP FWIP FWIP
FWIP FWIP FWIP
FWIP FWIP
SMWHACK!
GET OUT, QUICK!

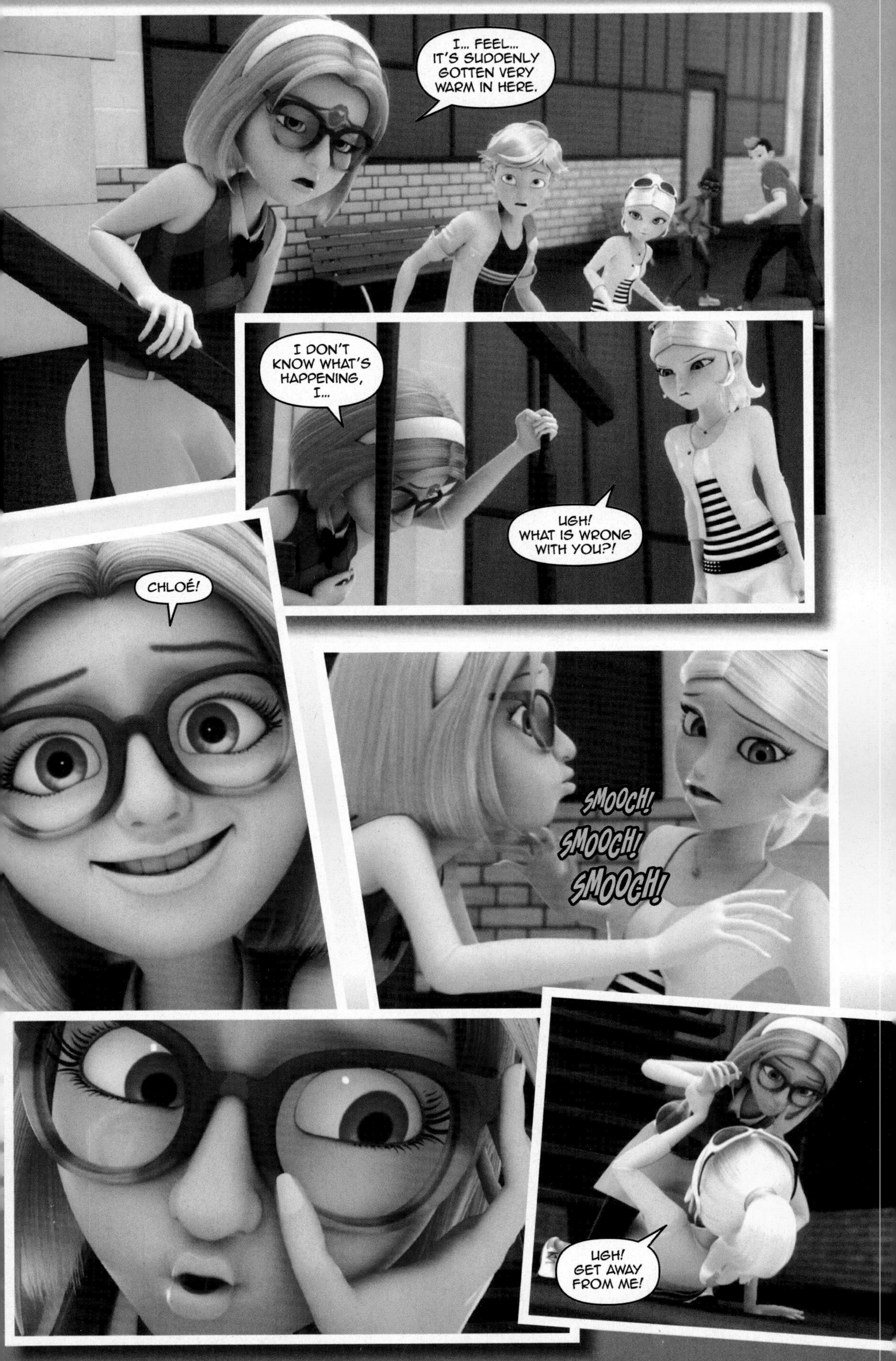
I... FEEL... IT'S SUDDENLY GOTTEN VERY WARM IN HERE.
I DON'T KNOW WHAT'S HAPPENING, I...
UGH! WHAT IS WRONG WITH YOU?!
CHLOÉ!
SMOOCH!
SMOOCH!
SMOOCH!
UGH! GET AWAY FROM ME!

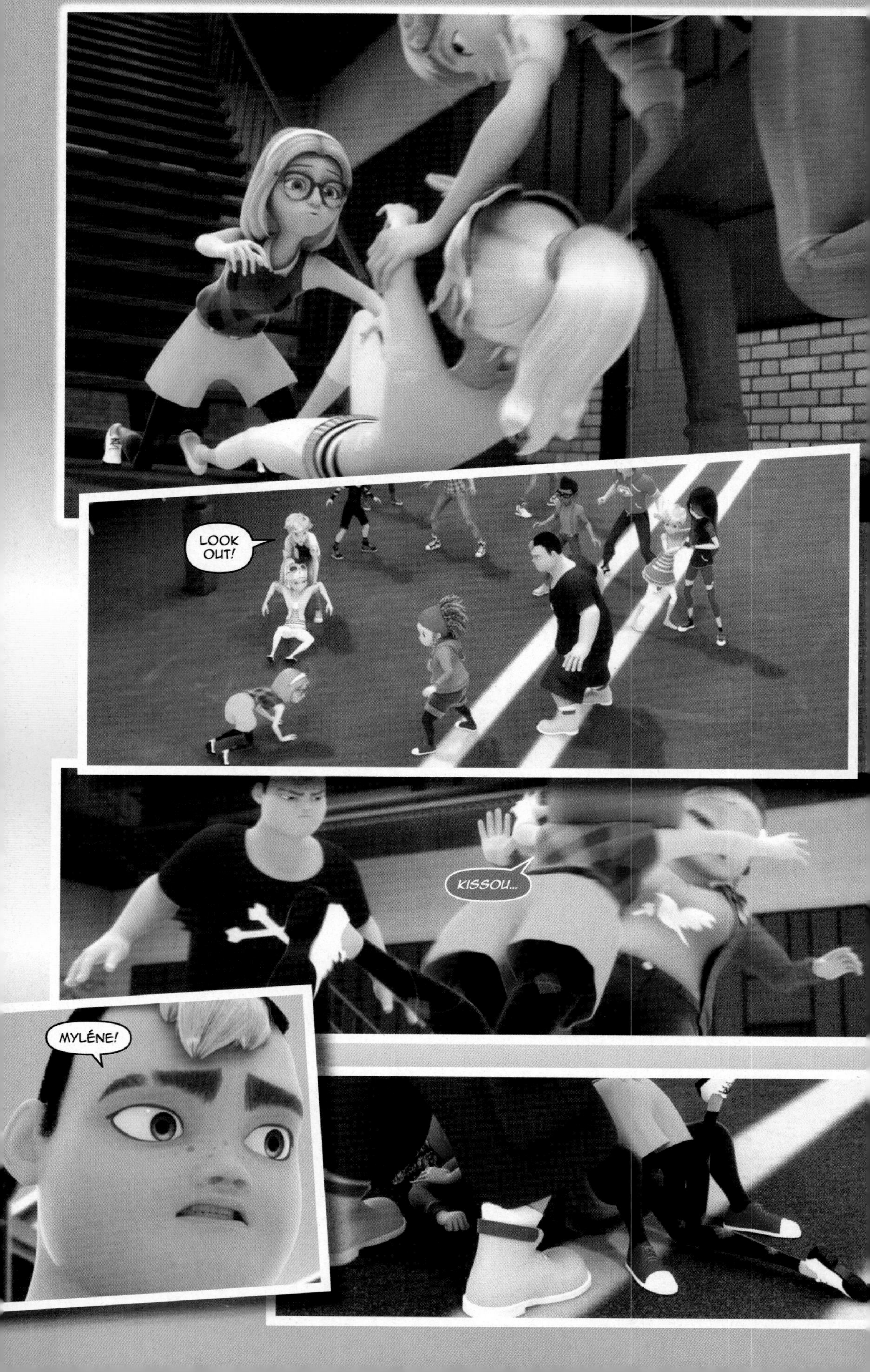
LOOK OUT!
KISSOU...
MYLÈNE!

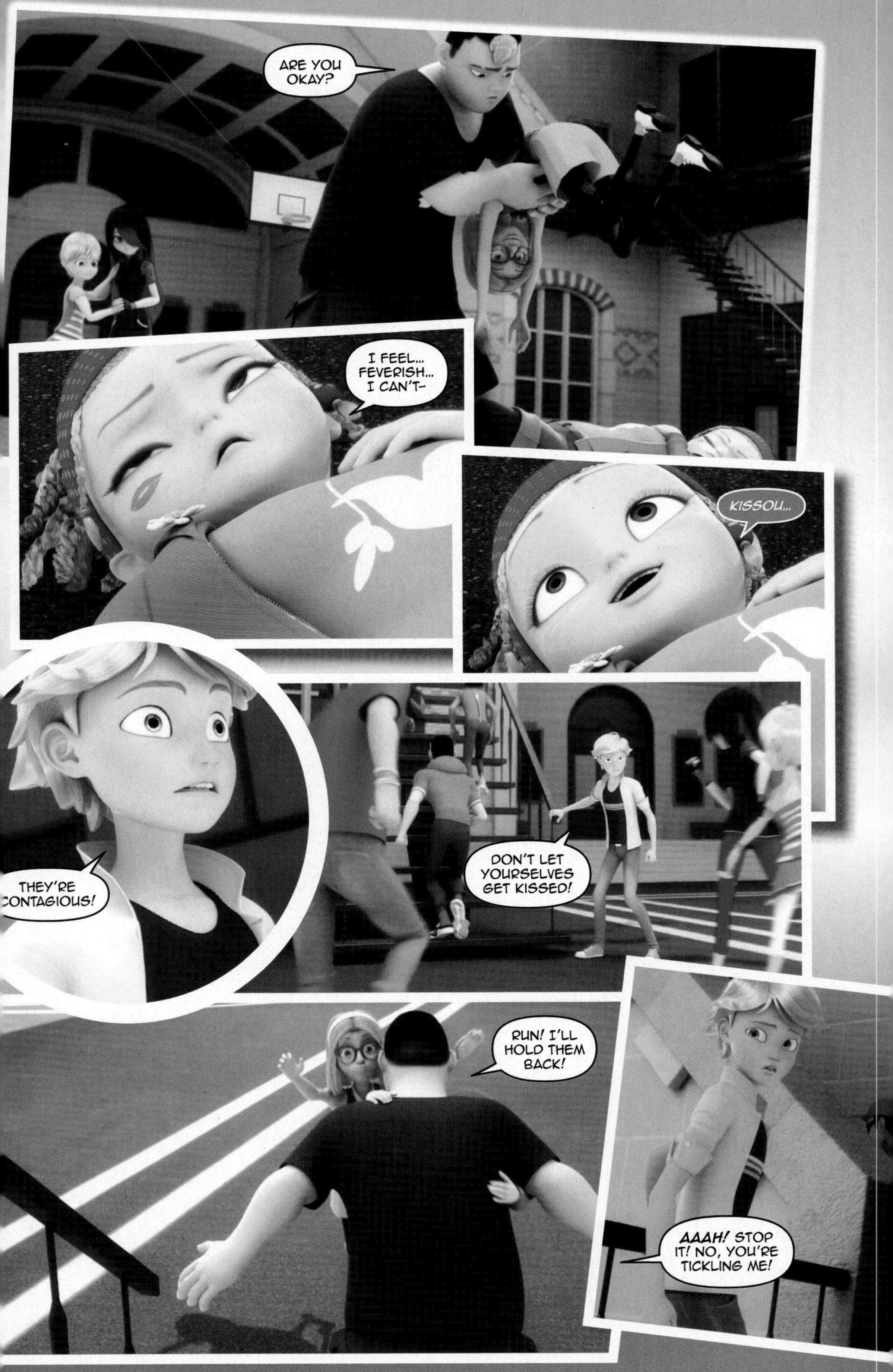
ARE YOU OKAY?
I FEEL... FEVERISH... I CAN'T-
KISSOU...
THEY'RE CONTAGIOUS!
DON'T LET YOURSELVES GET KISSED!
RUN! I'LL HOLD THEM BACK!
AAAH! STOP IT! NO, YOU'RE TICKLING ME!

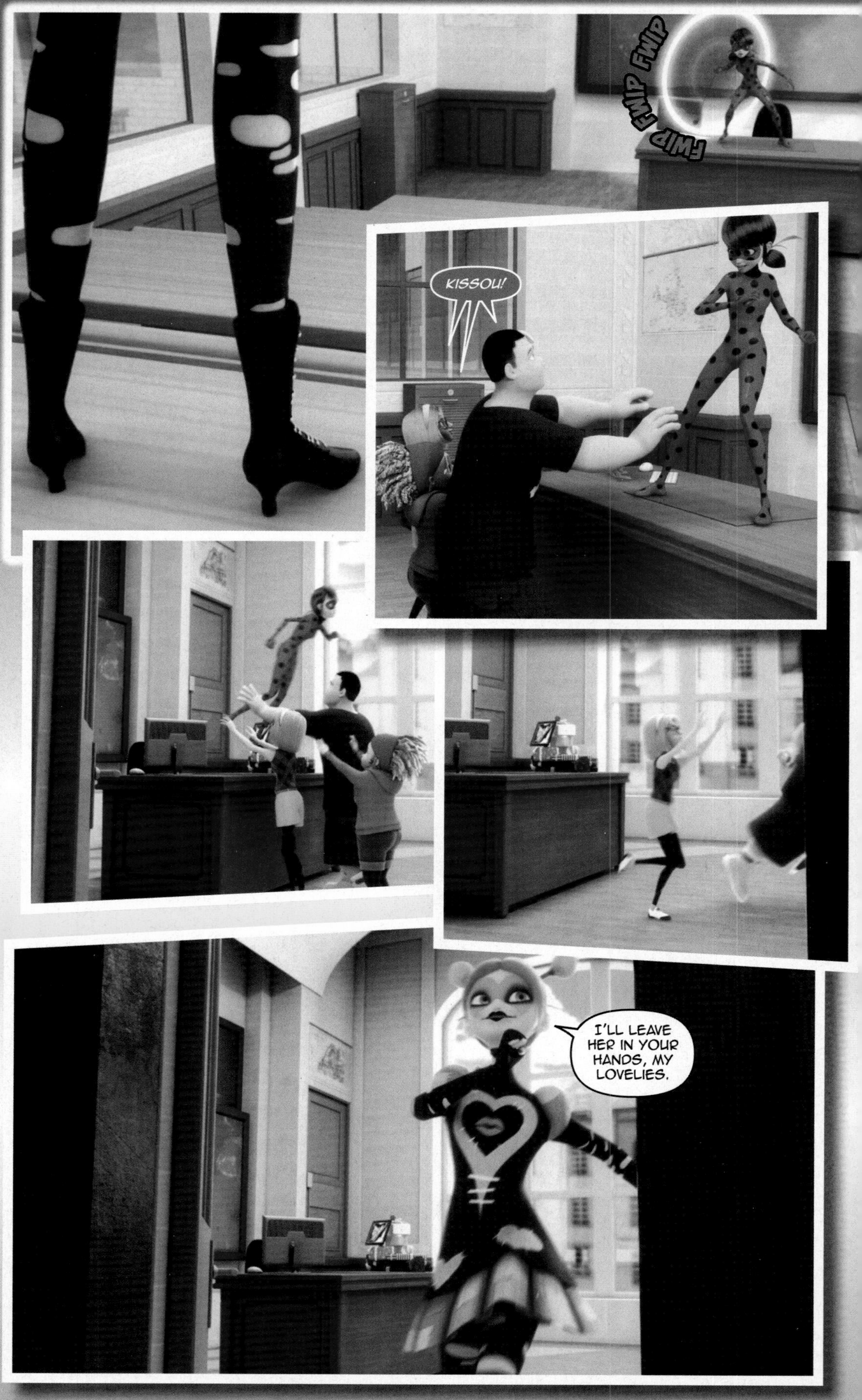
FWIP FWIP FWIP
KISSOU!
I'LL LEAVE HER IN YOUR HANDS, MY LOVELIES.

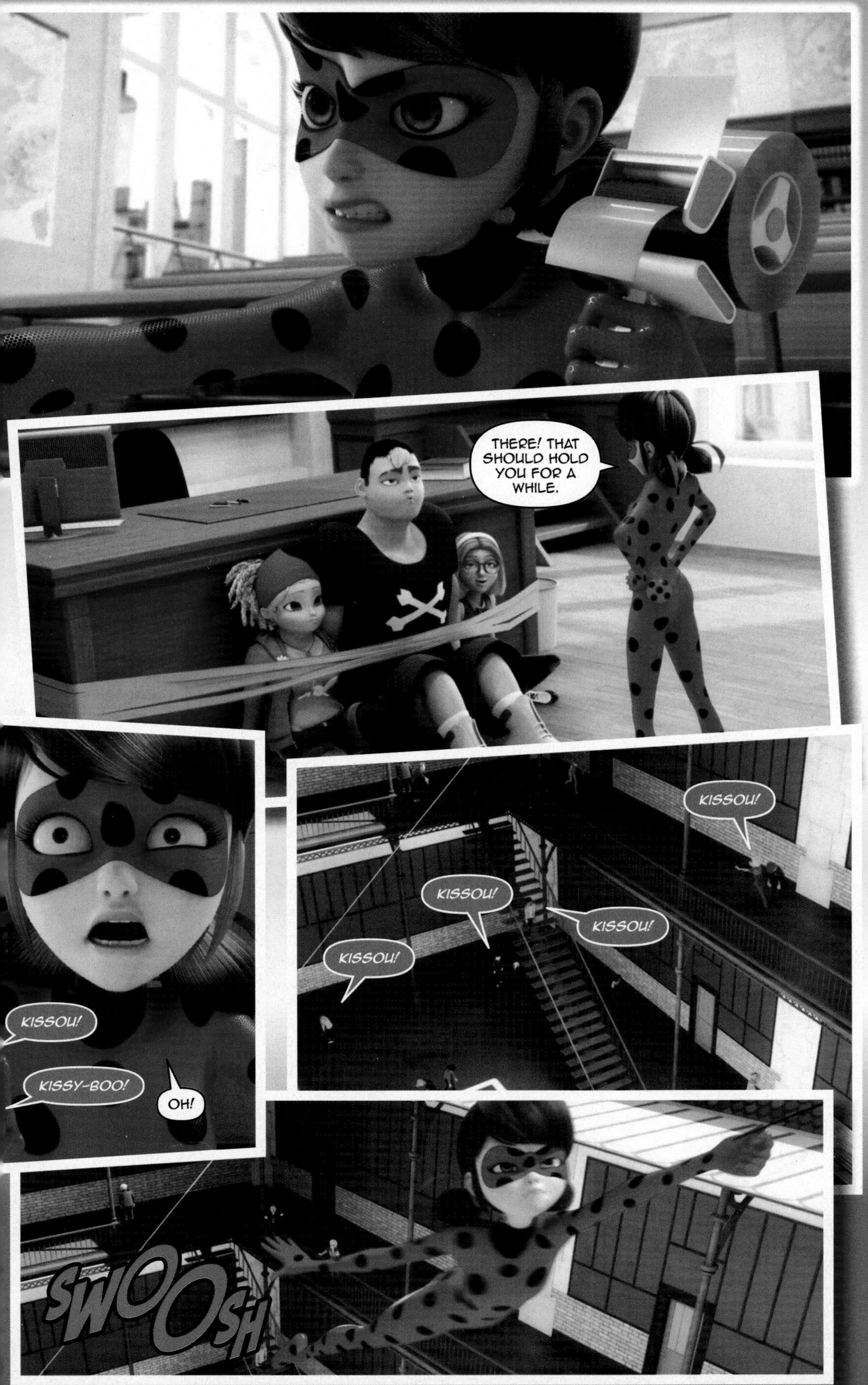
THERE! THAT SHOULD HOLD YOU FOR A WHILE.
KISSOU!
KISSY-BOO!
OH!
KISSOU!
KISSOU!
KISSOU!
KISSOU!
SWOOSH

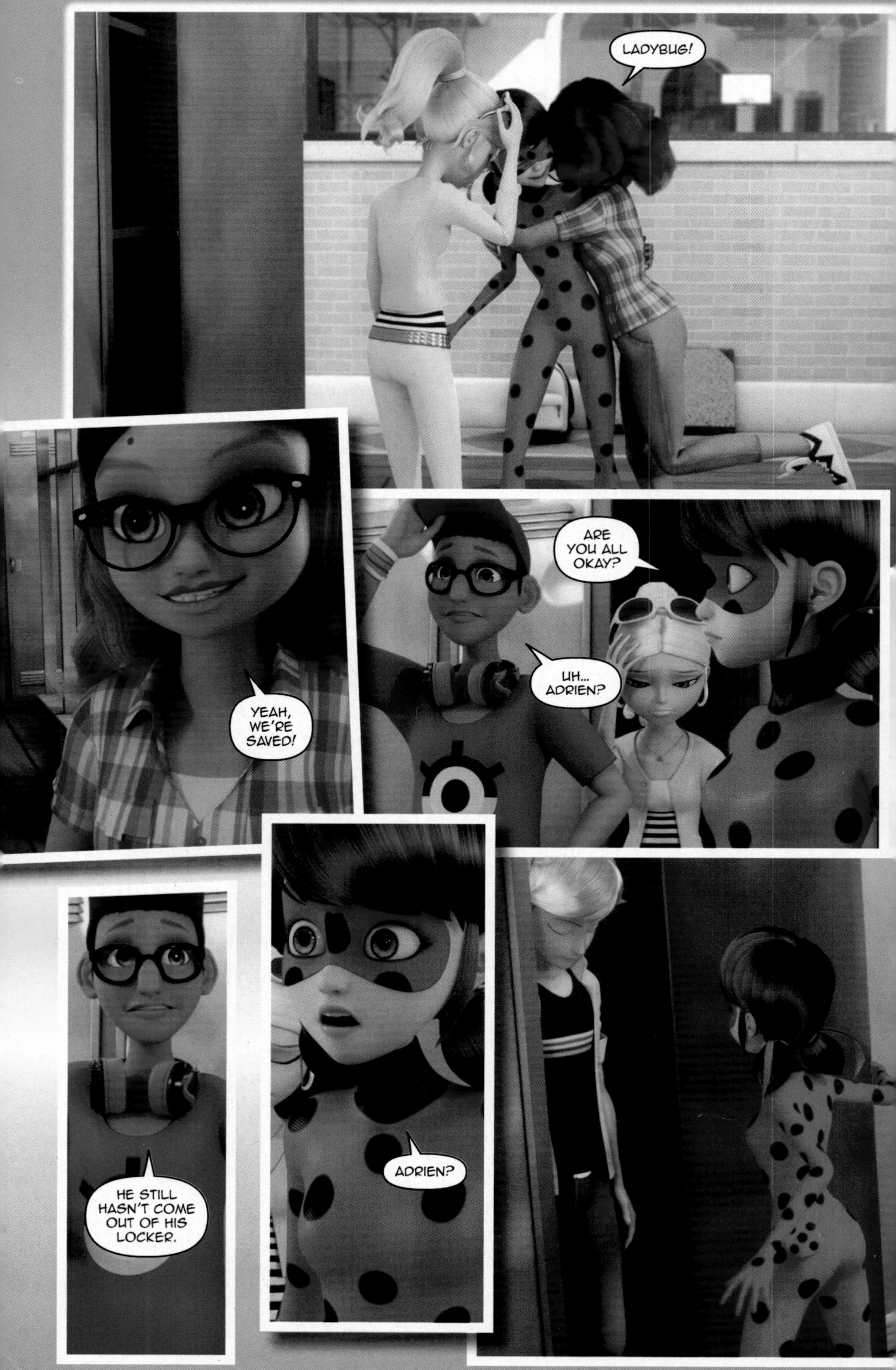
LADYBUG!
YEAH, WE'RE SAVED!
ARE YOU ALL OKAY?
UH... ADRIEN?
HE STILL HASN'T COME OUT OF HIS LOCKER.
ADRIEN?

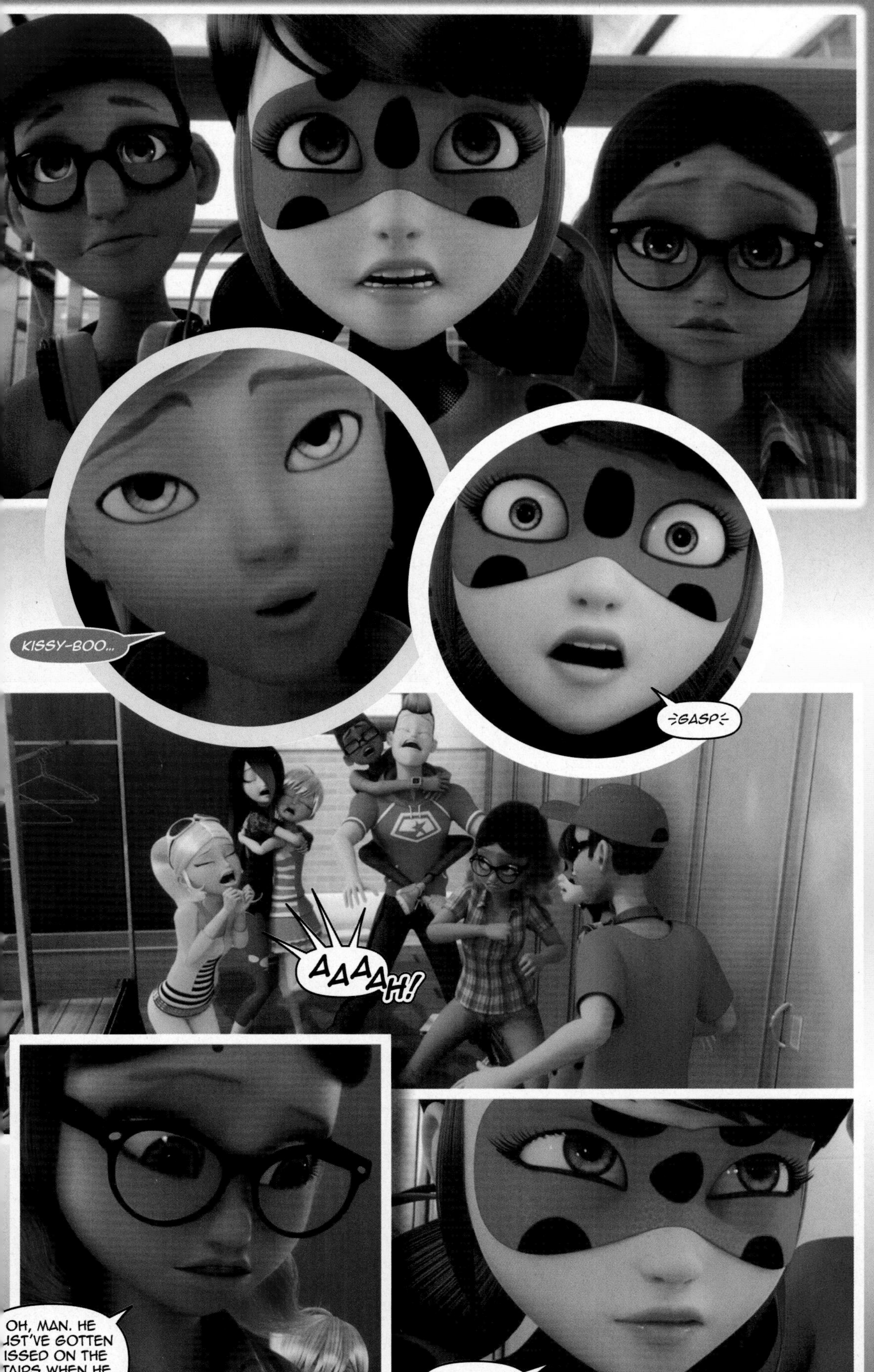
KISSY-BOO...
GASP
AAAAH!
OH, MAN. HE UST'VE GOTTEN ISSED ON THE TAIRS WHEN HE WAS SAVING CHLOÉ.
WE NEED TO HEAD TO THE ROOF.

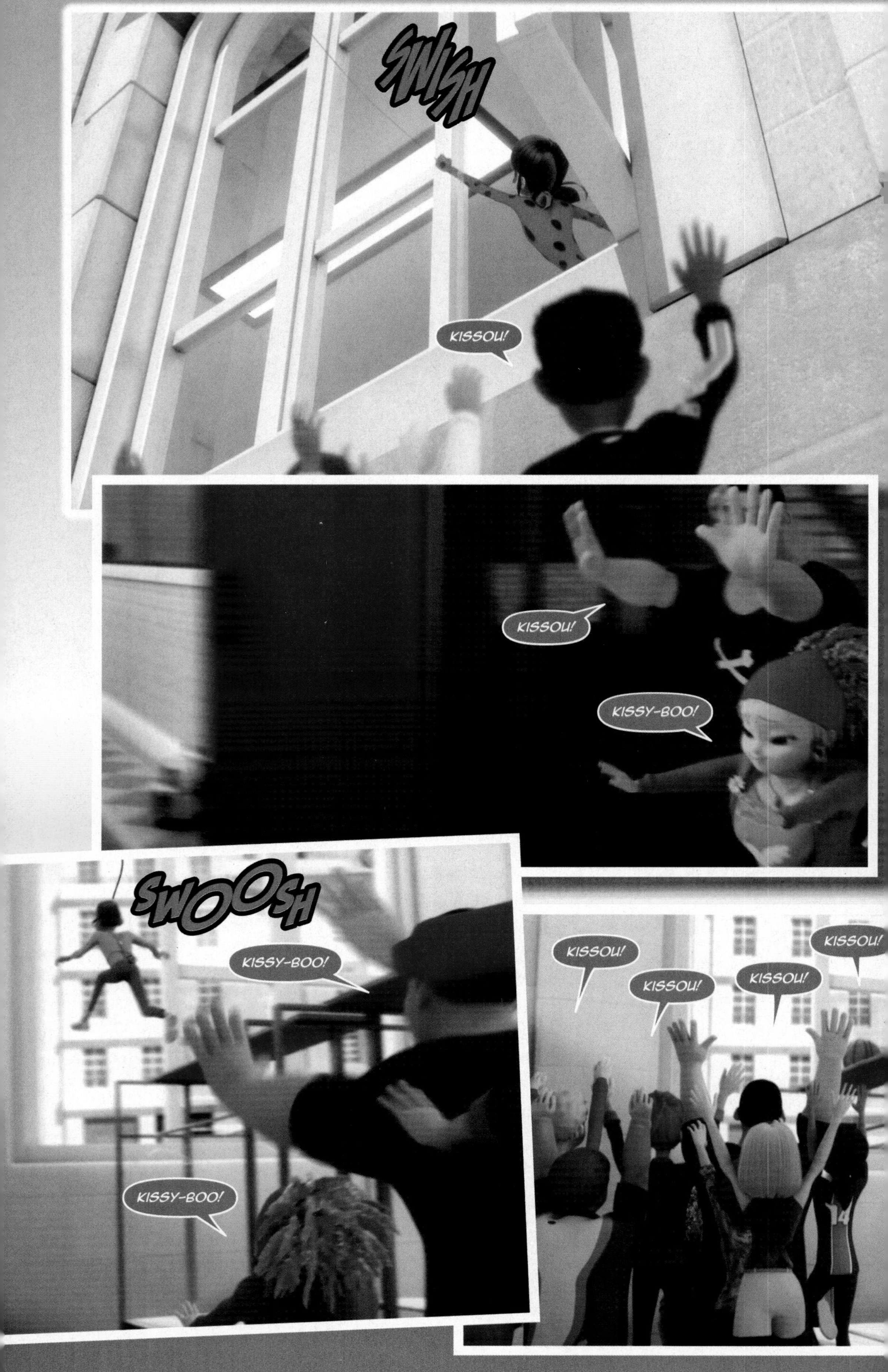
SWISH
KISSOU!
KISSOU!
KISSY-BOO!
SWOOSH
KISSY-BOO!
KISSY-BOO!
KISSOU!
KISSOU!
KISSOU!
KISSOU!

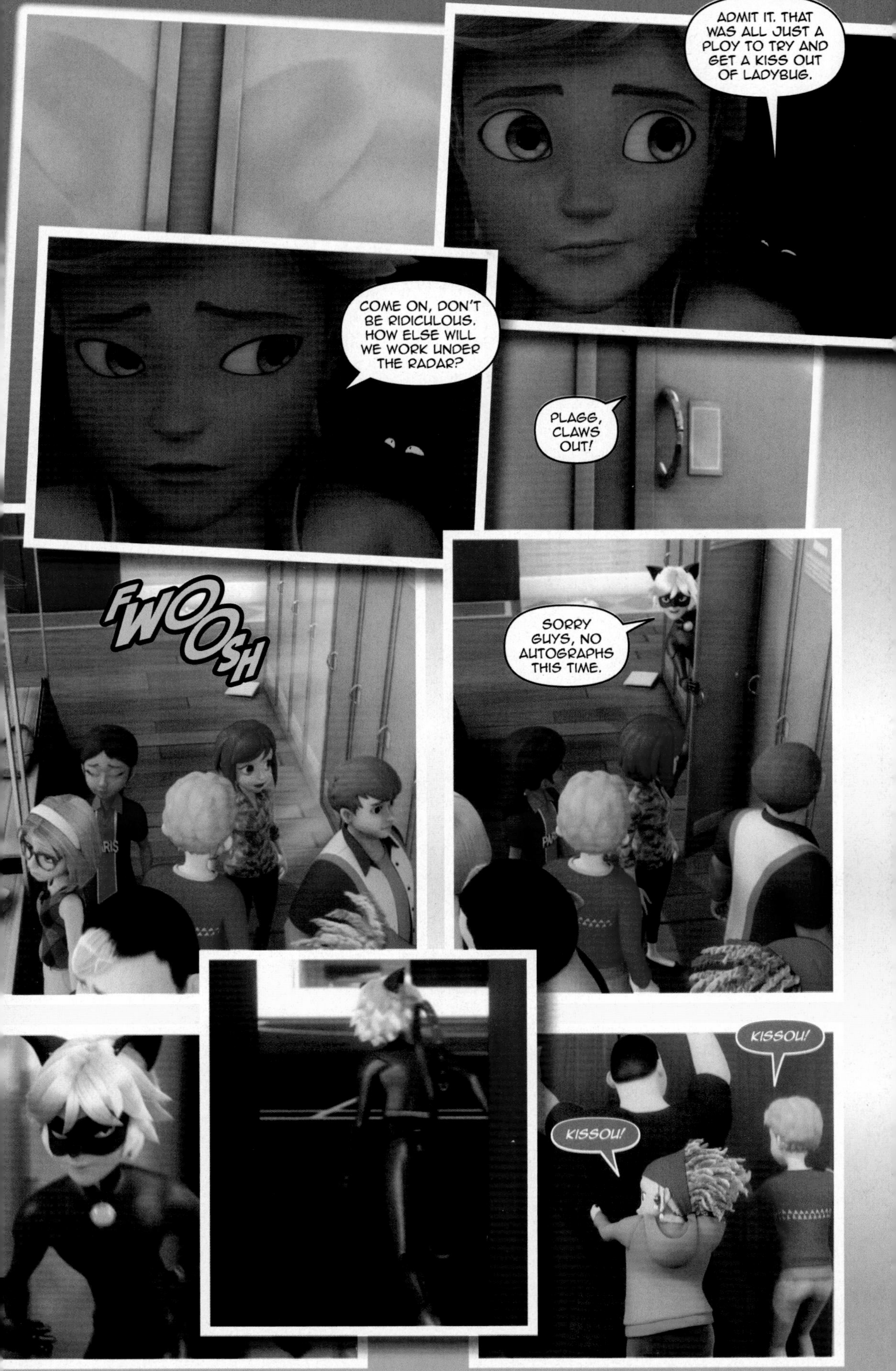
ADMIT IT. THAT WAS ALL JUST A PLOY TO TRY AND GET A KISS OUT OF LADYBUG.
COME ON, DON'T BE RIDICULOUS. HOW ELSE WILL WE WORK UNDER THE RADAR?
PLAGG, CLAWS OUT!
FWOOSH
SORRY GUYS, NO AUTOGRAPHS THIS TIME.
KISSOU!
KISSOU!

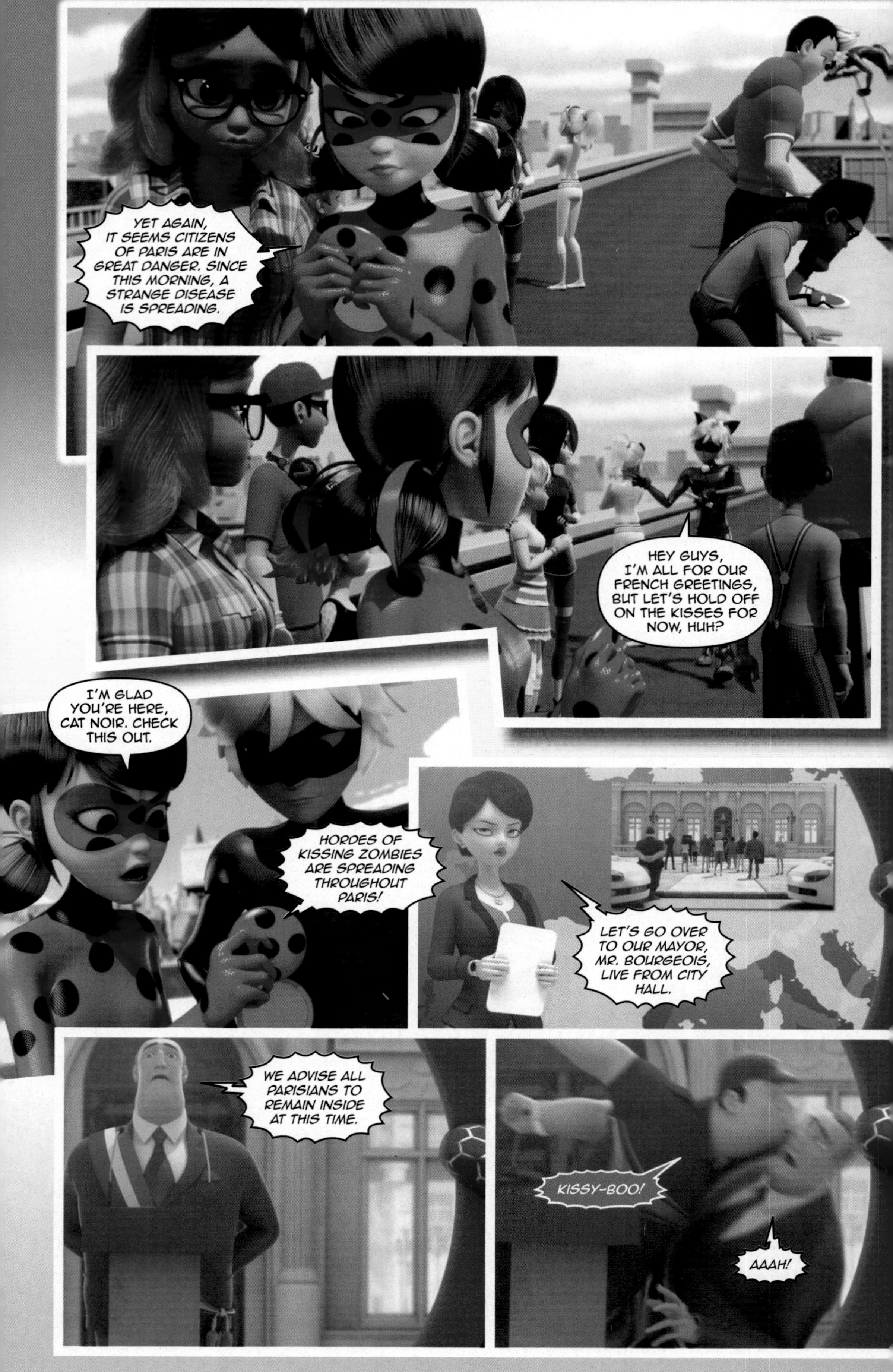
YET AGAIN, IT SEEMS CITIZENS OF PARIS ARE IN GREAT DANGER. SINCE THIS MORNING, A STRANGE DISEASE IS SPREADING.
HEY GUYS, I'M ALL FOR OUR FRENCH GREETINGS, BUT LET'S HOLD OFF ON THE KISSES FOR NOW, HUH?
I'M GLAD YOU'RE HERE, CAT NOIR. CHECK THIS OUT.
HORDES OF KISSING ZOMBIES ARE SPREADING THROUGHOUT PARIS!
LET'S GO OVER TO OUR MAYOR, MR. BOURGEOIS, LIVE FROM CITY HALL.
WE ADVISE ALL PARISIANS TO REMAIN INSIDE AT THIS TIME.
KISSY-BOO!
AAAH!

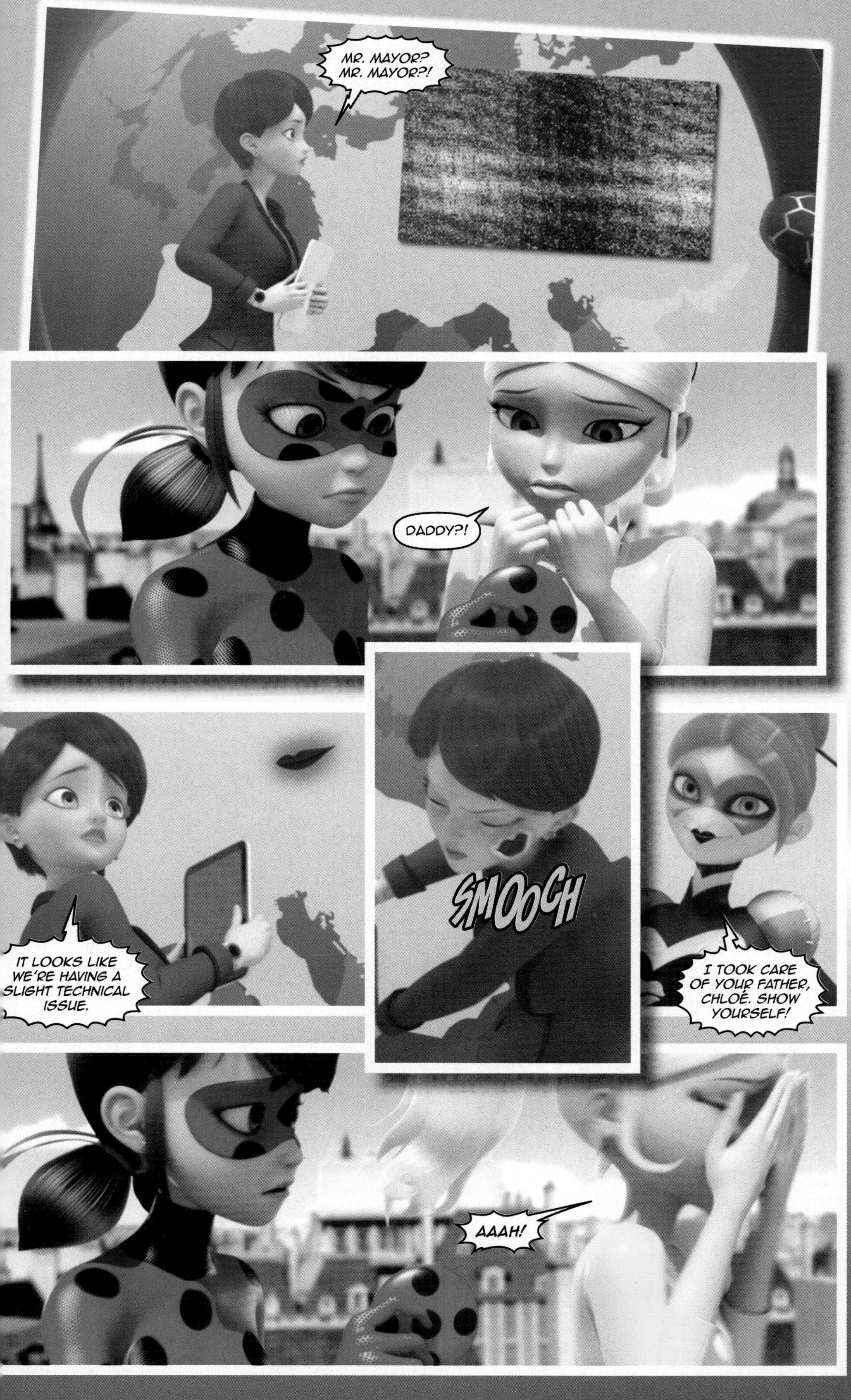
MR. MAYOR?
MR. MAYOR?!
DADDY?!
IT LOOKS LIKE WE'RE HAVING A SLIGHT TECHNICAL ISSUE.
SMOOCH
I TOOK CARE OF YOUR FATHER, CHLOÉ. SHOW YOURSELF!
AAAH!

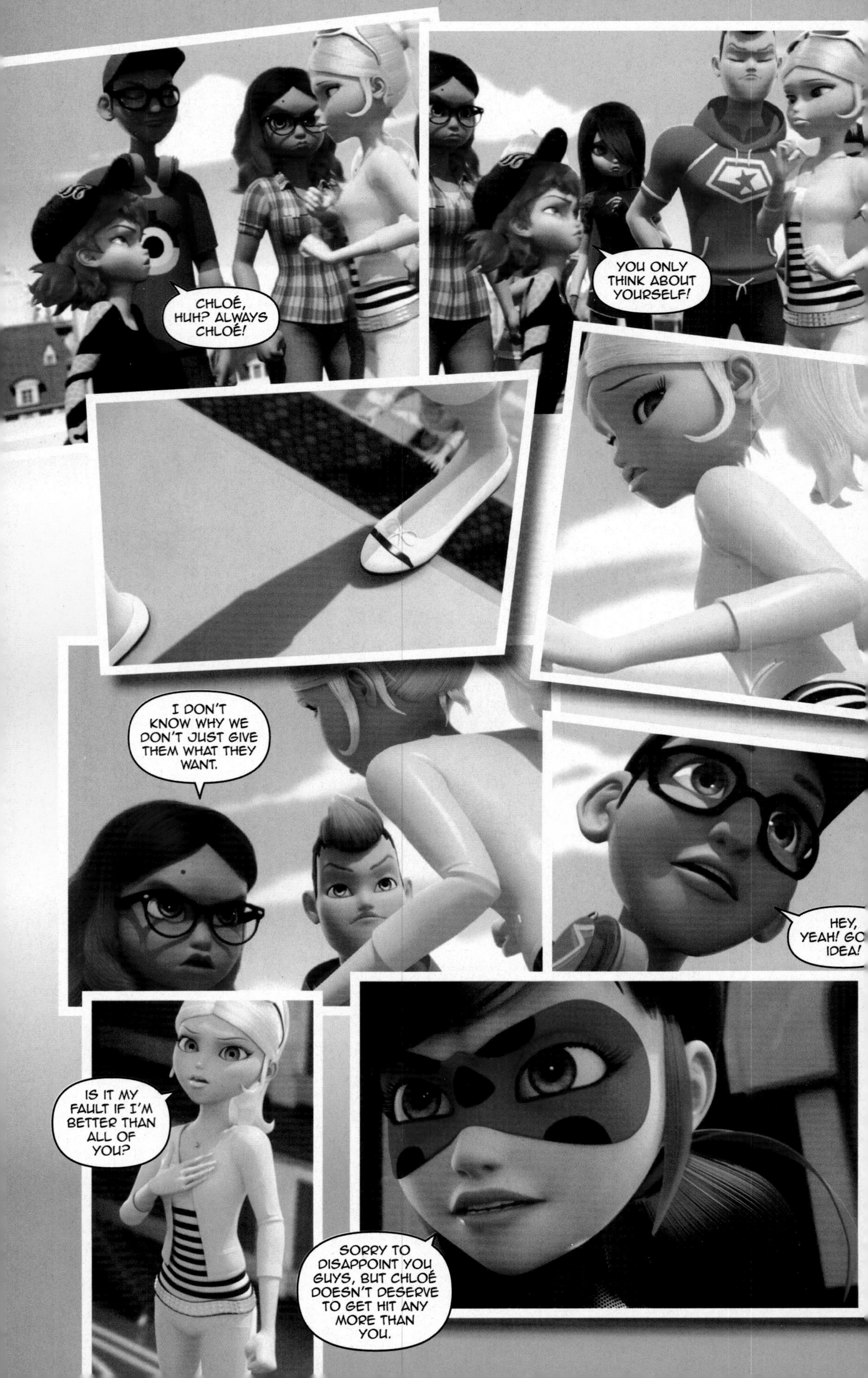
CHLOÉ, HUH? ALWAYS CHLOÉ!
YOU ONLY THINK ABOUT YOURSELF!
I DON'T KNOW WHY WE DON'T JUST GIVE THEM WHAT THEY WANT.
HEY, YEAH! GO IDEA!
IS IT MY FAULT IF I'M BETTER THAN ALL OF YOU?
SORRY TO DISAPPOINT YOU GUYS, BUT CHLOÉ DOESN'T DESERVE TO GET HIT ANY MORE THAN YOU.

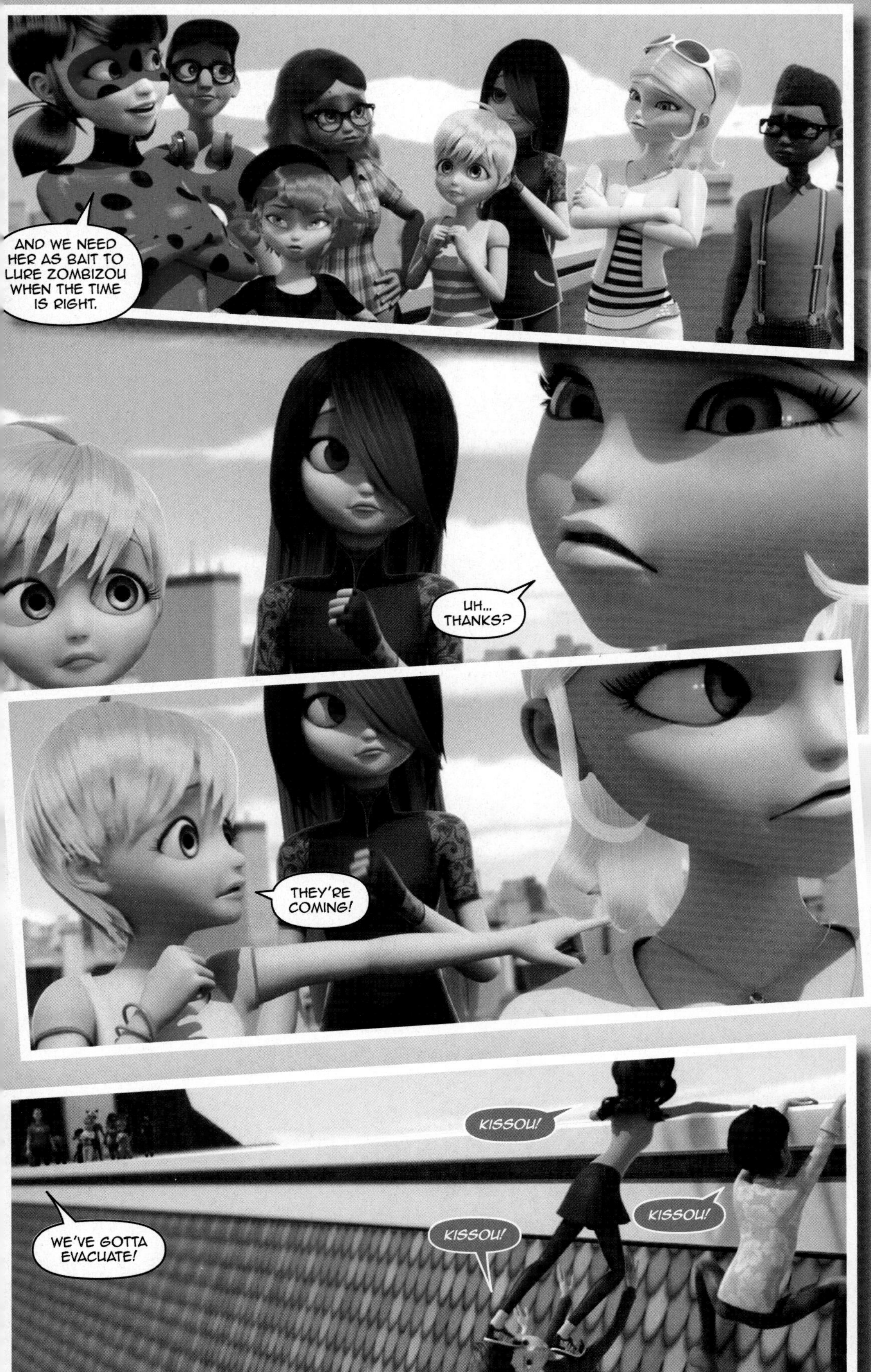
AND WE NEED HER AS BAIT TO LURE ZOMBIZOU WHEN THE TIME IS RIGHT.
UH... THANKS?
THEY'RE COMING!
KISSOU!
WE'VE GOTTA EVACUATE!
KISSOU!
KISSOU!

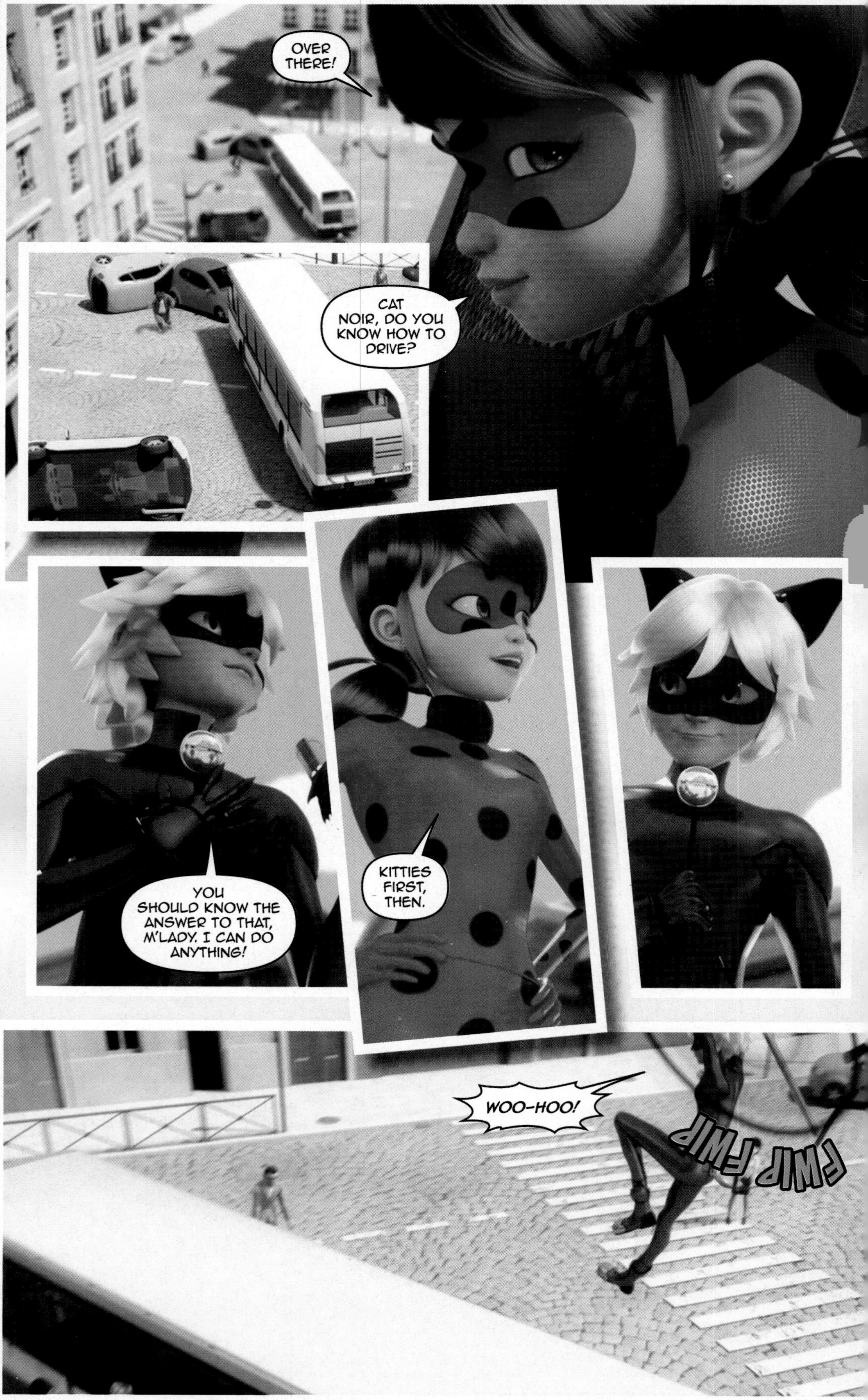
OVER THERE!
CAT NOIR, DO YOU KNOW HOW TO DRIVE?
YOU SHOULD KNOW THE ANSWER TO THAT, M'LADY. I CAN DO ANYTHING!
KITTIES FIRST, THEN.
WOO-HOO!
FWIP FWIP

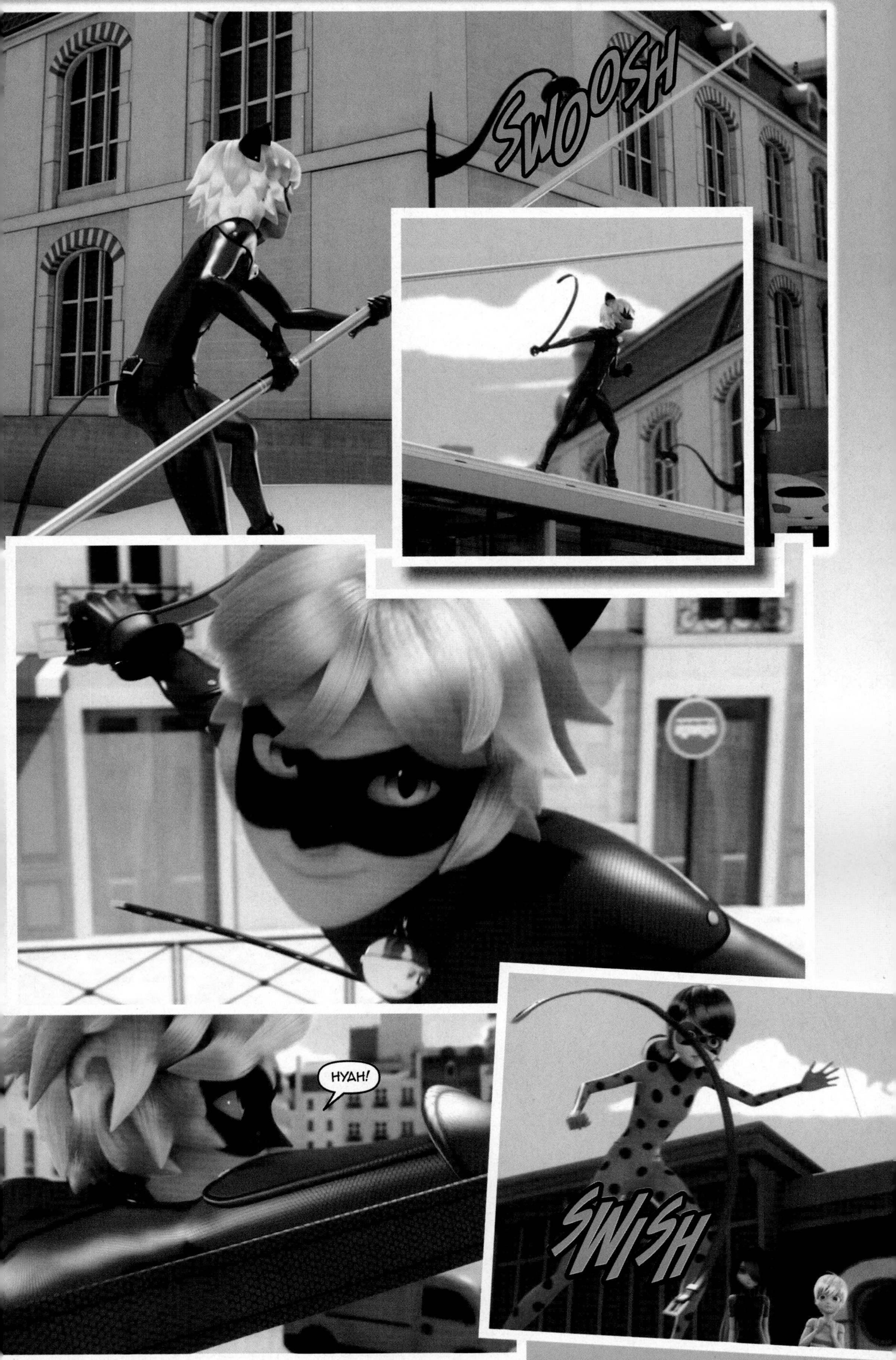
SWOOSH
HYAH!
SWISH

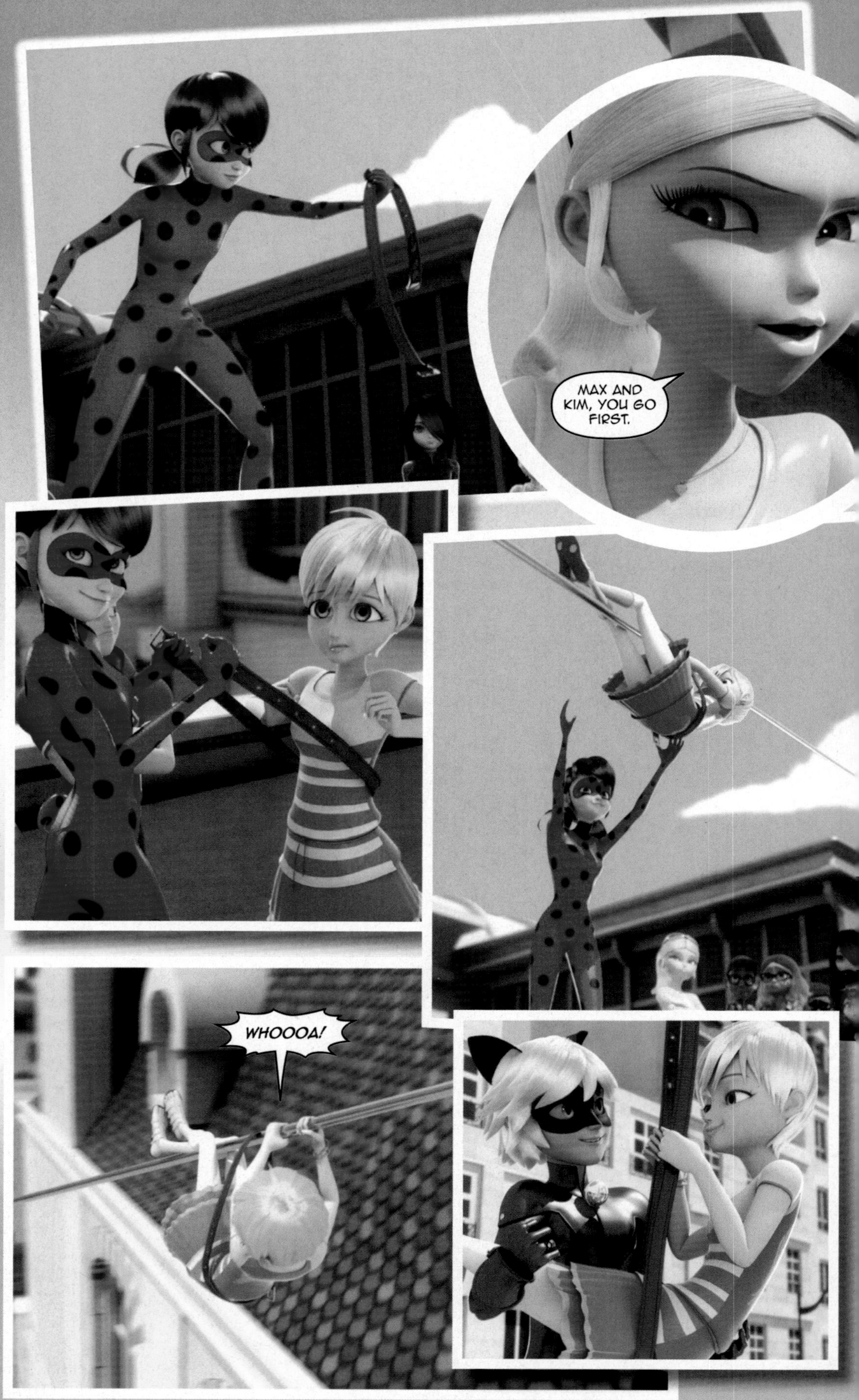
MAX AND KIM, YOU GO FIRST.
WHOOOA!

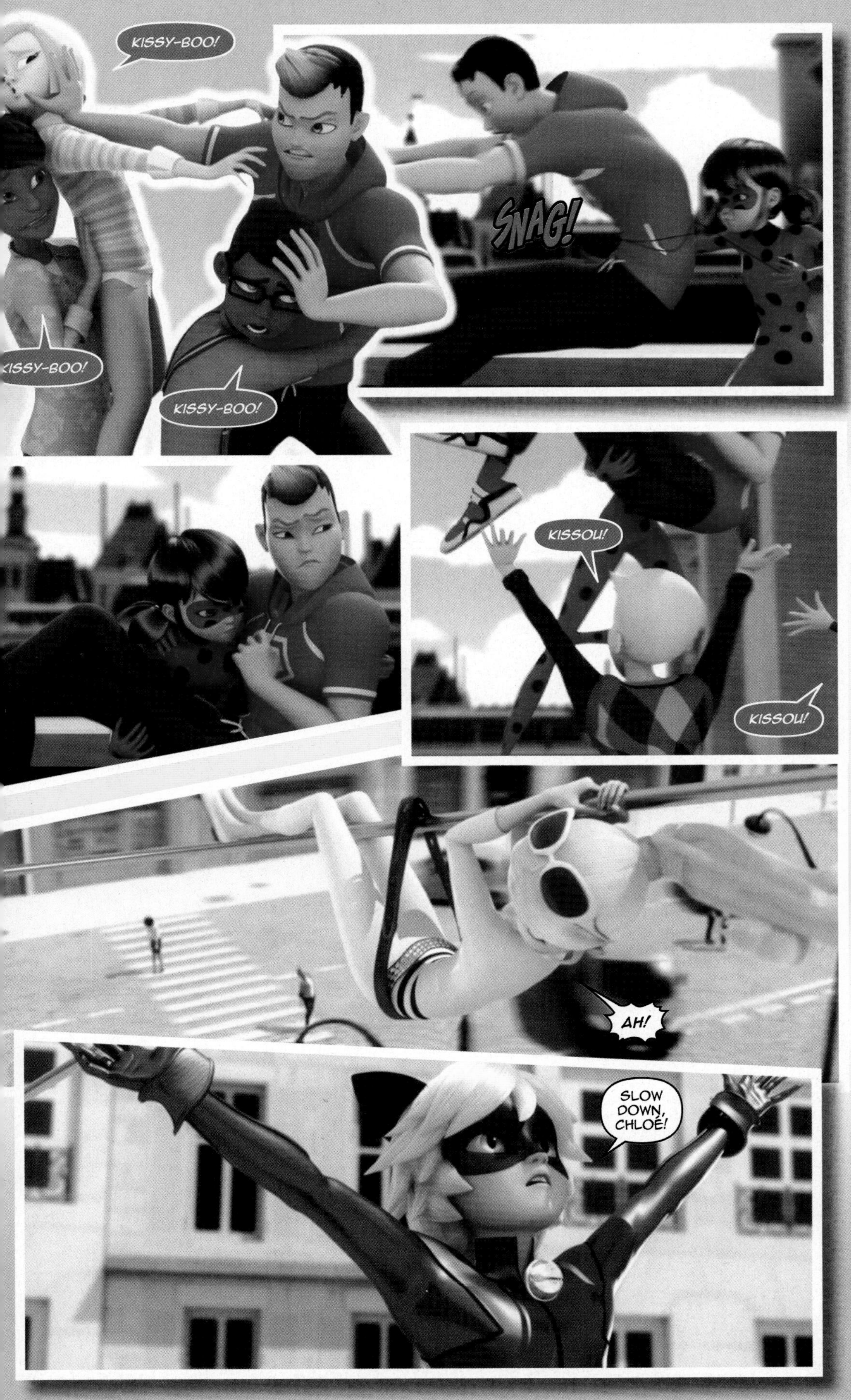
KISSY-BOO!
KISSY-BOO!
KISSY-BOO!
SNAG!
KISSOU!
KISSOU!
AH!
SLOW DOWN, CHLOÉ!

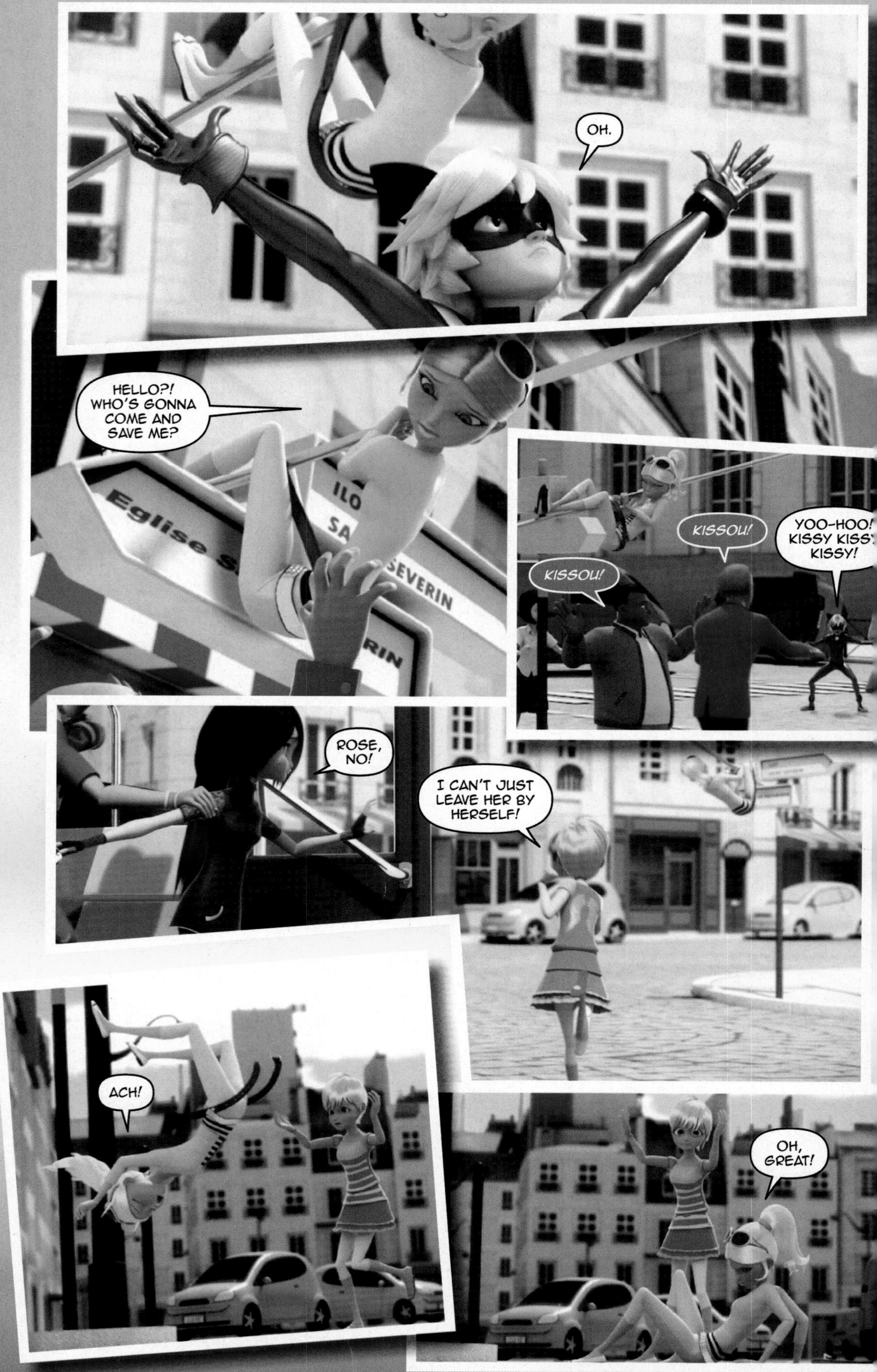
OH.
HELLO?! WHO'S GONNA COME AND SAVE ME?
KISSOU!
KISSOU!
YOO-HOO! KISSY KISSY KISSY!
ROSE, NO!
I CAN'T JUST LEAVE HER BY HERSELF!
ACH!
OH, GREAT!

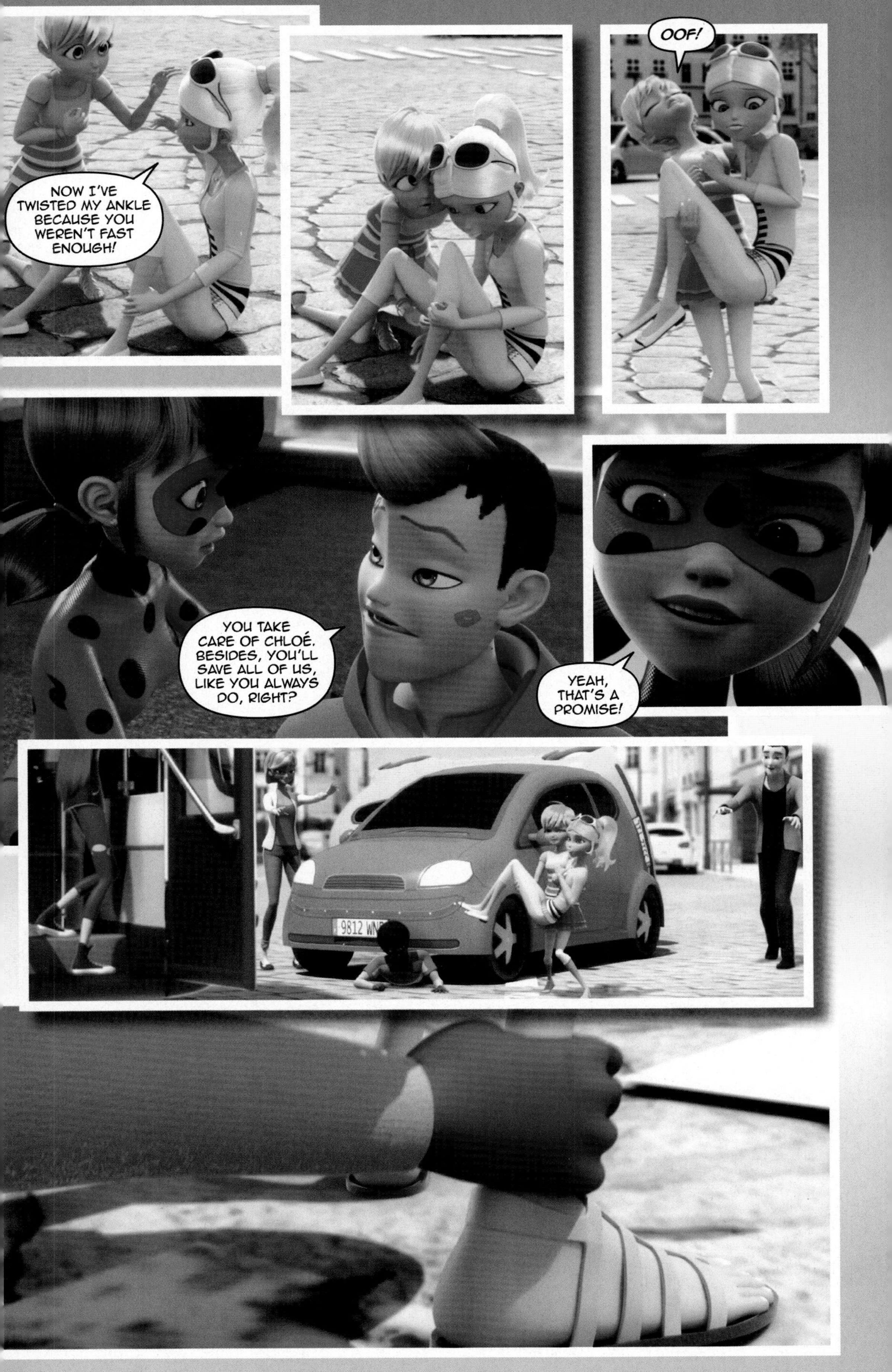
NOW I'VE TWISTED MY ANKLE BECAUSE YOU WEREN'T FAST ENOUGH!
OOF!
YOU TAKE CARE OF CHLOÉ. BESIDES, YOU'LL SAVE ALL OF US, LIKE YOU ALWAYS DO, RIGHT?
YEAH, THAT'S A PROMISE!

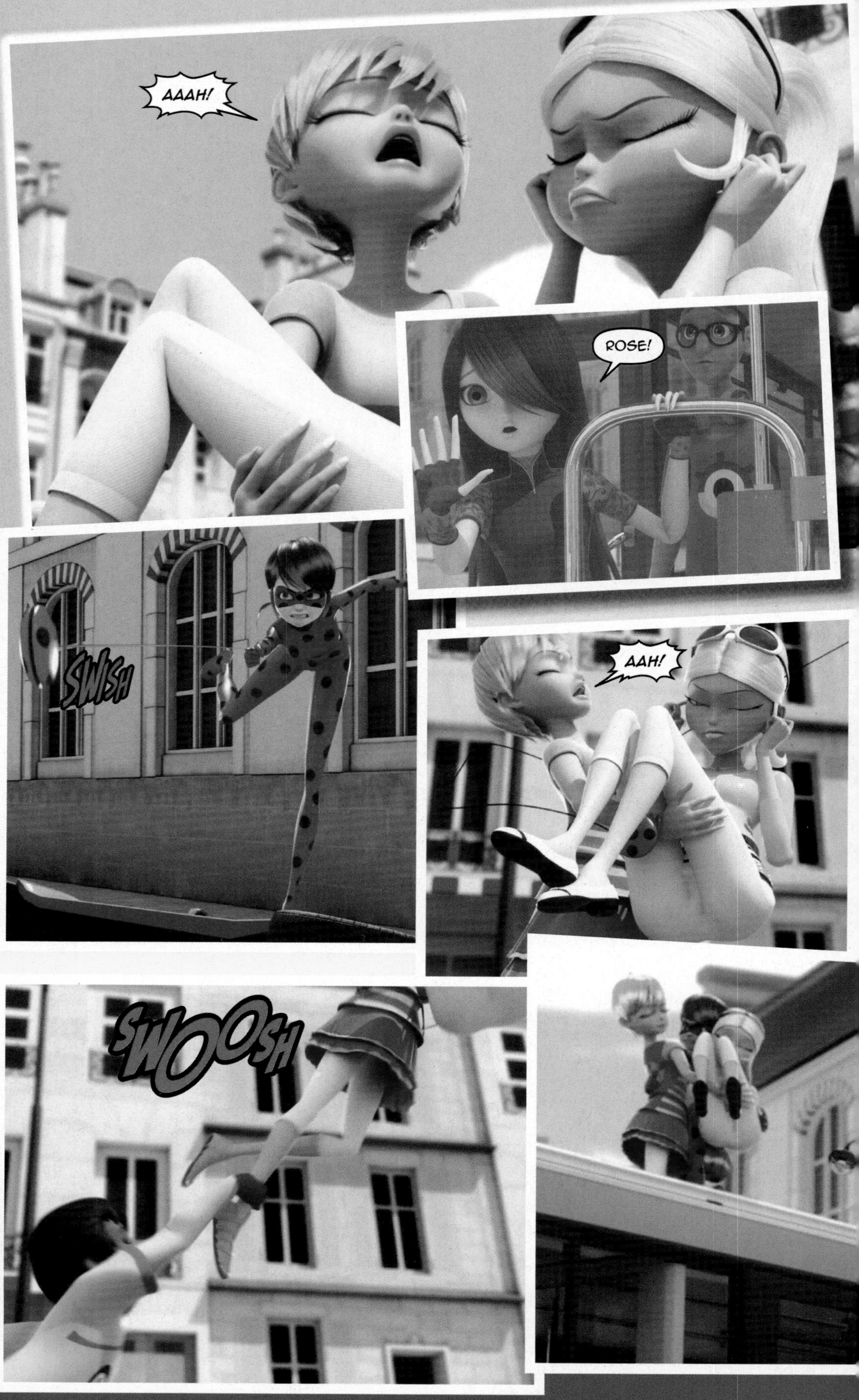
AAAH!
ROSE!
SWISH
AAH!
SWOOSH

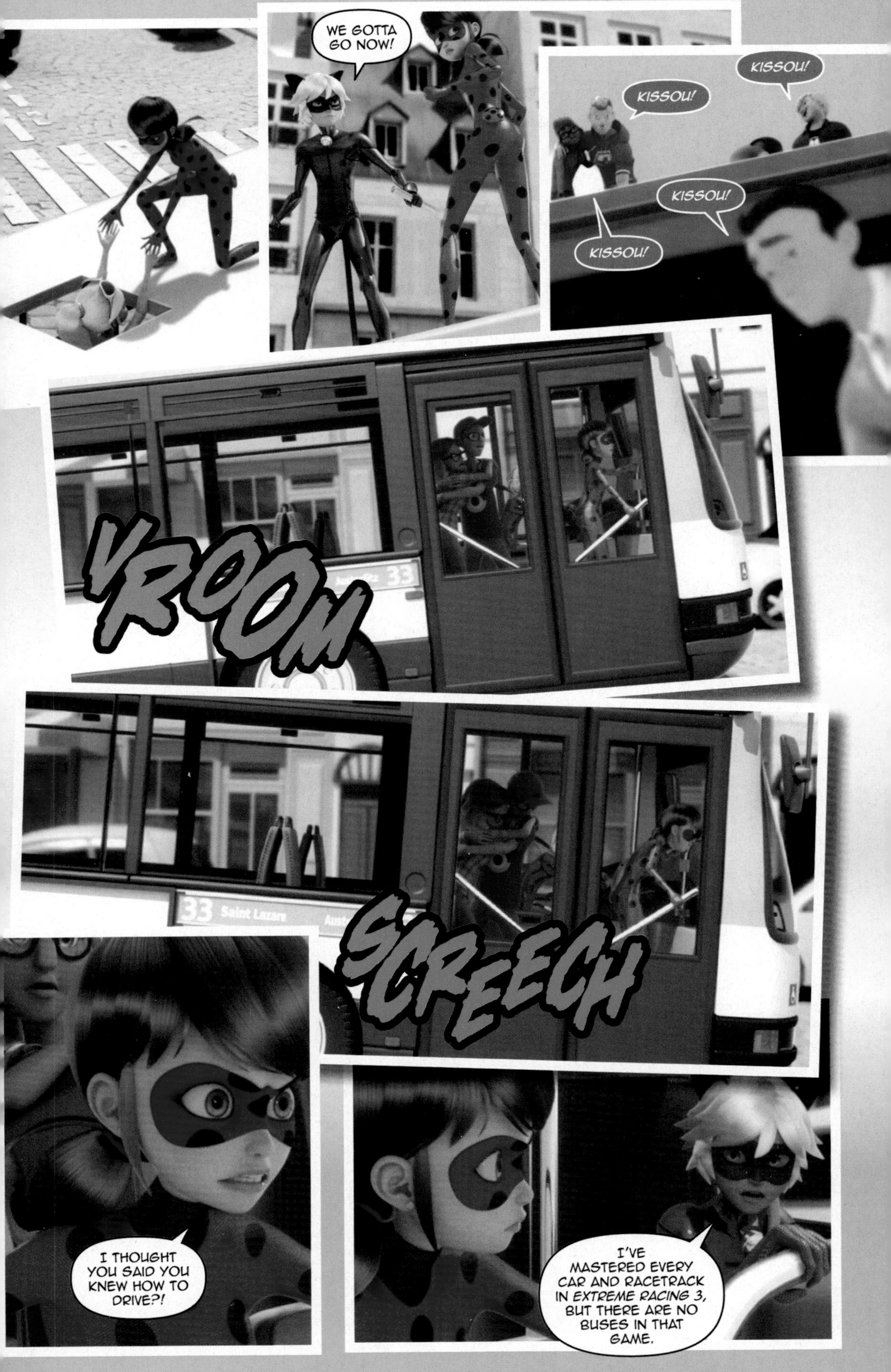
WE GOTTA GO NOW!
KISSOU!
KISSOU!
KISSOU!
KISSOU!
VROOM
SCREECH
I THOUGHT YOU SAID YOU KNEW HOW TO DRIVE?!
I'VE MASTERED EVERY CAR AND RACETRACK IN *EXTREME RACING 3*, BUT THERE ARE NO BUSES IN THAT GAME.

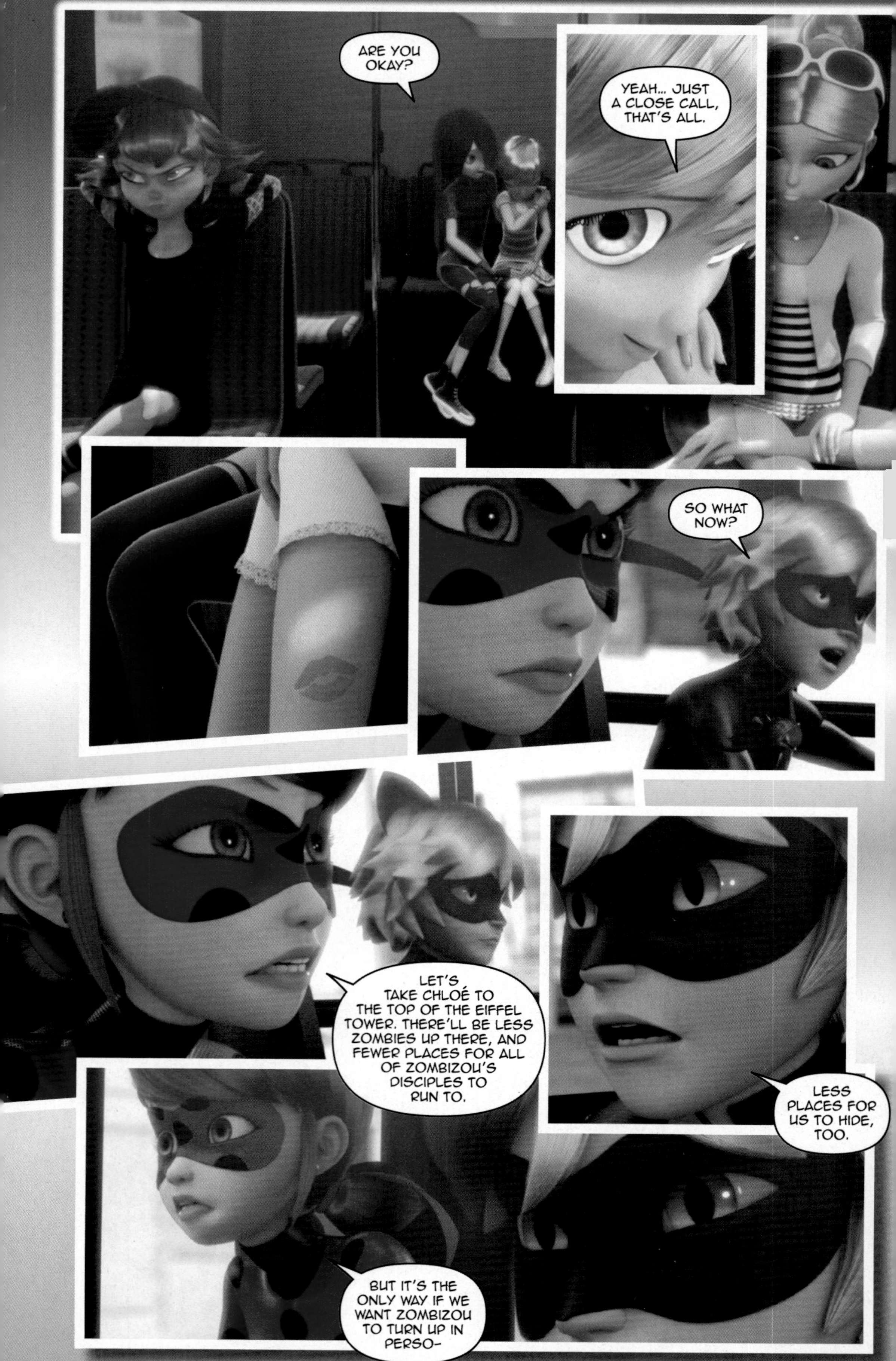
ARE YOU OKAY?
YEAH... JUST A CLOSE CALL, THAT'S ALL.
SO WHAT NOW?
LET'S TAKE CHLOÉ TO THE TOP OF THE EIFFEL TOWER. THERE'LL BE LESS ZOMBIES UP THERE, AND FEWER PLACES FOR ALL OF ZOMBIZOU'S DISCIPLES TO RUN TO.
LESS PLACES FOR US TO HIDE, TOO.
BUT IT'S THE ONLY WAY IF WE WANT ZOMBIZOU TO TURN UP IN PERSO-

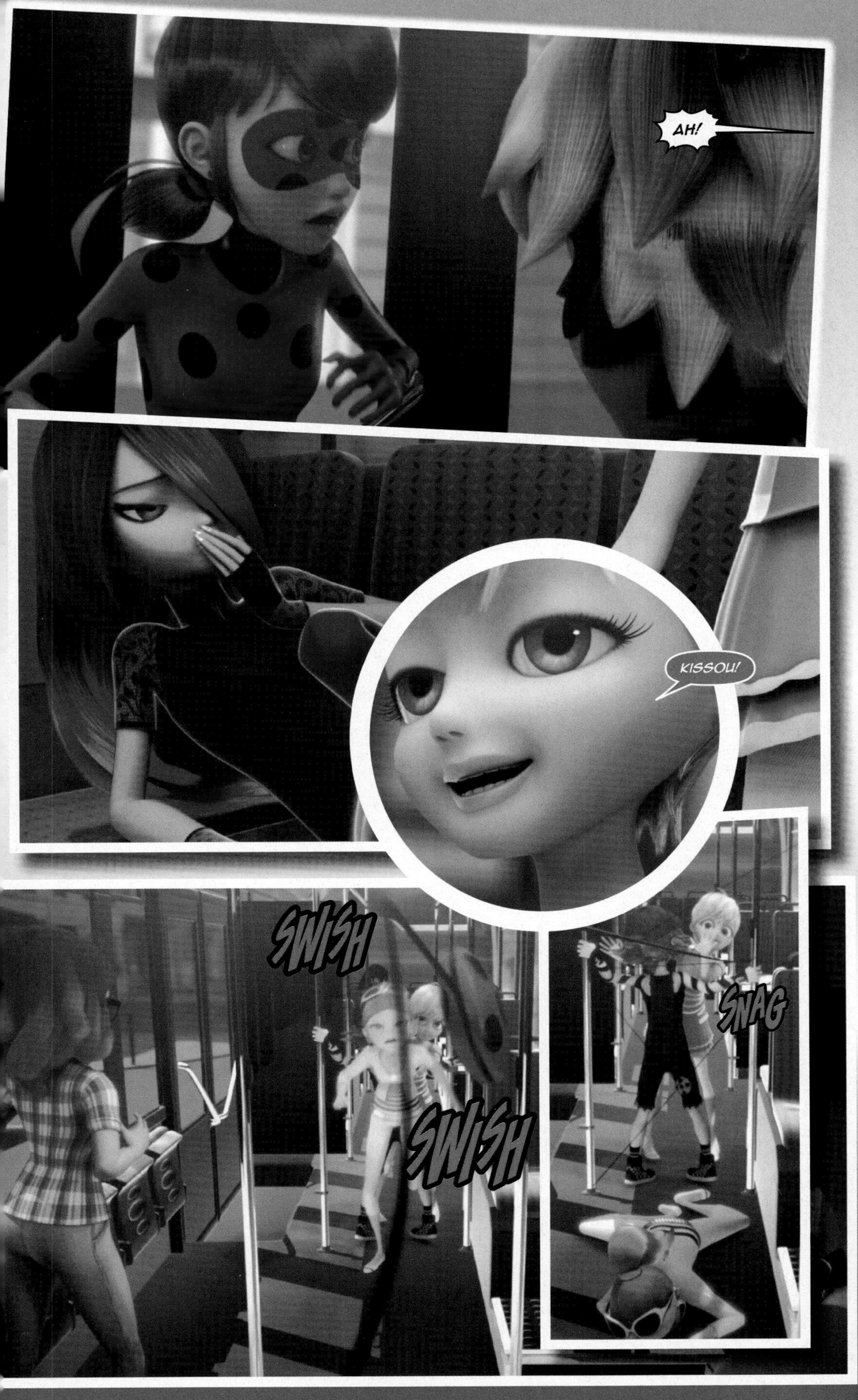
AH!
KISSOU!
SWISH
SWISH
SNAG

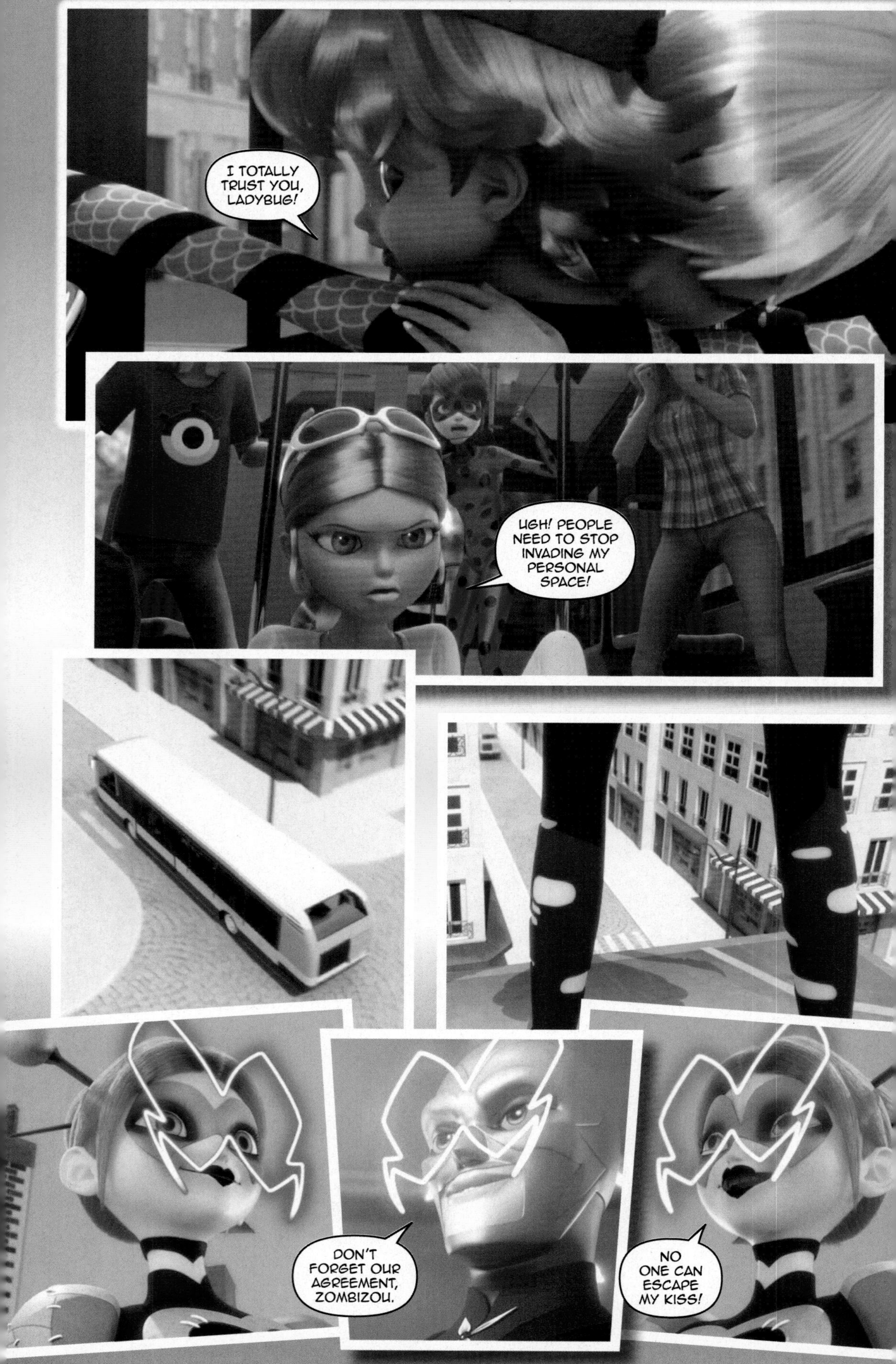
I TOTALLY TRUST YOU, LADYBUG!
UGH! PEOPLE NEED TO STOP INVADING MY PERSONAL SPACE!
DON'T FORGET OUR AGREEMENT, ZOMBIZOU.
NO ONE CAN ESCAPE MY KISS!

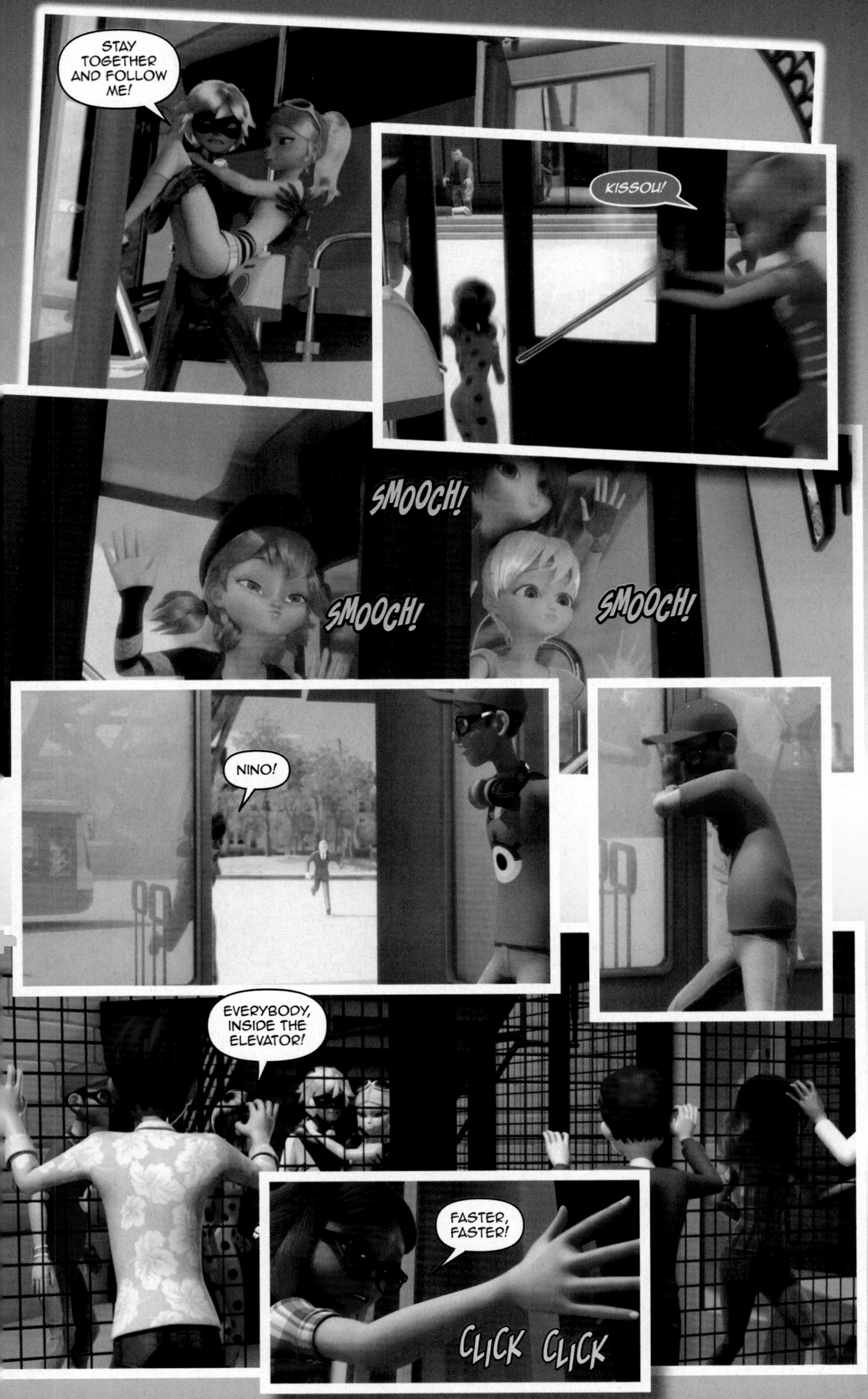
STAY TOGETHER AND FOLLOW ME!
KISSOU!
SMOOCH!
SMOOCH!
SMOOCH!
NINO!
EVERYBODY, INSIDE THE ELEVATOR!
FASTER, FASTER!
CLICK CLICK

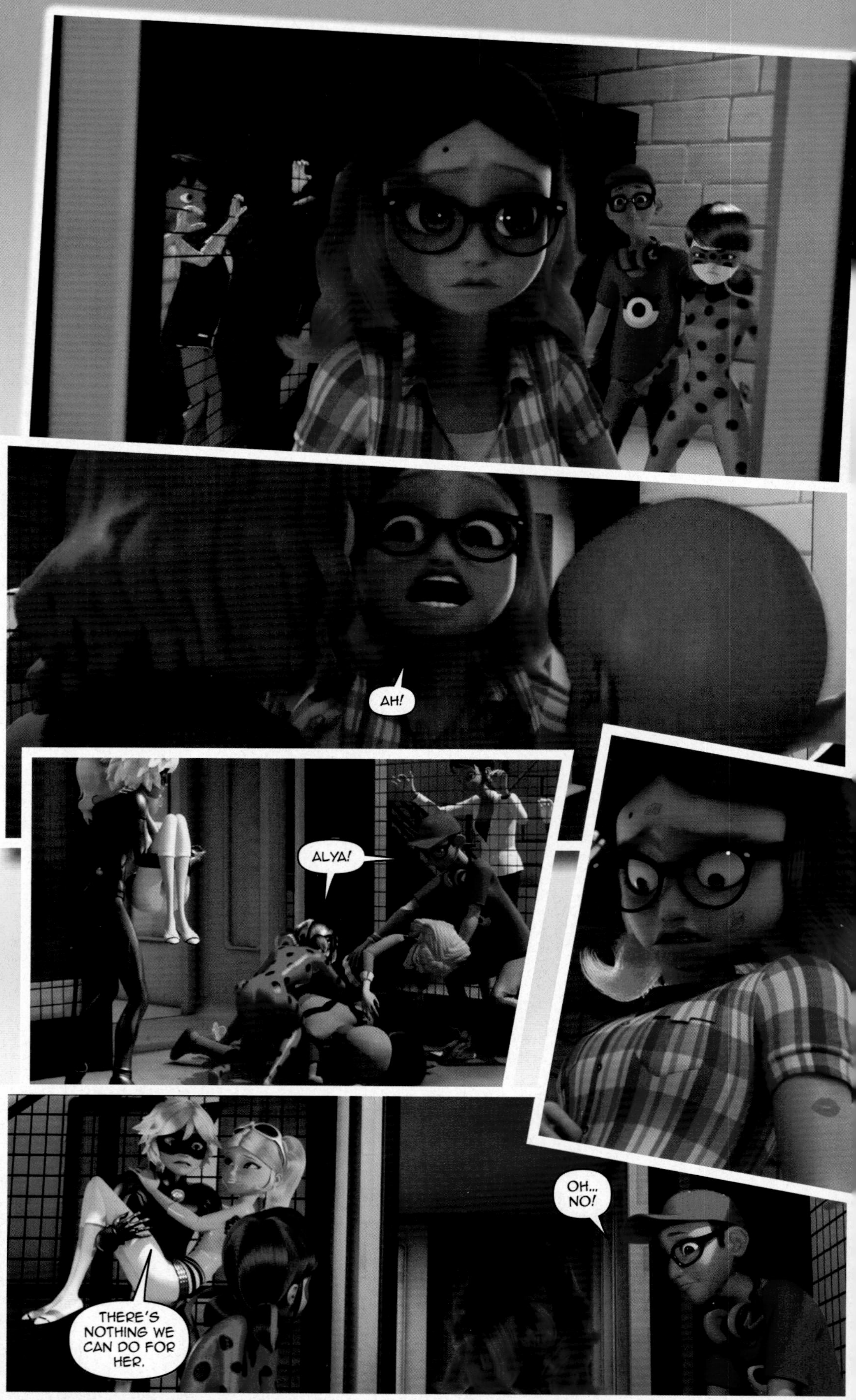
AH!
ALYA!
OH... NO!
THERE'S NOTHING WE CAN DO FOR HER.

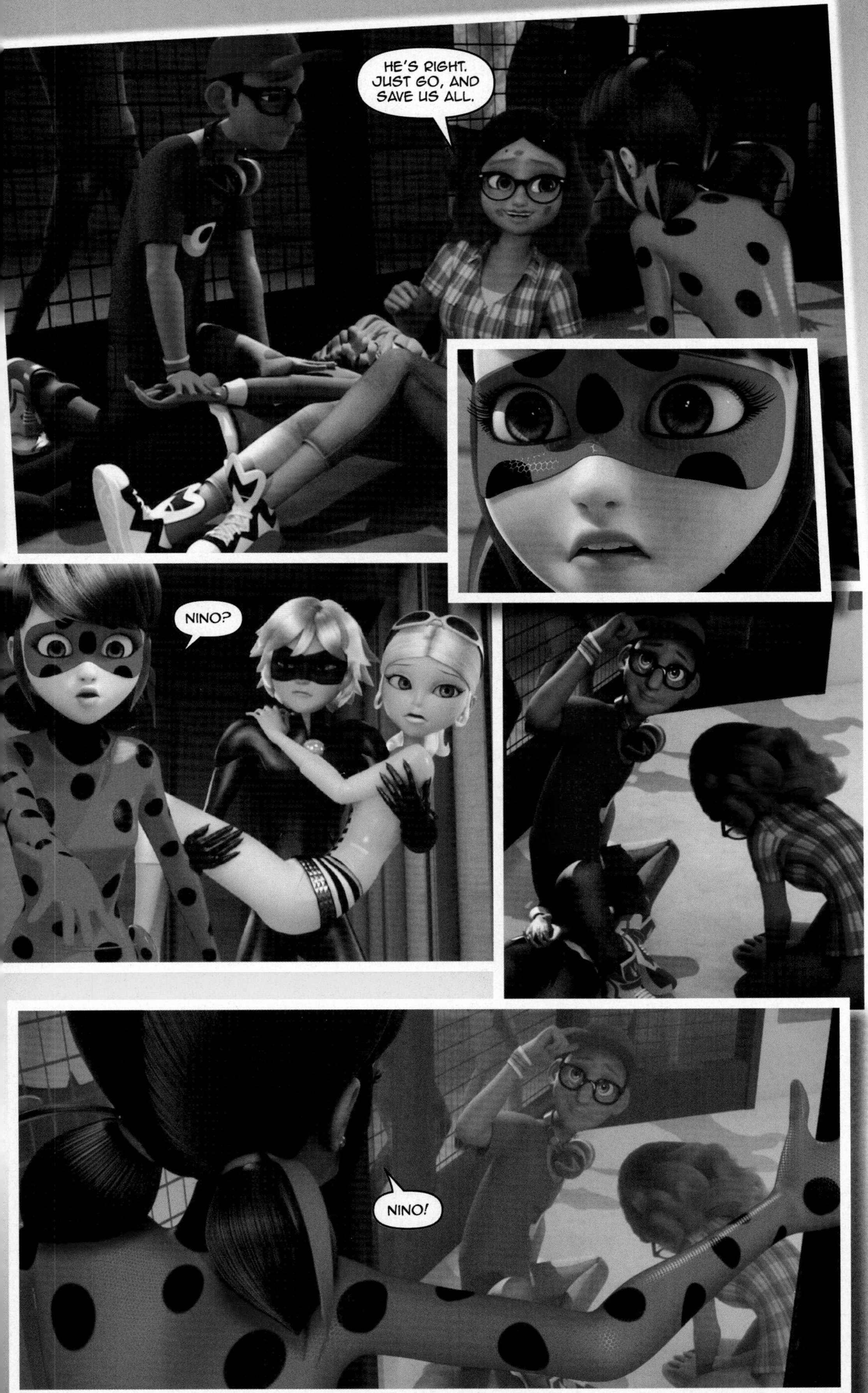
HE'S RIGHT. JUST GO, AND SAVE US ALL.
NINO?
NINO!

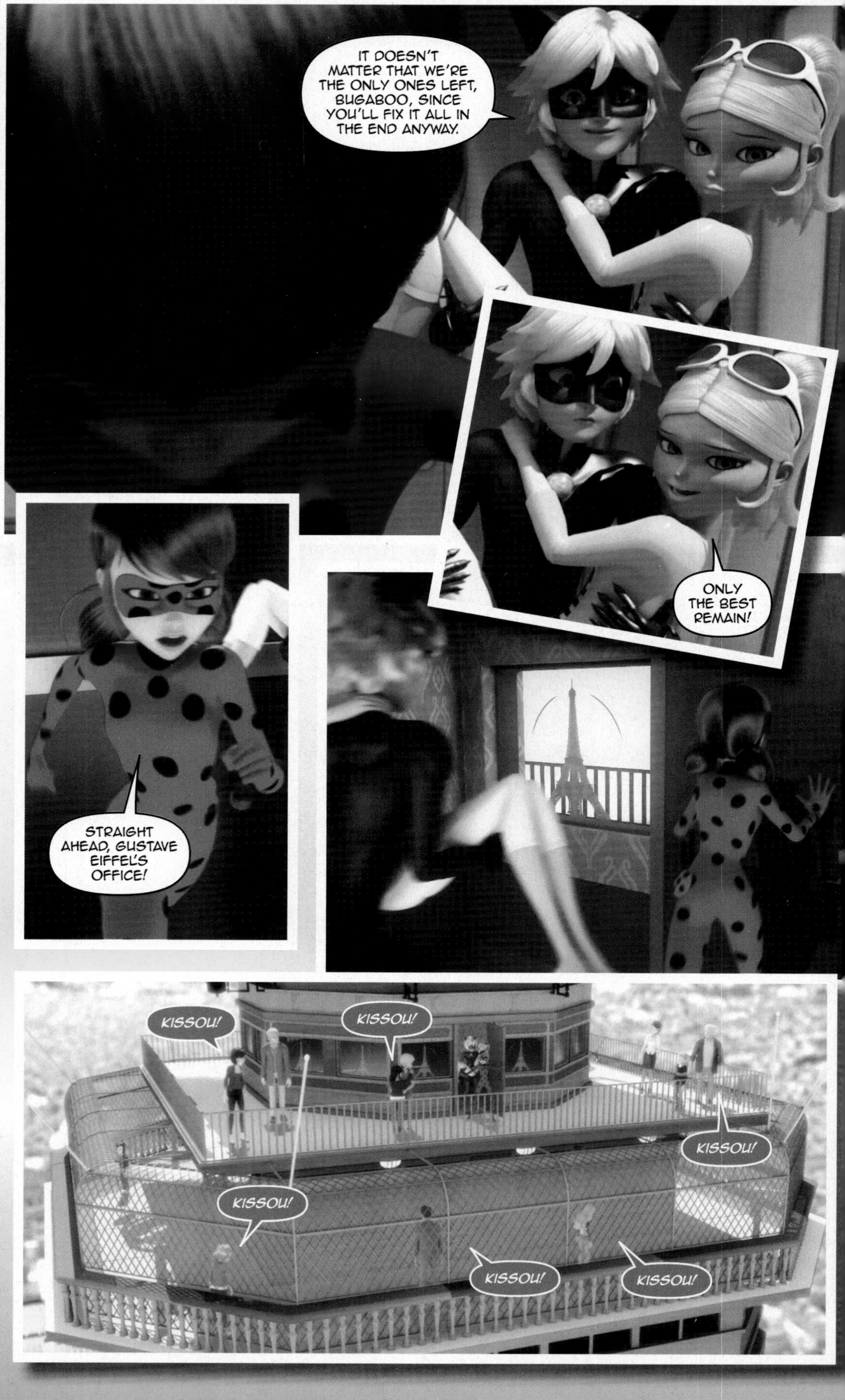
IT DOESN'T MATTER THAT WE'RE THE ONLY ONES LEFT, BUGABOO, SINCE YOU'LL FIX IT ALL IN THE END ANYWAY.
ONLY THE BEST REMAIN!
STRAIGHT AHEAD, GUSTAVE EIFFEL'S OFFICE!
KISSOU!
KISSOU!
KISSOU!
KISSOU!
KISSOU!
KISSOU!

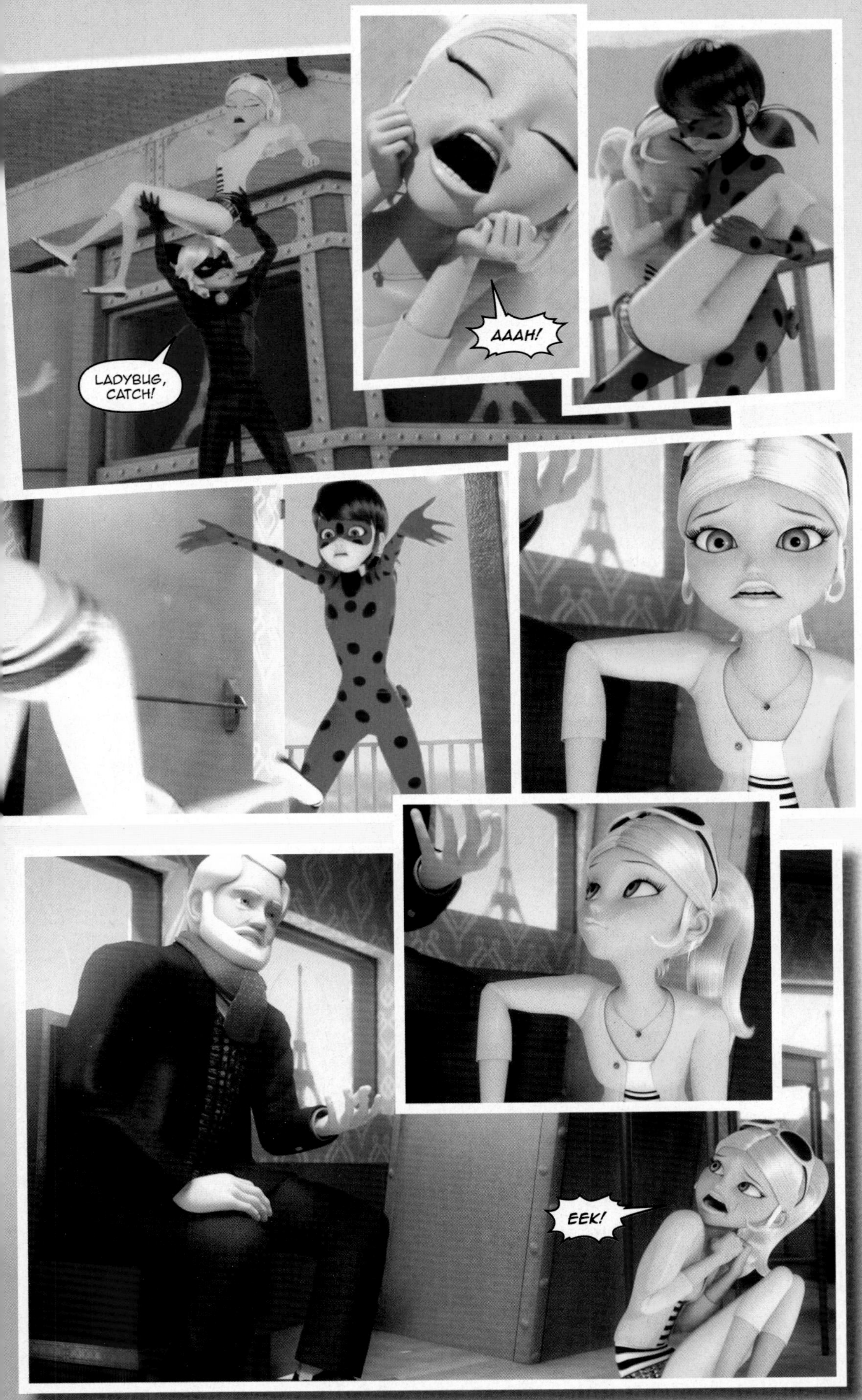
LADYBUG, CATCH!
AAAH!
EEK!

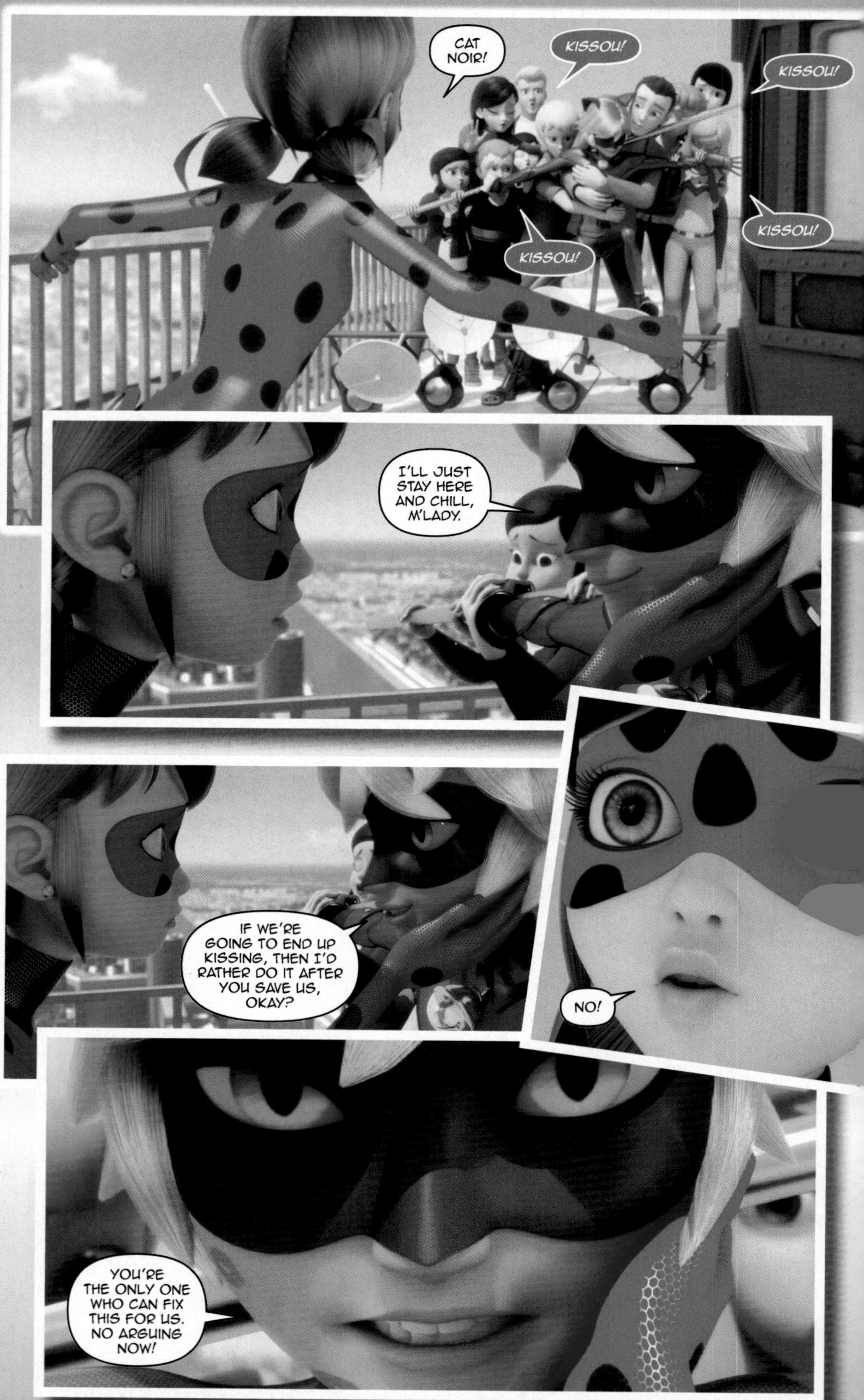
CAT NOIR!
KISSOU!
KISSOU!
KISSOU!
KISSOU!
I'LL JUST STAY HERE AND CHILL, M'LADY.
IF WE'RE GOING TO END UP KISSING, THEN I'D RATHER DO IT AFTER YOU SAVE US, OKAY?
NO!
YOU'RE THE ONLY ONE WHO CAN FIX THIS FOR US. NO ARGUING NOW!

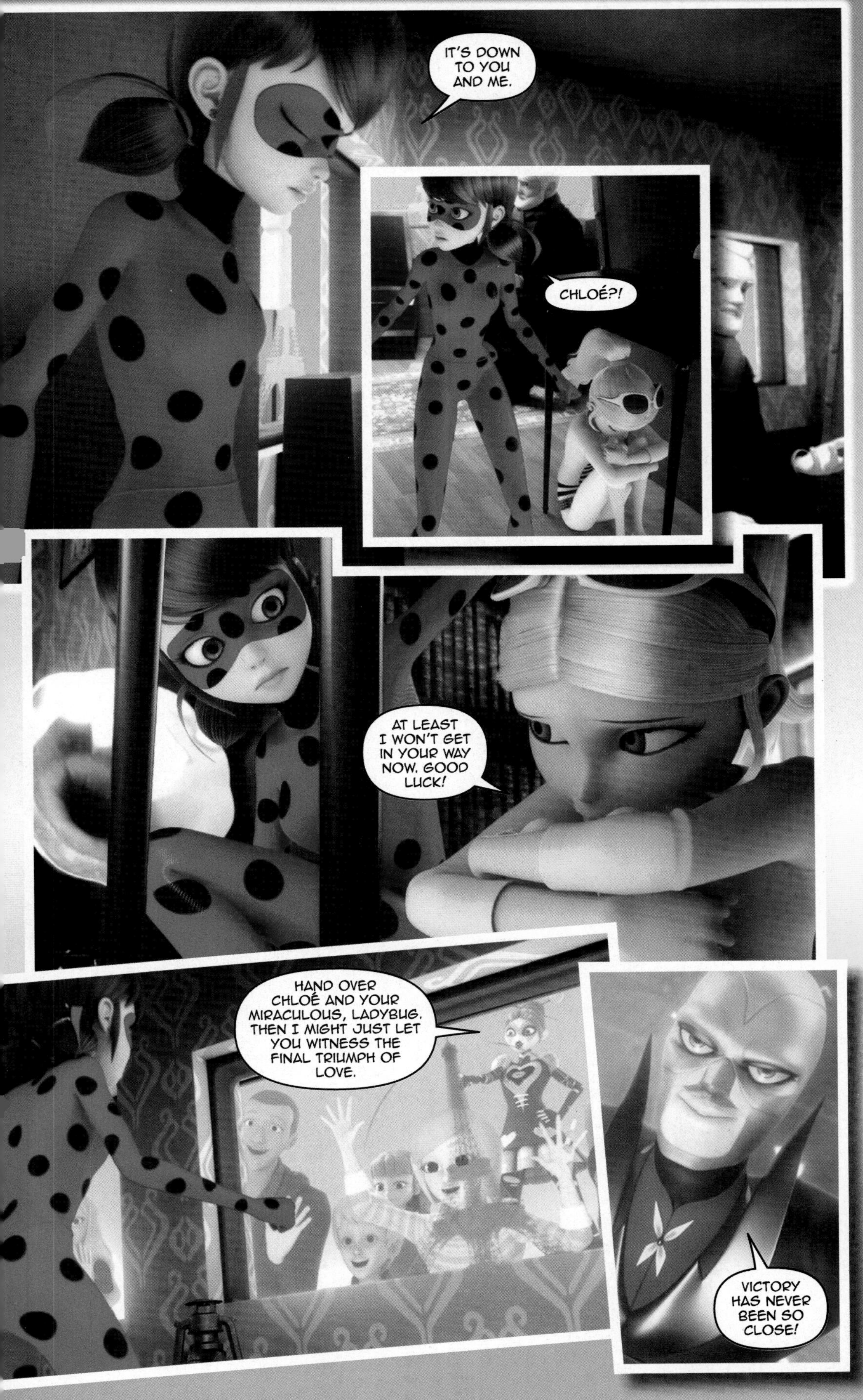
IT'S DOWN TO YOU AND ME.
CHLOÉ?!
AT LEAST I WON'T GET IN YOUR WAY NOW. GOOD LUCK!
HAND OVER CHLOÉ AND YOUR MIRACULOUS, LADYBUG. THEN I MIGHT JUST LET YOU WITNESS THE FINAL TRIUMPH OF LOVE.
VICTORY HAS NEVER BEEN SO CLOSE!

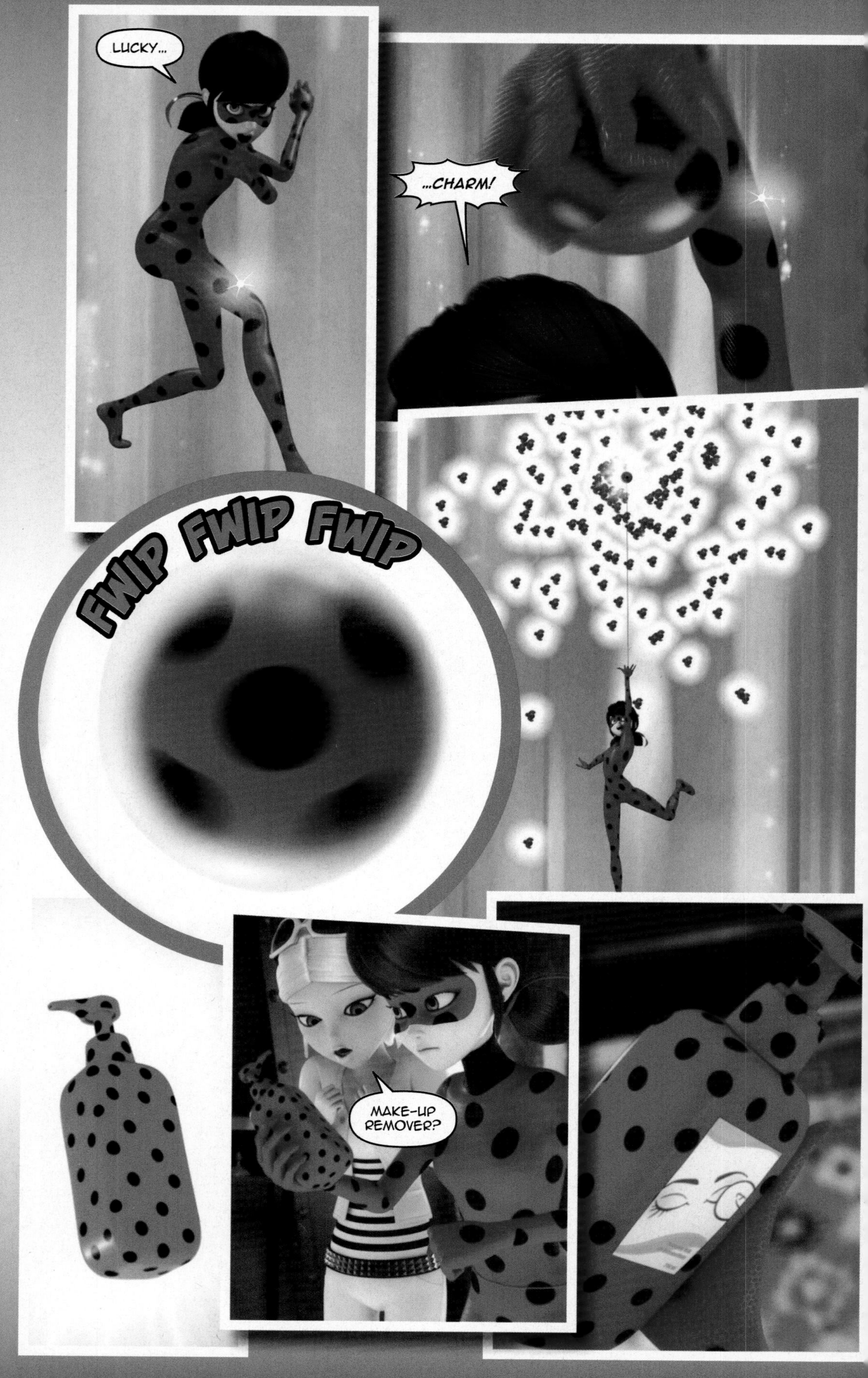
LUCKY...
...CHARM!
FWIP FWIP FWIP
MAKE-UP REMOVER?

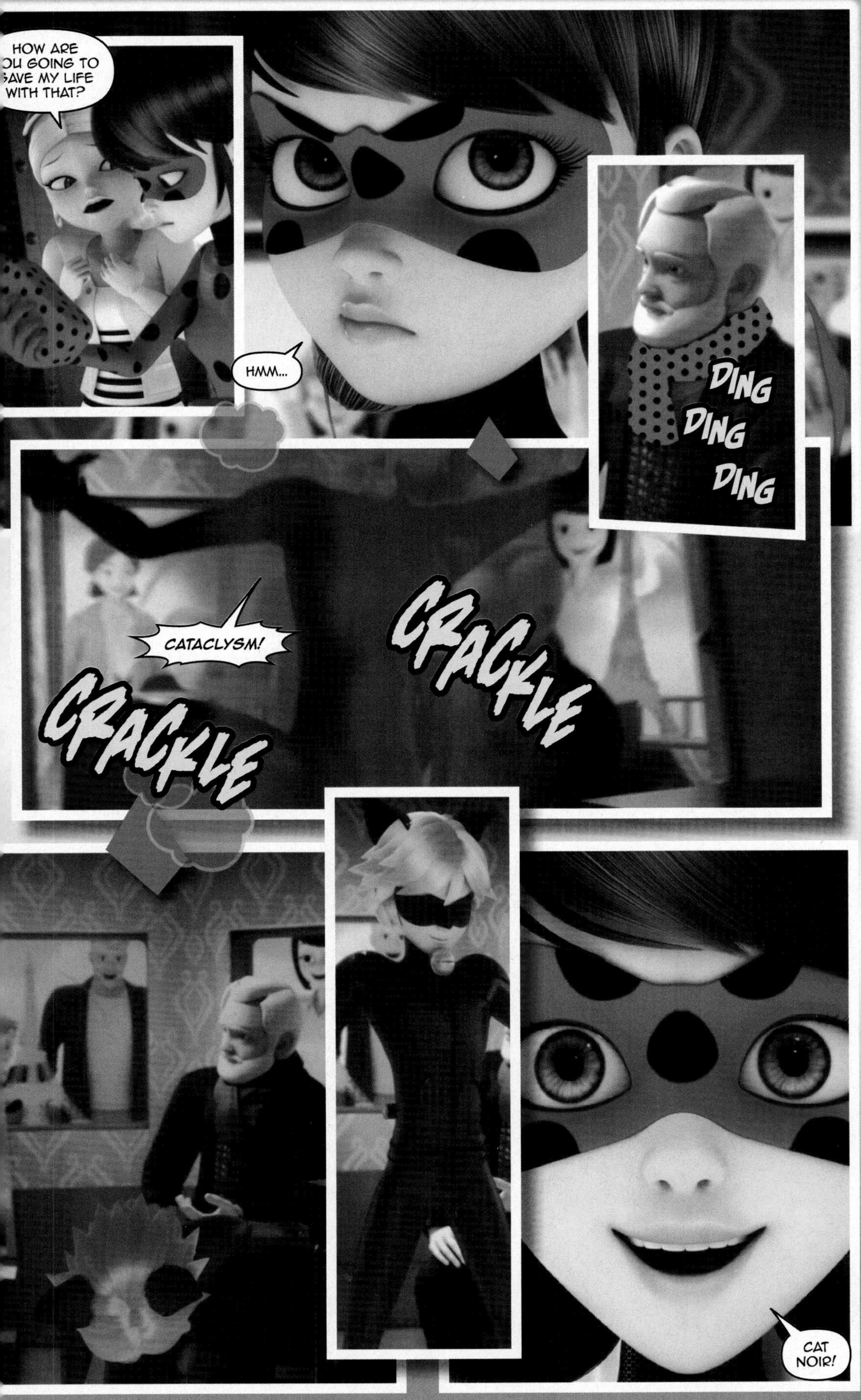
HOW ARE OU GOING TO SAVE MY LIFE WITH THAT?
HMM...
DING
DING
DING
CATACLYSM!
CRACKLE
CRACKLE
CAT NOIR!

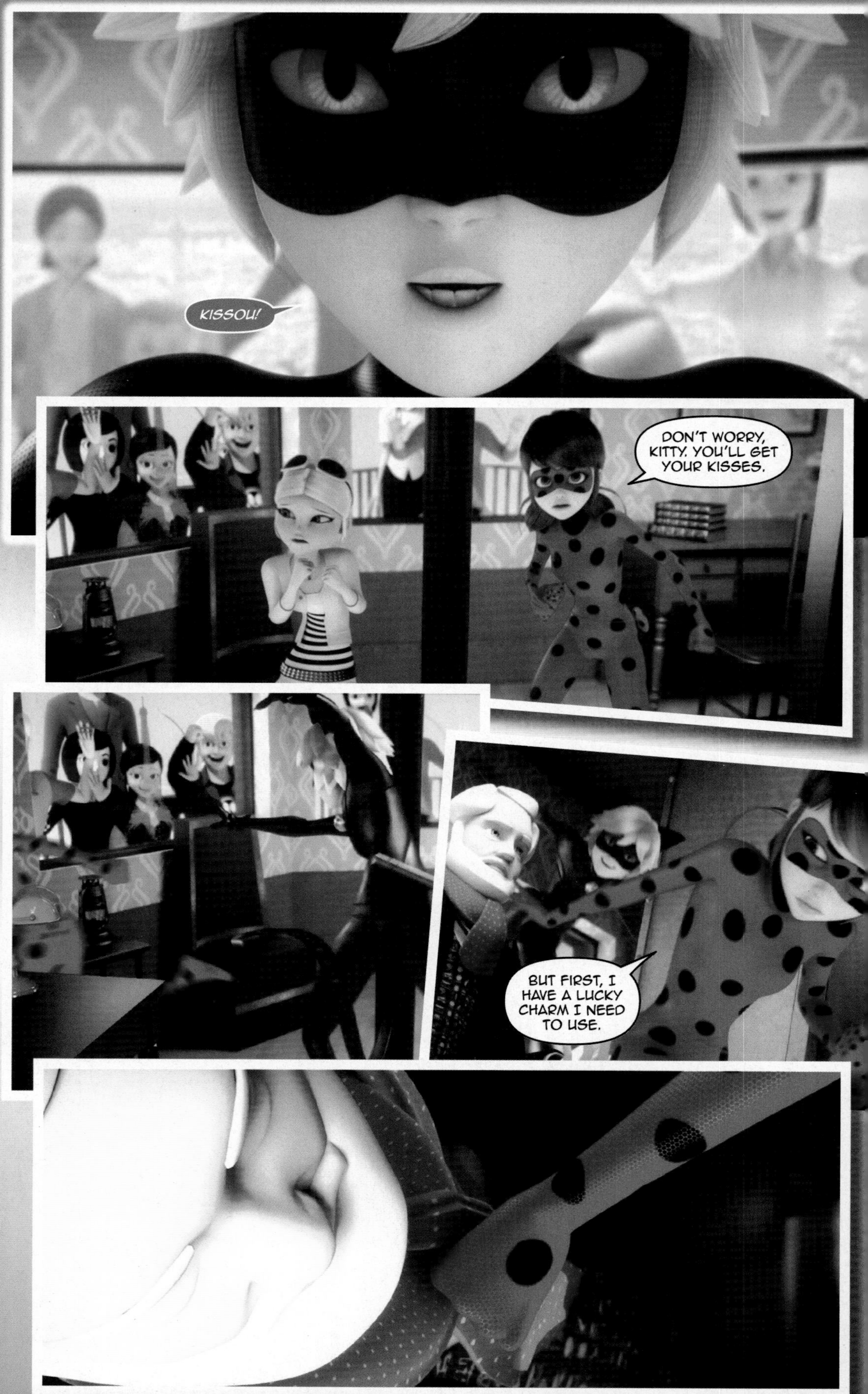
KISSOU!
DON'T WORRY, KITTY. YOU'LL GET YOUR KISSES.
BUT FIRST, I HAVE A LUCKY CHARM I NEED TO USE.

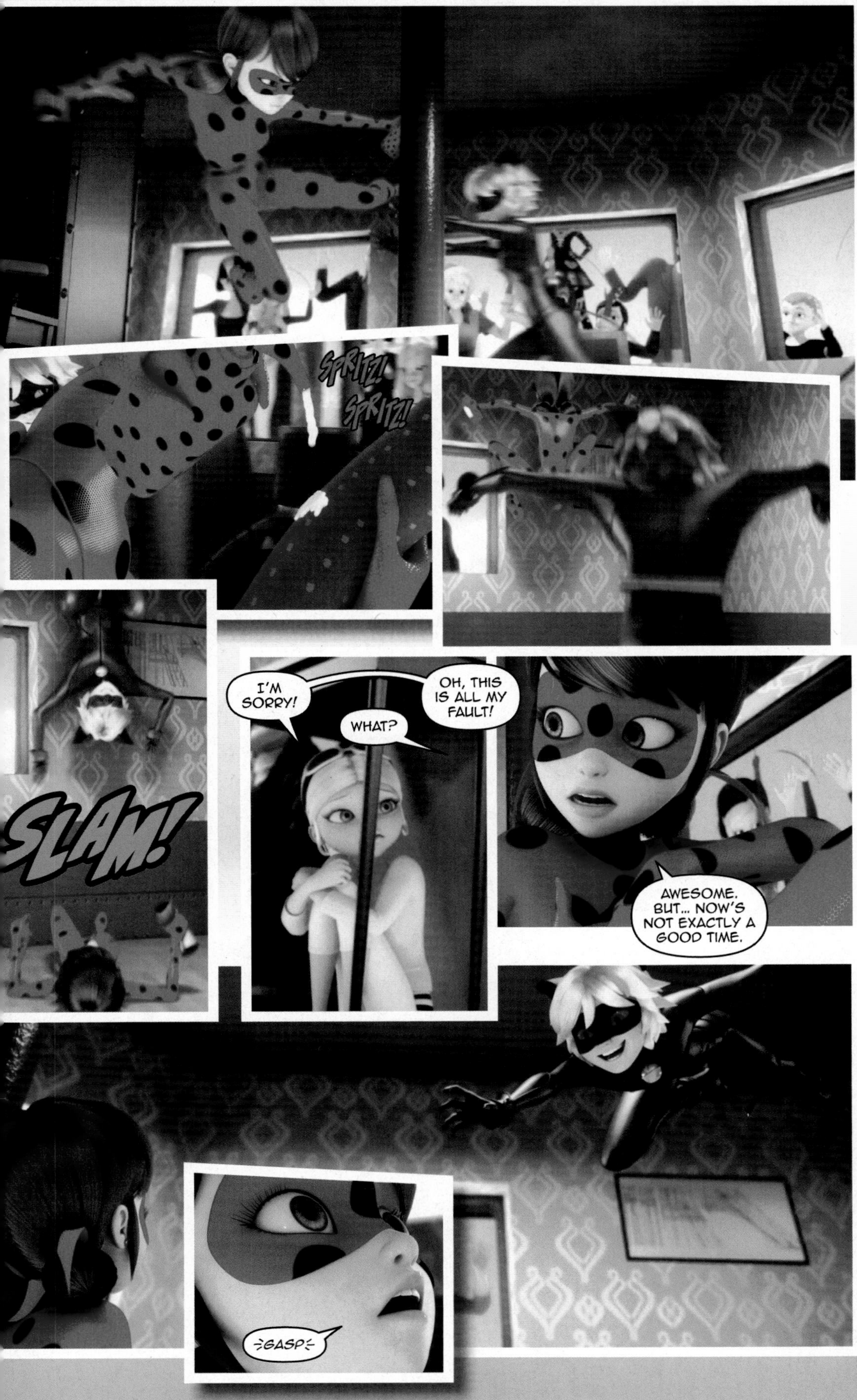

SPRITZ! SPRITZ!
SLAM!
I'M SORRY!
WHAT?
OH, THIS IS ALL MY FAULT!
AWESOME. BUT... NOW'S NOT EXACTLY A GOOD TIME.
GASP

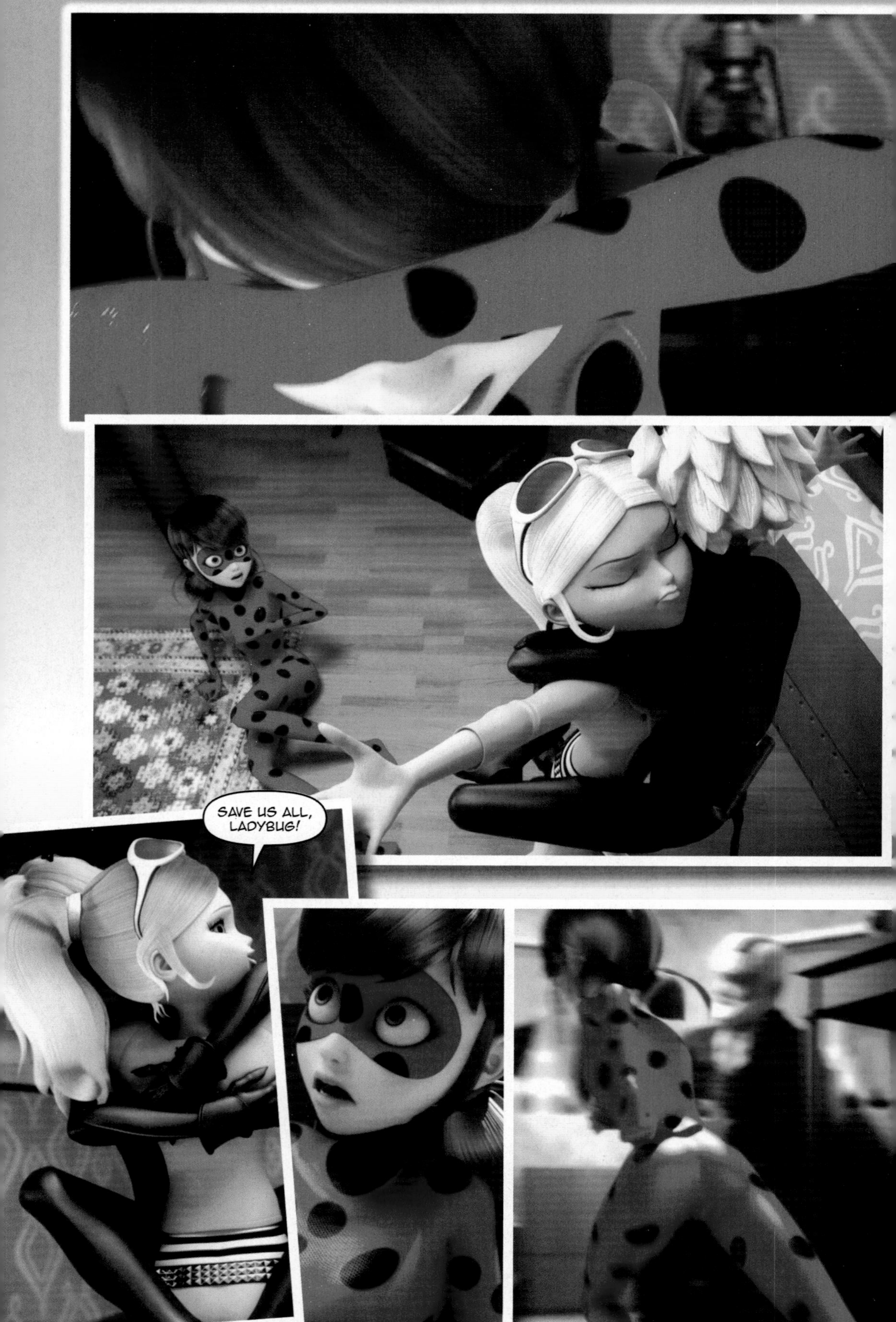
SAVE US ALL, LADYBUG!

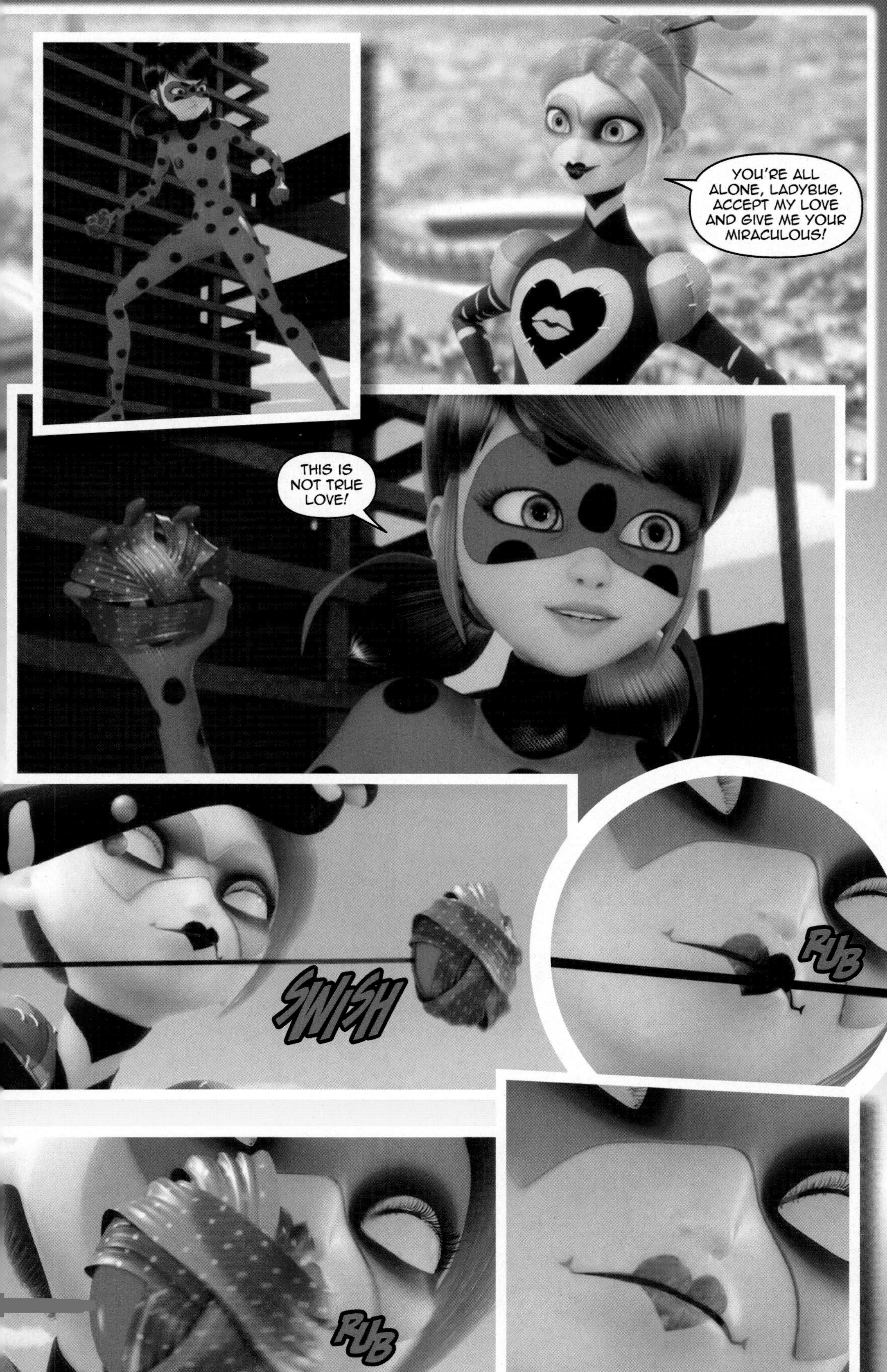
YOU'RE ALL ALONE, LADYBUG. ACCEPT MY LOVE AND GIVE ME YOUR MIRACULOUS!
THIS IS NOT TRUE LOVE!
SWISH
RUB
RUB

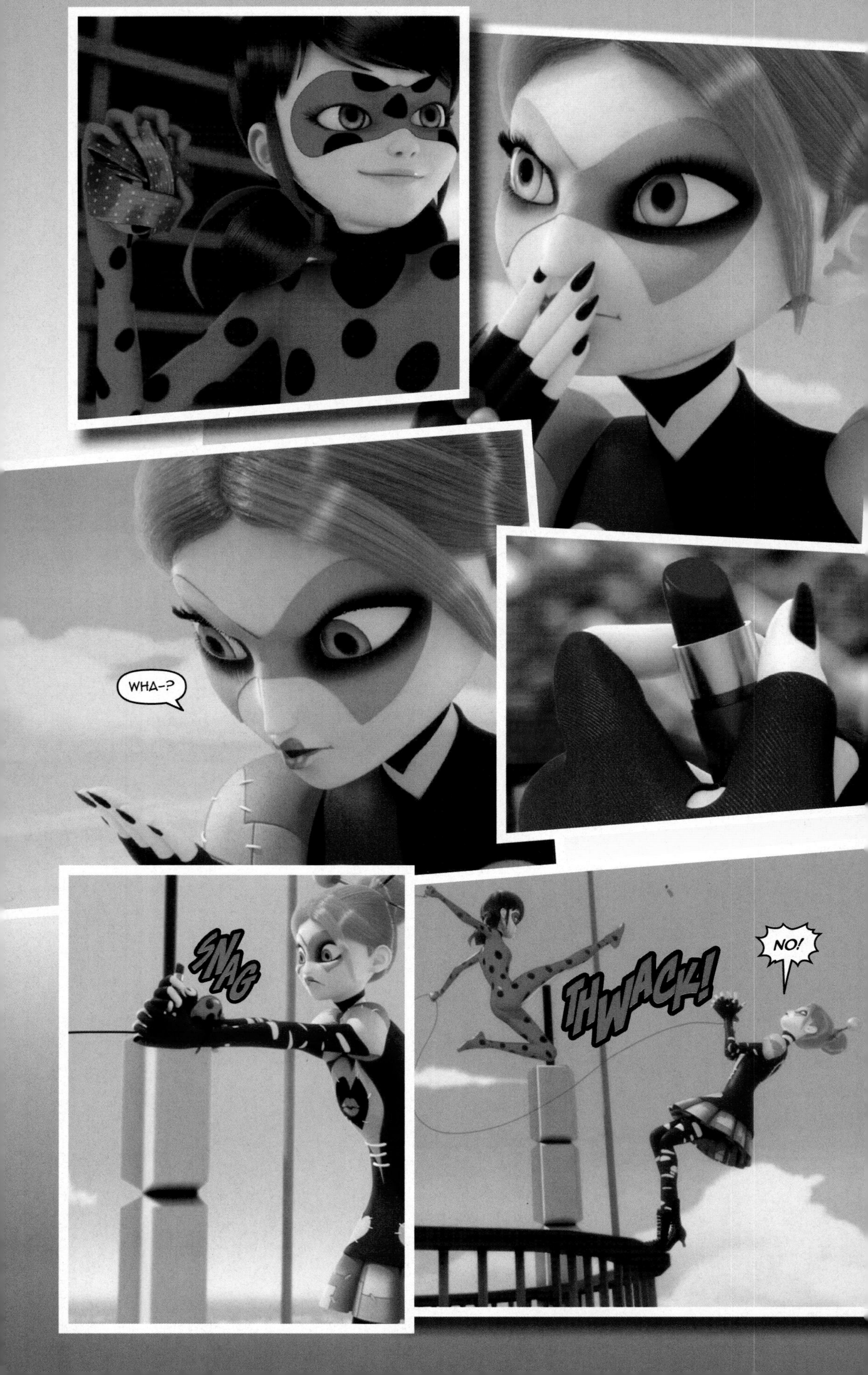
WHA-?
SNAG
THWACK!
NO!

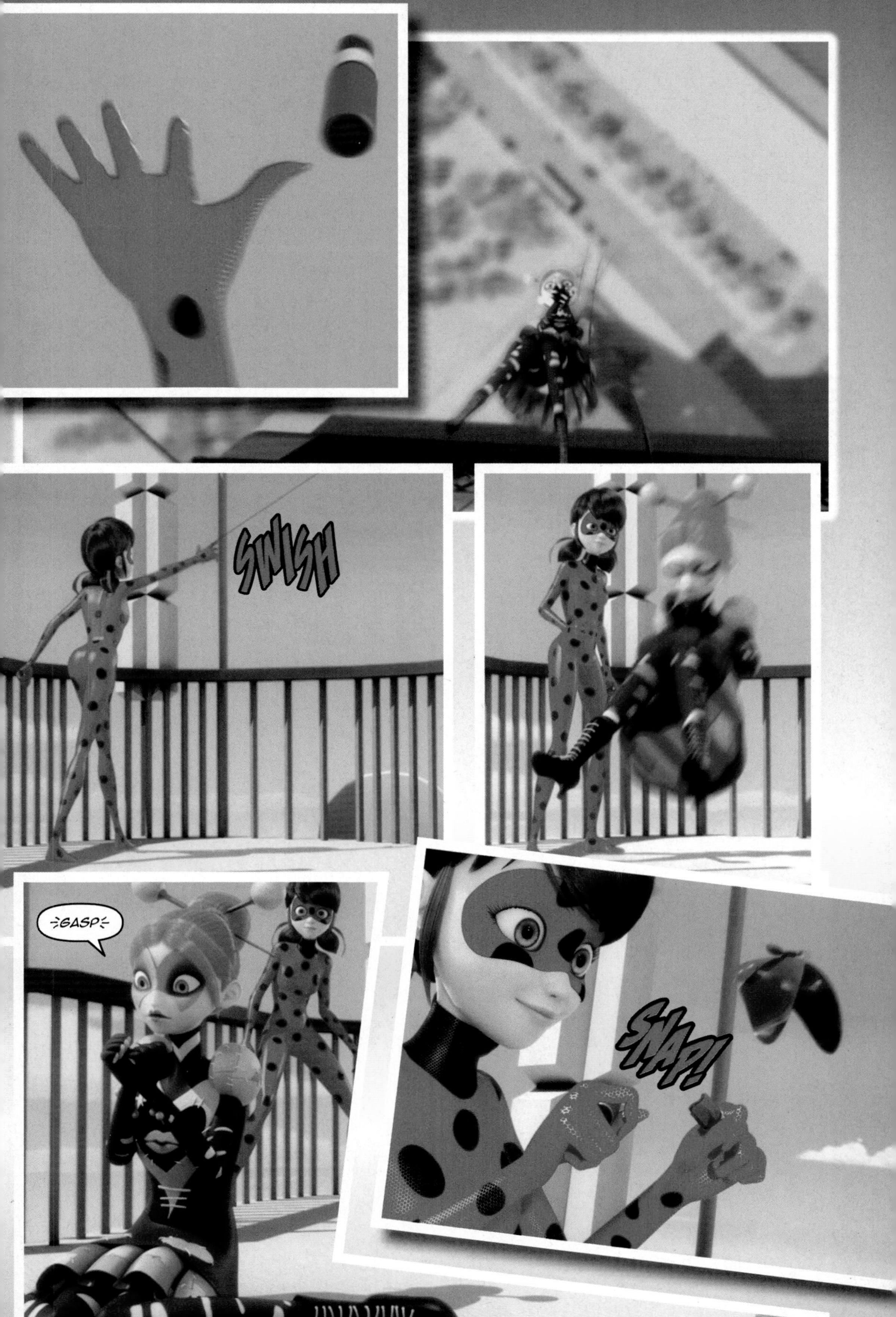
SWISH
GASP
SNAP!

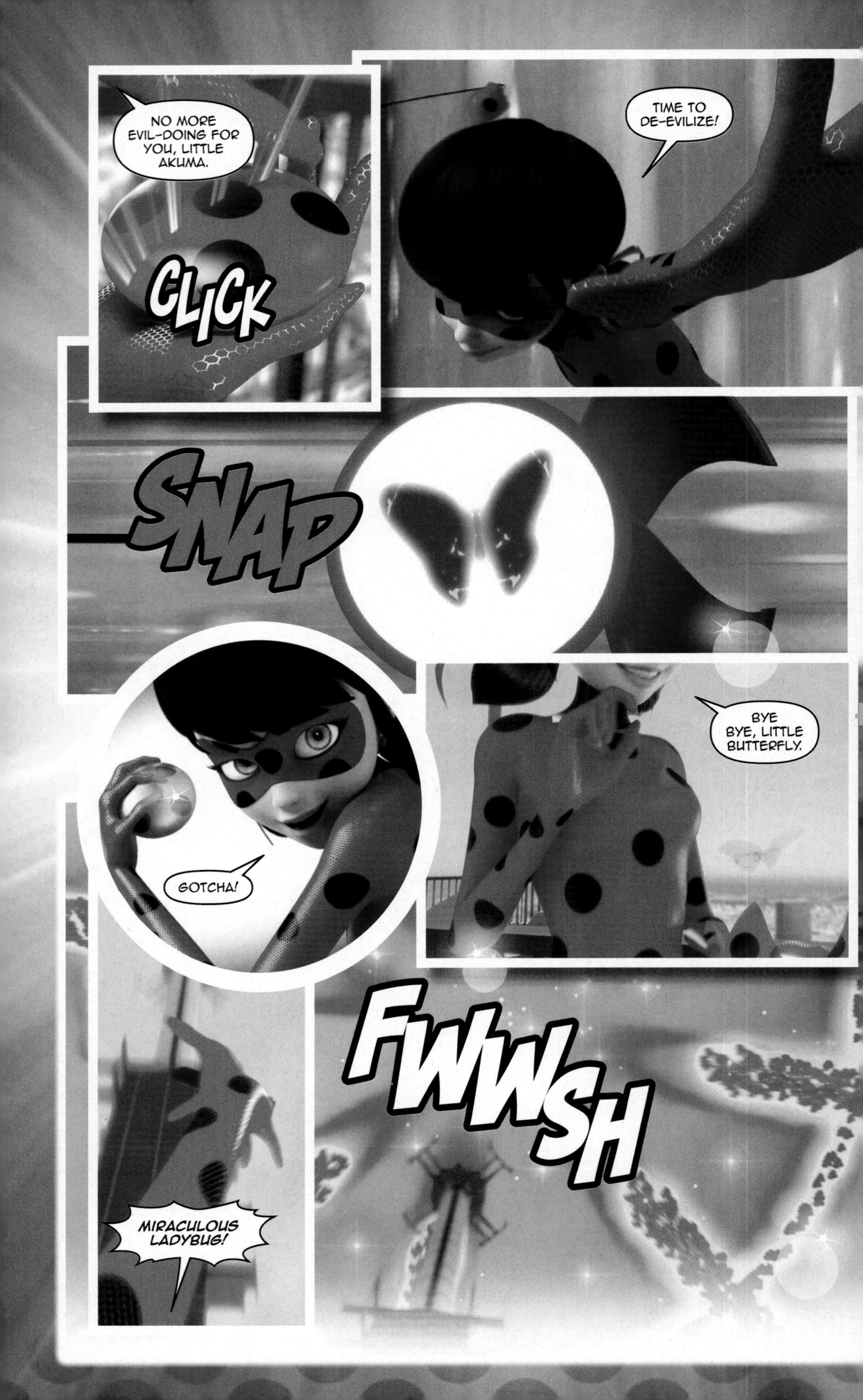
NO MORE EVIL-DOING FOR YOU, LITTLE AKUMA.
CLICK
TIME TO DE-EVILIZE!
SNAP
GOTCHA!
BYE BYE, LITTLE BUTTERFLY.
FWWSH
MIRACULOUS LADYBUG!

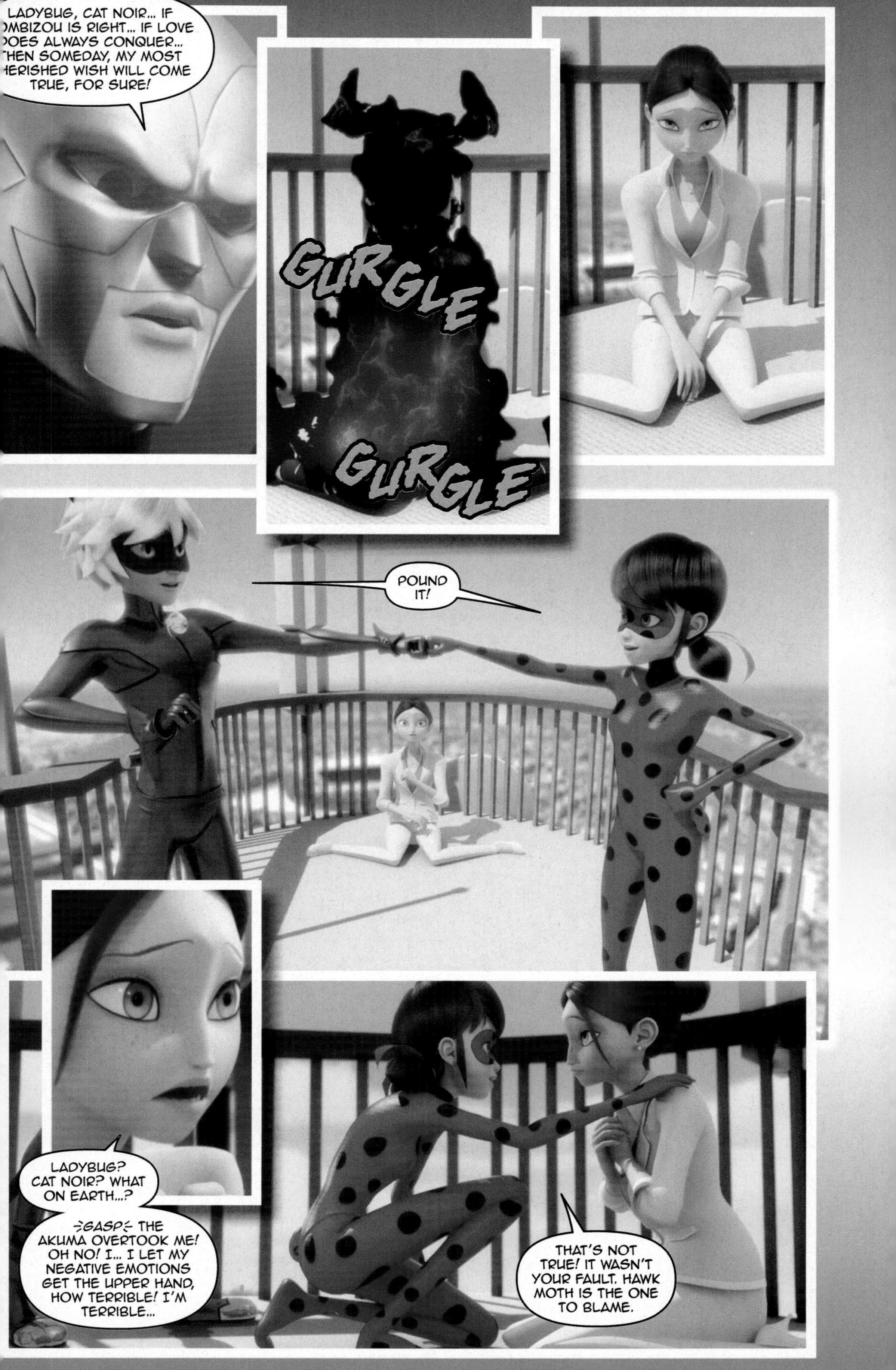

LADYBUG, CAT NOIR... IF OMBIZOU IS RIGHT... IF LOVE DOES ALWAYS CONQUER... THEN SOMEDAY, MY MOST CHERISHED WISH WILL COME TRUE, FOR SURE!
GURGLE
GURGLE
POUND IT!
LADYBUG? CAT NOIR? WHAT ON EARTH...?
GASP THE AKUMA OVERTOOK ME! OH NO! I... I LET MY NEGATIVE EMOTIONS GET THE UPPER HAND, HOW TERRIBLE! I'M TERRIBLE...
THAT'S NOT TRUE! IT WASN'T YOUR FAULT. HAWK MOTH IS THE ONE TO BLAME.

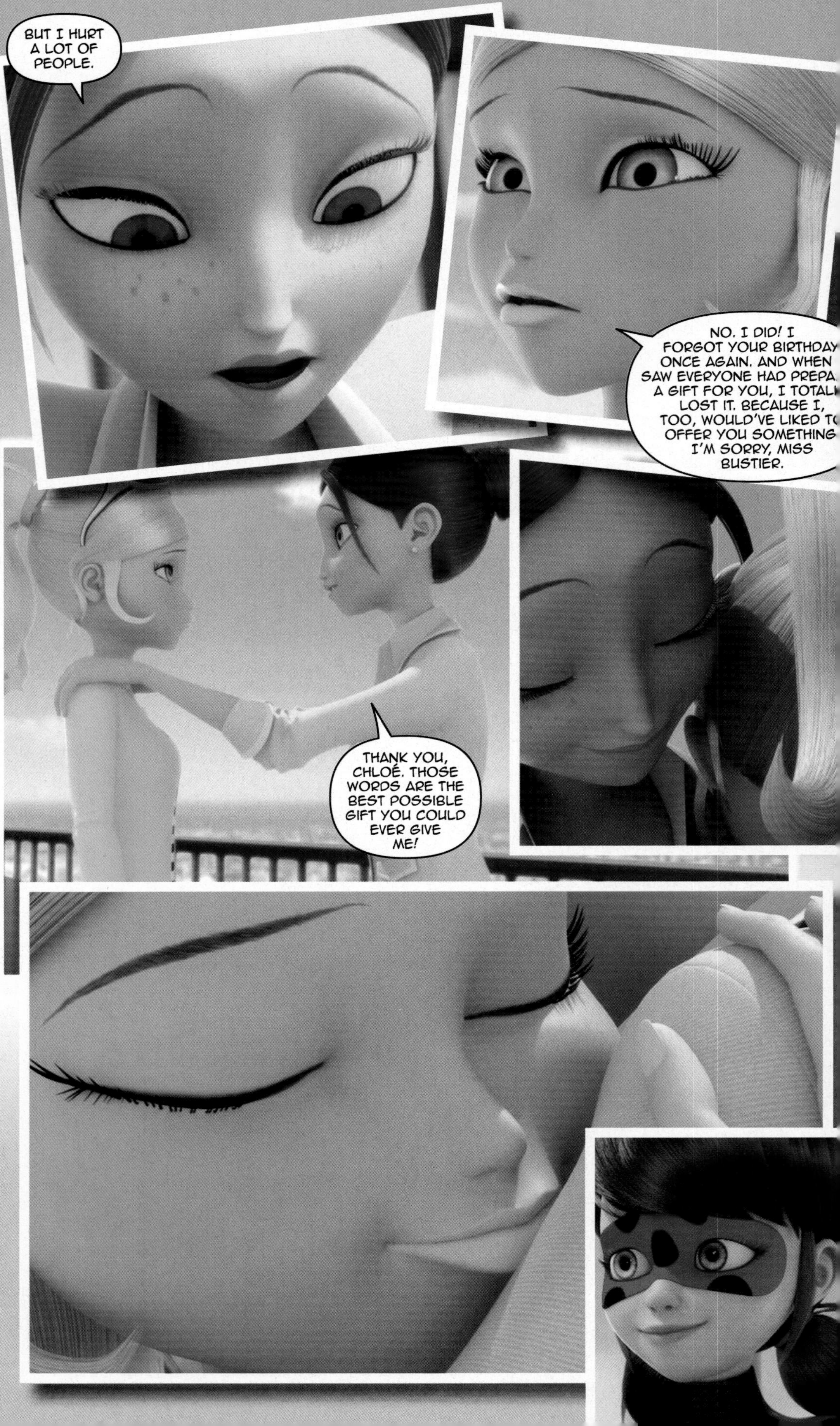
BUT I HURT A LOT OF PEOPLE.
NO. I DID! I FORGOT YOUR BIRTHDAY ONCE AGAIN. AND WHEN SAW EVERYONE HAD PREPA A GIFT FOR YOU, I TOTAL LOST IT. BECAUSE I, TOO, WOULD'VE LIKED T OFFER YOU SOMETHING I'M SORRY, MISS BUSTIER.
THANK YOU, CHLOÉ. THOSE WORDS ARE THE BEST POSSIBLE GIFT YOU COULD EVER GIVE ME!

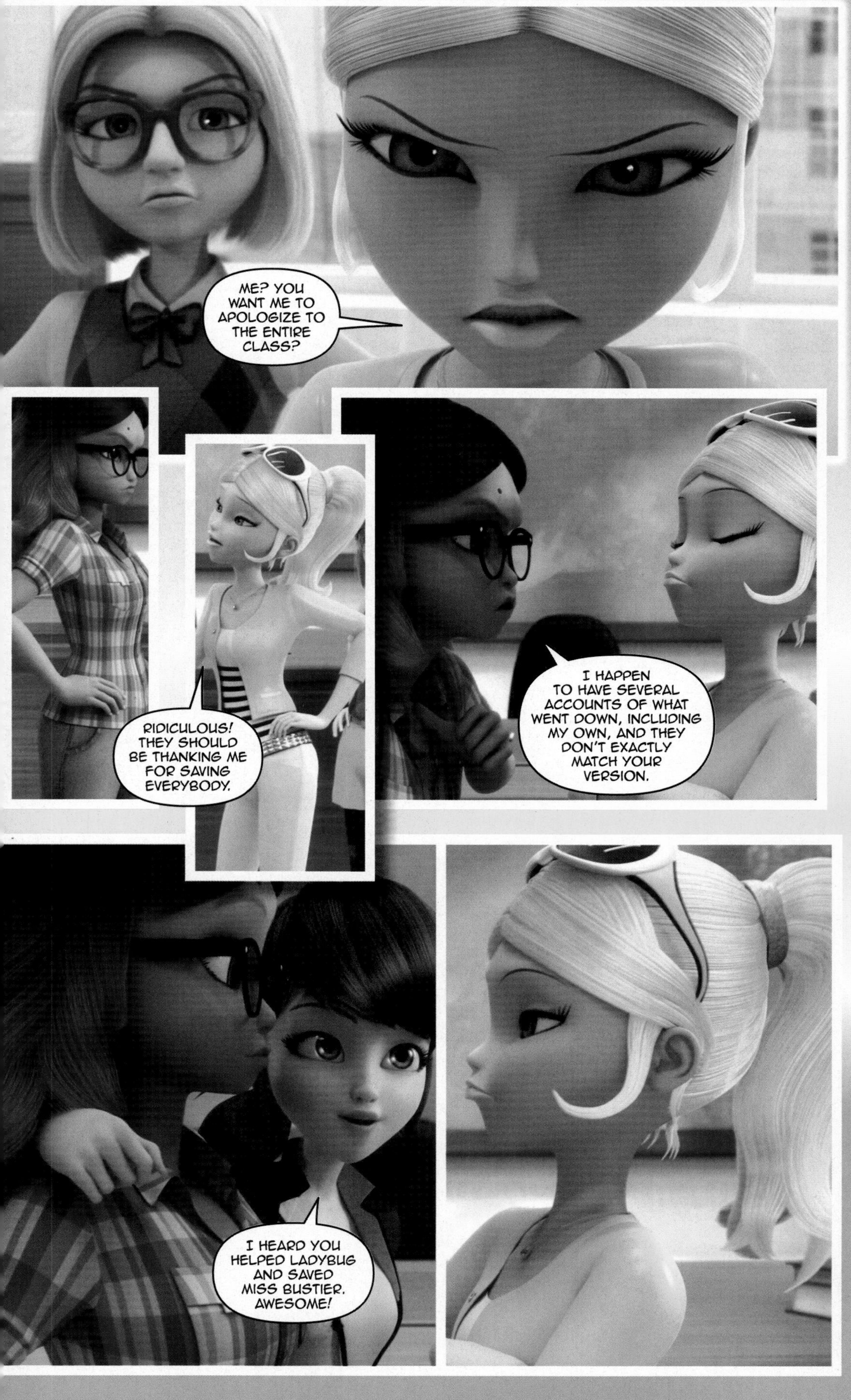
ME? YOU WANT ME TO APOLOGIZE TO THE ENTIRE CLASS?
RIDICULOUS! THEY SHOULD BE THANKING ME FOR SAVING EVERYBODY.
I HAPPEN TO HAVE SEVERAL ACCOUNTS OF WHAT WENT DOWN, INCLUDING MY OWN, AND THEY DON'T EXACTLY MATCH YOUR VERSION.
I HEARD YOU HELPED LADYBUG AND SAVED MISS BUSTIER. AWESOME!

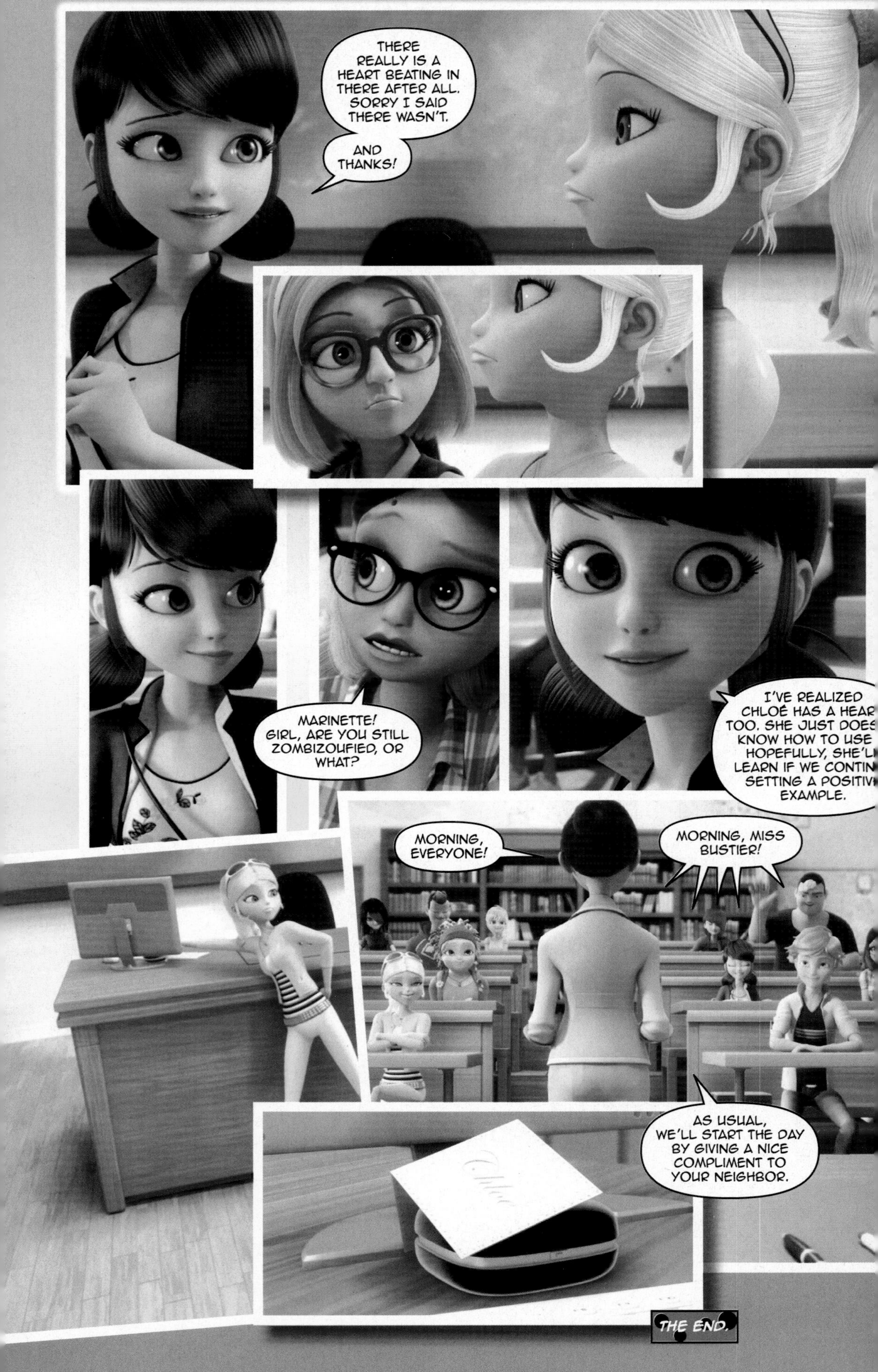
THERE REALLY IS A HEART BEATING IN THERE AFTER ALL. SORRY I SAID THERE WASN'T.
AND THANKS!
MARINETTE! GIRL, ARE YOU STILL ZOMBIZOUFIED, OR WHAT?
I'VE REALIZED CHLOÉ HAS A HEAR TOO. SHE JUST DOES KNOW HOW TO USE HOPEFULLY, SHE'L LEARN IF WE CONTIN SETTING A POSITIV EXAMPLE.
MORNING, EVERYONE!
MORNING, MISS BUSTIER!
AS USUAL, WE'LL START THE DAY BY GIVING A NICE COMPLIMENT TO YOUR NEIGHBOR.
THE END.

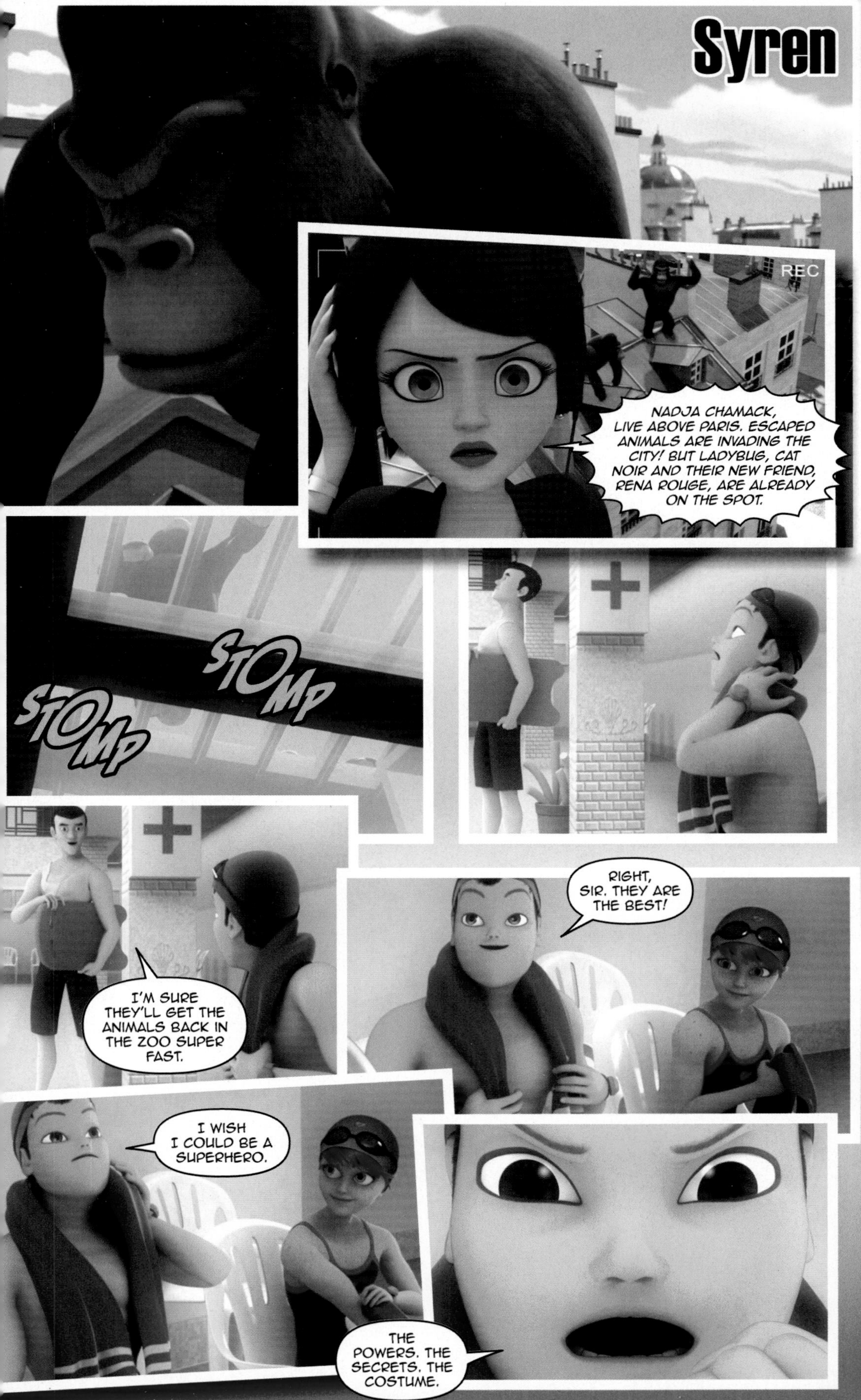

Syren
REC
NADJA CHAMACK, LIVE ABOVE PARIS. ESCAPED ANIMALS ARE INVADING THE CITY! BUT LADYBUG, CAT NOIR AND THEIR NEW FRIEND, RENA ROUGE, ARE ALREADY ON THE SPOT.
STOMP
STOMP
I'M SURE THEY'LL GET THE ANIMALS BACK IN THE ZOO SUPER FAST.
RIGHT, SIR. THEY ARE THE BEST!
I WISH I COULD BE A SUPERHERO.
THE POWERS. THE SECRETS. THE COSTUME.

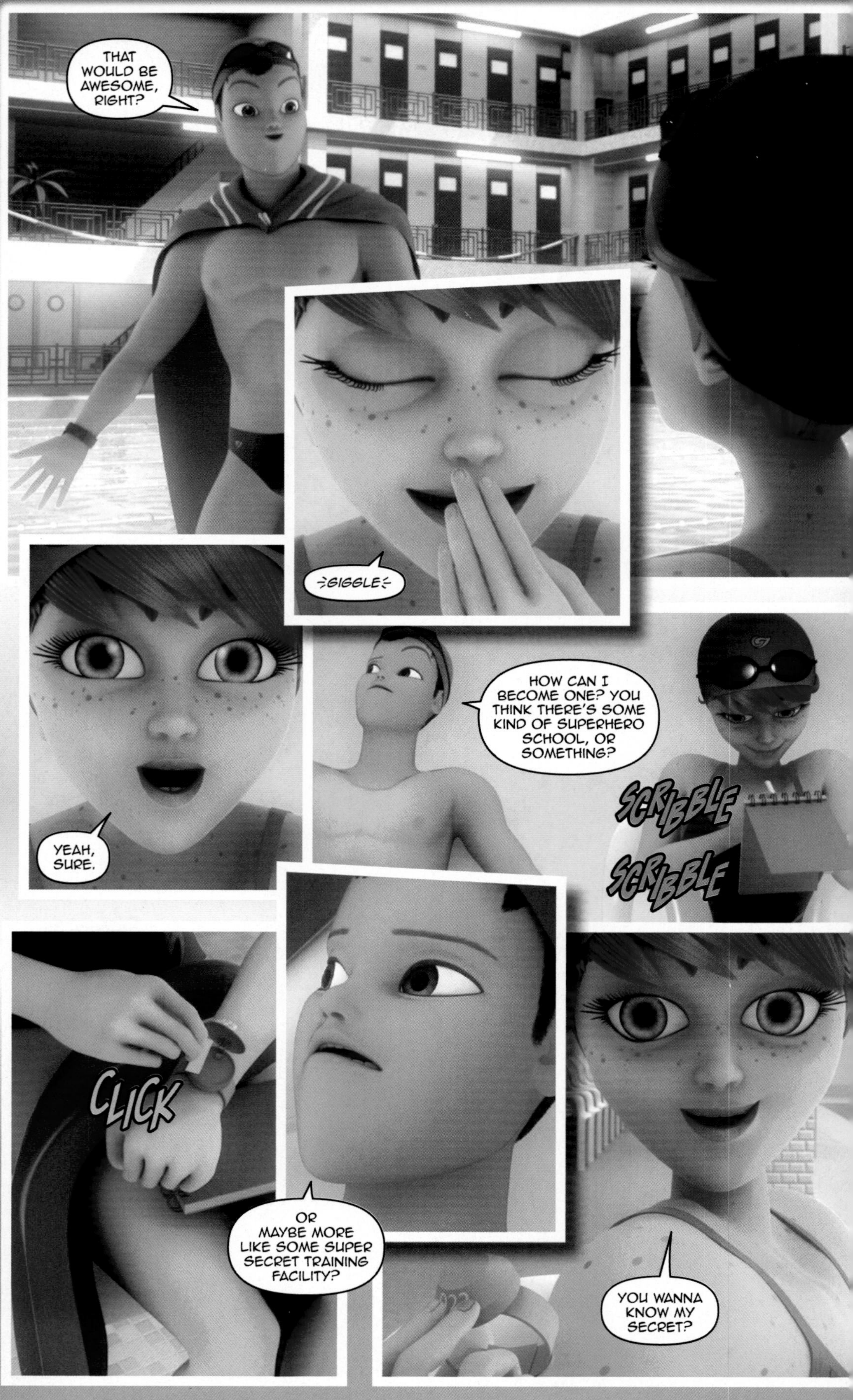
THAT WOULD BE AWESOME, RIGHT?
GIGGLE
YEAH, SURE.
HOW CAN I BECOME ONE? YOU THINK THERE'S SOME KIND OF SUPERHERO SCHOOL, OR SOMETHING?
SCRIBBLE
SCRIBBLE
CLICK
OR MAYBE MORE LIKE SOME SUPER SECRET TRAINING FACILITY?
YOU WANNA KNOW MY SECRET?

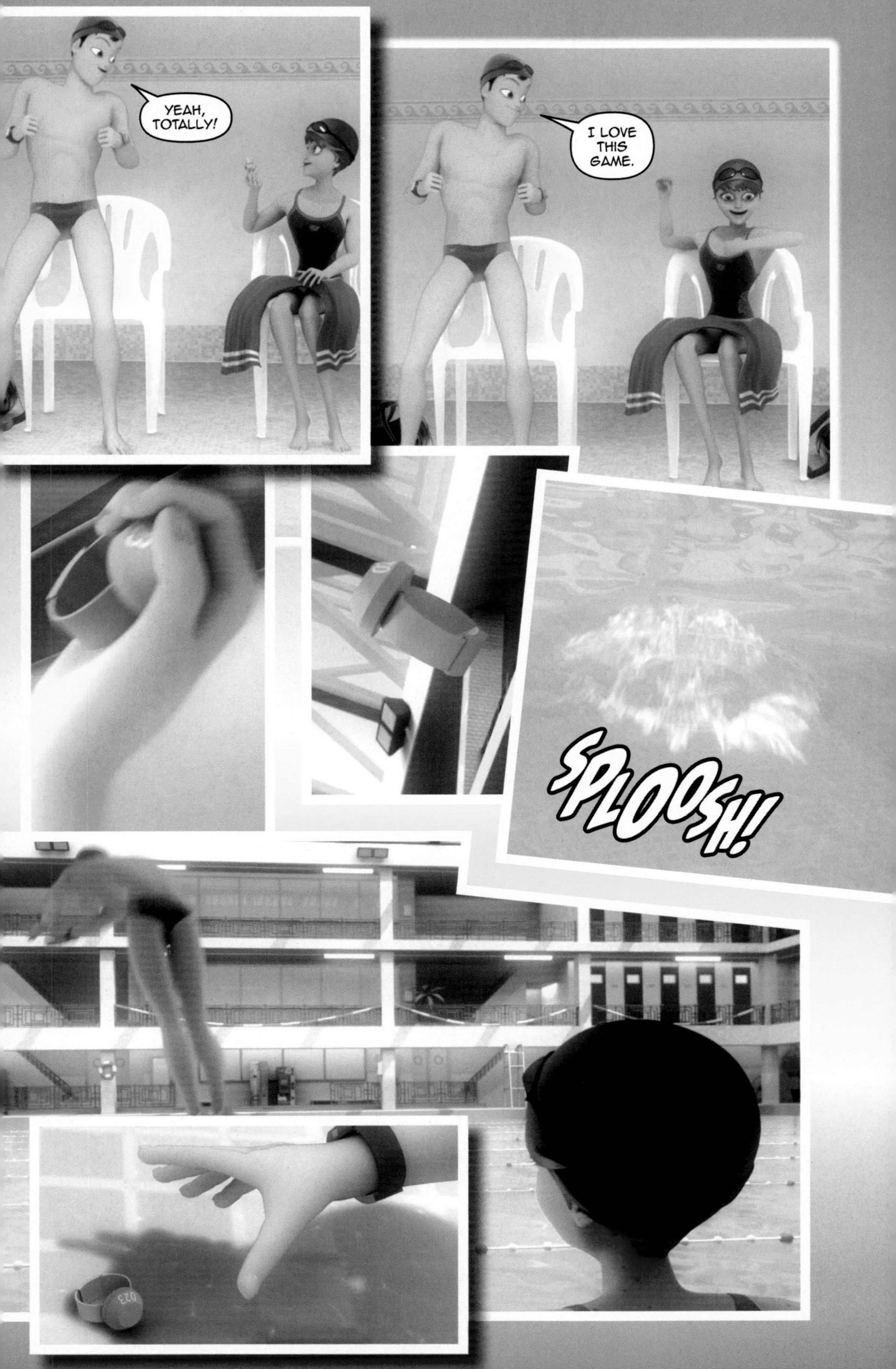
YEAH, TOTALLY!
I LOVE THIS GAME.
SPLOOSH!

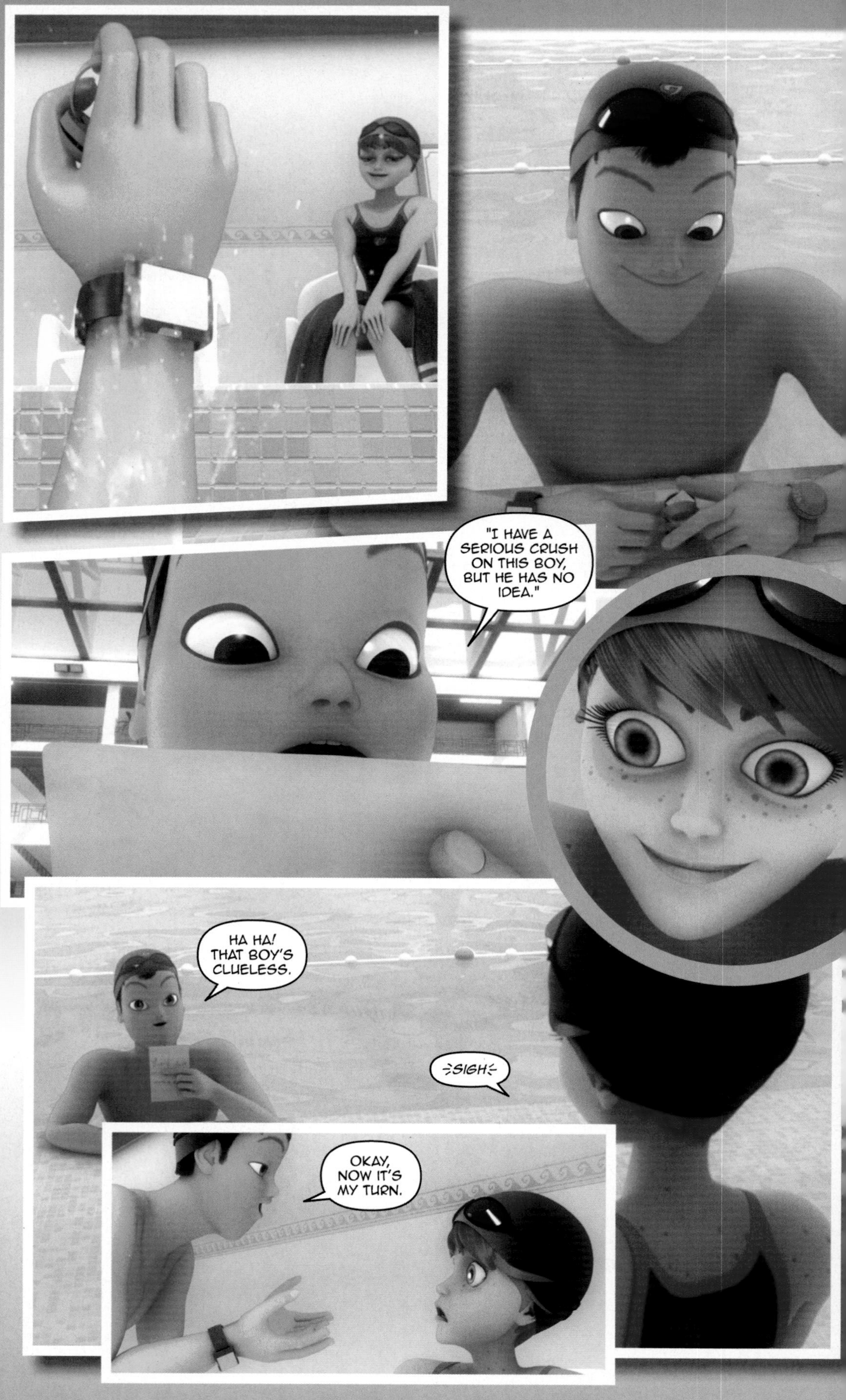
"I HAVE A SERIOUS CRUSH ON THIS BOY, BUT HE HAS NO IDEA."
HA HA! THAT BOY'S CLUELESS.
SIGH
OKAY, NOW IT'S MY TURN.

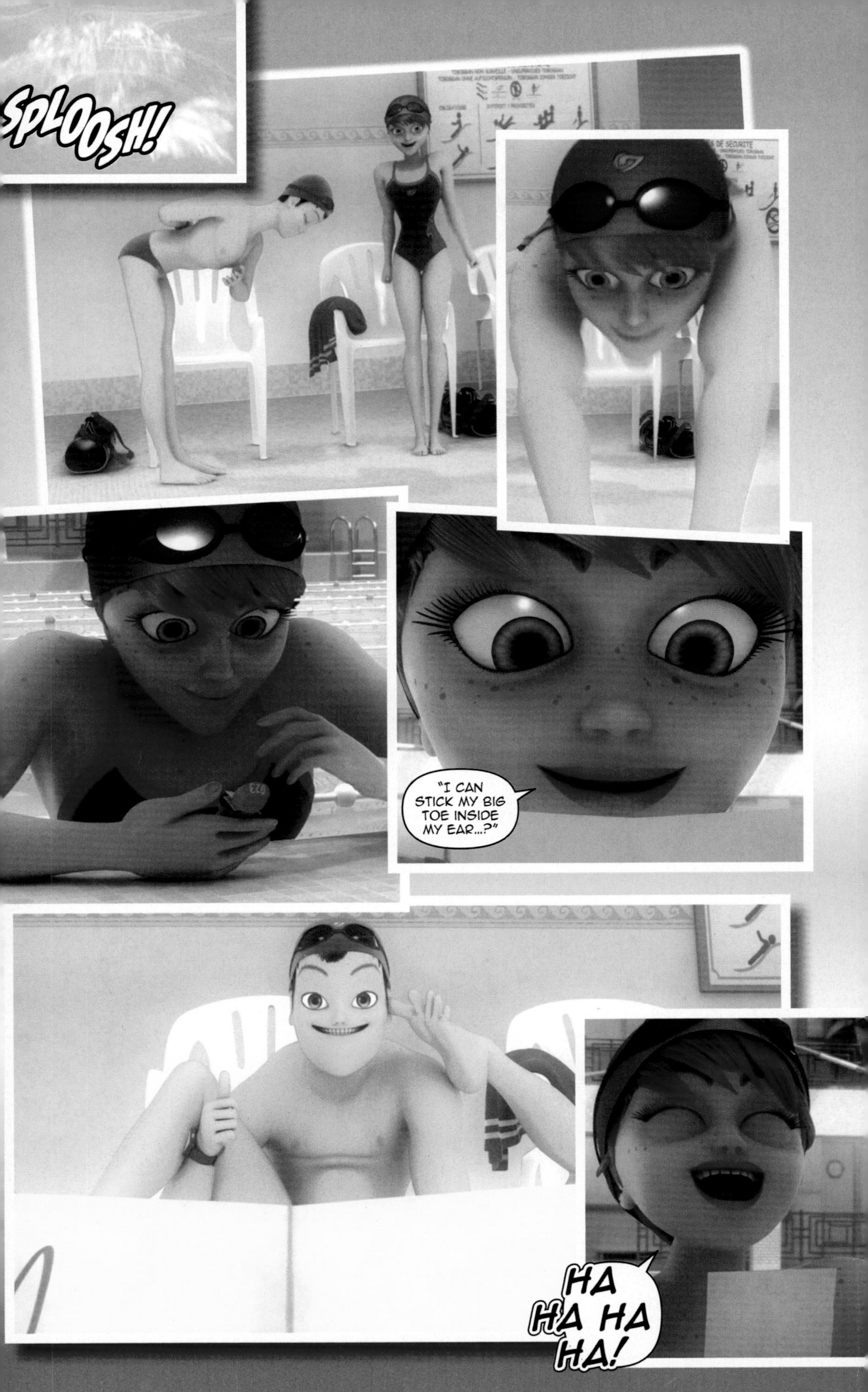
SPLOOSH!
"I CAN STICK MY BIG TOE INSIDE MY EAR...?"
HA HA HA HA!

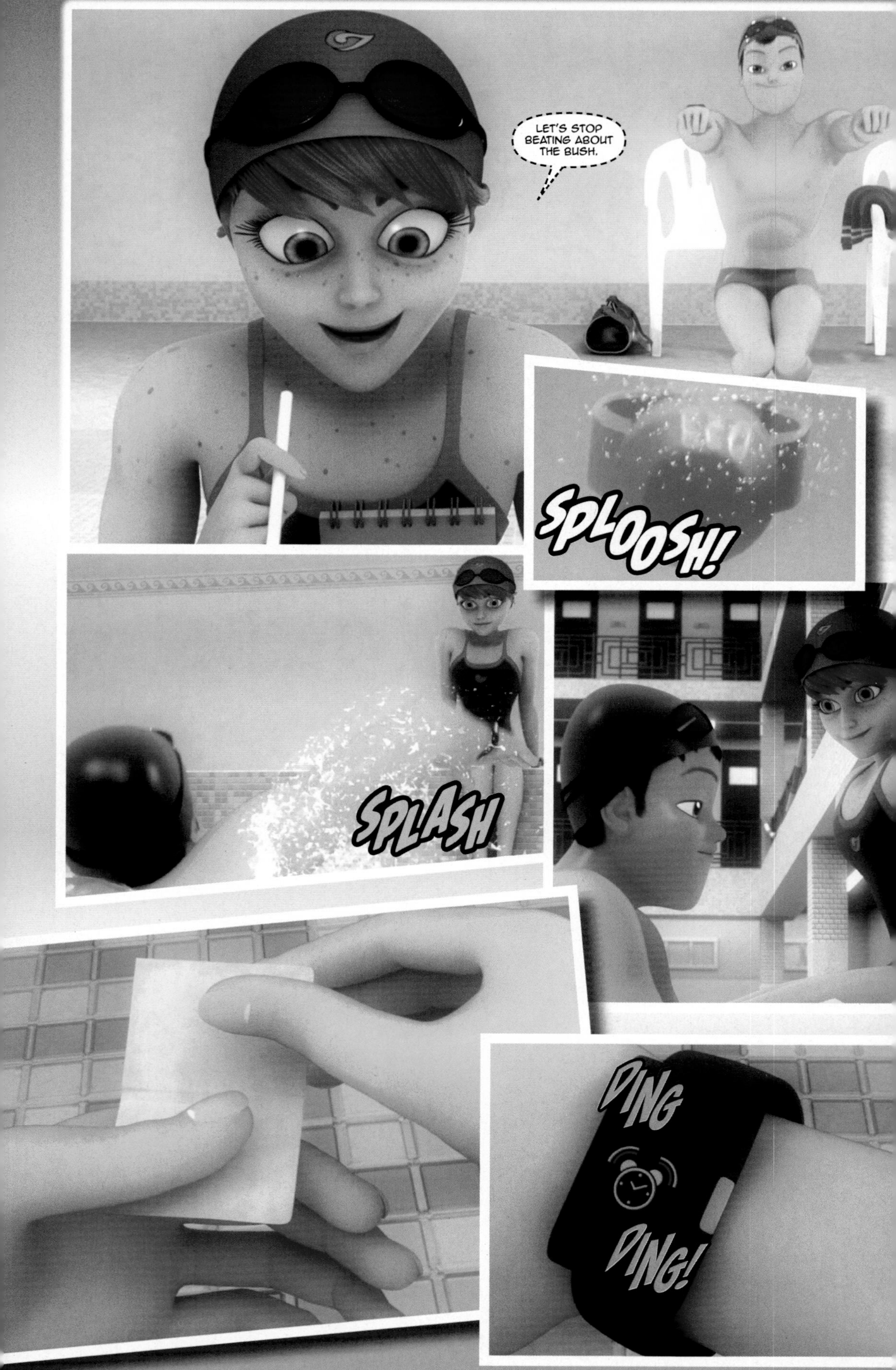

LET'S STOP BEATING ABOUT THE BUSH.
SPLOOSH!
SPLASH
DING
DING!

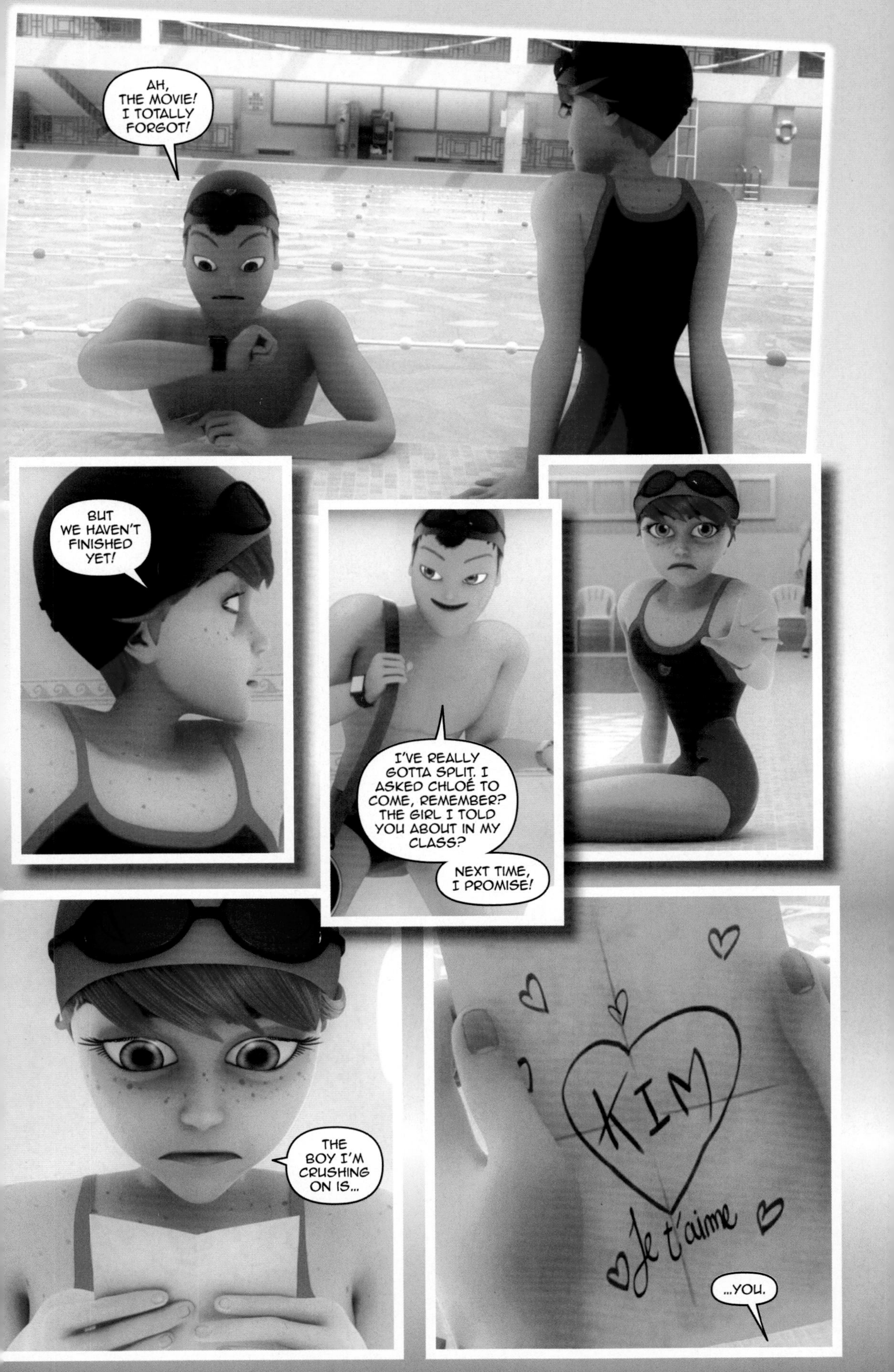
AH, THE MOVIE! I TOTALLY FORGOT!
BUT WE HAVEN'T FINISHED YET!
I'VE REALLY GOTTA SPLIT. I ASKED CHLOÉ TO COME, REMEMBER? THE GIRL I TOLD YOU ABOUT IN MY CLASS?
NEXT TIME, I PROMISE!
THE BOY I'M CRUSHING ON IS...
KIM
Je t'aime
...YOU.

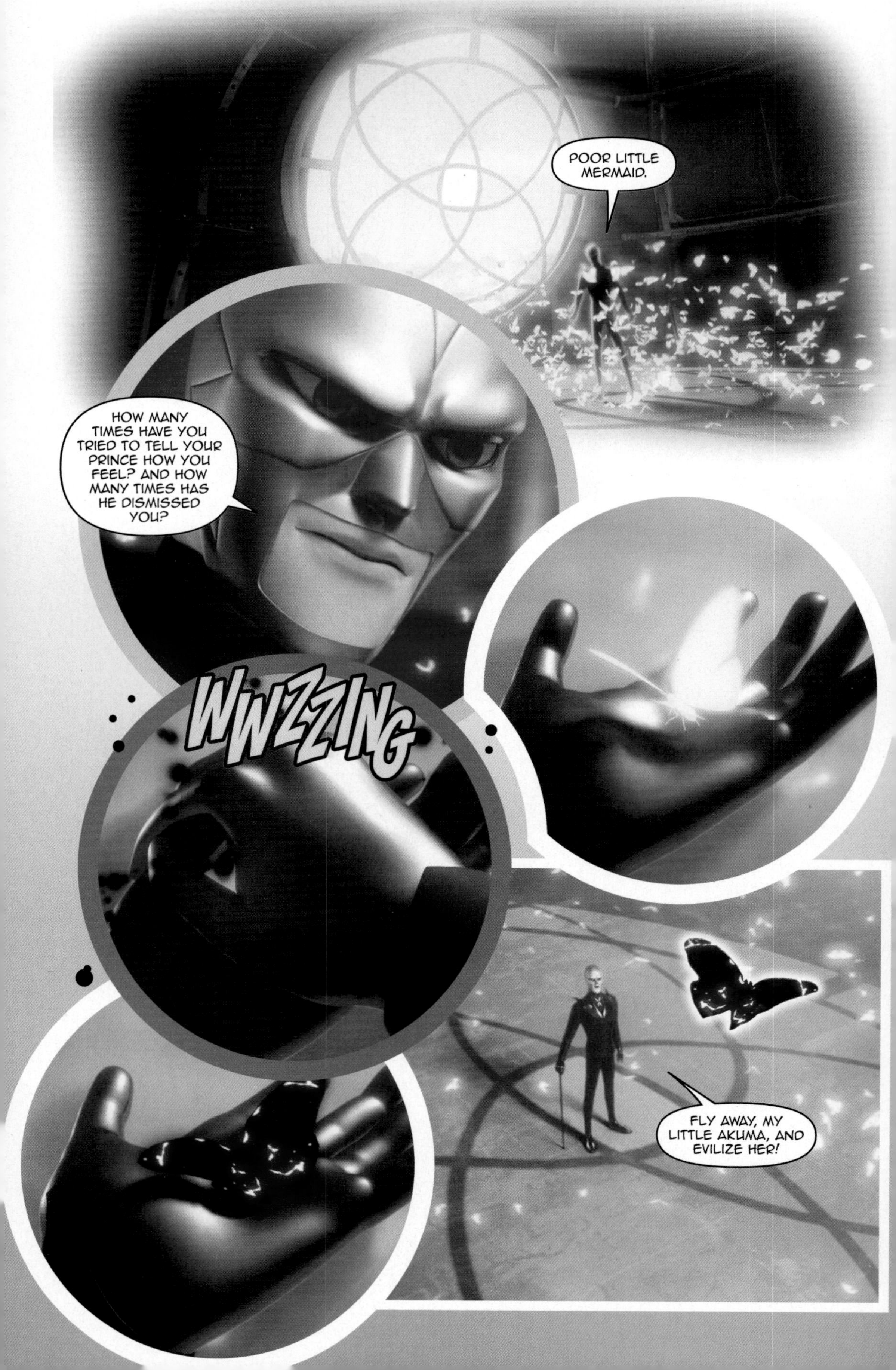
POOR LITTLE MERMAID.
HOW MANY TIMES HAVE YOU TRIED TO TELL YOUR PRINCE HOW YOU FEEL? AND HOW MANY TIMES HAS HE DISMISSED YOU?
WWZZING
FLY AWAY, MY LITTLE AKUMA, AND EVILIZE HER!

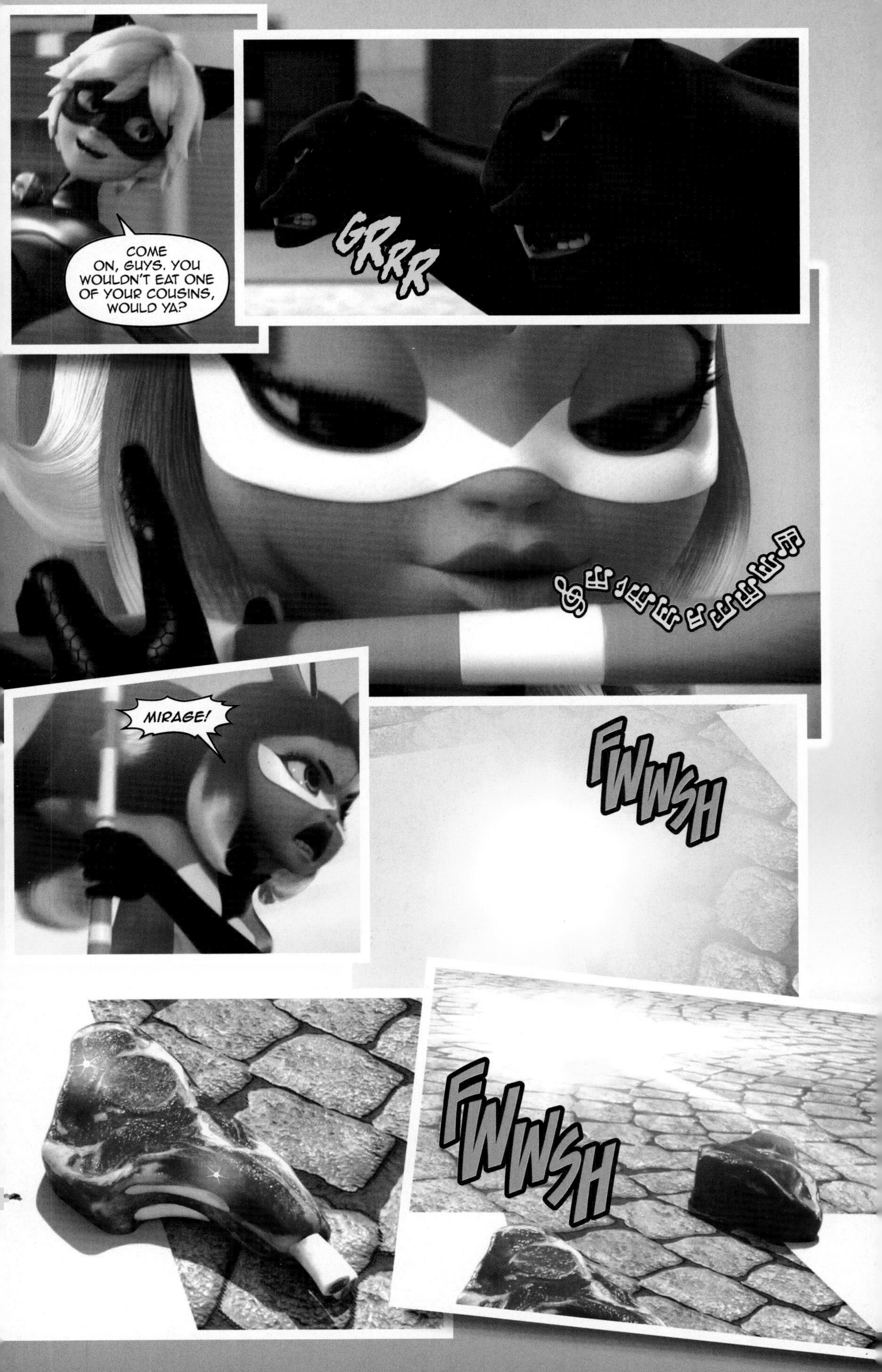
COME ON, GUYS. YOU WOULDN'T EAT ONE OF YOUR COUSINS, WOULD YA?
GRRR
MIRAGE!
FWWSH
FWWSH

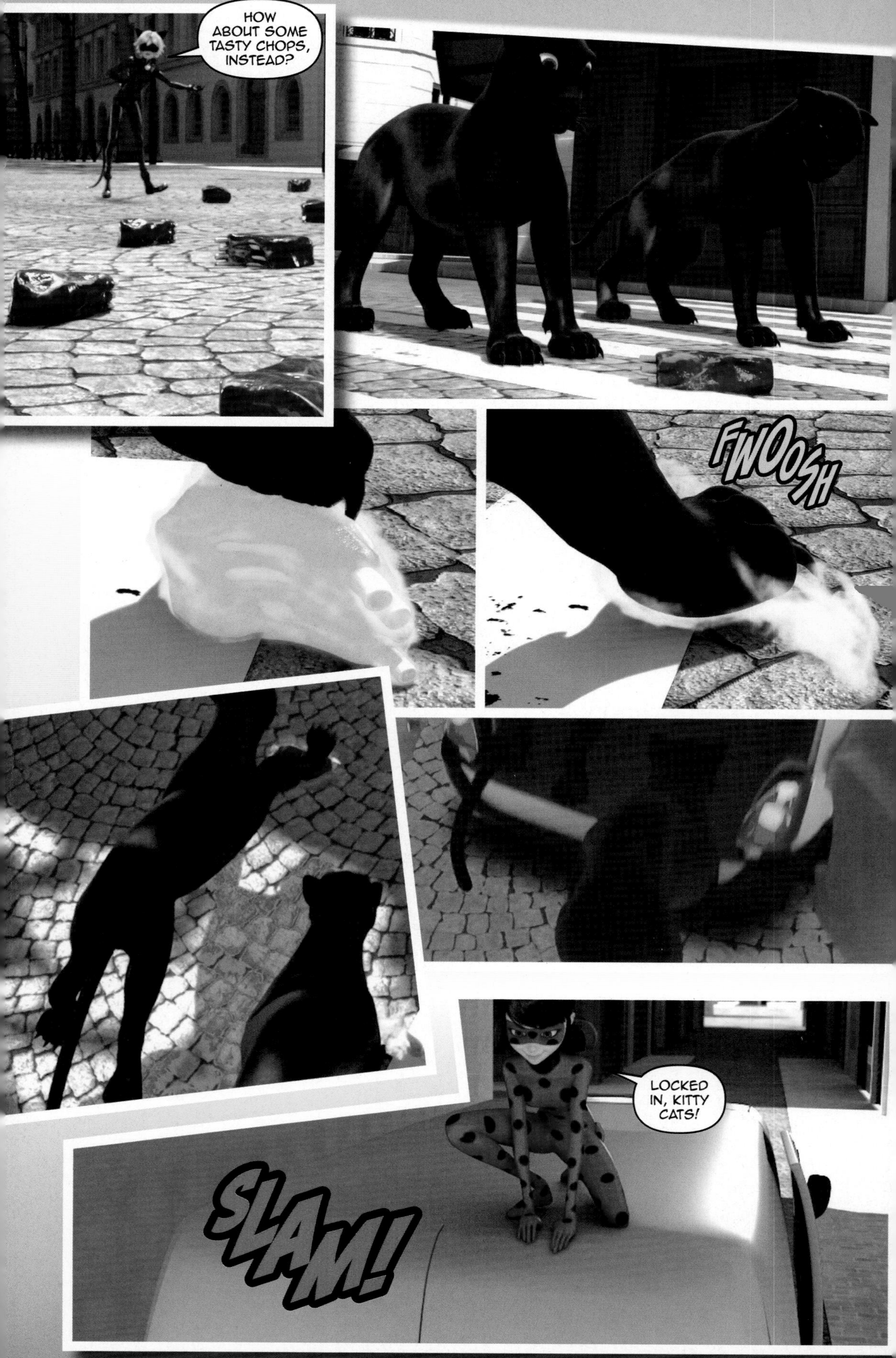
HOW ABOUT SOME TASTY CHOPS, INSTEAD?
FWOOSH
LOCKED IN, KITTY CATS!
SLAM!

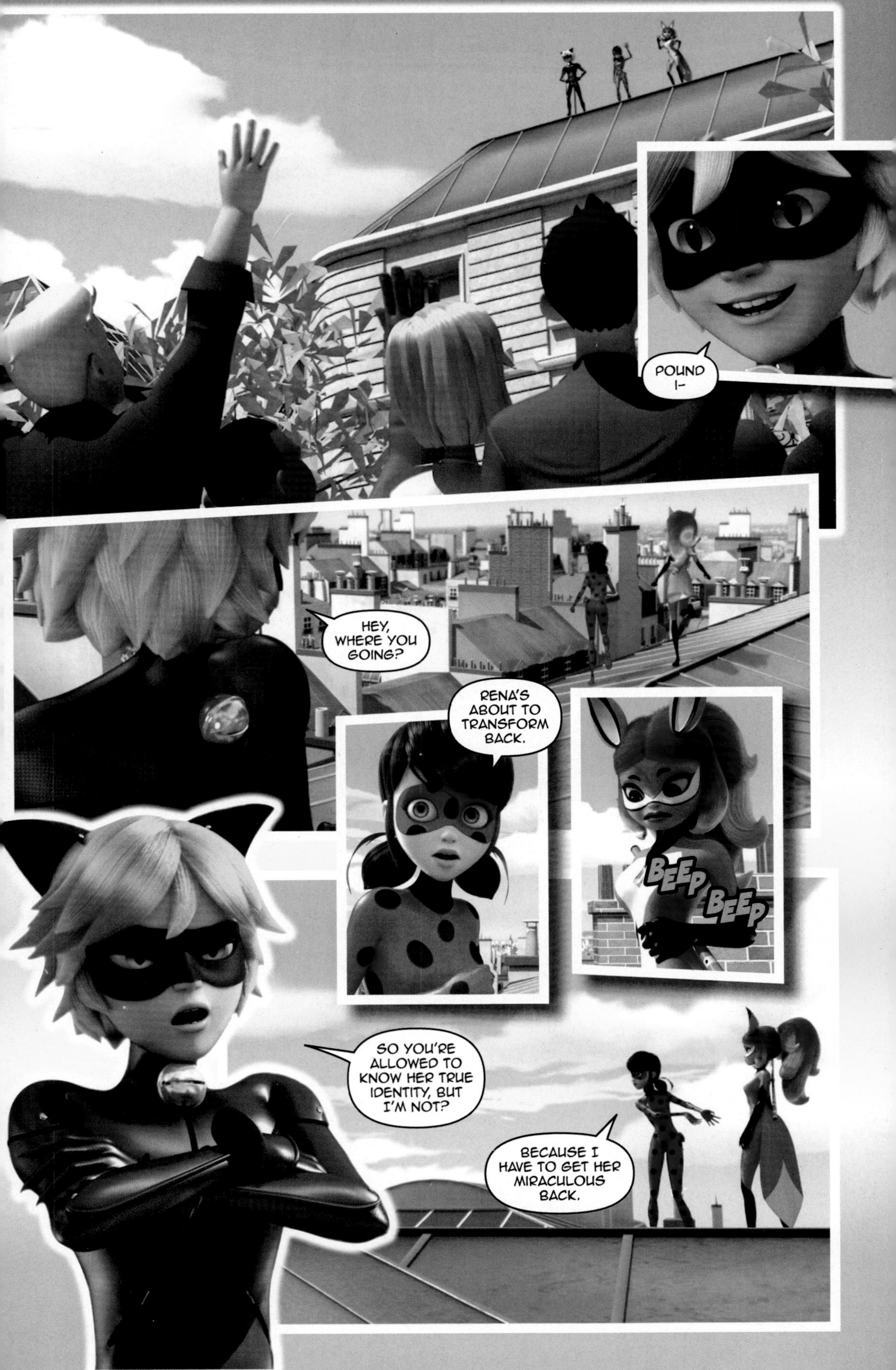
POUND I–
HEY, WHERE YOU GOING?
RENA'S ABOUT TO TRANSFORM BACK.
BEEP BEEP
SO YOU'RE ALLOWED TO KNOW HER TRUE IDENTITY, BUT I'M NOT?
BECAUSE I HAVE TO GET HER MIRACULOUS BACK.

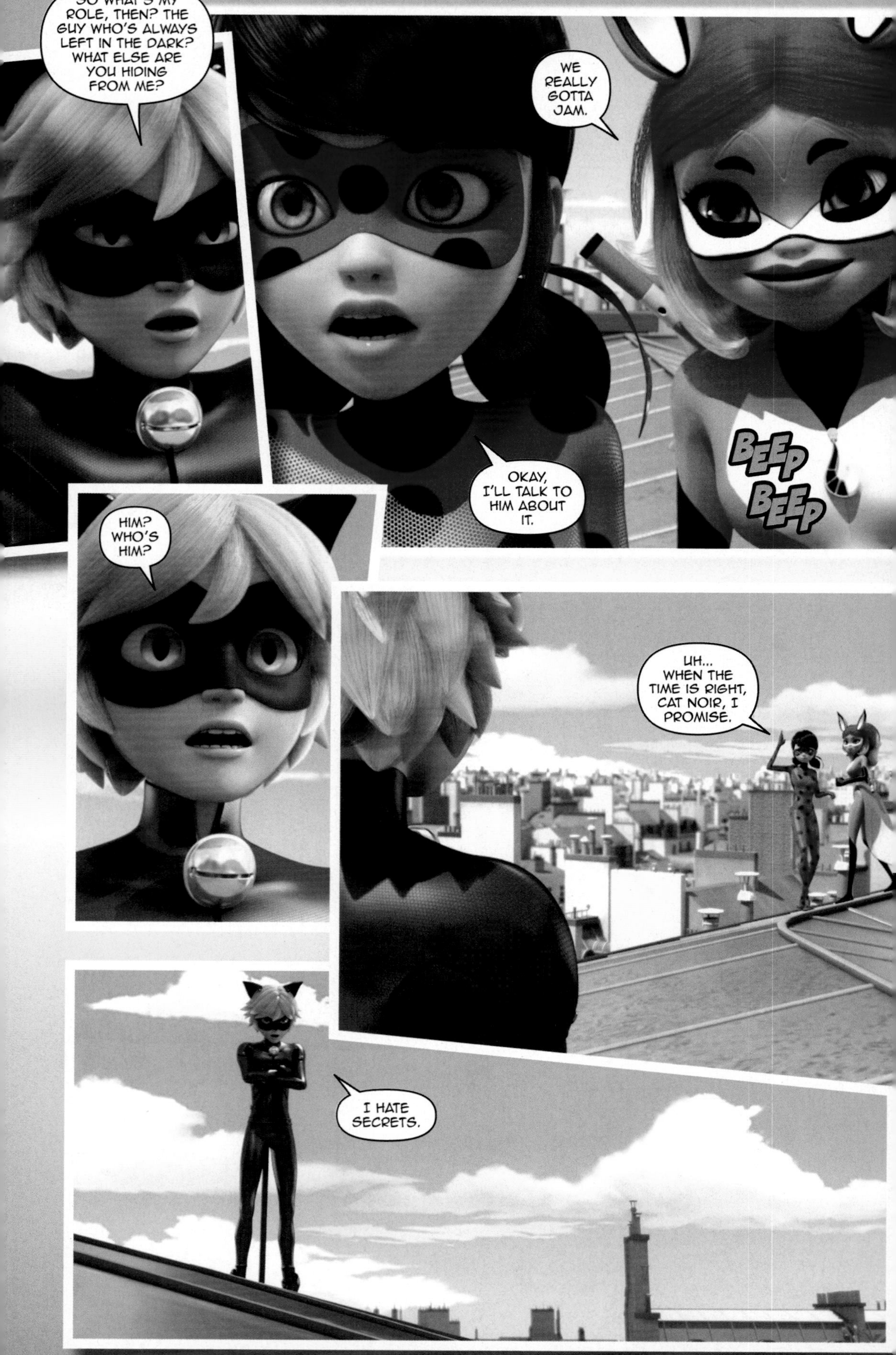
SO WHAT'S MY ROLE, THEN? THE GUY WHO'S ALWAYS LEFT IN THE DARK? WHAT ELSE ARE YOU HIDING FROM ME?
WE REALLY GOTTA JAM.
OKAY, I'LL TALK TO HIM ABOUT IT.
BEEP BEEP
HIM? WHO'S HIM?
UH... WHEN THE TIME IS RIGHT, CAT NOIR, I PROMISE.
I HATE SECRETS.

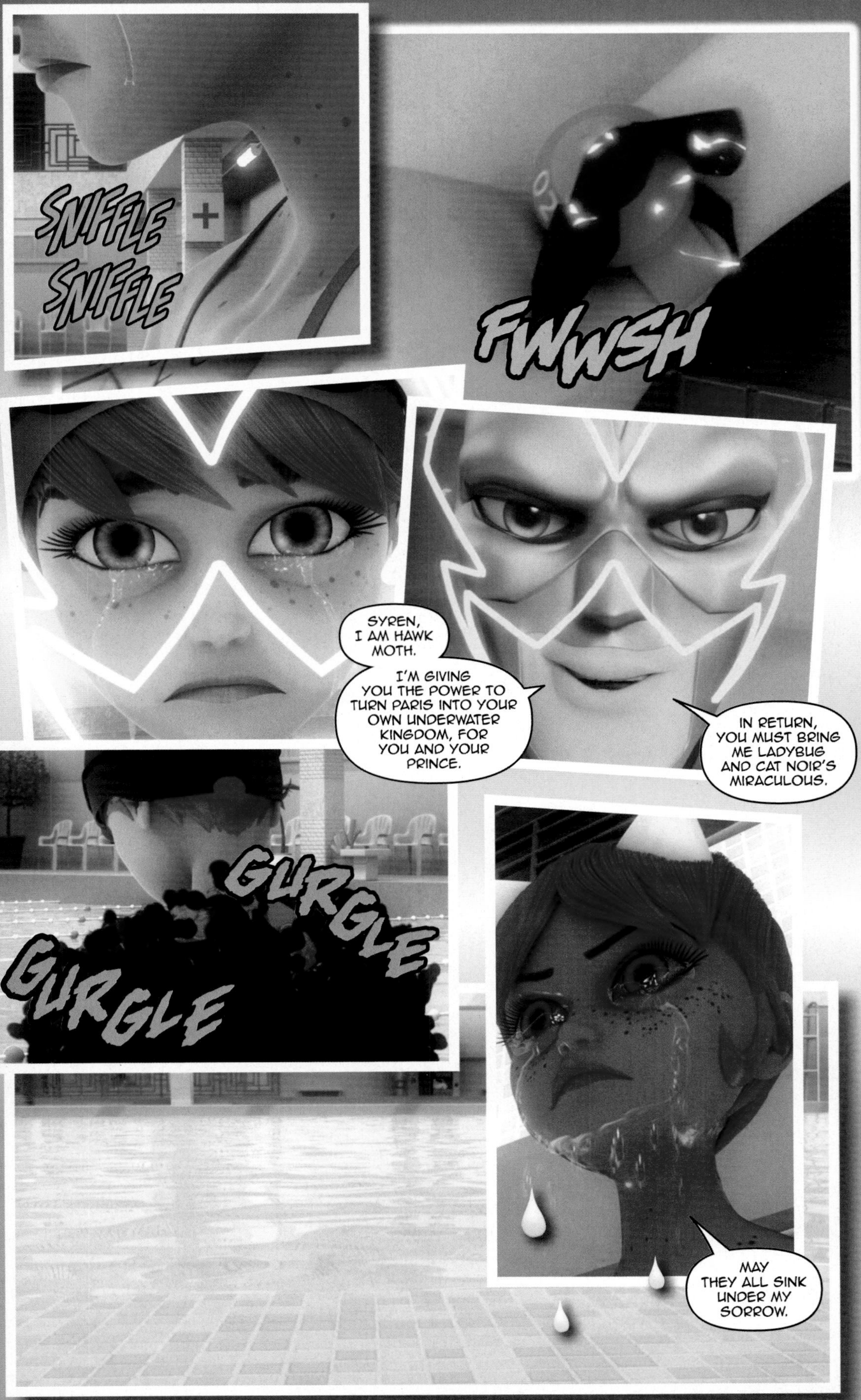
SNIFFLE
SNIFFLE
FWWSH
SYREN, I AM HAWK MOTH.
I'M GIVING YOU THE POWER TO TURN PARIS INTO YOUR OWN UNDERWATER KINGDOM, FOR YOU AND YOUR PRINCE.
IN RETURN, YOU MUST BRING ME LADYBUG AND CAT NOIR'S MIRACULOUS.
GURGLE
GURGLE
MAY THEY ALL SINK UNDER MY SORROW.

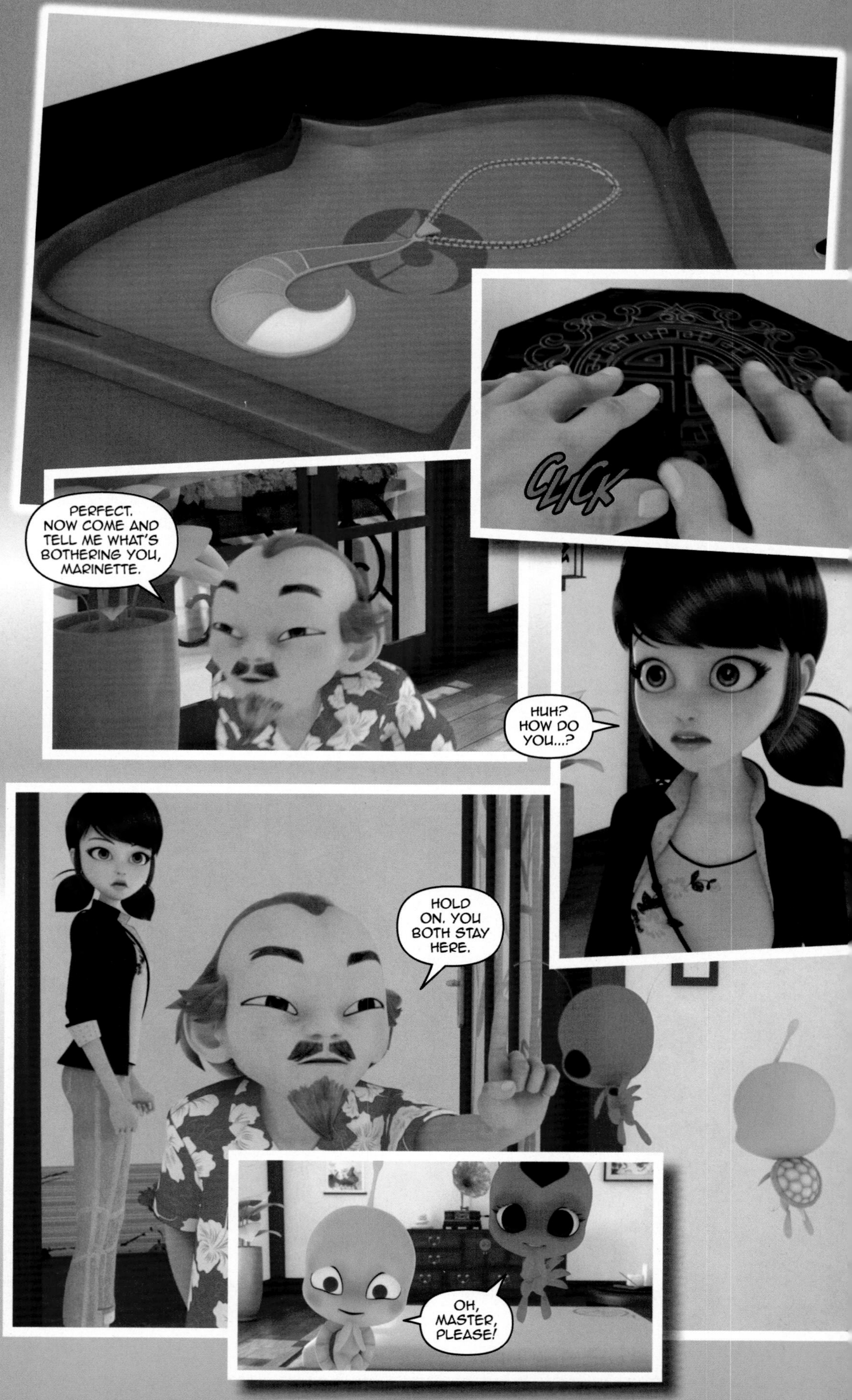
CLICK
PERFECT. NOW COME AND TELL ME WHAT'S BOTHERING YOU, MARINETTE.
HUH? HOW DO YOU...?
HOLD ON. YOU BOTH STAY HERE.
OH, MASTER, PLEASE!

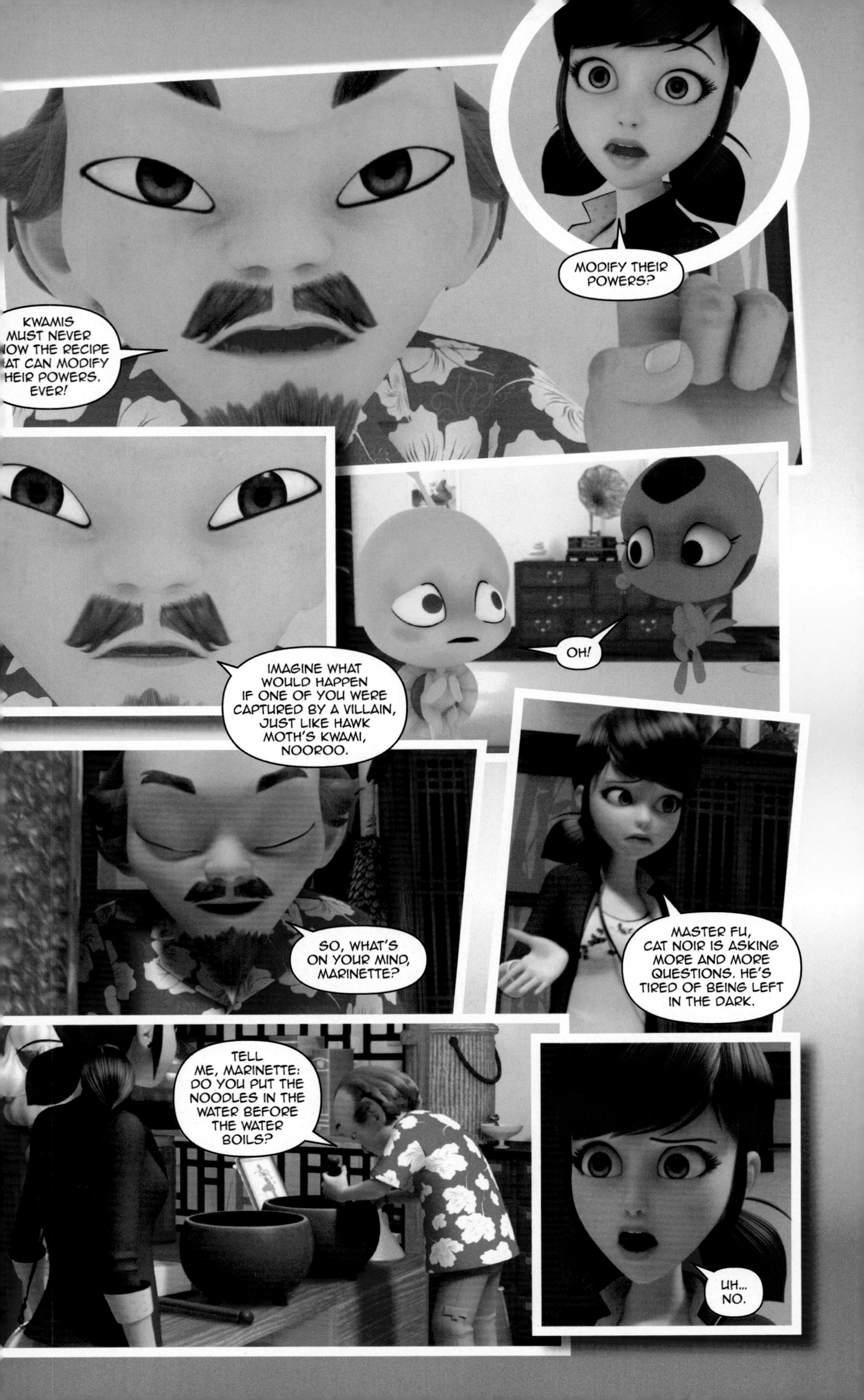
MODIFY THEIR POWERS?
KWAMIS MUST NEVER
OW THE RECIPE
AT CAN MODIFY
HEIR POWERS.
EVER!
OH!
IMAGINE WHAT WOULD HAPPEN IF ONE OF YOU WERE CAPTURED BY A VILLAIN, JUST LIKE HAWK MOTH'S KWAMI, NOOROO.
SO, WHAT'S ON YOUR MIND, MARINETTE?
MASTER FU, CAT NOIR IS ASKING MORE AND MORE QUESTIONS. HE'S TIRED OF BEING LEFT IN THE DARK.
TELL ME, MARINETTE: DO YOU PUT THE NOODLES IN THE WATER BEFORE THE WATER BOILS?
UH... NO.

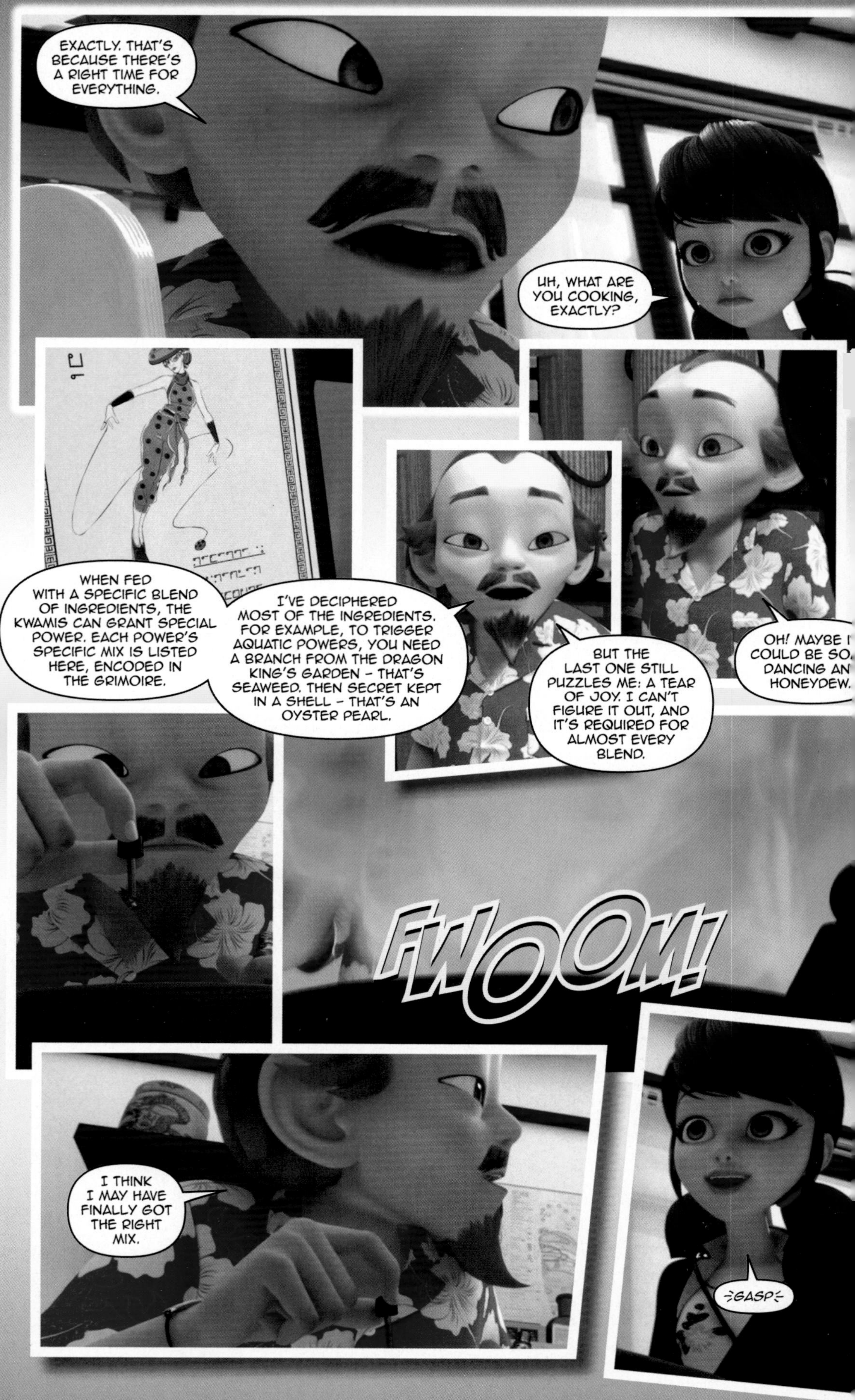
EXACTLY. THAT'S BECAUSE THERE'S A RIGHT TIME FOR EVERYTHING.
UH, WHAT ARE YOU COOKING, EXACTLY?
WHEN FED WITH A SPECIFIC BLEND OF INGREDIENTS, THE KWAMIS CAN GRANT SPECIAL POWER. EACH POWER'S SPECIFIC MIX IS LISTED HERE, ENCODED IN THE GRIMOIRE.
I'VE DECIPHERED MOST OF THE INGREDIENTS. FOR EXAMPLE, TO TRIGGER AQUATIC POWERS, YOU NEED A BRANCH FROM THE DRAGON KING'S GARDEN – THAT'S SEAWEED. THEN SECRET KEPT IN A SHELL – THAT'S AN OYSTER PEARL.
BUT THE LAST ONE STILL PUZZLES ME: A TEAR OF JOY. I CAN'T FIGURE IT OUT, AND IT'S REQUIRED FOR ALMOST EVERY BLEND.
OH! MAYBE I COULD BE SO DANCING AN HONEYDEW.
FWOOM!
I THINK I MAY HAVE FINALLY GOT THE RIGHT MIX.
GASP

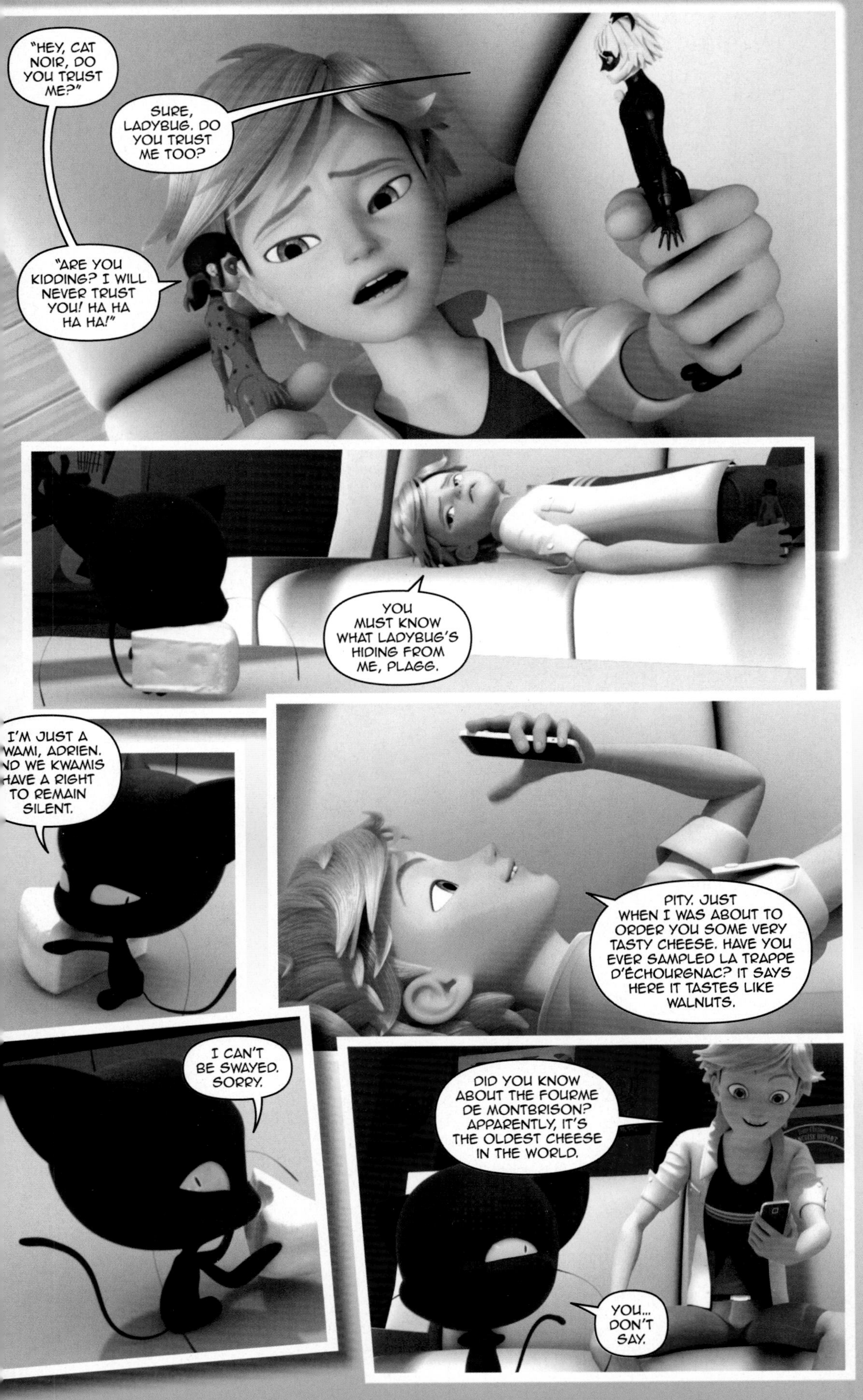
"HEY, CAT NOIR, DO YOU TRUST ME?"
SURE, LADYBUG. DO YOU TRUST ME TOO?
"ARE YOU KIDDING? I WILL NEVER TRUST YOU! HA HA HA HA!"
YOU MUST KNOW WHAT LADYBUG'S HIDING FROM ME, PLAGG.
I'M JUST A WAMI, ADRIEN. ND WE KWAMIS HAVE A RIGHT TO REMAIN SILENT.
PITY. JUST WHEN I WAS ABOUT TO ORDER YOU SOME VERY TASTY CHEESE. HAVE YOU EVER SAMPLED LA TRAPPE D'ÉCHOURGNAC? IT SAYS HERE IT TASTES LIKE WALNUTS.
I CAN'T BE SWAYED. SORRY.
DID YOU KNOW ABOUT THE FOURME DE MONTBRISON? APPARENTLY, IT'S THE OLDEST CHEESE IN THE WORLD.
YOU... DON'T SAY.

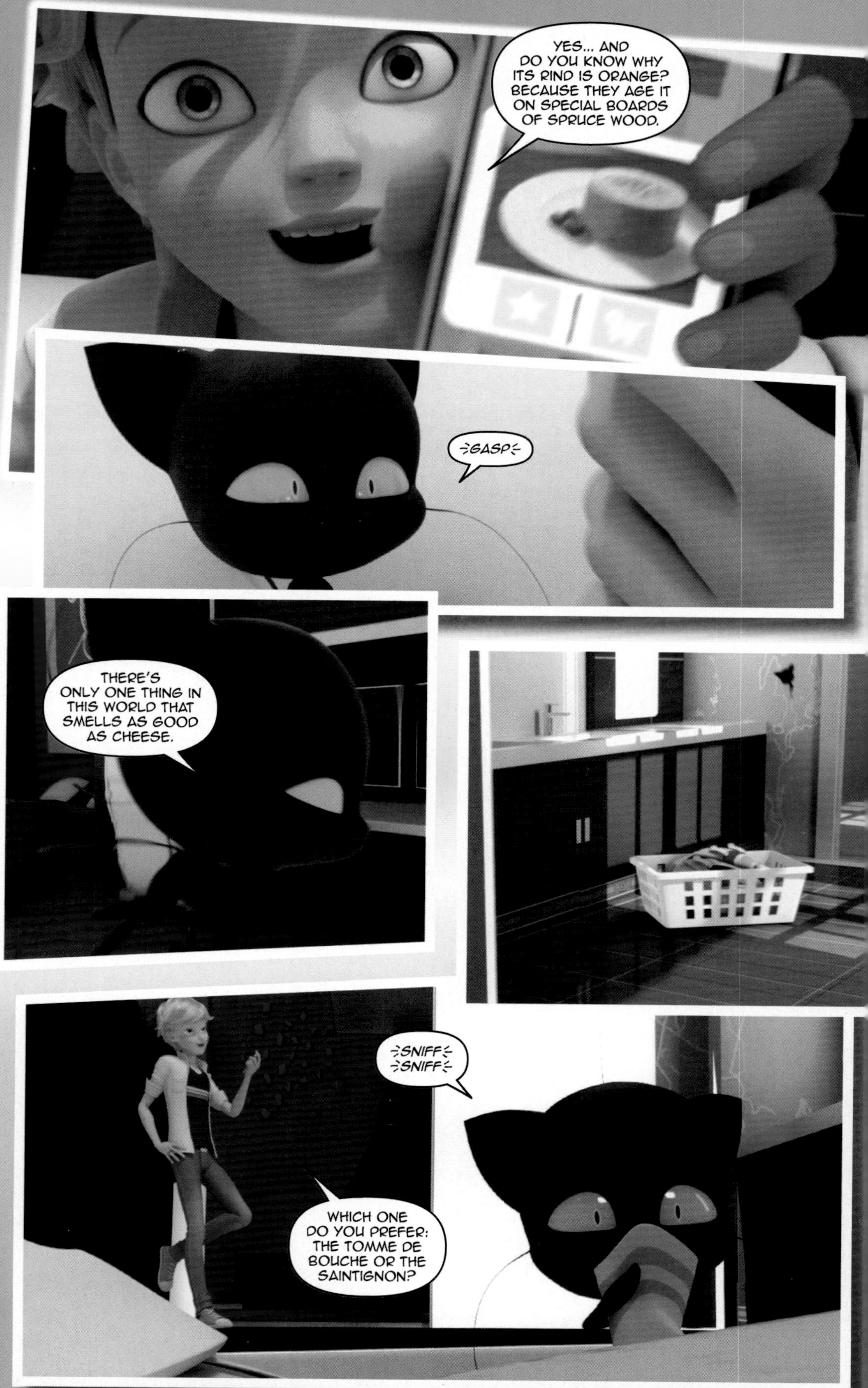
YES... AND DO YOU KNOW WHY ITS RIND IS ORANGE? BECAUSE THEY AGE IT ON SPECIAL BOARDS OF SPRUCE WOOD.
GASP
THERE'S ONLY ONE THING IN THIS WORLD THAT SMELLS AS GOOD AS CHEESE.
SNIFF SNIFF
WHICH ONE DO YOU PREFER: THE TOMME DE BOUCHE OR THE SAINTIGNON?

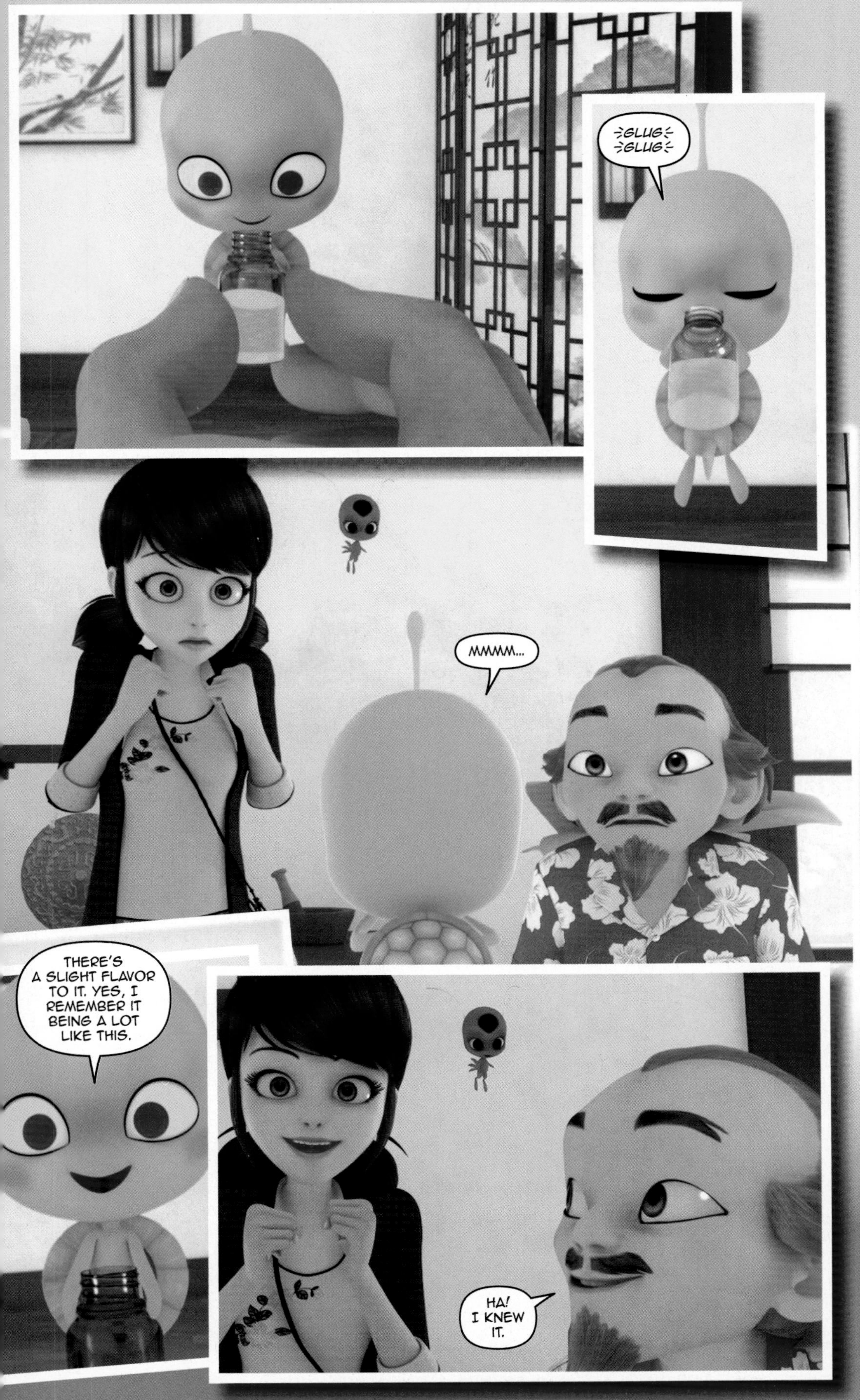

GLUG GLUG
MMMM...
THERE'S A SLIGHT FLAVOR TO IT. YES, I REMEMBER IT BEING A LOT LIKE THIS.
HA! I KNEW IT.

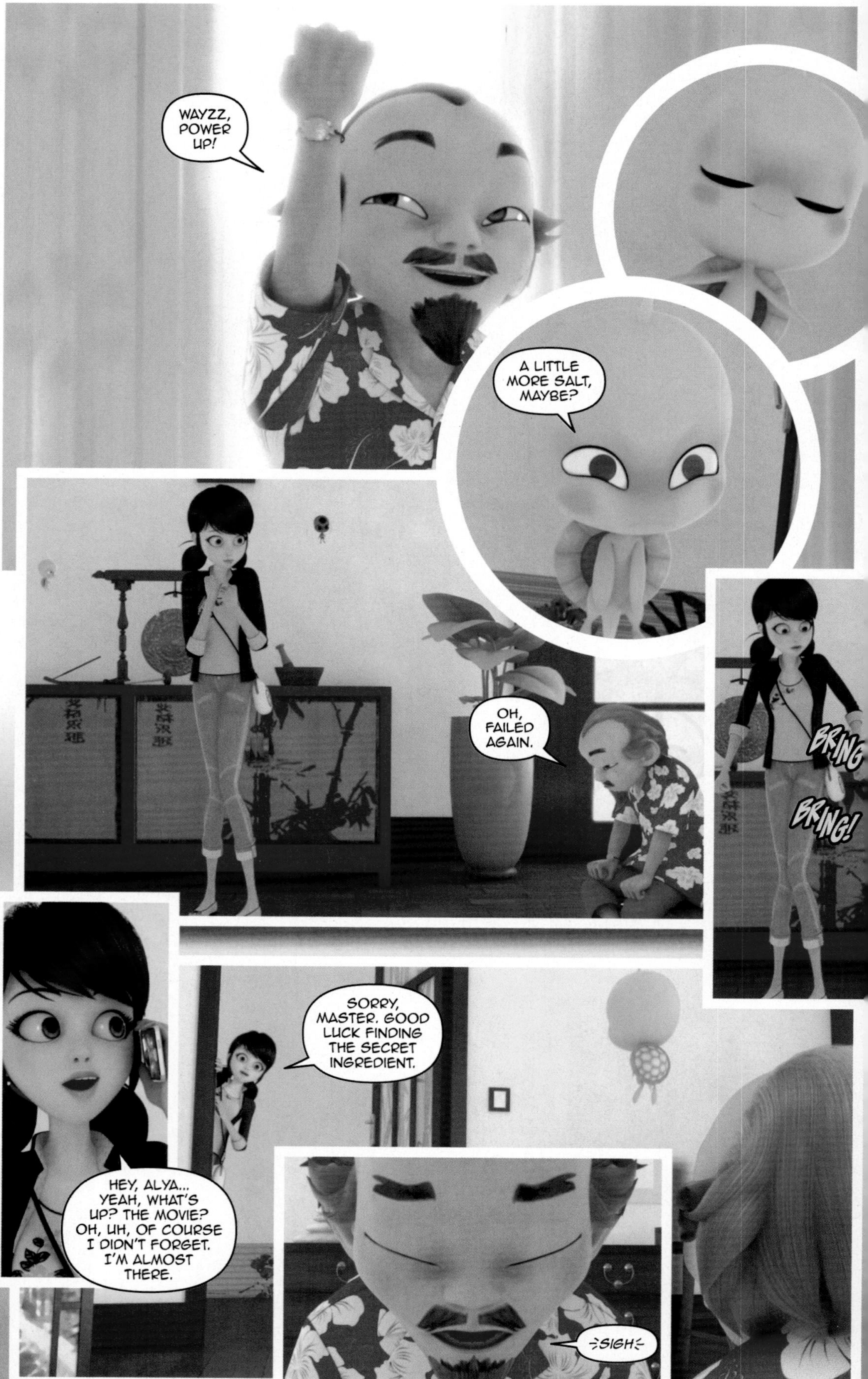
WAYZZ, POWER UP!
A LITTLE MORE SALT, MAYBE?
OH, FAILED AGAIN.
BRING
BRING!
SORRY, MASTER. GOOD LUCK FINDING THE SECRET INGREDIENT.
HEY, ALYA... YEAH, WHAT'S UP? THE MOVIE? OH, UH, OF COURSE I DIDN'T FORGET. I'M ALMOST THERE.
SIGH

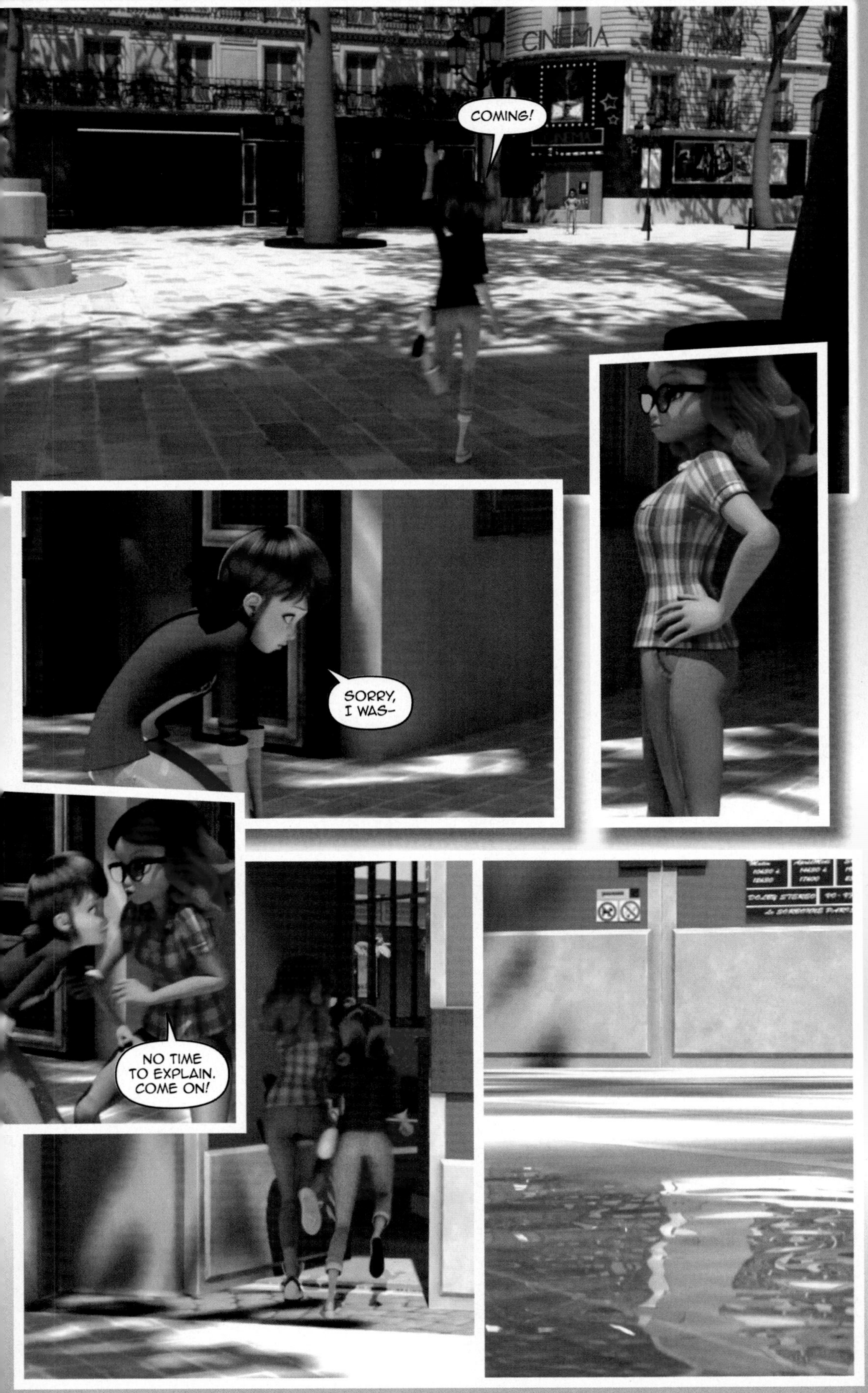
COMING!
SORRY, I WAS-
NO TIME TO EXPLAIN. COME ON!

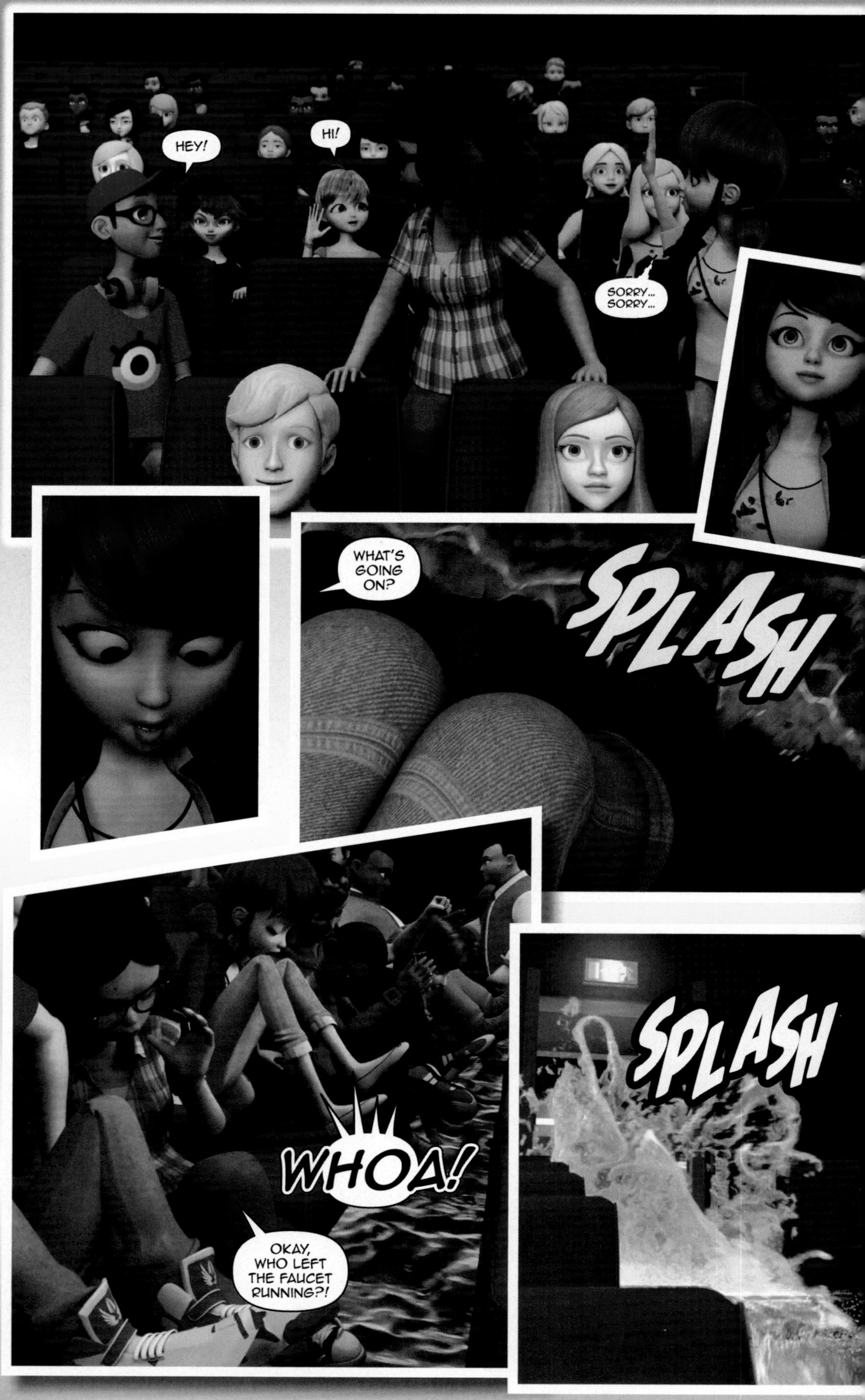
HEY!
HI!
SORRY... SORRY...
WHAT'S GOING ON?
SPLASH
WHOA!
OKAY, WHO LEFT THE FAUCET RUNNING?!
SPLASH

THE STAIRS! QUICK!

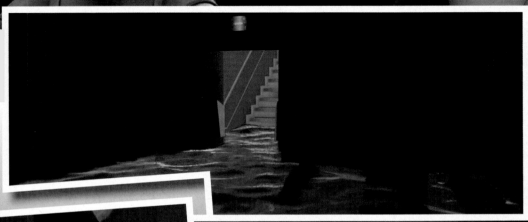

EVERYONE, UP ON THE ROOF!

SPLASH

SPLASH

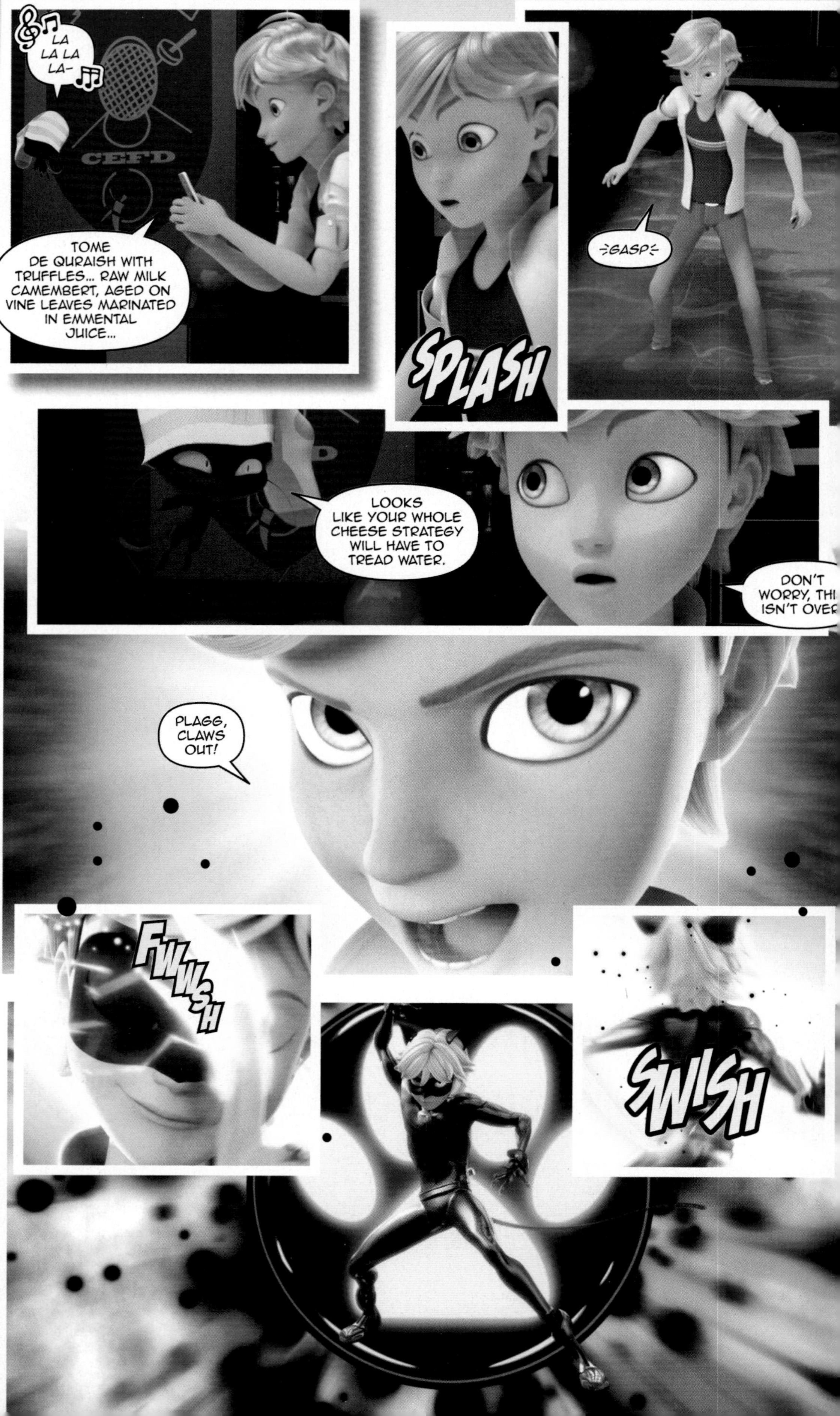
LA LA LA LA-
TOME DE QURAISH WITH TRUFFLES... RAW MILK CAMEMBERT, AGED ON VINE LEAVES MARINATED IN EMMENTAL JUICE...
SPLASH
GASP
LOOKS LIKE YOUR WHOLE CHEESE STRATEGY WILL HAVE TO TREAD WATER.
DON'T WORRY, THI ISN'T OVER
PLAGG, CLAWS OUT!
FWWSH
SWISH

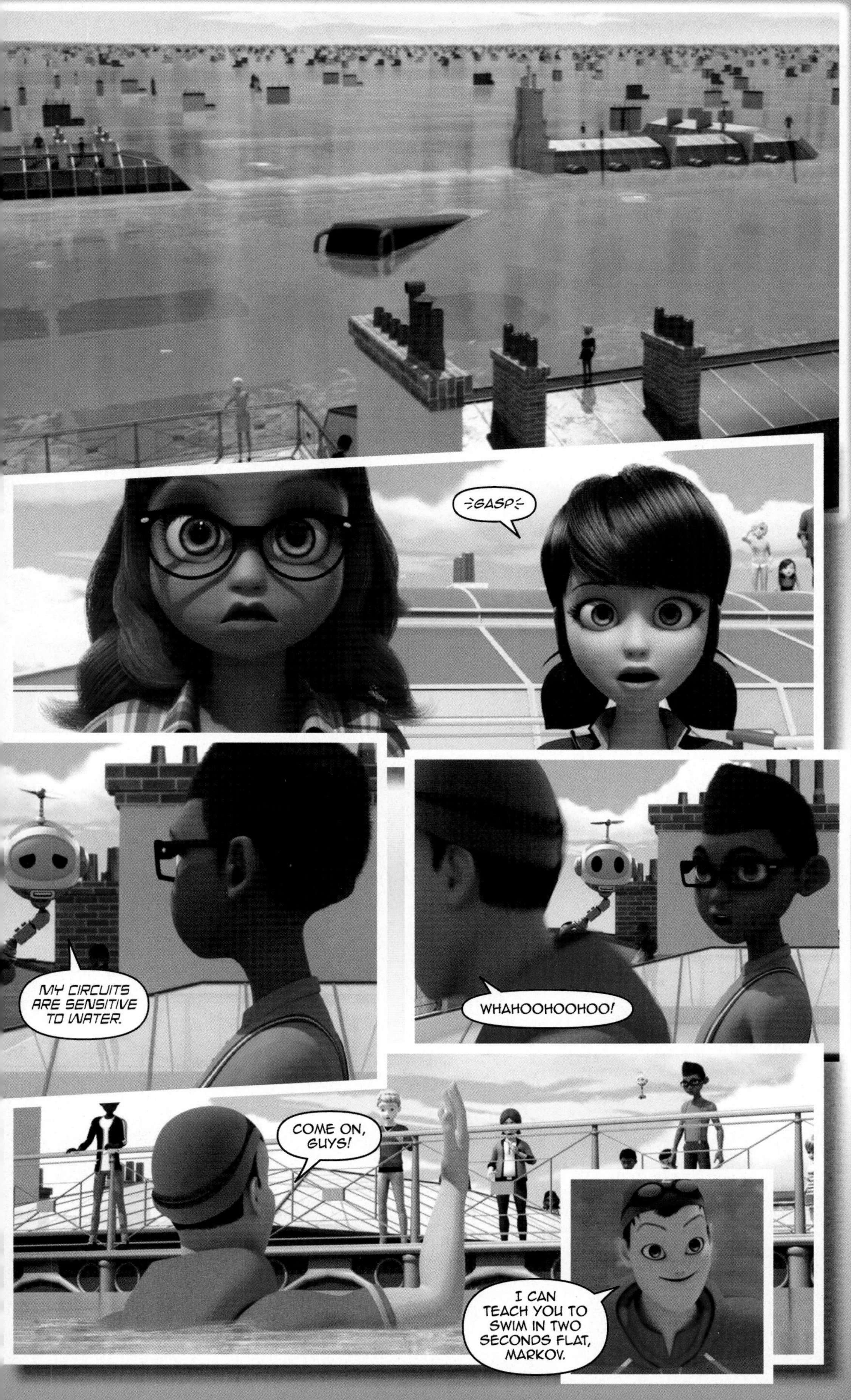
-GASP-
MY CIRCUITS ARE SENSITIVE TO WATER.
WHAHOOHOOHOO!
COME ON, GUYS!
I CAN TEACH YOU TO SWIM IN TWO SECONDS FLAT, MARKOV.

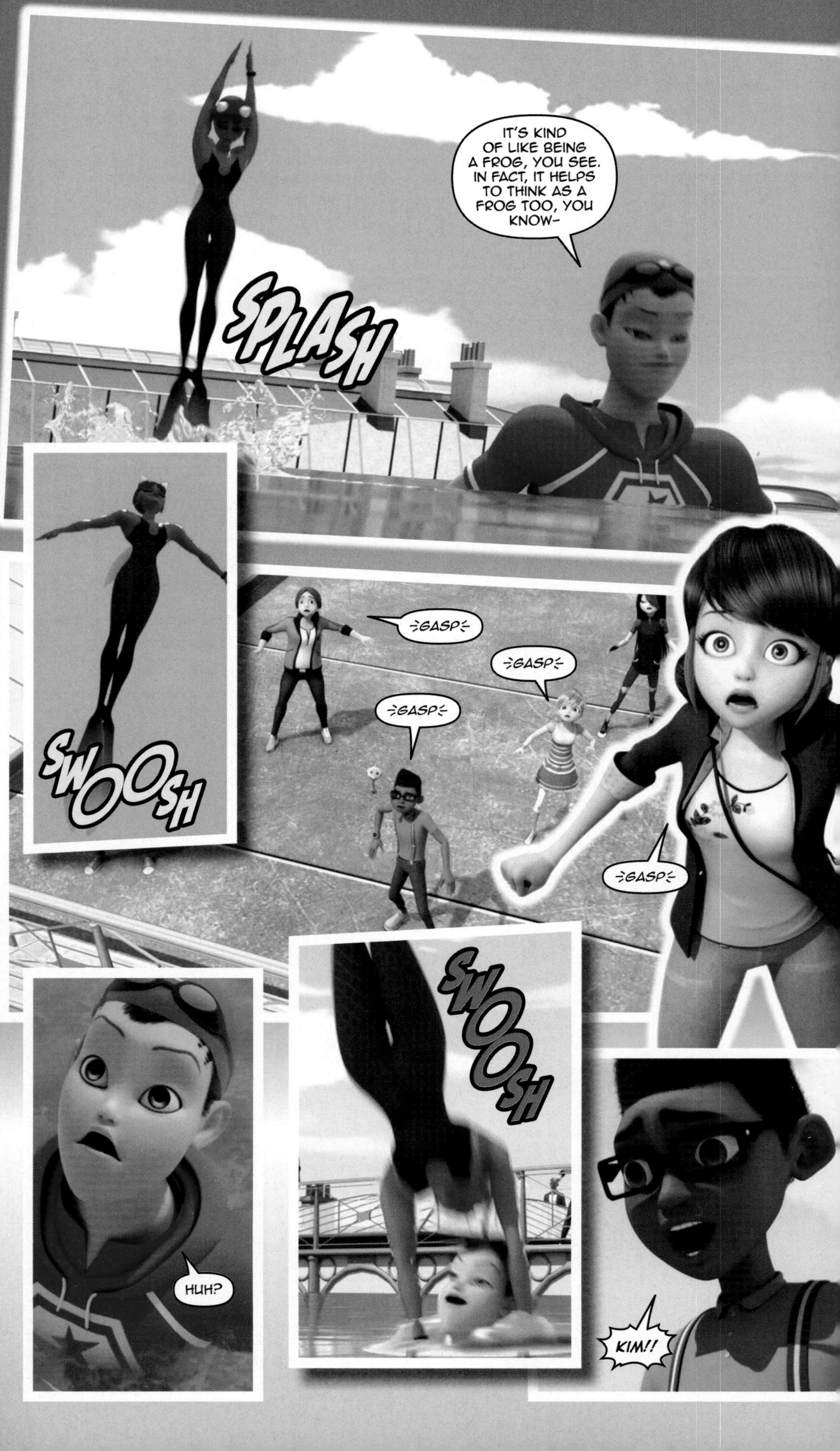
IT'S KIND OF LIKE BEING A FROG, YOU SEE. IN FACT, IT HELPS TO THINK AS A FROG TOO, YOU KNOW-
SPLASH
SWOOSH
GASP
GASP
GASP
GASP
HUH?
SWOOSH
KIM!!

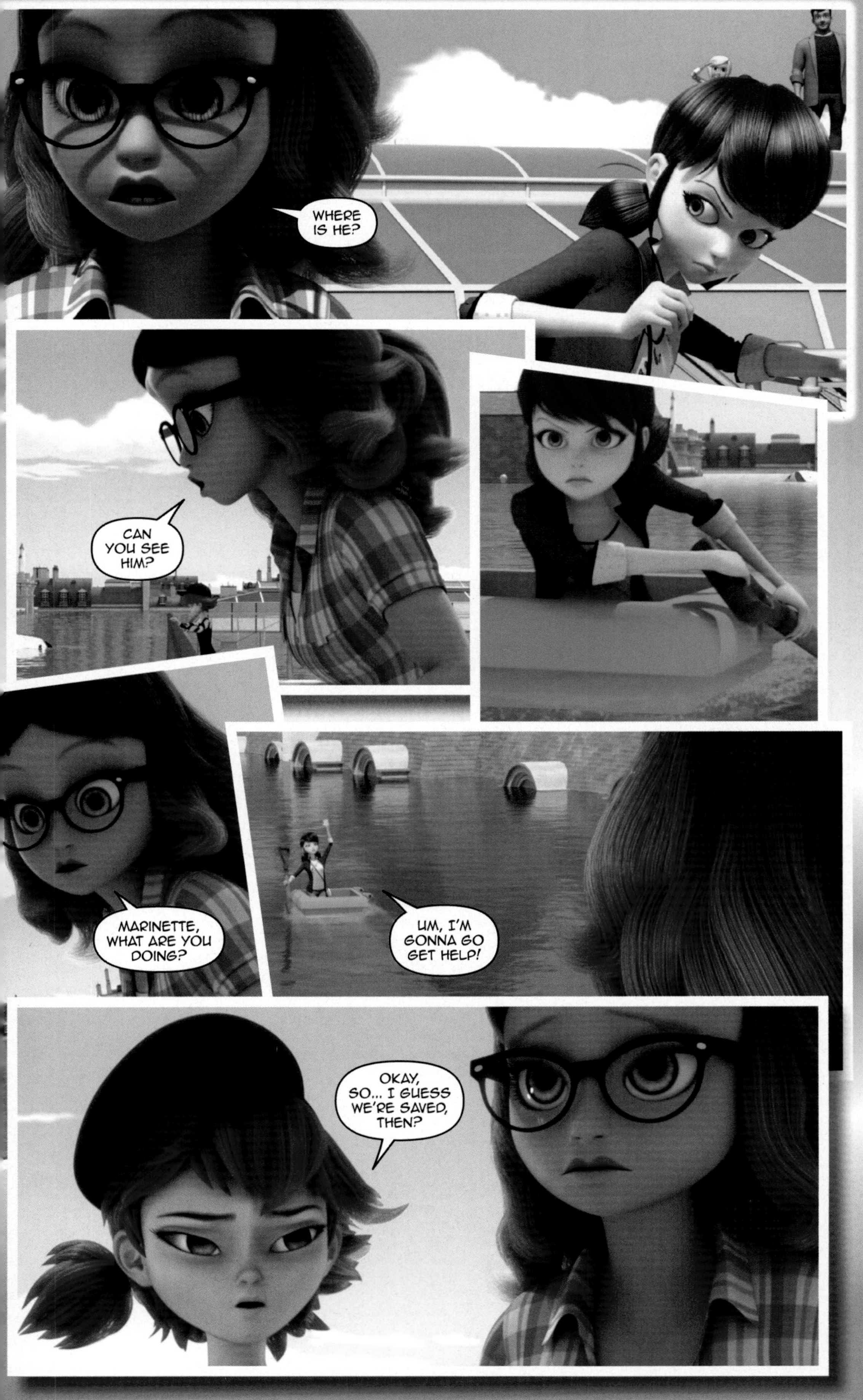
WHERE IS HE?
CAN YOU SEE HIM?
MARINETTE, WHAT ARE YOU DOING?
UM, I'M GONNA GO GET HELP!
OKAY, SO... I GUESS WE'RE SAVED, THEN?

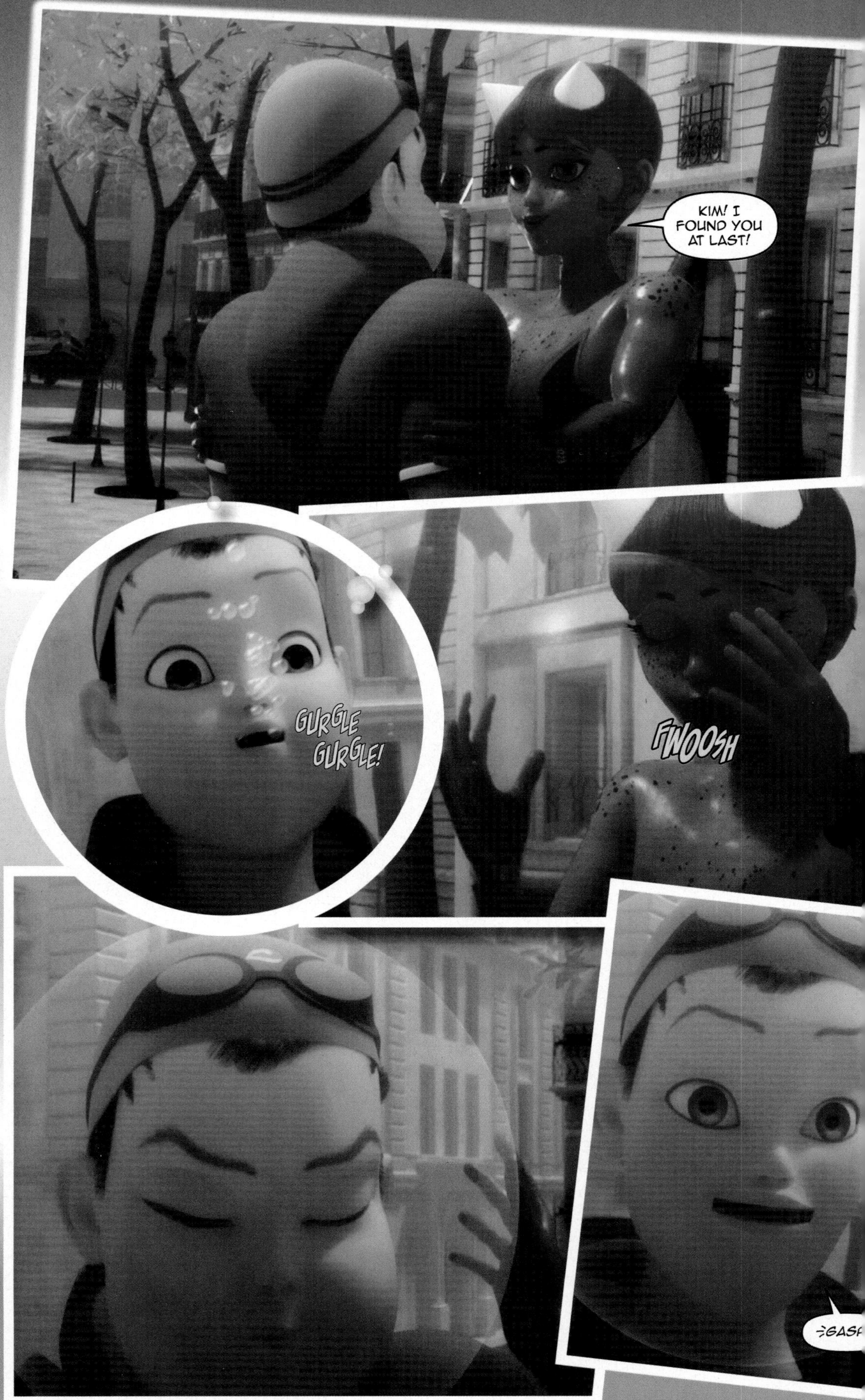
KIM! I FOUND YOU AT LAST!
GURGLE GURGLE!
FWOOSH
GASP

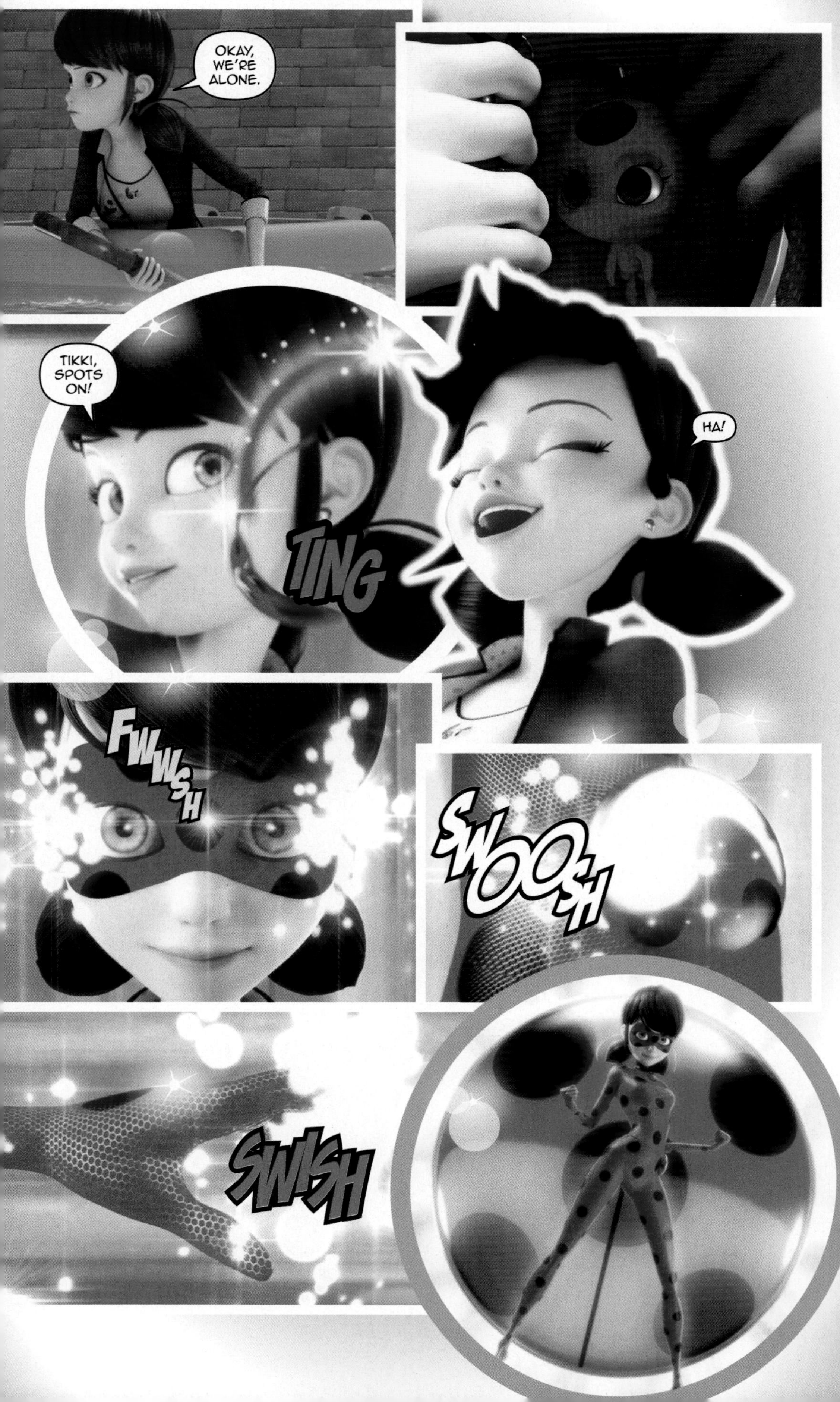
OKAY, WE'RE ALONE.
TIKKI, SPOTS ON!
TING
HA!
FWWSH
SWOOSH
SWISH

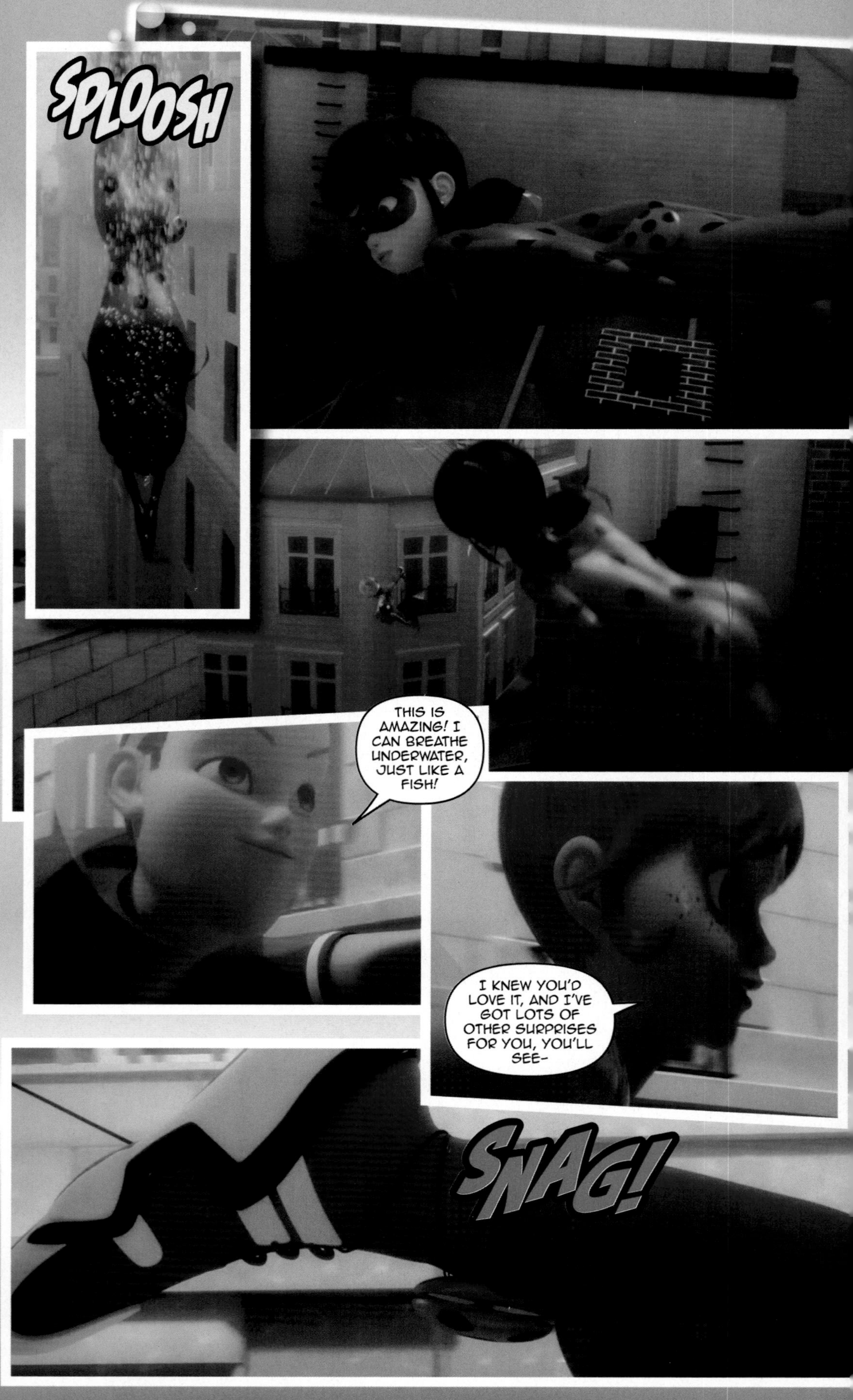
SPLOOSH
THIS IS AMAZING! I CAN BREATHE UNDERWATER, JUST LIKE A FISH!
I KNEW YOU'D LOVE IT, AND I'VE GOT LOTS OF OTHER SURPRISES FOR YOU, YOU'LL SEE-
SNAG!

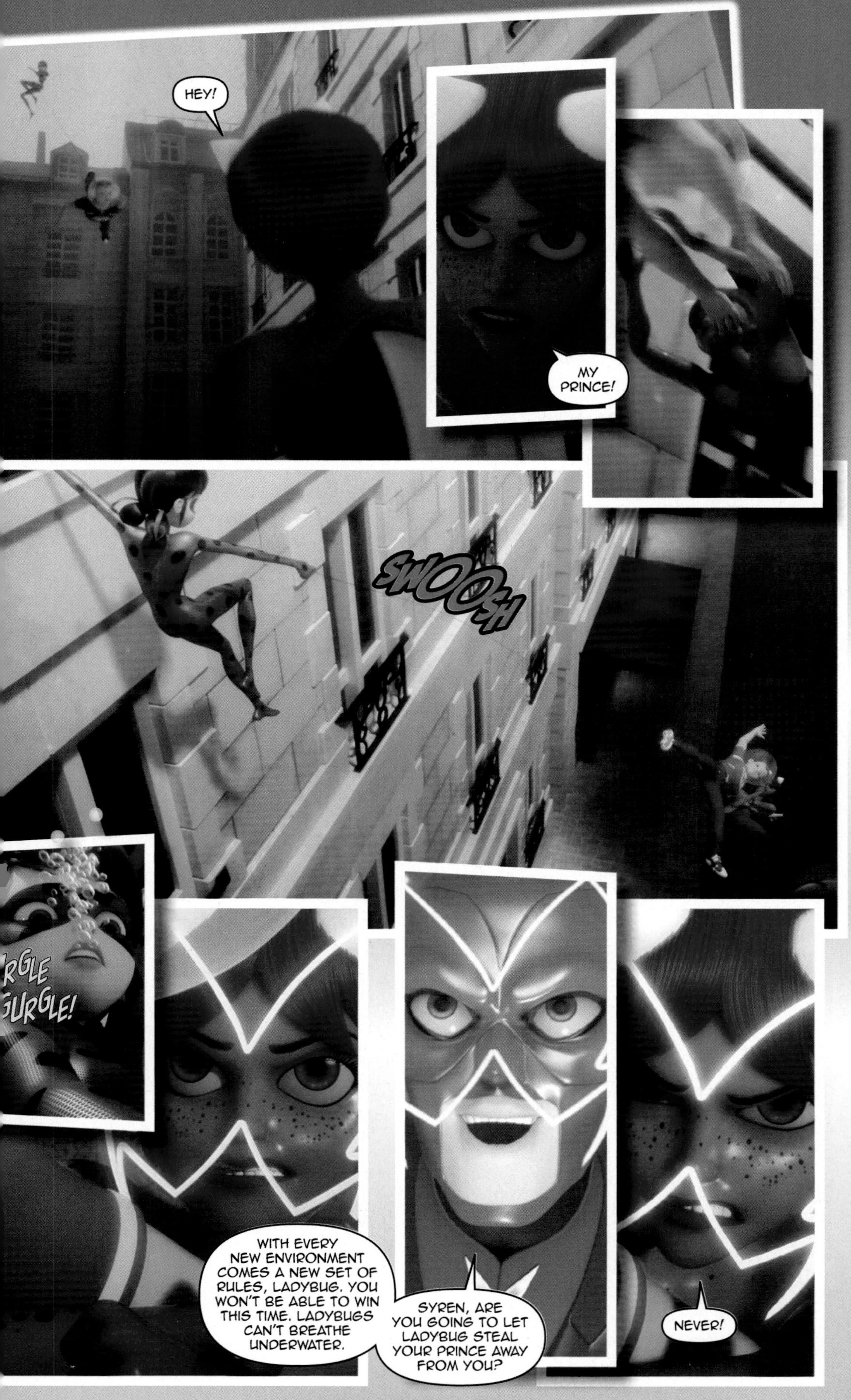
HEY!
MY PRINCE!
SWOOSH
WITH EVERY NEW ENVIRONMENT COMES A NEW SET OF RULES, LADYBUG. YOU WON'T BE ABLE TO WIN THIS TIME. LADYBUGS CAN'T BREATHE UNDERWATER.
SYREN, ARE YOU GOING TO LET LADYBUG STEAL YOUR PRINCE AWAY FROM YOU?
NEVER!

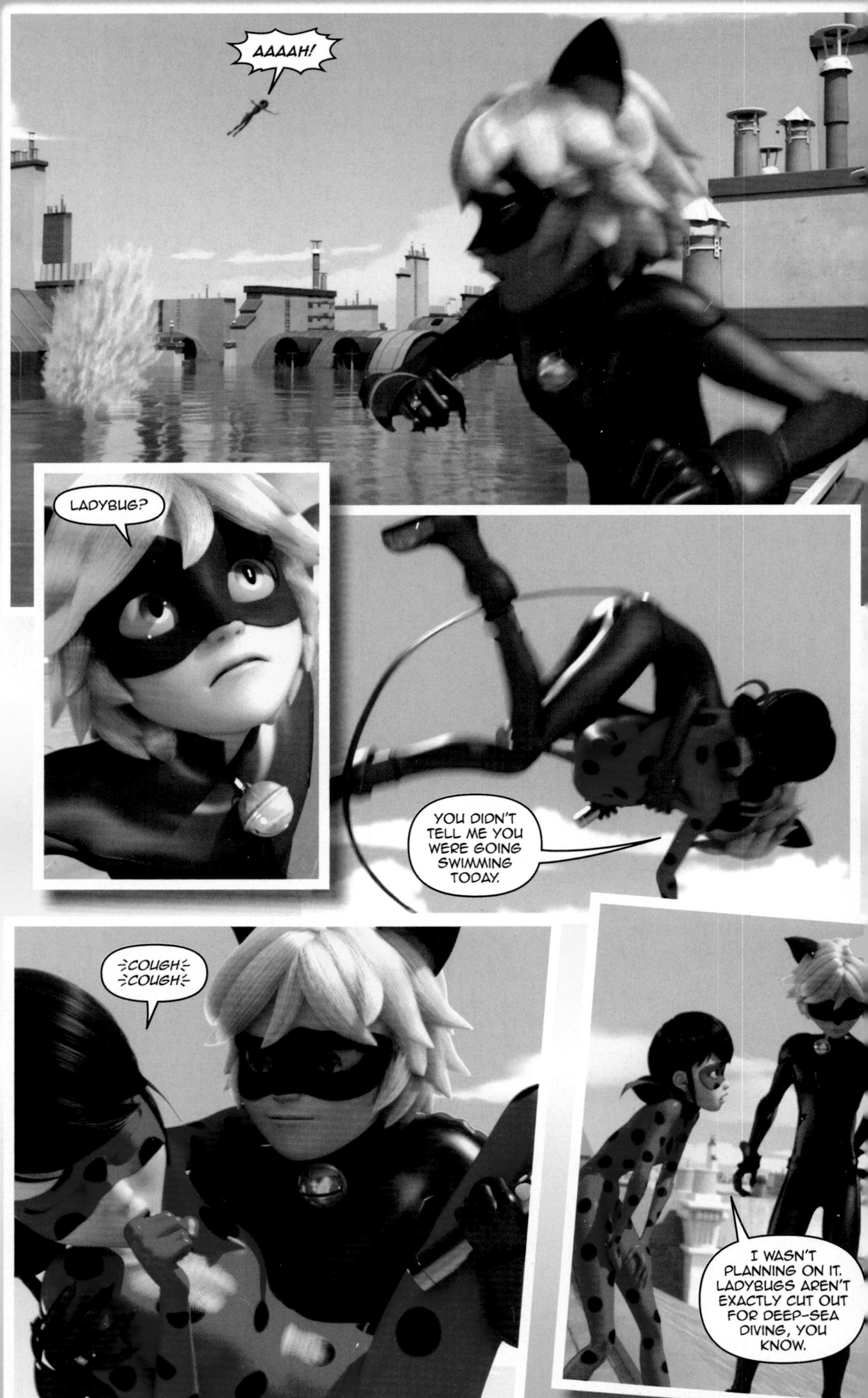
AAAAH!
LADYBUG?
YOU DIDN'T TELL ME YOU WERE GOING SWIMMING TODAY.
COUGH COUGH
I WASN'T PLANNING ON IT. LADYBUGS AREN'T EXACTLY CUT OUT FOR DEEP-SEA DIVING, YOU KNOW.

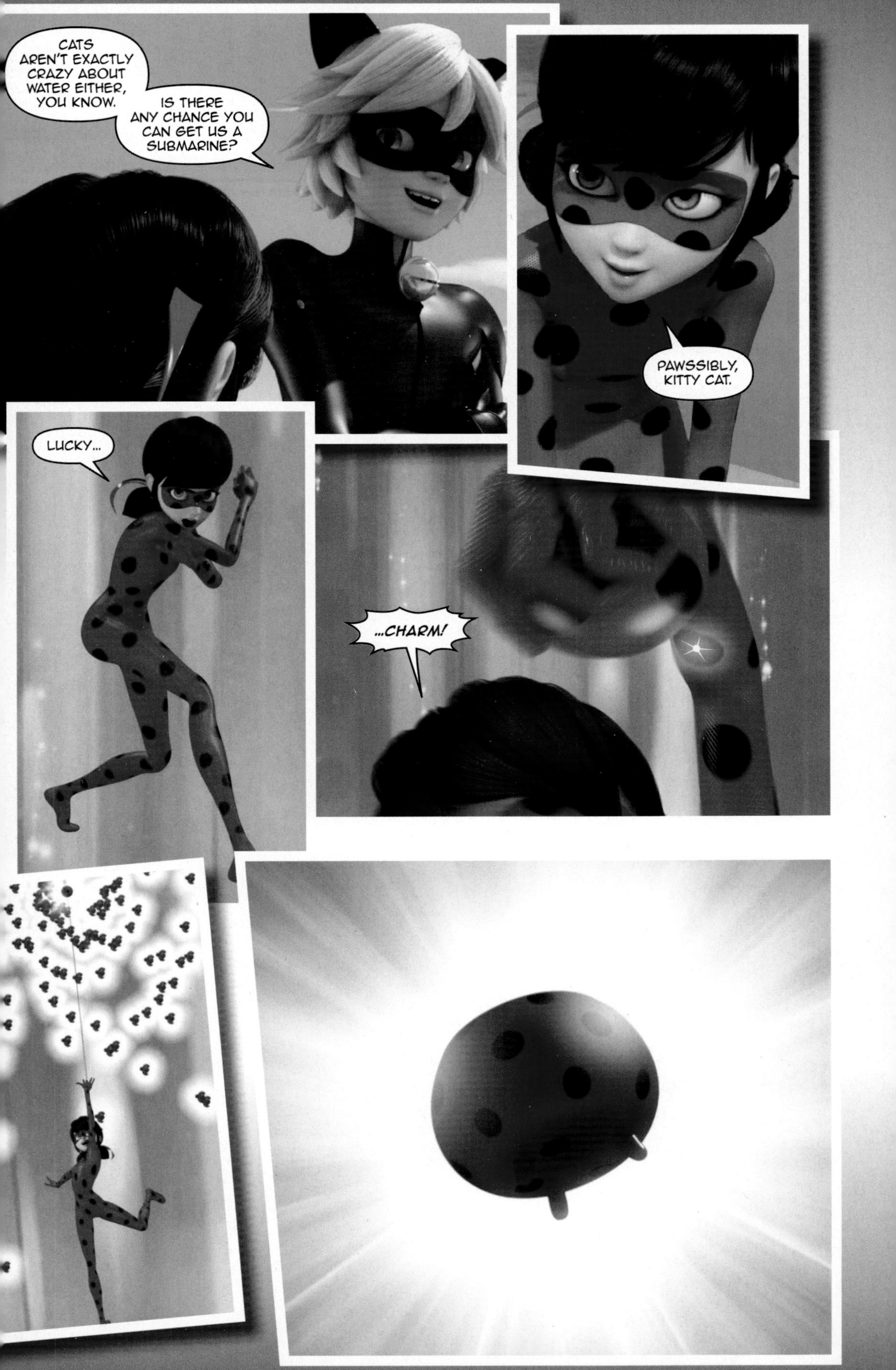
CATS AREN'T EXACTLY CRAZY ABOUT WATER EITHER, YOU KNOW.
IS THERE ANY CHANCE YOU CAN GET US A SUBMARINE?
PAWSSIBLY, KITTY CAT.
LUCKY...
...CHARM!

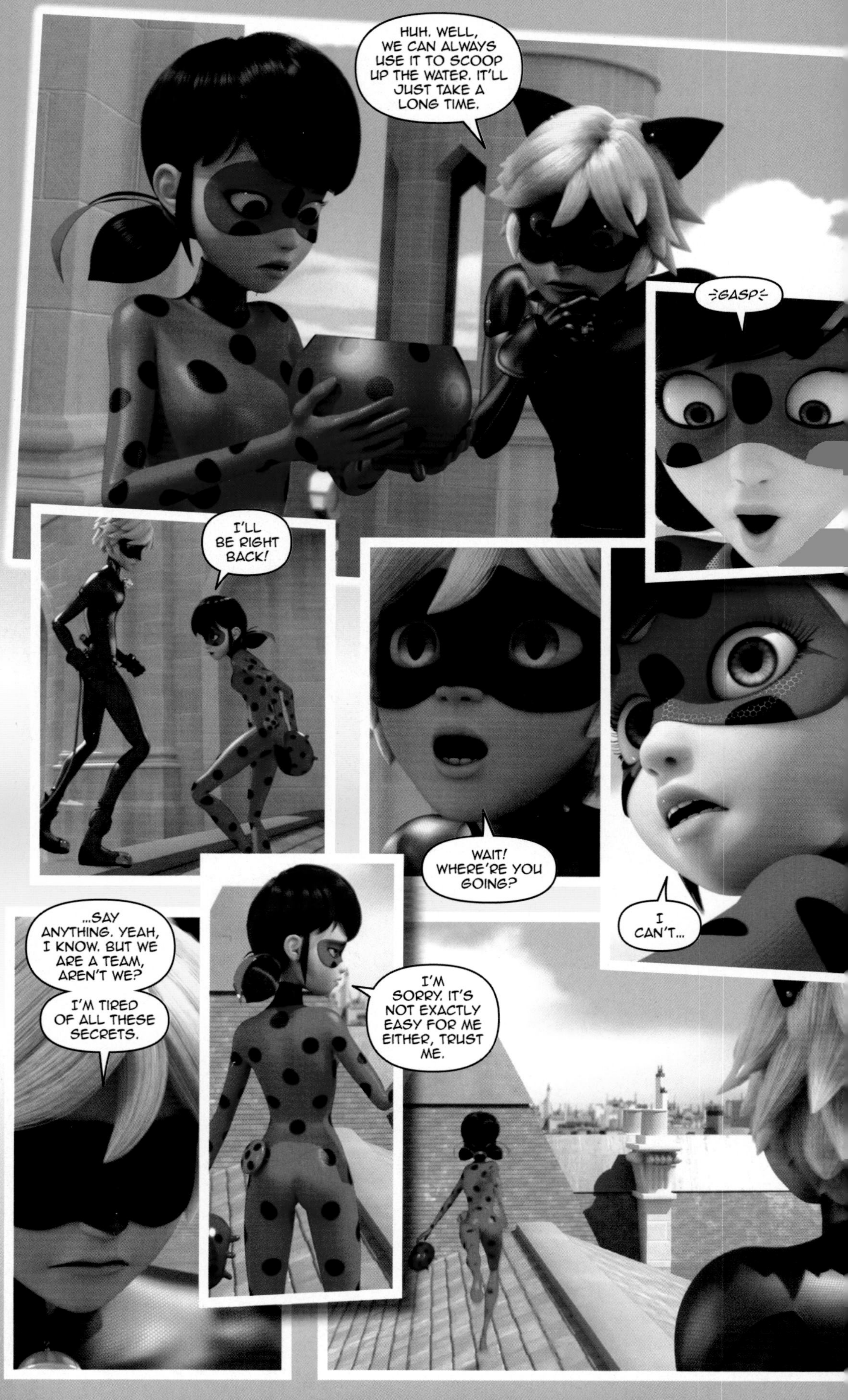
HUH. WELL, WE CAN ALWAYS USE IT TO SCOOP UP THE WATER. IT'LL JUST TAKE A LONG TIME.
GASP
I'LL BE RIGHT BACK!
WAIT! WHERE'RE YOU GOING?
I CAN'T...
...SAY ANYTHING. YEAH, I KNOW. BUT WE ARE A TEAM, AREN'T WE?
I'M TIRED OF ALL THESE SECRETS.
I'M SORRY. IT'S NOT EXACTLY EASY FOR ME EITHER, TRUST ME.

MASTER FU? MASTER?

CAT NOIR AND I CAN'T DEFEAT THE MERMAID UNDERWATER.

I KNOW. AND UNFORTUNATELY I HAVEN'T FOUND THE CORRECT BLEND THAT COULD HELP YOU BOTH OUT.

I'VE FAILED YOU.

NO WAY! WE ARE GONNA FIND THAT LAST INGREDIENT!

THE TEAR OF JOY? I'VE TRIED EVERYTHING. WATER FROM THE LAUGHING FOUNTAIN, MELTED SNOW FROM THE MOUNTAIN OF JUBILATION, DROPS OF PURE CHOCOLATE EXTRACT.

BUT HAVE YOU TRIED A REAL TEAR OF JOY?

WHAT?!

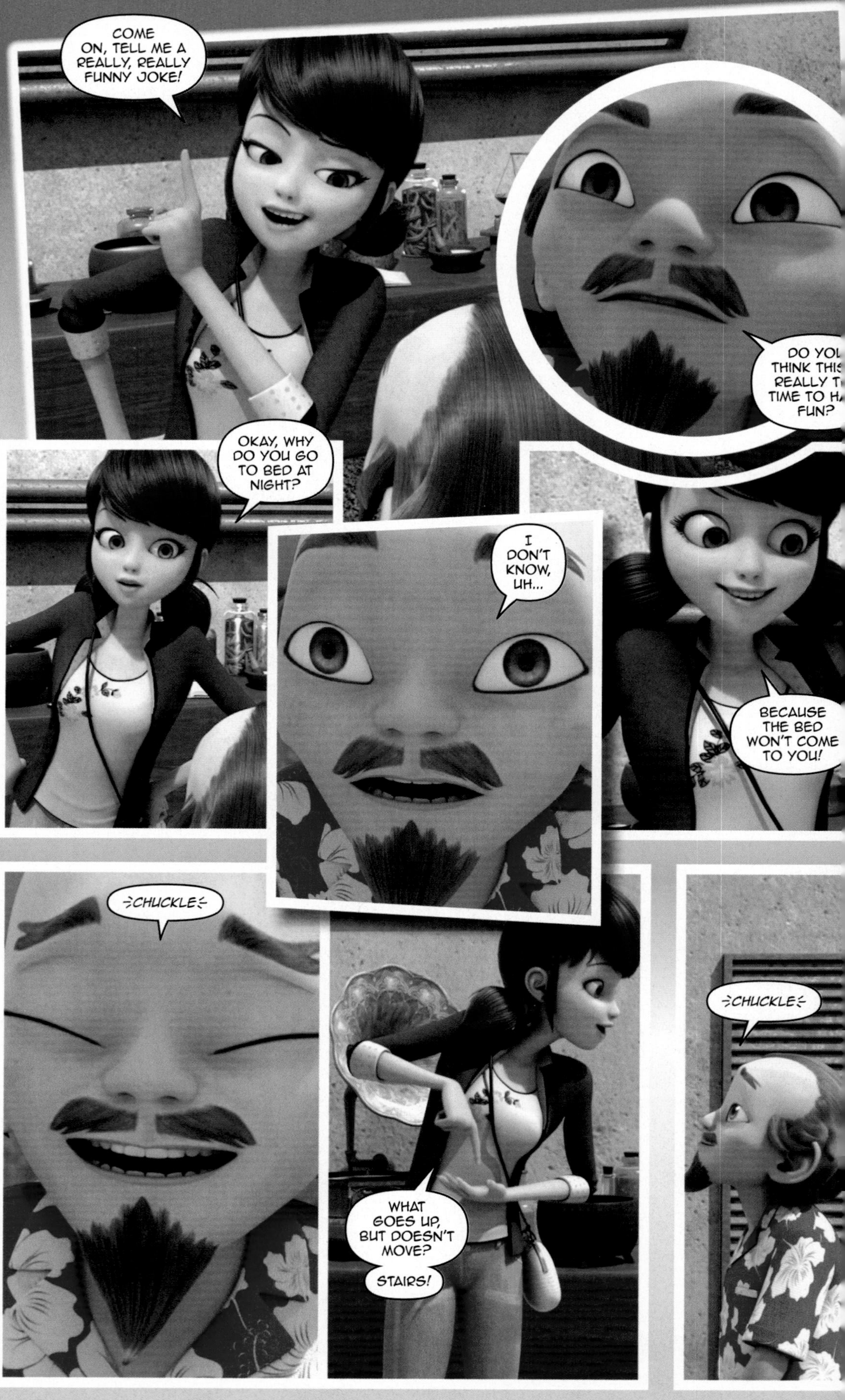
COME ON, TELL ME A REALLY, REALLY FUNNY JOKE!
DO YOU THINK THIS REALLY T TIME TO HA FUN?
OKAY, WHY DO YOU GO TO BED AT NIGHT?
I DON'T KNOW, UH...
BECAUSE THE BED WON'T COME TO YOU!
CHUCKLE
WHAT GOES UP, BUT DOESN'T MOVE?
STAIRS!
CHUCKLE

WHAT DOES A NAIL SAY WHEN T'S RIDING ON A TURTLE'S BACK?

WOOHOO!

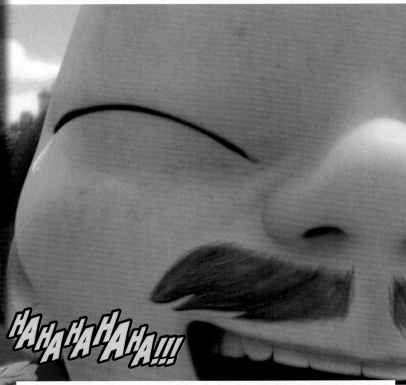

HAHAHAHAHA!!!

GASP

HA HA HA!!!

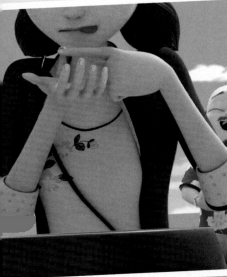

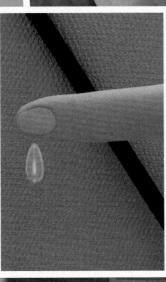

PLOP!

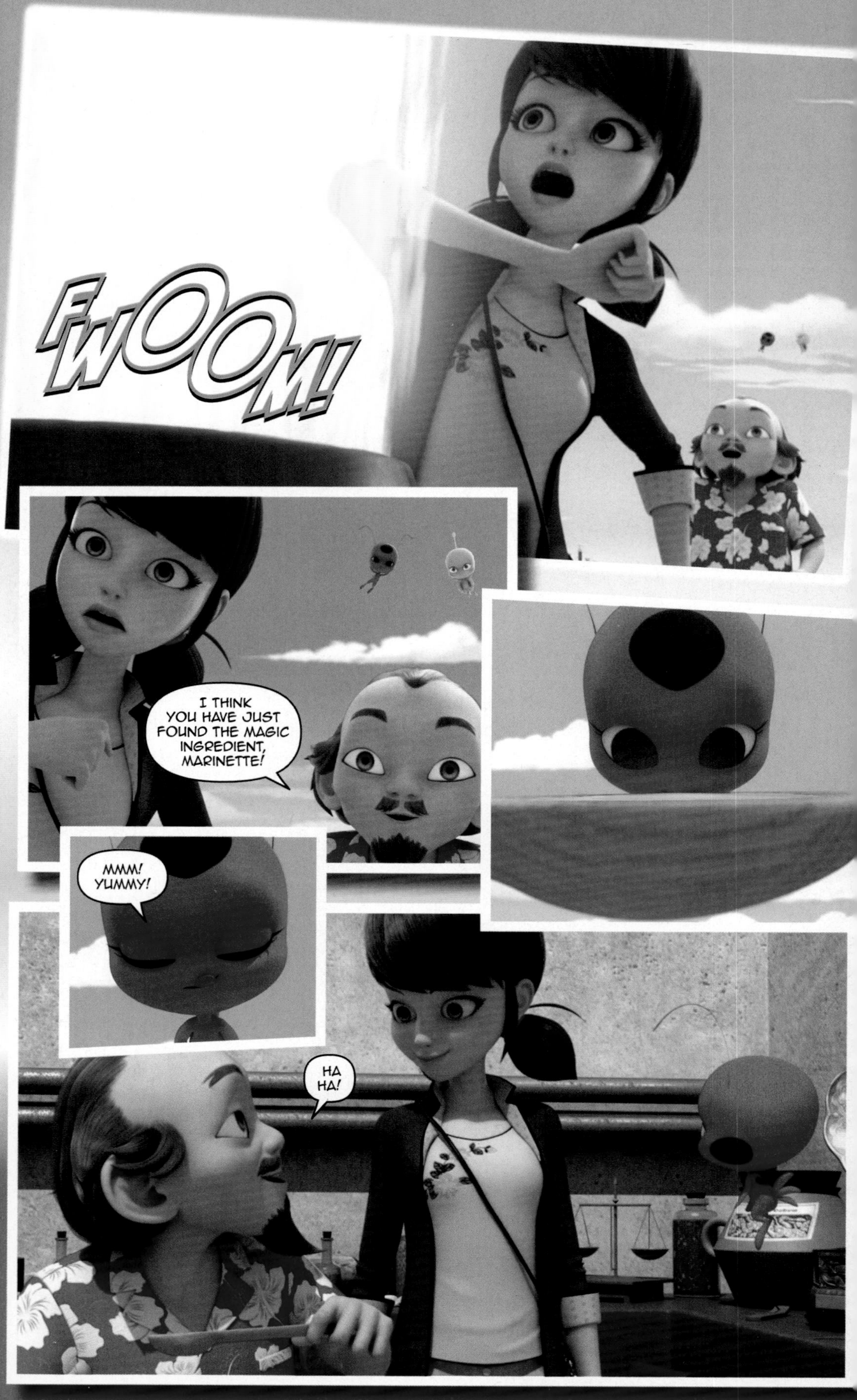
FWOOM!
I THINK YOU HAVE JUST FOUND THE MAGIC INGREDIENT, MARINETTE!
MMM! YUMMY!
HA HA!

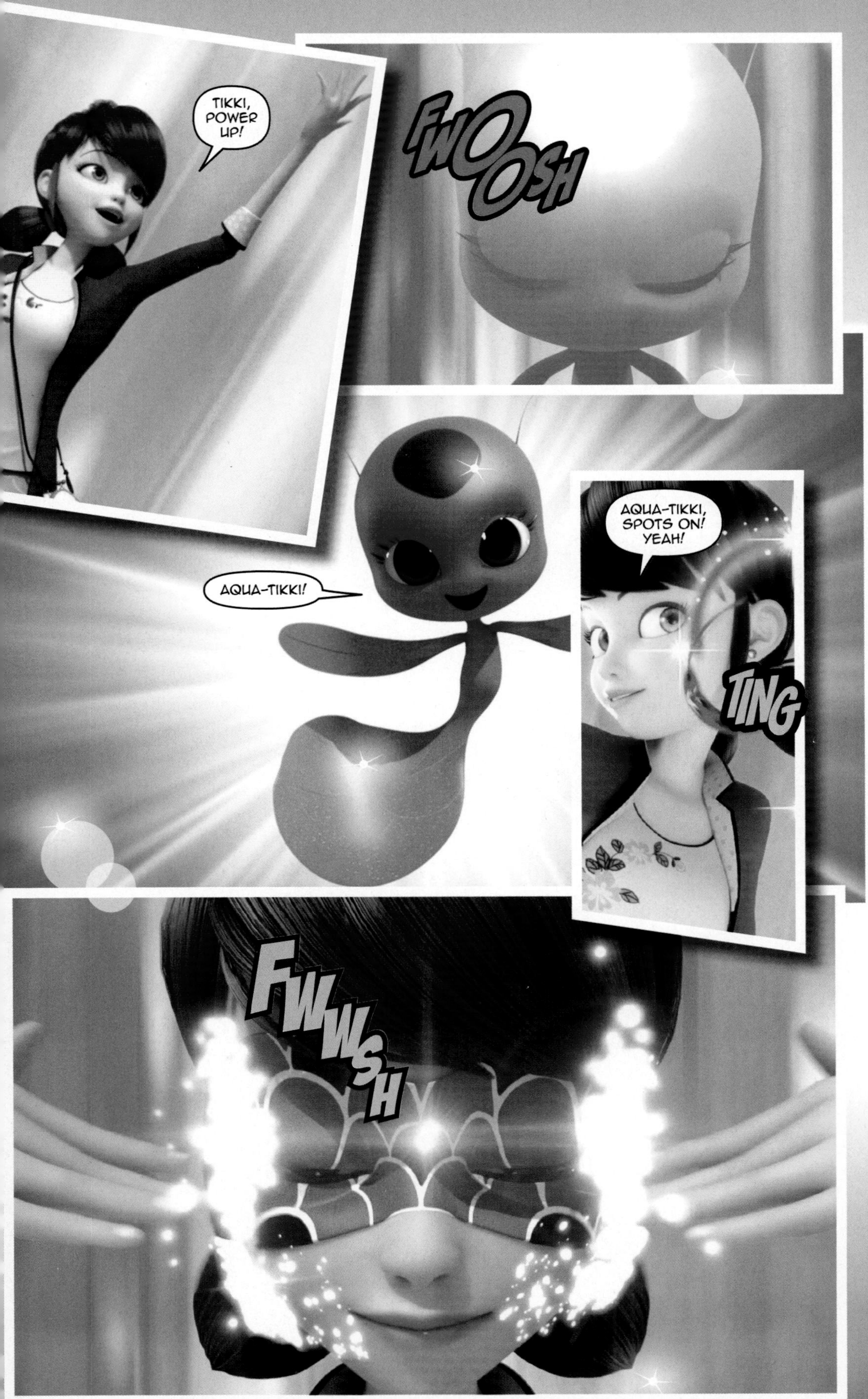
TIKKI, POWER UP!
FWOOSH
AQUA-TIKKI!
AQUA-TIKKI, SPOTS ON! YEAH!
TING
FWWSH

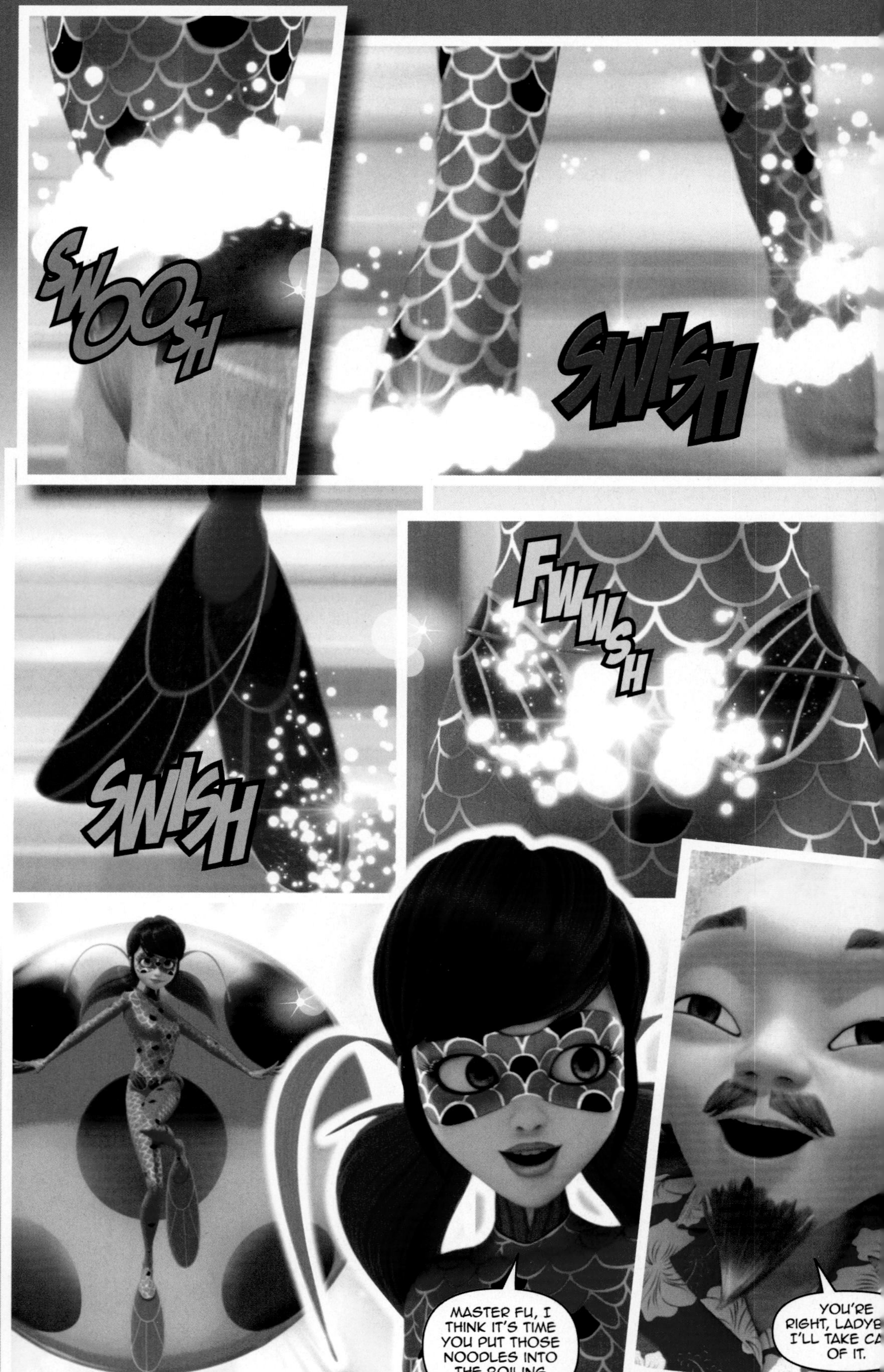
SWOOSH
SWISH
SWISH
FWWSH
MASTER FU, I THINK IT'S TIME YOU PUT THOSE NOODLES INTO THE BOILING WATER.
YOU'RE RIGHT, LADYB I'LL TAKE CA OF IT.

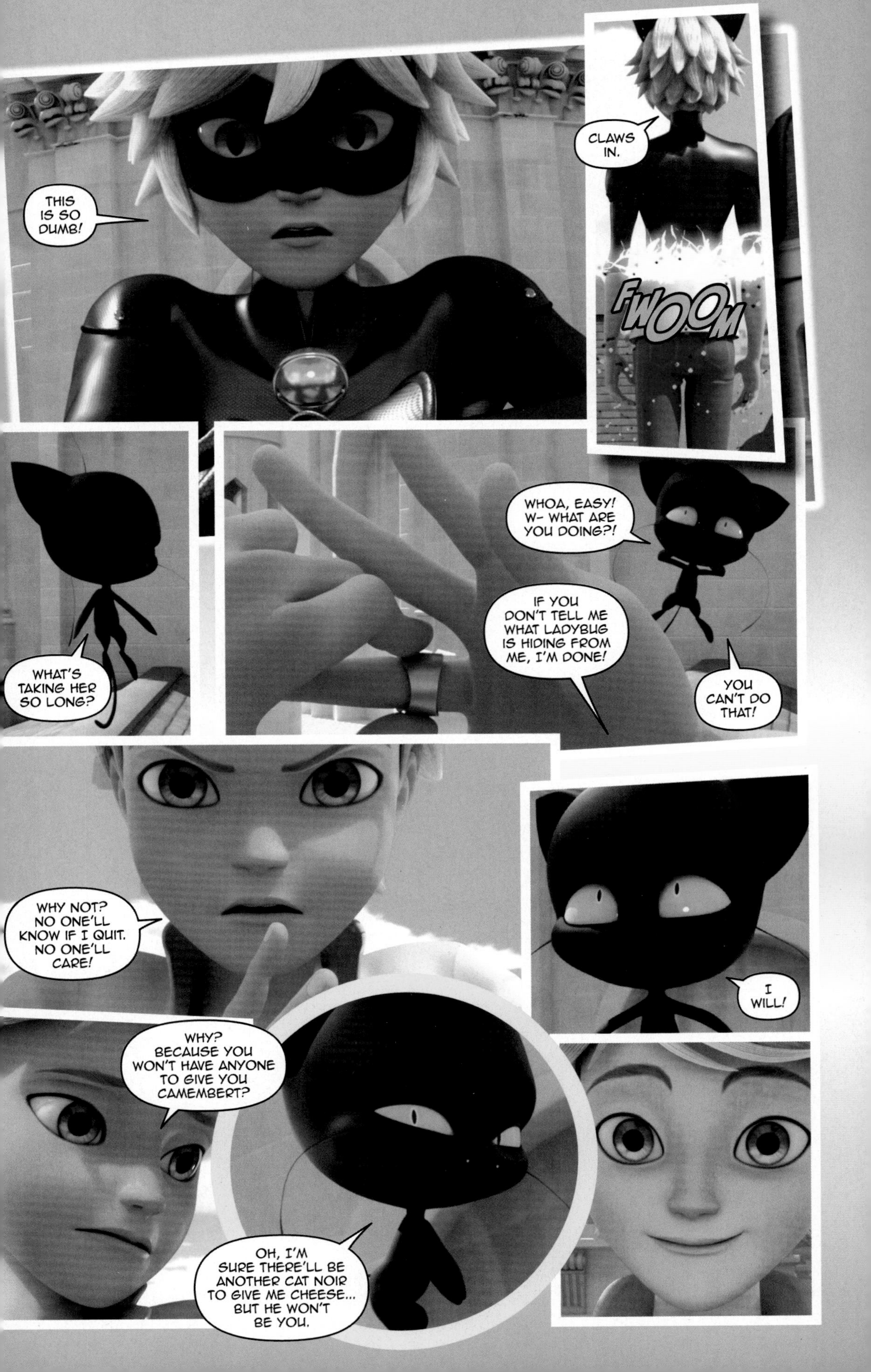
THIS IS SO DUMB!
CLAWS IN.
FWOOM
WHAT'S TAKING HER SO LONG?
WHOA, EASY! W- WHAT ARE YOU DOING?!
IF YOU DON'T TELL ME WHAT LADYBUG IS HIDING FROM ME, I'M DONE!
YOU CAN'T DO THAT!
WHY NOT? NO ONE'LL KNOW IF I QUIT. NO ONE'LL CARE!
I WILL!
WHY? BECAUSE YOU WON'T HAVE ANYONE TO GIVE YOU CAMEMBERT?
OH, I'M SURE THERE'LL BE ANOTHER CAT NOIR TO GIVE ME CHEESE... BUT HE WON'T BE YOU.

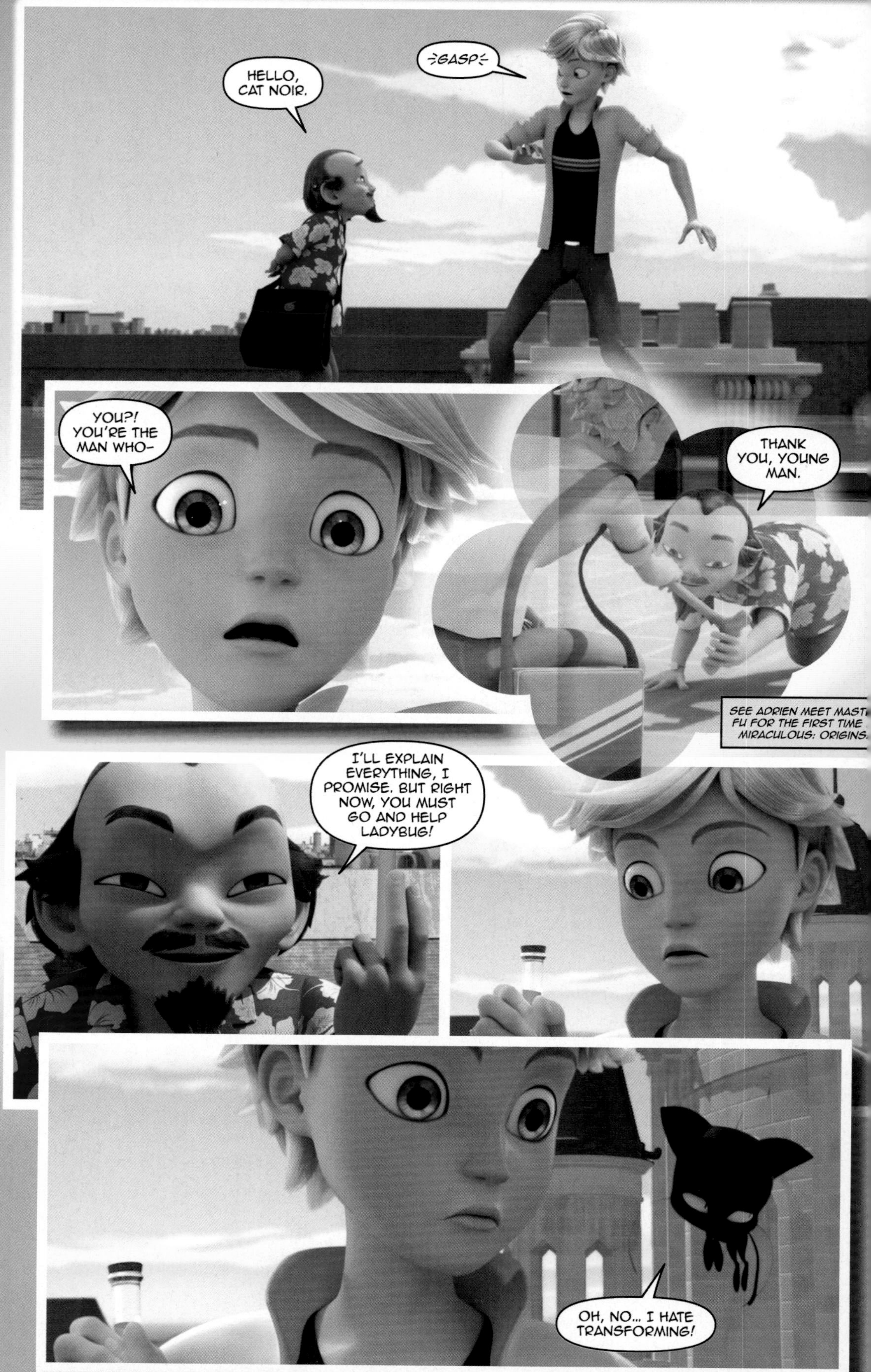
HELLO, CAT NOIR.
GASP
YOU?! YOU'RE THE MAN WHO-
THANK YOU, YOUNG MAN.
SEE ADRIEN MEET MAST
FU FOR THE FIRST TIME
MIRACULOUS: ORIGINS.
I'LL EXPLAIN EVERYTHING, I PROMISE. BUT RIGHT NOW, YOU MUST GO AND HELP LADYBUG!
OH, NO... I HATE TRANSFORMING!

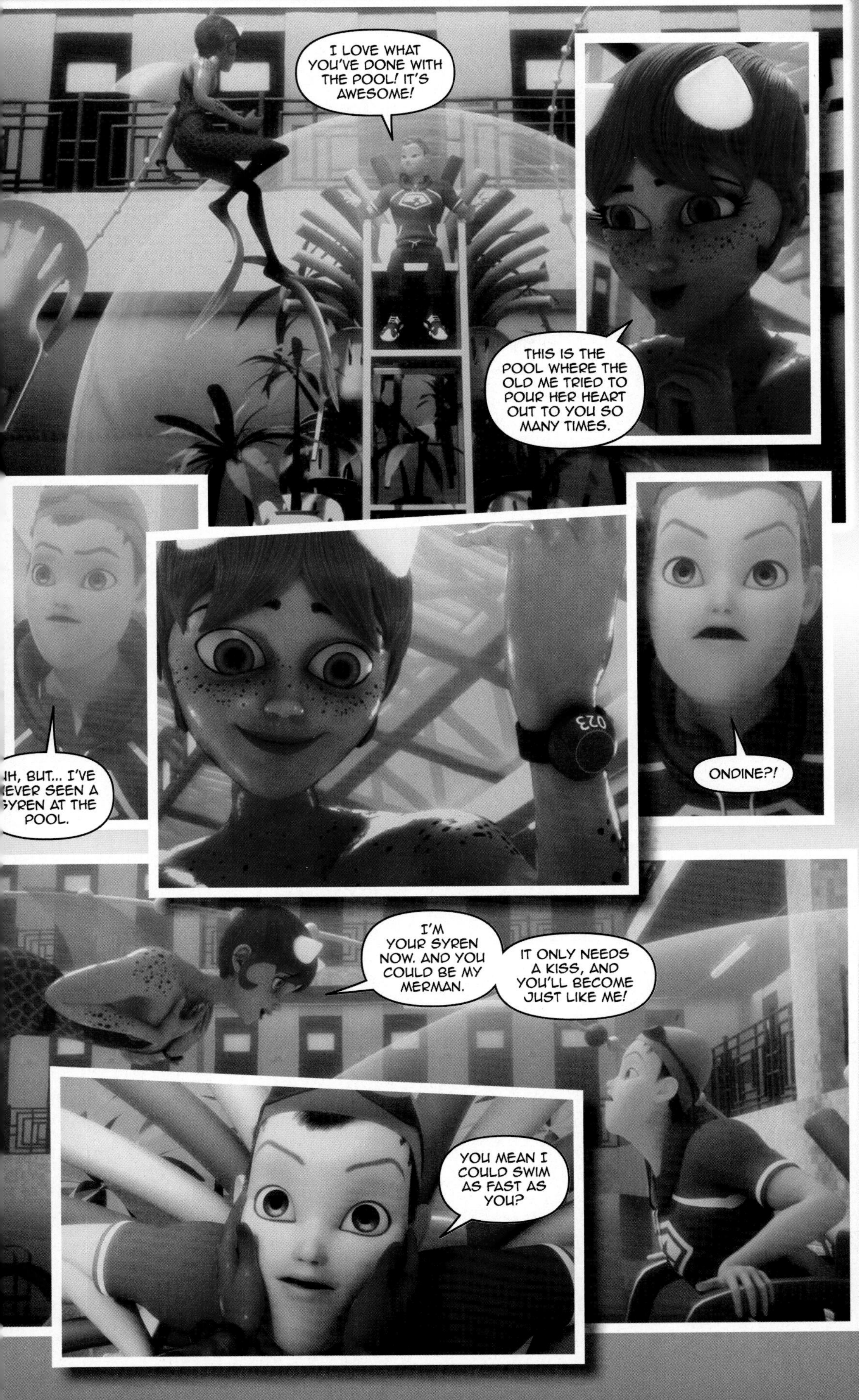
I LOVE WHAT YOU'VE DONE WITH THE POOL! IT'S AWESOME!
THIS IS THE POOL WHERE THE OLD ME TRIED TO POUR HER HEART OUT TO YOU SO MANY TIMES.
H, BUT... I'VE EVER SEEN A SYREN AT THE POOL.
ONDINE?!
I'M YOUR SYREN NOW. AND YOU COULD BE MY MERMAN.
IT ONLY NEEDS A KISS, AND YOU'LL BECOME JUST LIKE ME!
YOU MEAN I COULD SWIM AS FAST AS YOU?

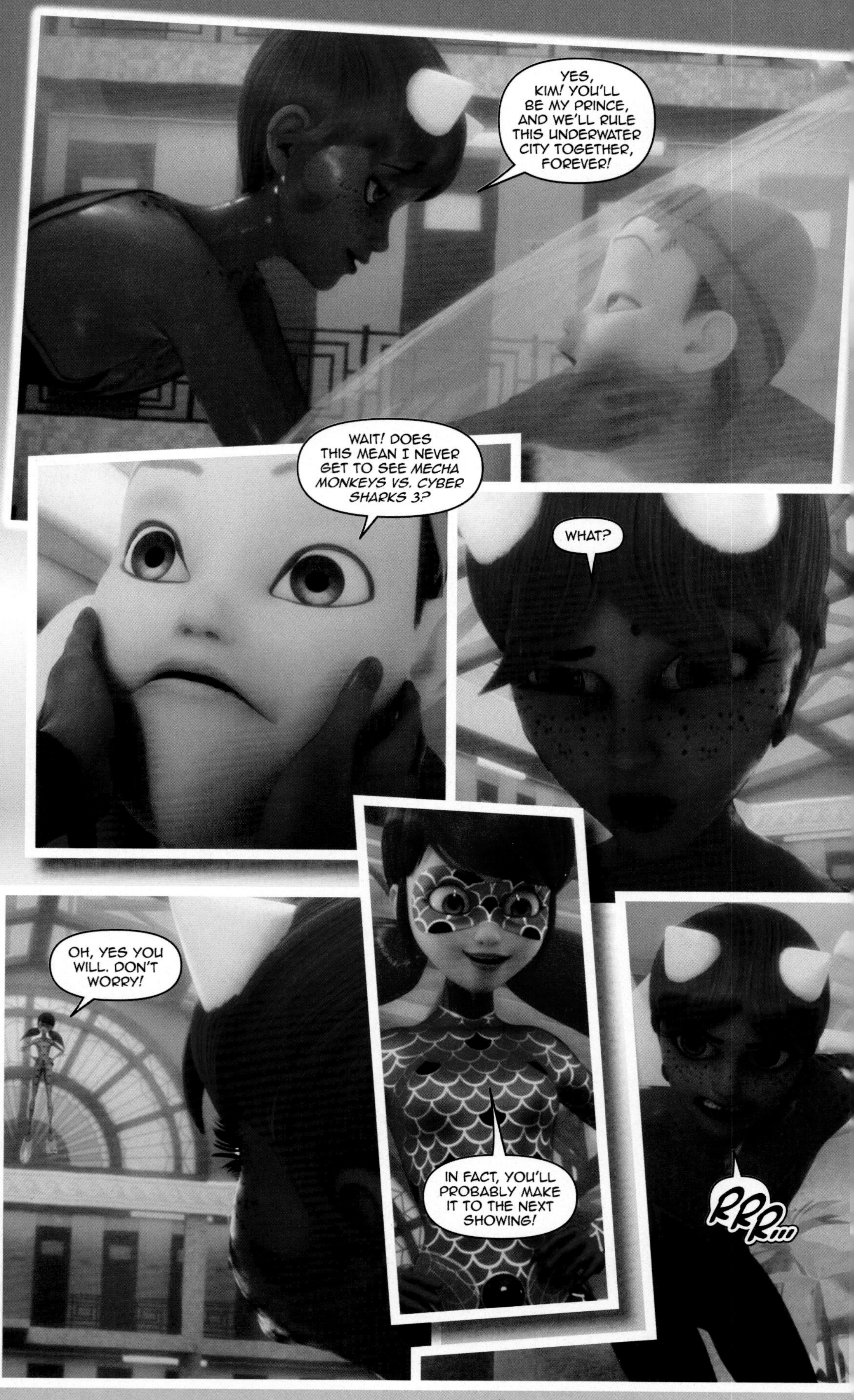
YES, KIM! YOU'LL BE MY PRINCE, AND WE'LL RULE THIS UNDERWATER CITY TOGETHER, FOREVER!
WAIT! DOES THIS MEAN I NEVER GET TO SEE *MECHA MONKEYS VS. CYBER SHARKS 3*?
WHAT?
OH, YES YOU WILL. DON'T WORRY!
IN FACT, YOU'LL PROBABLY MAKE IT TO THE NEXT SHOWING!
RRR...

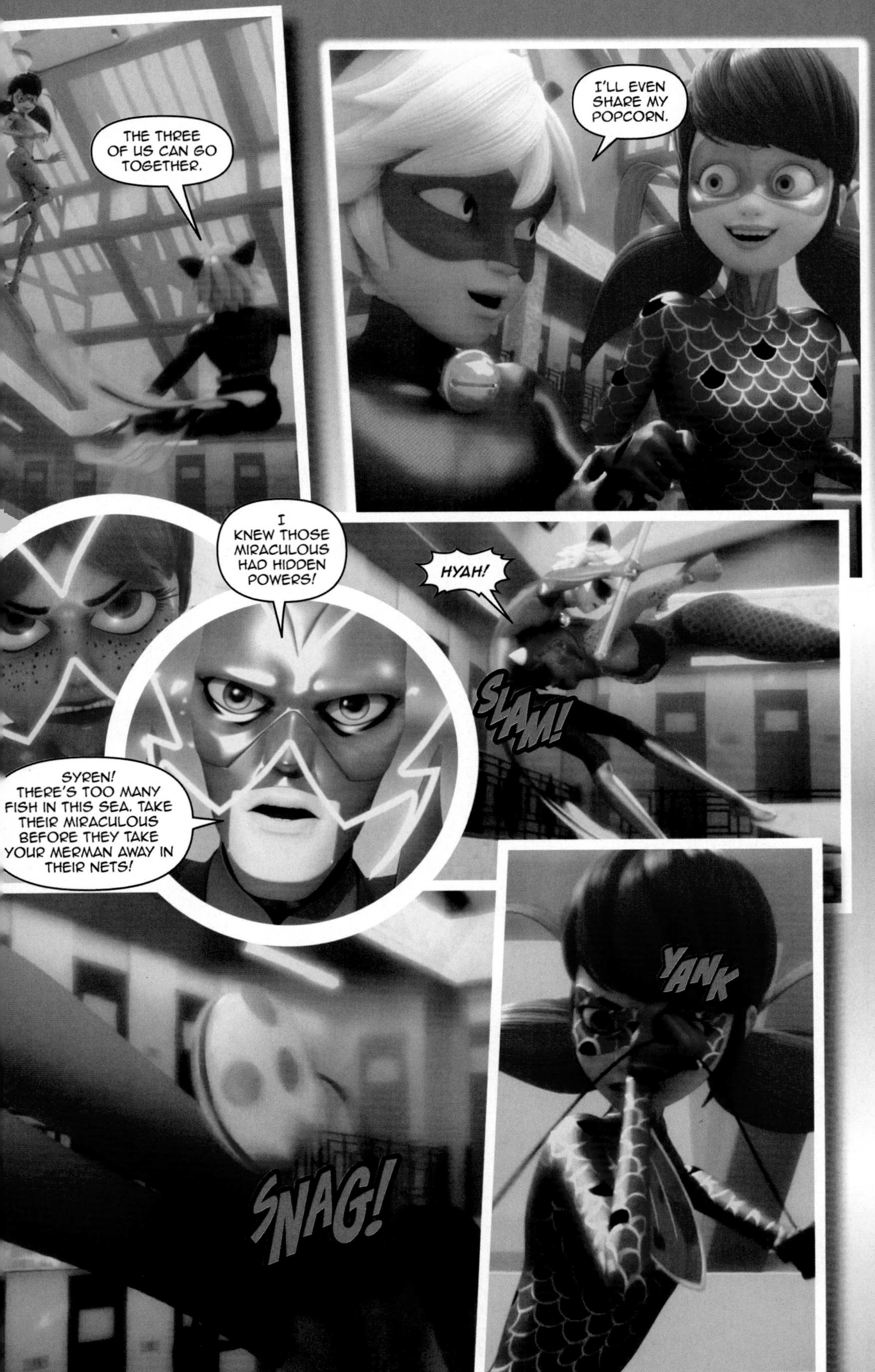
THE THREE OF US CAN GO TOGETHER.
I'LL EVEN SHARE MY POPCORN.
I KNEW THOSE MIRACULOUS HAD HIDDEN POWERS!
SYREN! THERE'S TOO MANY FISH IN THIS SEA. TAKE THEIR MIRACULOUS BEFORE THEY TAKE YOUR MERMAN AWAY IN THEIR NETS!
HYAH!
SLAM!
SNAG!
YANK

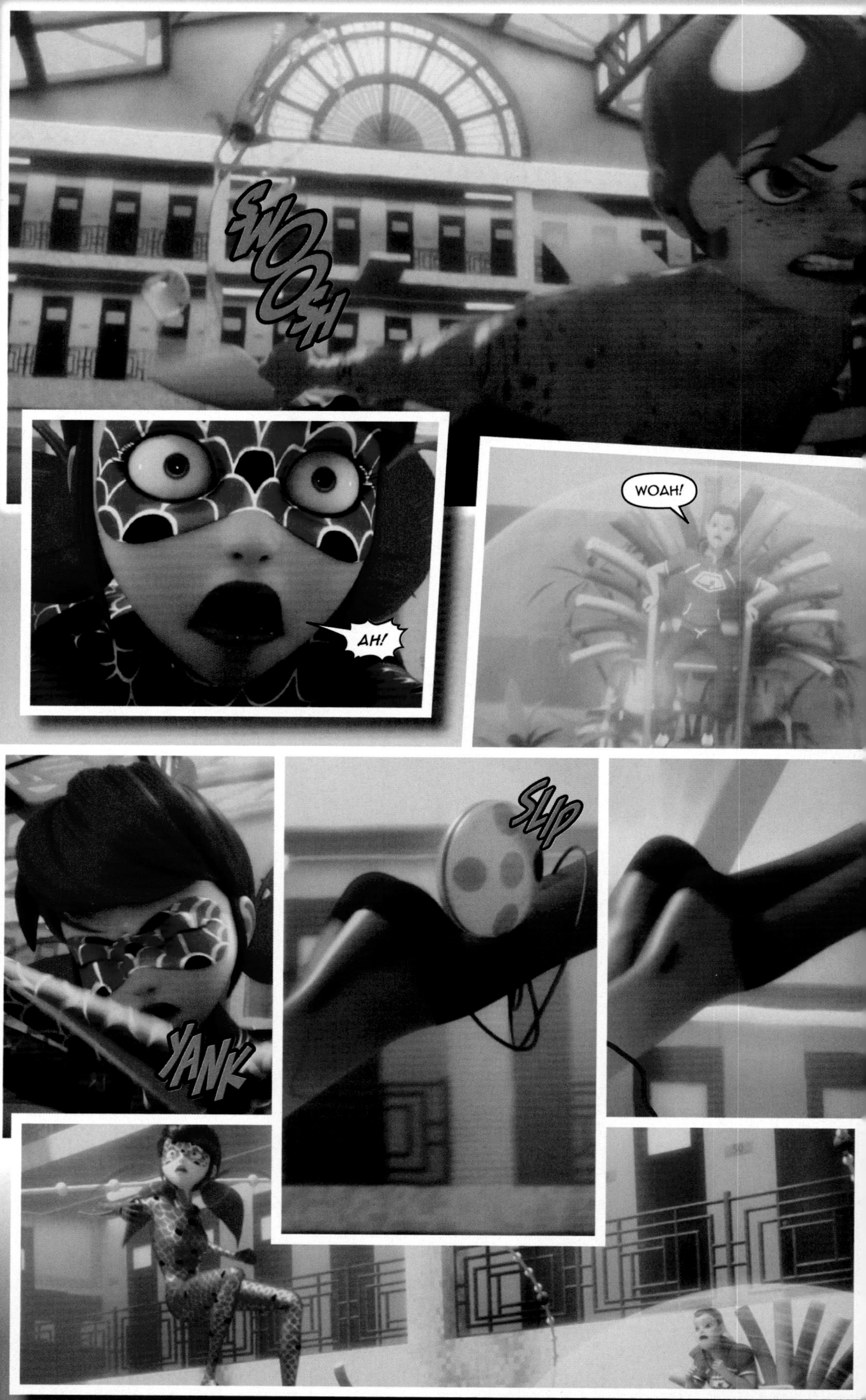
SWOOSH
AH!
WOAH!
YANK
SLIP

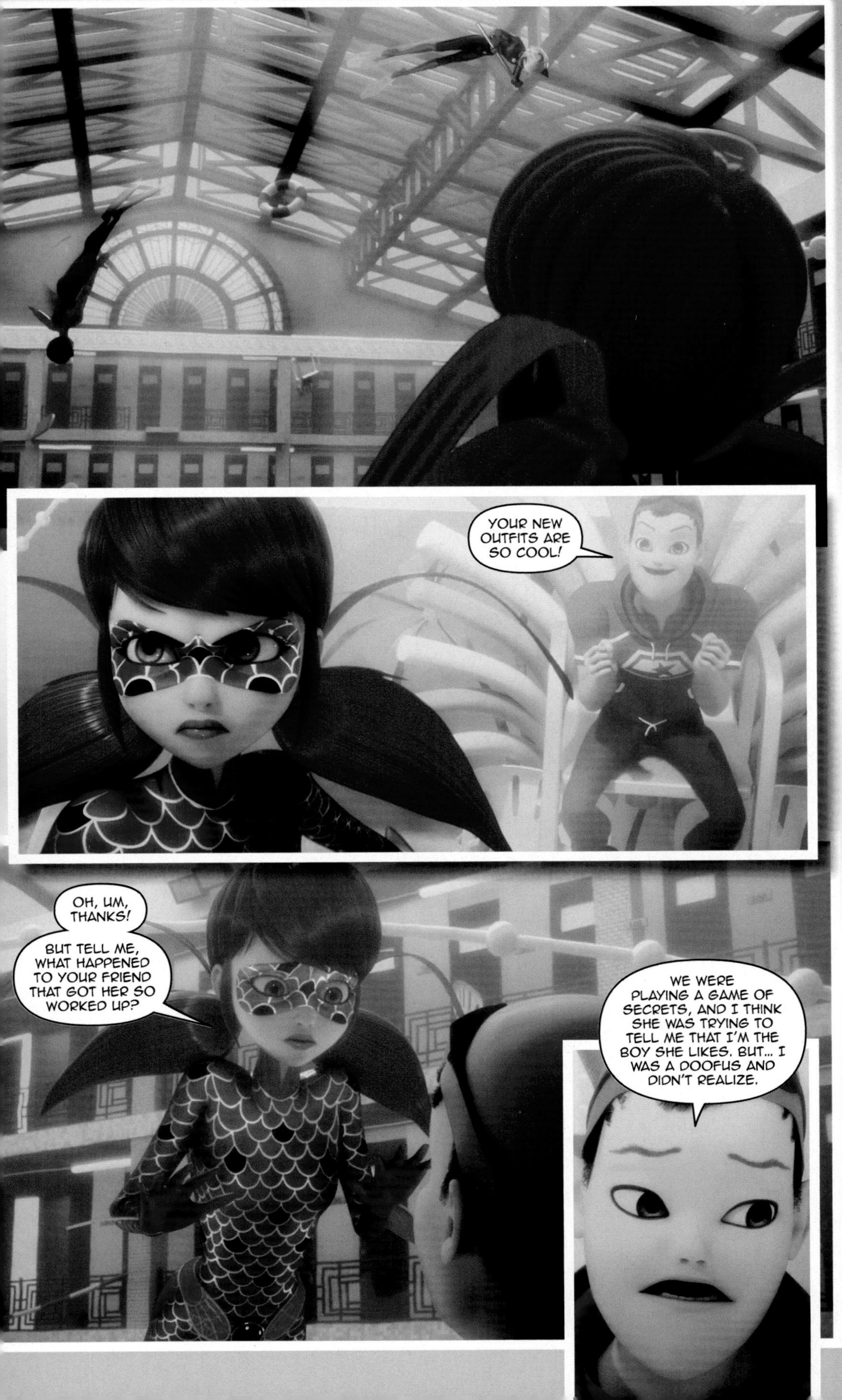
YOUR NEW OUTFITS ARE SO COOL!
OH, UM, THANKS!
BUT TELL ME, WHAT HAPPENED TO YOUR FRIEND THAT GOT HER SO WORKED UP?
WE WERE PLAYING A GAME OF SECRETS, AND I THINK SHE WAS TRYING TO TELL ME THAT I'M THE BOY SHE LIKES. BUT... I WAS A DOOFUS AND DIDN'T REALIZE.

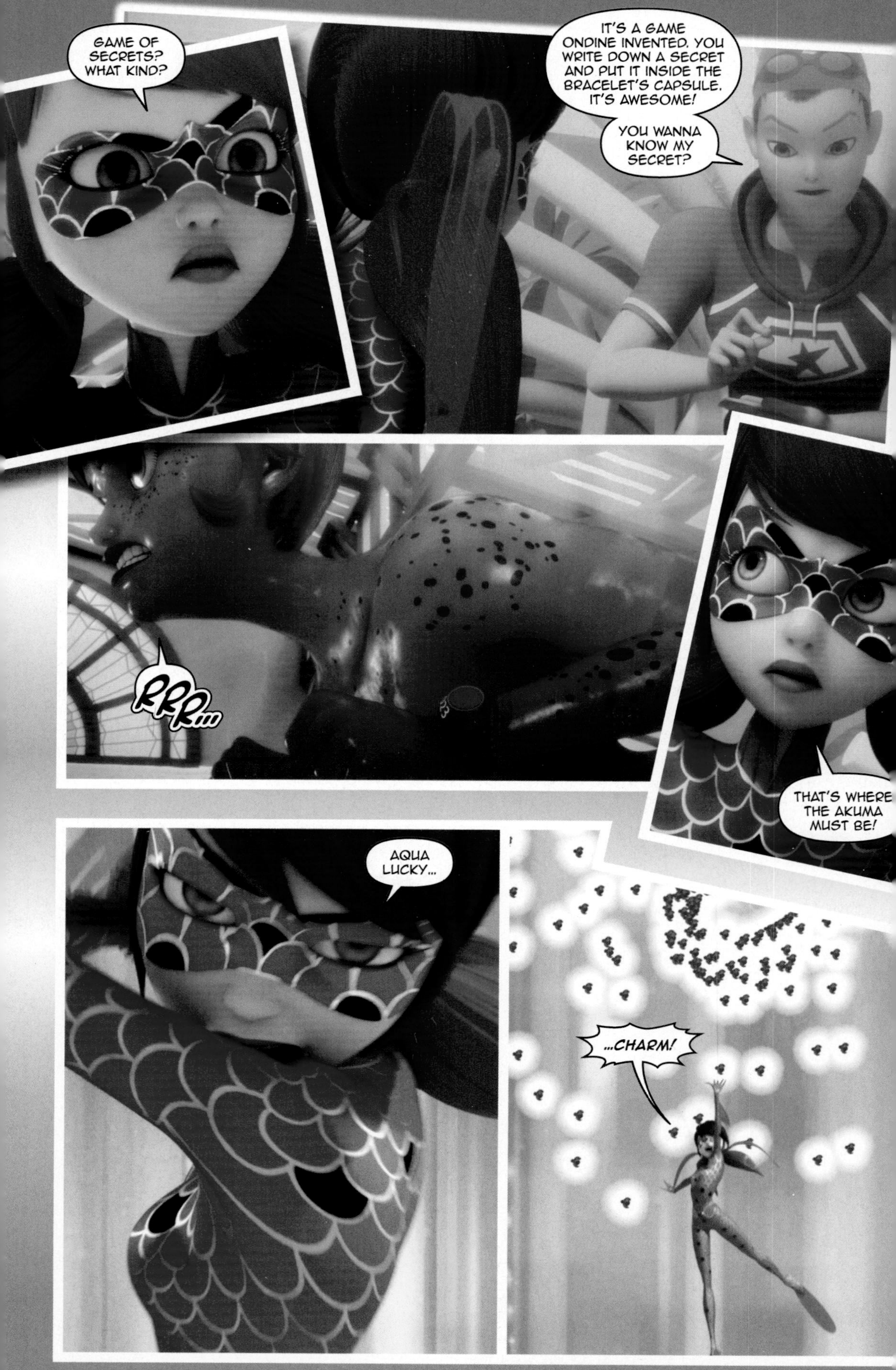
GAME OF SECRETS? WHAT KIND?
IT'S A GAME ONDINE INVENTED. YOU WRITE DOWN A SECRET AND PUT IT INSIDE THE BRACELET'S CAPSULE. IT'S AWESOME!
YOU WANNA KNOW MY SECRET?
RRR...
THAT'S WHERE THE AKUMA MUST BE!
AQUA LUCKY...
...CHARM!

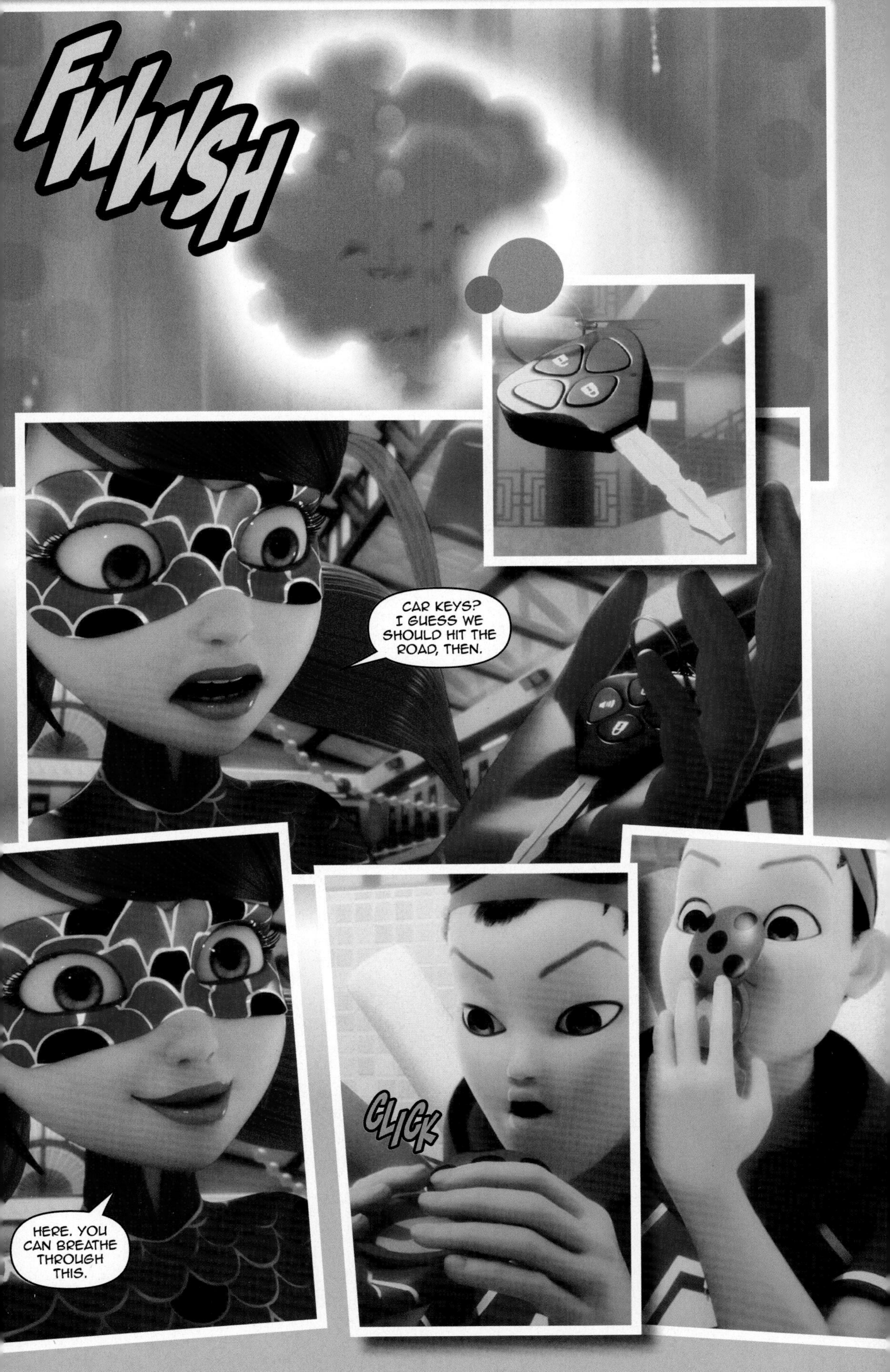
FWWSH
CAR KEYS? I GUESS WE SHOULD HIT THE ROAD, THEN.
HERE. YOU CAN BREATHE THROUGH THIS.
CLICK

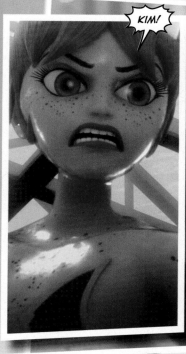

KIM!

SWOOSH

HEY! WE'RE NOT DONE YET!

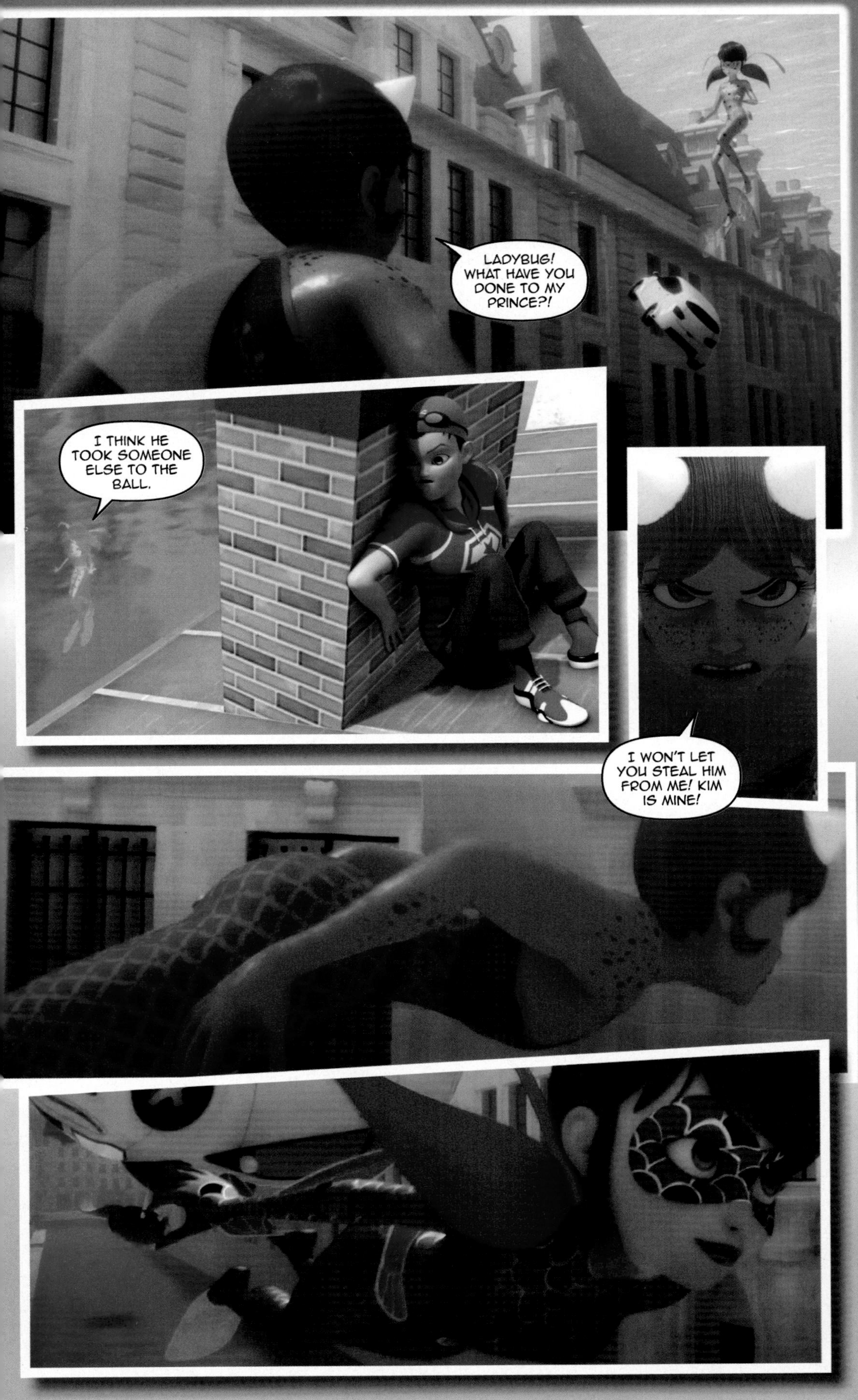
LADYBUG! WHAT HAVE YOU DONE TO MY PRINCE?!
I THINK HE TOOK SOMEONE ELSE TO THE BALL.
I WON'T LET YOU STEAL HIM FROM ME! KIM IS MINE!

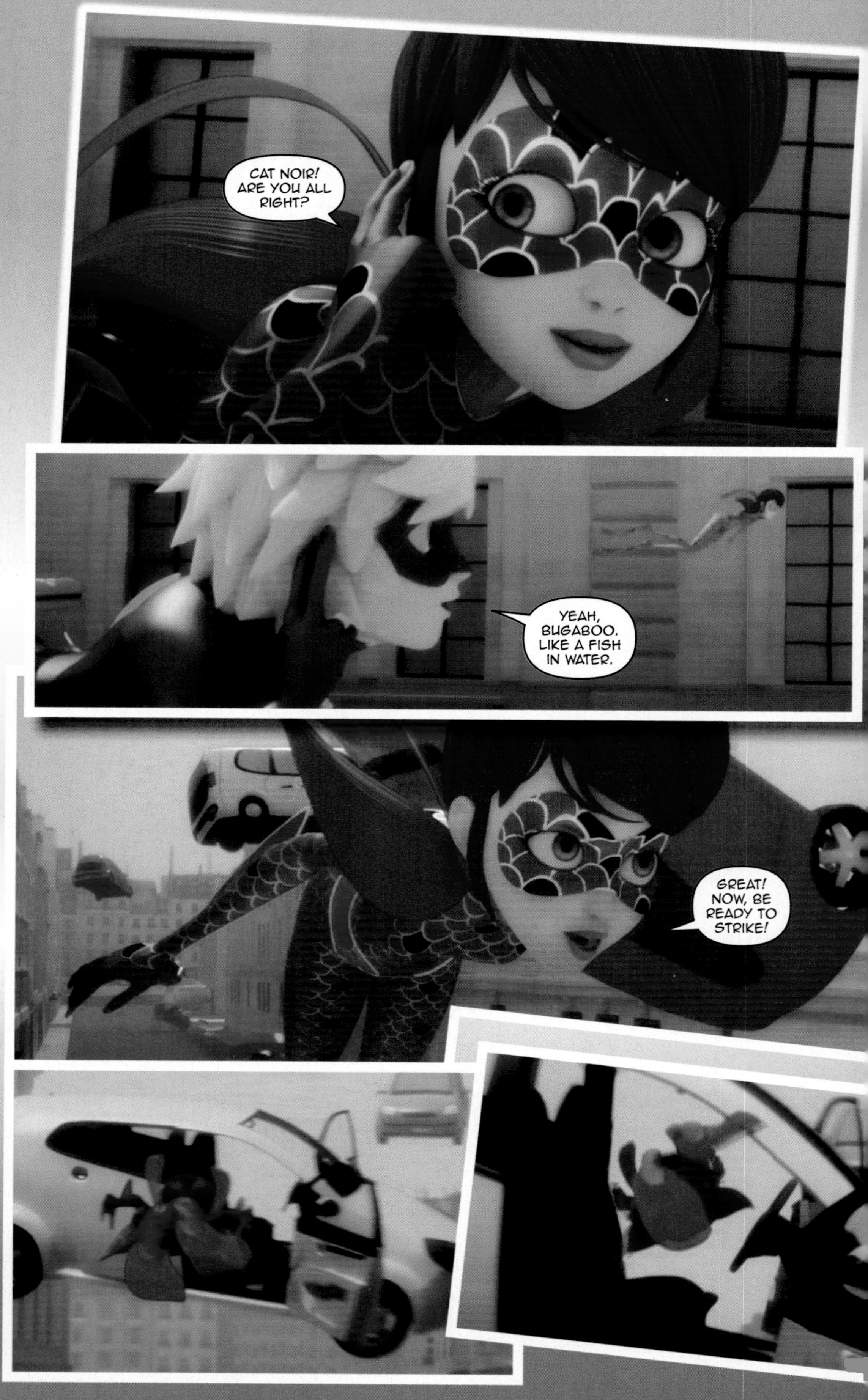
CAT NOIR! ARE YOU ALL RIGHT?
YEAH, BUGABOO. LIKE A FISH IN WATER.
GREAT! NOW, BE READY TO STRIKE!

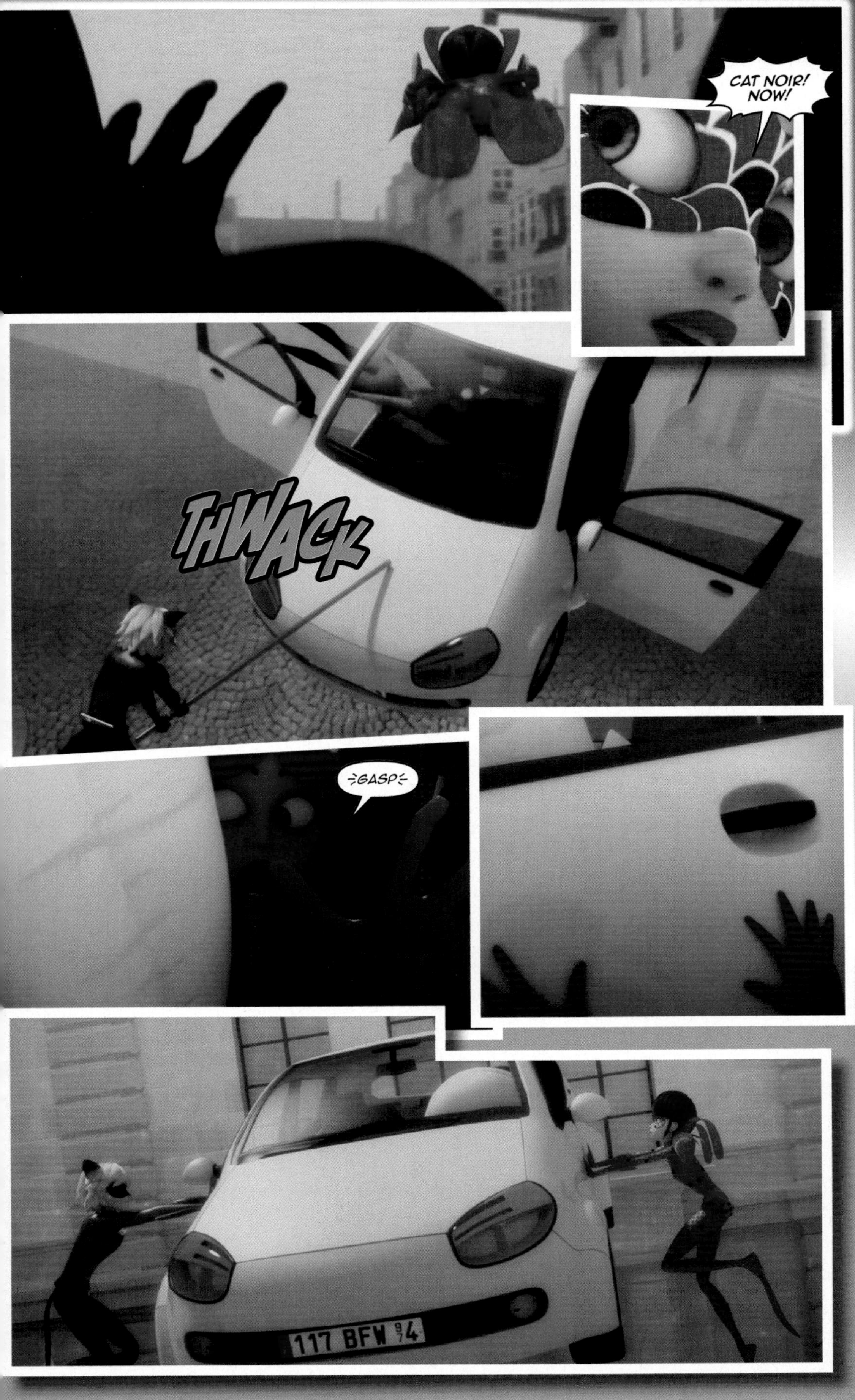
CAT NOIR! NOW!
THWACK
GASP
117 BFW 94

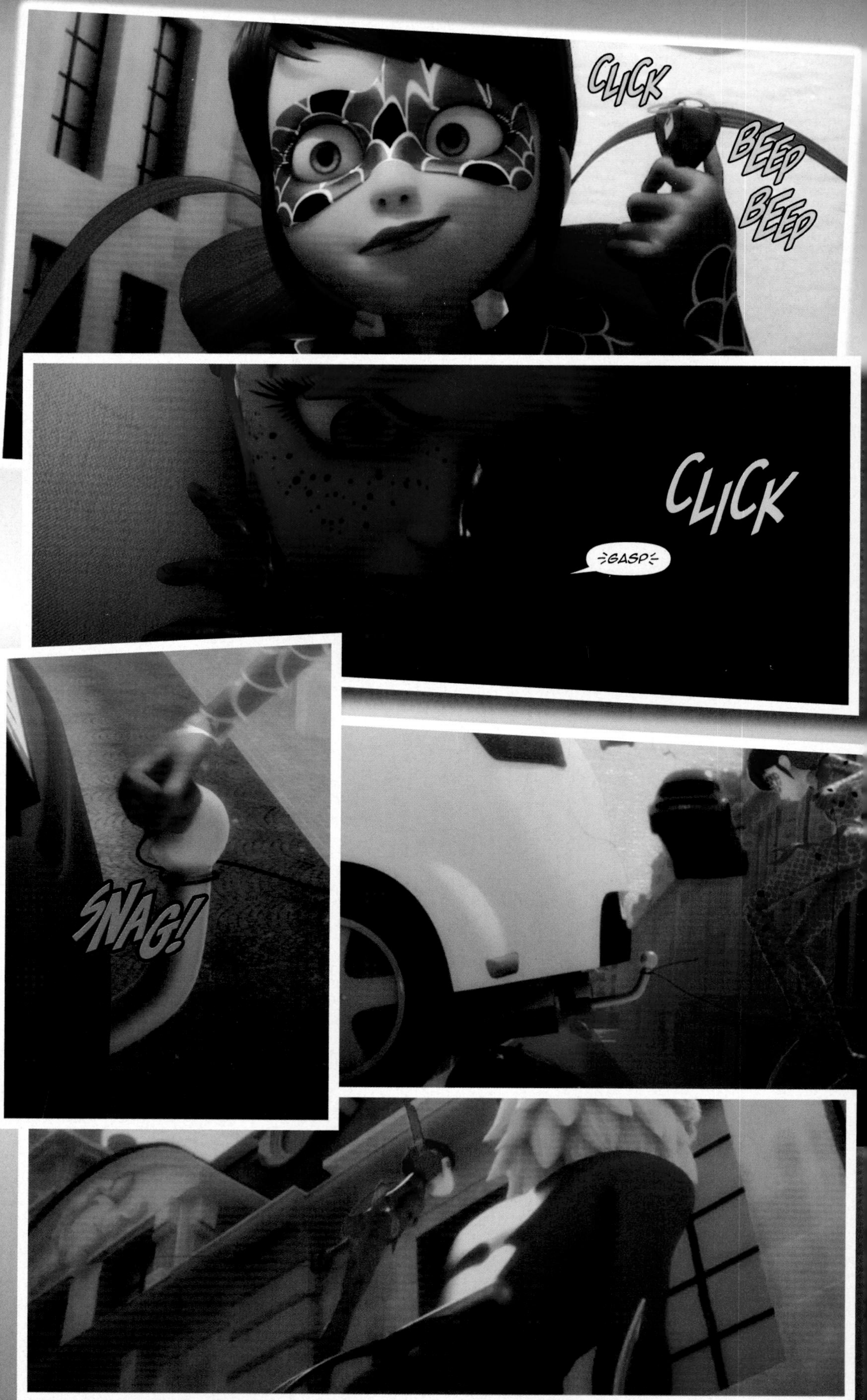
CLICK
BEEP
BEEP
CLICK
GASP
SNAG!

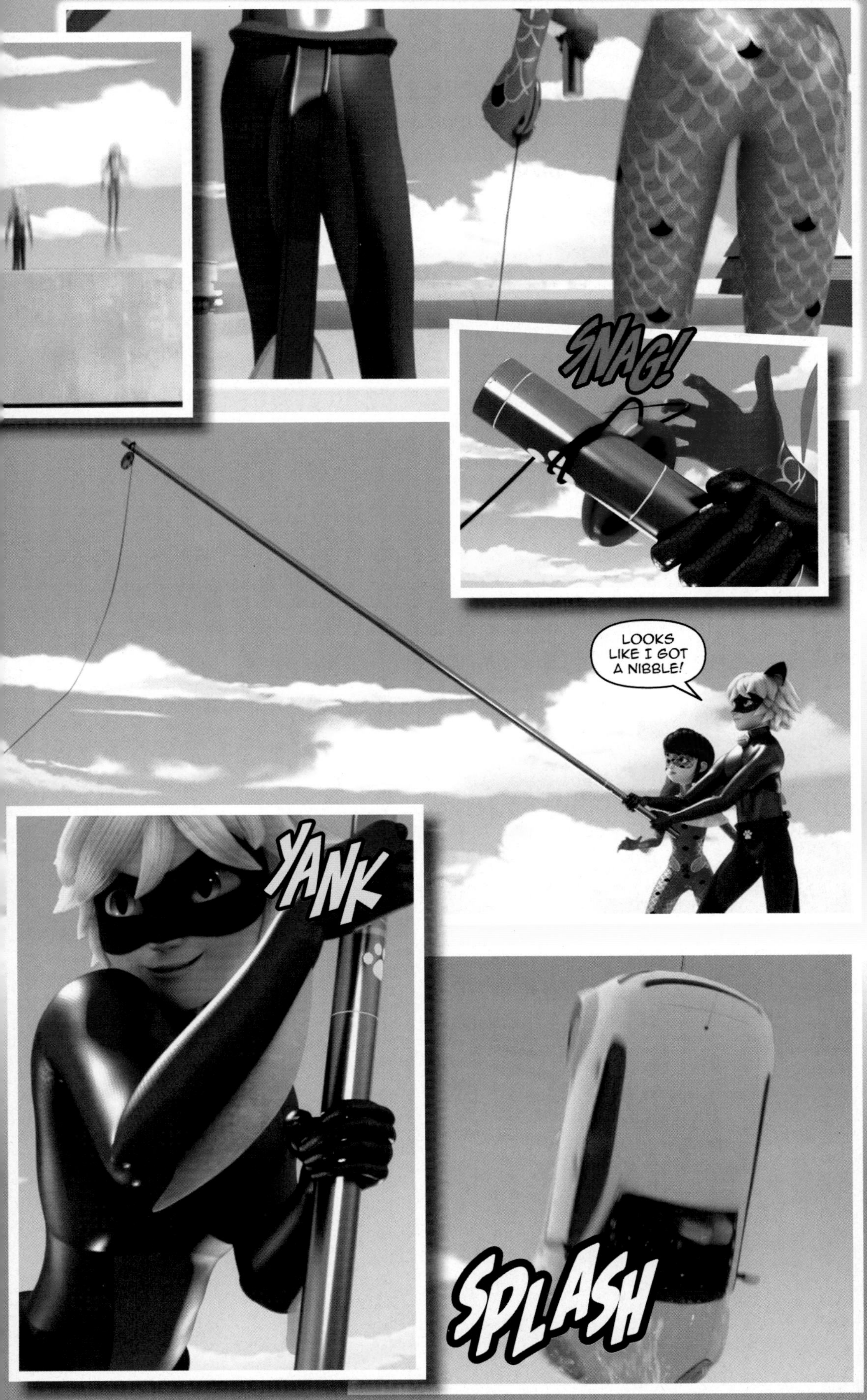
SNAG!
LOOKS LIKE I GOT A NIBBLE!
YANK
SPLASH

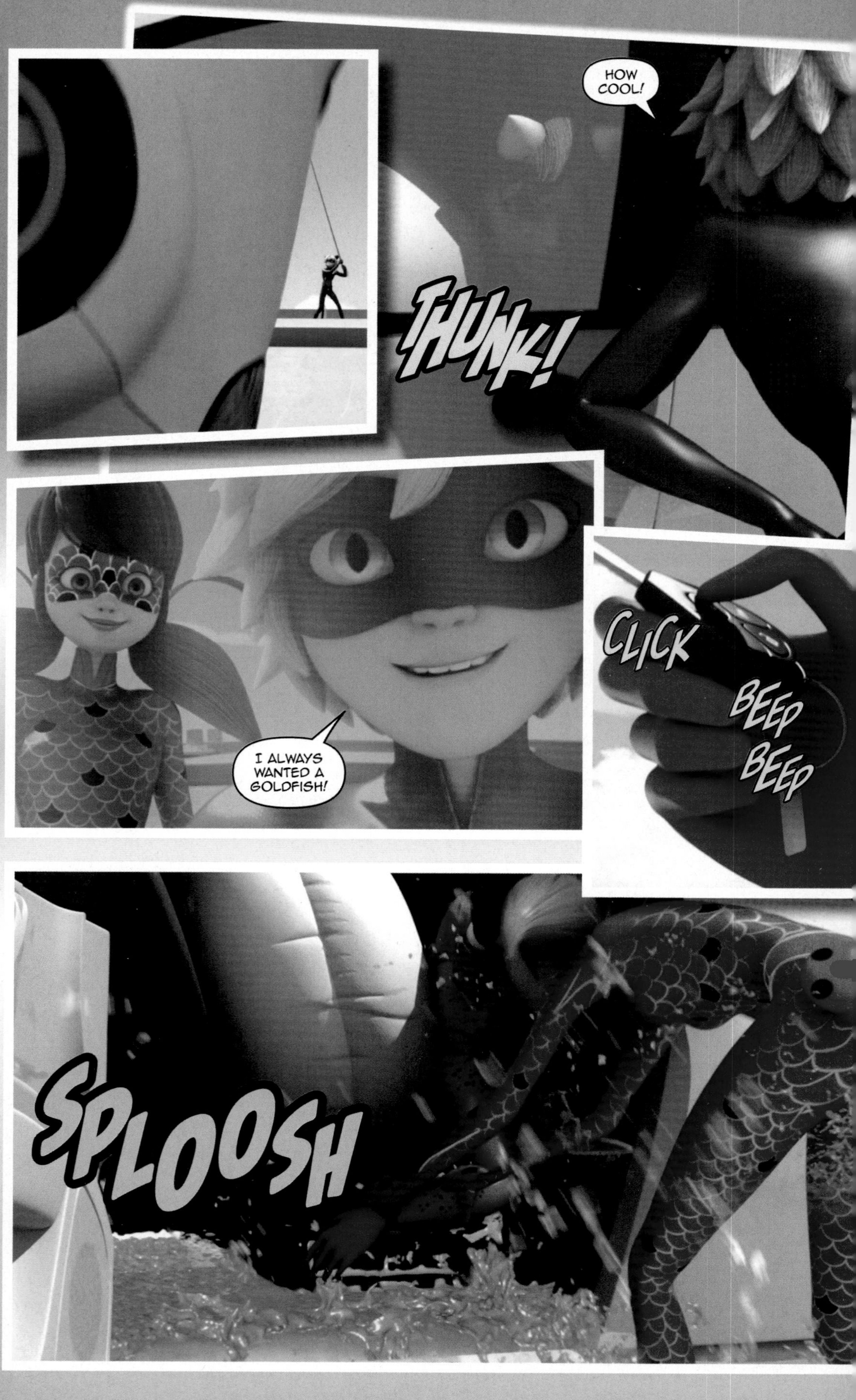
HOW COOL!
THUNK!
I ALWAYS WANTED A GOLDFISH!
CLICK
BEEP BEEP
SPLOOSH

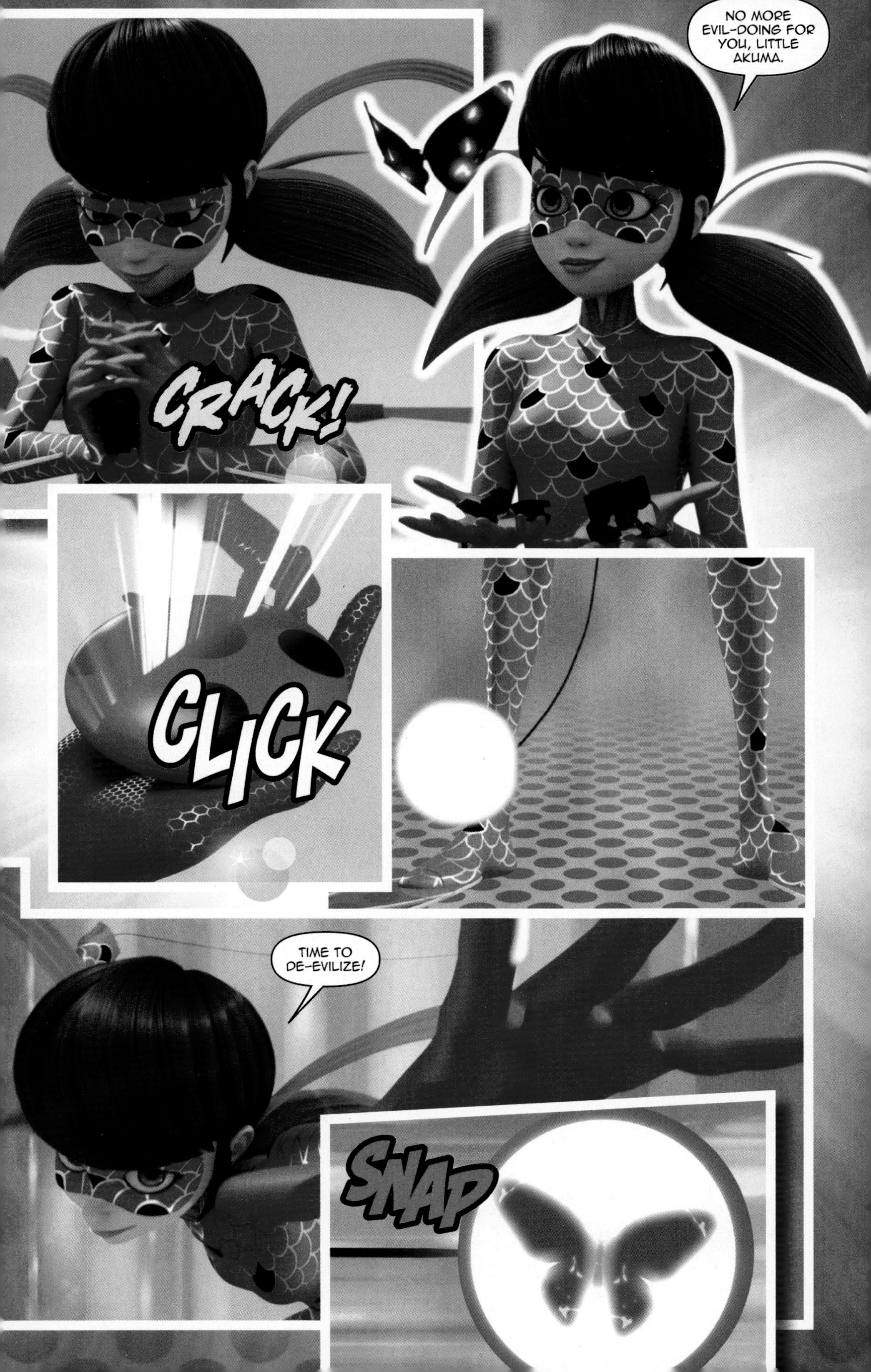

CRACK!
NO MORE EVIL-DOING FOR YOU, LITTLE AKUMA.
CLICK
TIME TO DE-EVILIZE!
SNAP

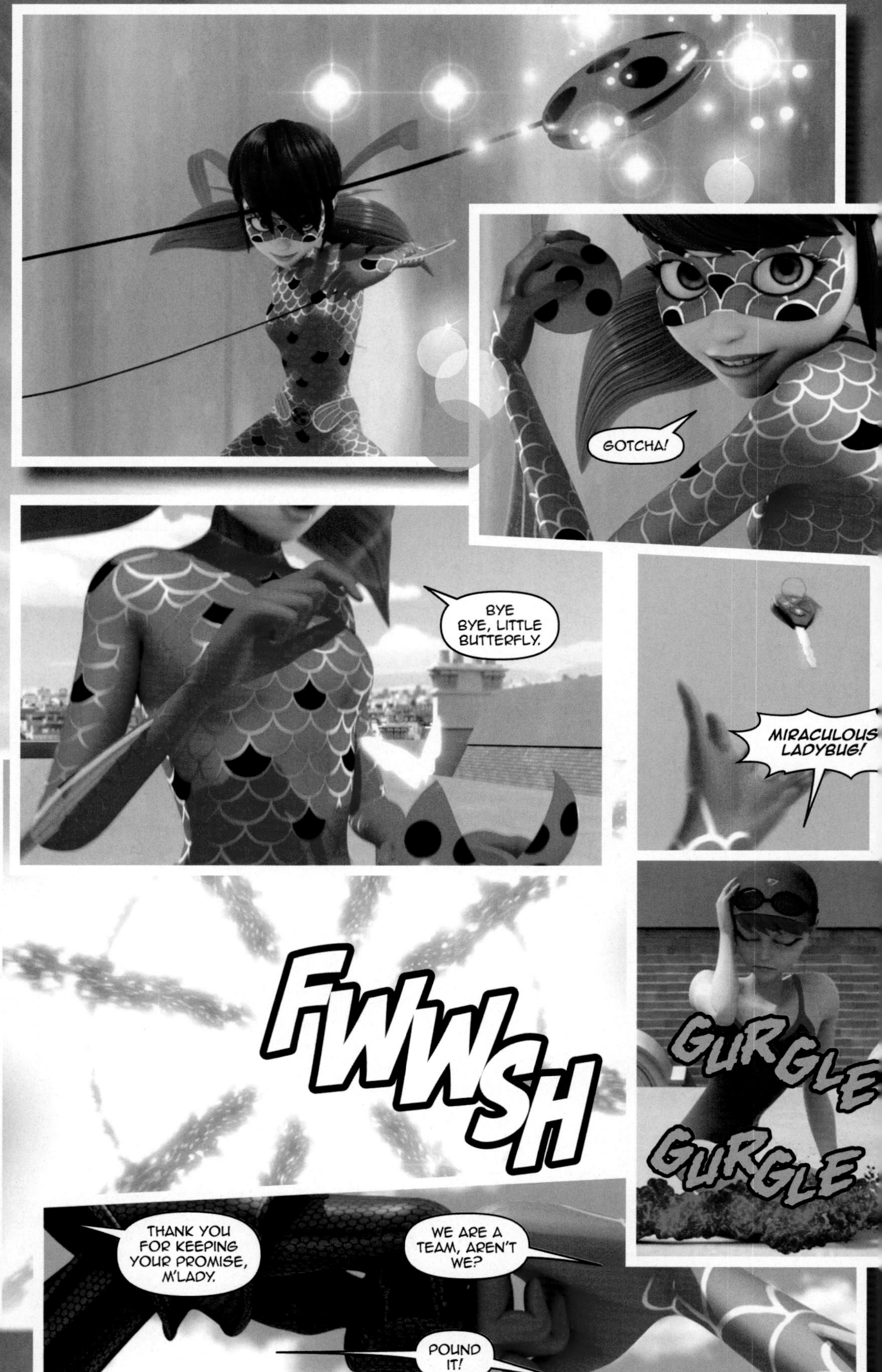
GOTCHA!
BYE BYE, LITTLE BUTTERFLY.
MIRACULOUS LADYBUG!
FWWSH
GURGLE
GURGLE
THANK YOU FOR KEEPING YOUR PROMISE, M'LADY.
WE ARE A TEAM, AREN'T WE?
POUND IT!

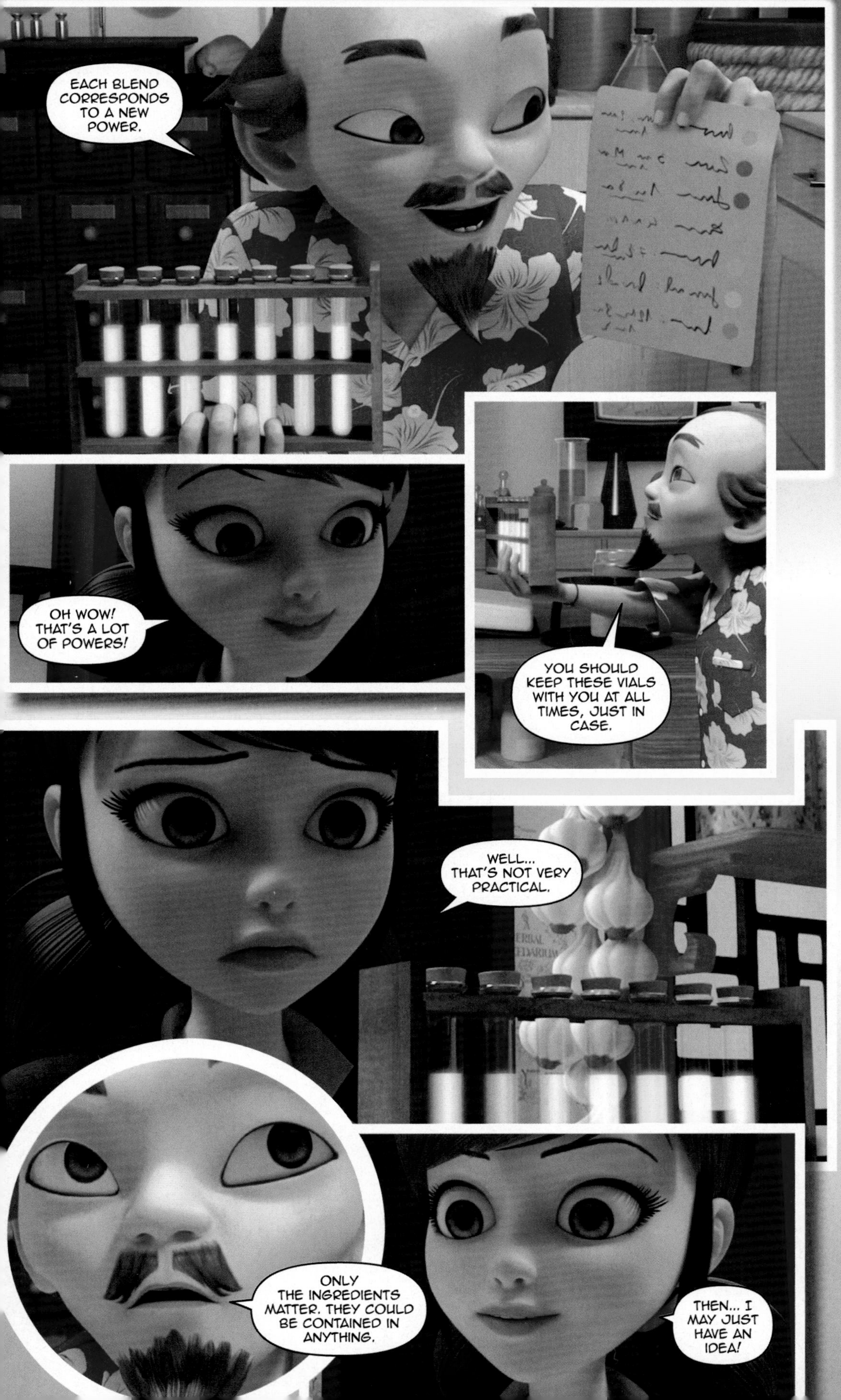
EACH BLEND CORRESPONDS TO A NEW POWER.
OH WOW! THAT'S A LOT OF POWERS!
YOU SHOULD KEEP THESE VIALS WITH YOU AT ALL TIMES, JUST IN CASE.
WELL... THAT'S NOT VERY PRACTICAL.
ONLY THE INGREDIENTS MATTER. THEY COULD BE CONTAINED IN ANYTHING.
THEN... I MAY JUST HAVE AN IDEA!

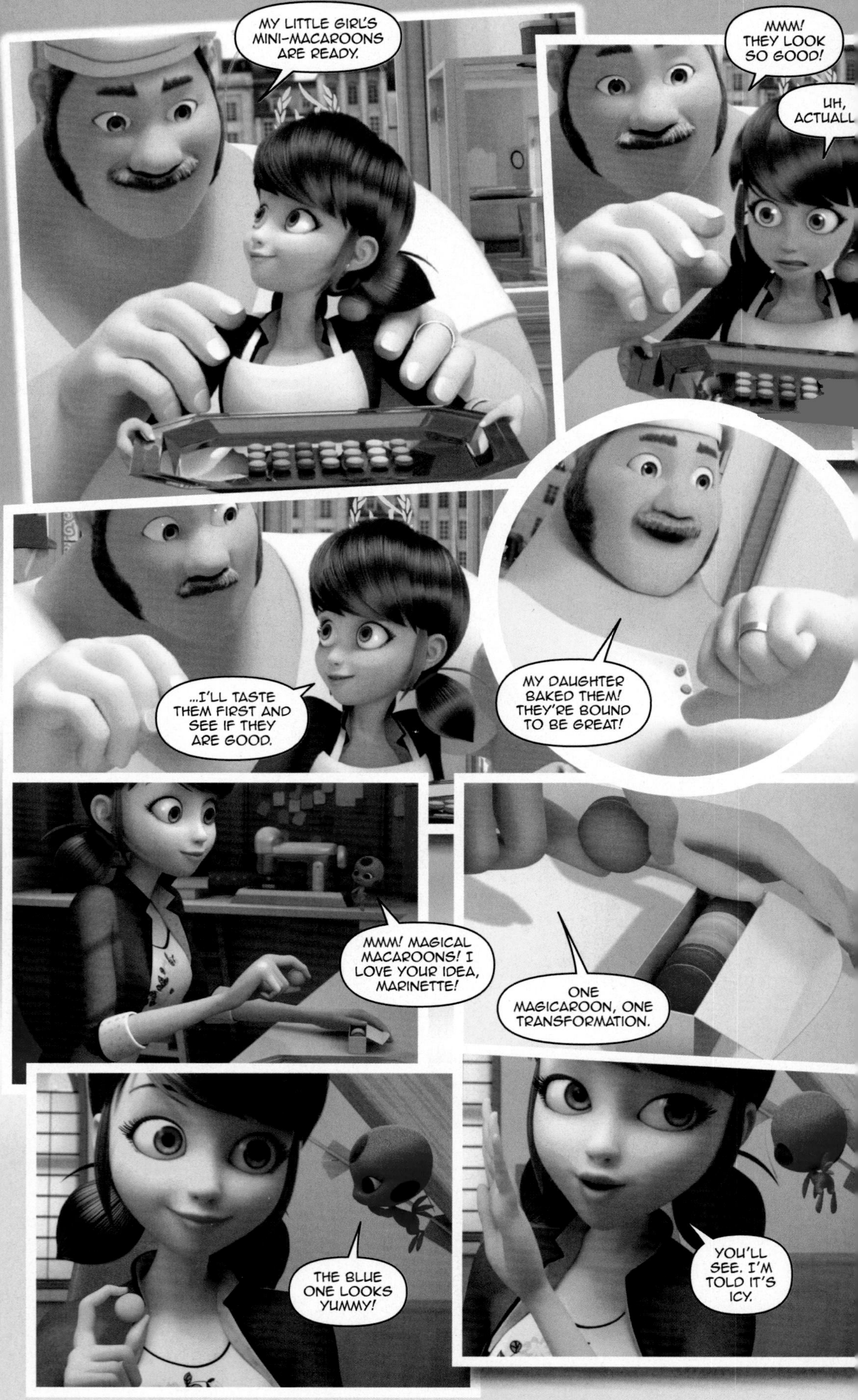
MY LITTLE GIRL'S MINI-MACAROONS ARE READY.
MMM! THEY LOOK SO GOOD!
UH, ACTUALL
...I'LL TASTE THEM FIRST AND SEE IF THEY ARE GOOD.
MY DAUGHTER BAKED THEM! THEY'RE BOUND TO BE GREAT!
MMM! MAGICAL MACAROONS! I LOVE YOUR IDEA, MARINETTE!
ONE MAGICAROON, ONE TRANSFORMATION.
THE BLUE ONE LOOKS YUMMY!
YOU'LL SEE. I'M TOLD IT'S ICY.

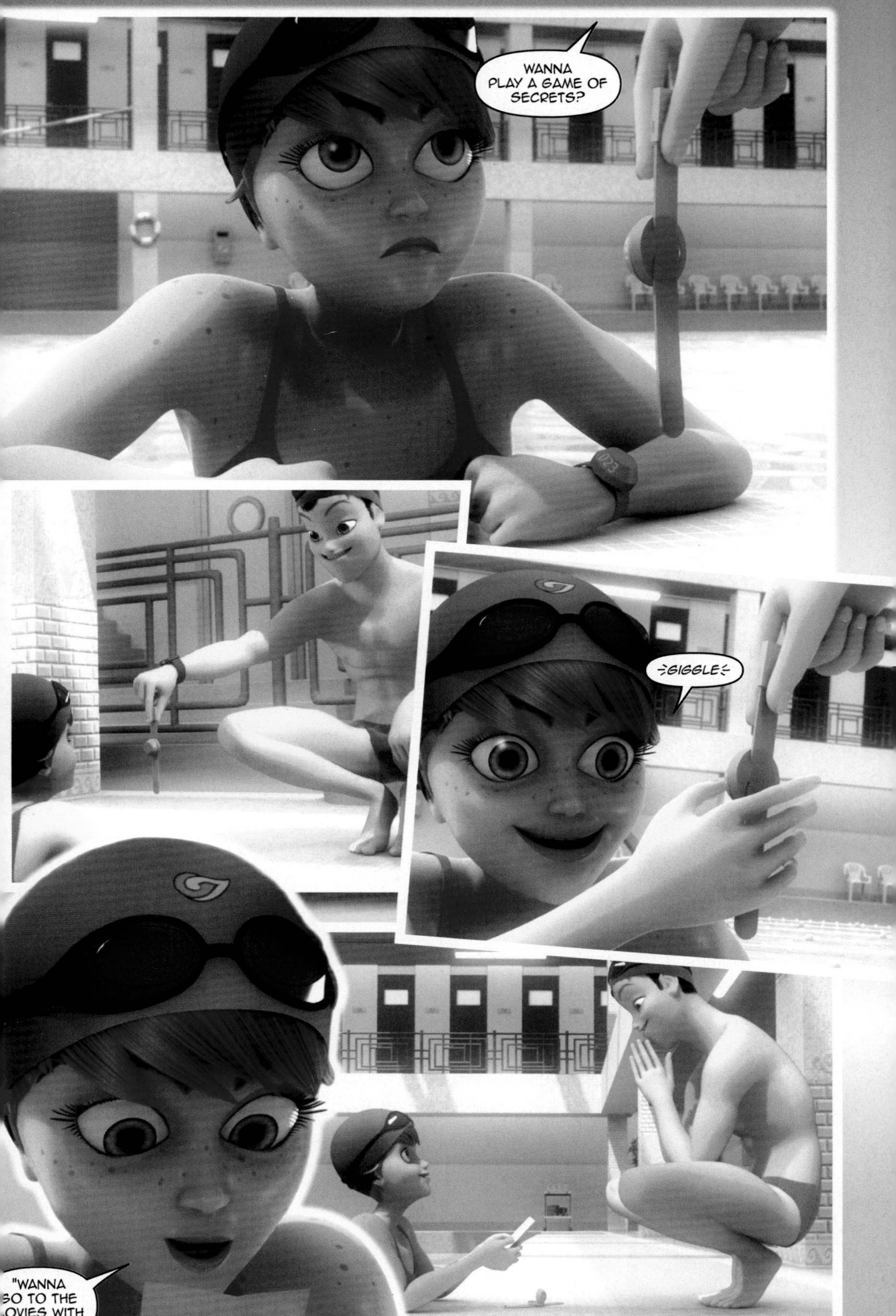
WANNA PLAY A GAME OF SECRETS?
GIGGLE
"WANNA GO TO THE MOVIES WITH ME?"

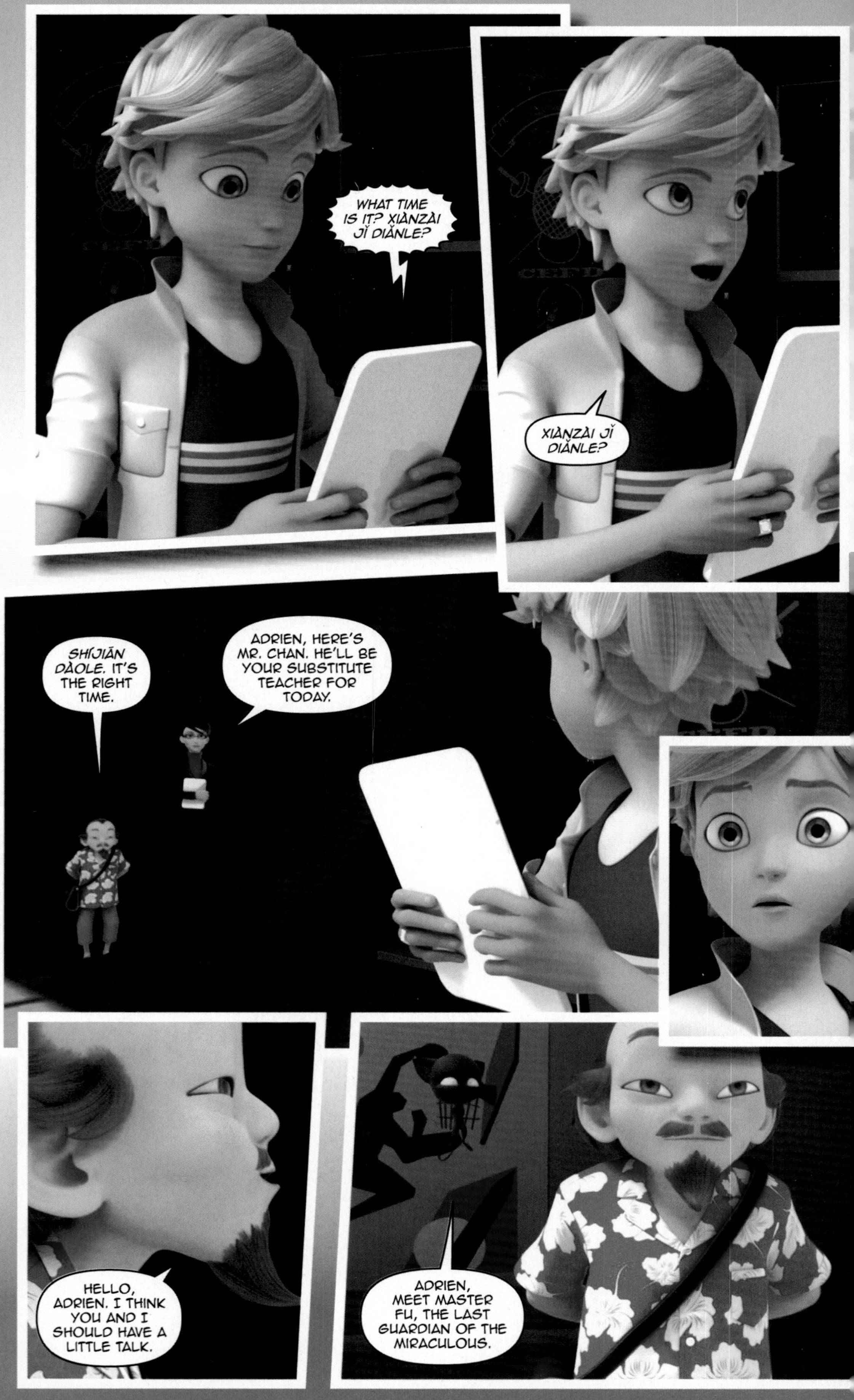
WHAT TIME IS IT? XIÀNZÀI JǏ DIǍNLE?
XIÀNZÀI JǏ DIǍNLE?
SHÍJIĀN DÀOLE. IT'S THE RIGHT TIME.
ADRIEN, HERE'S MR. CHAN. HE'LL BE YOUR SUBSTITUTE TEACHER FOR TODAY.
HELLO, ADRIEN. I THINK YOU AND I SHOULD HAVE A LITTLE TALK.
ADRIEN, MEET MASTER FU, THE LAST GUARDIAN OF THE MIRACULOUS.

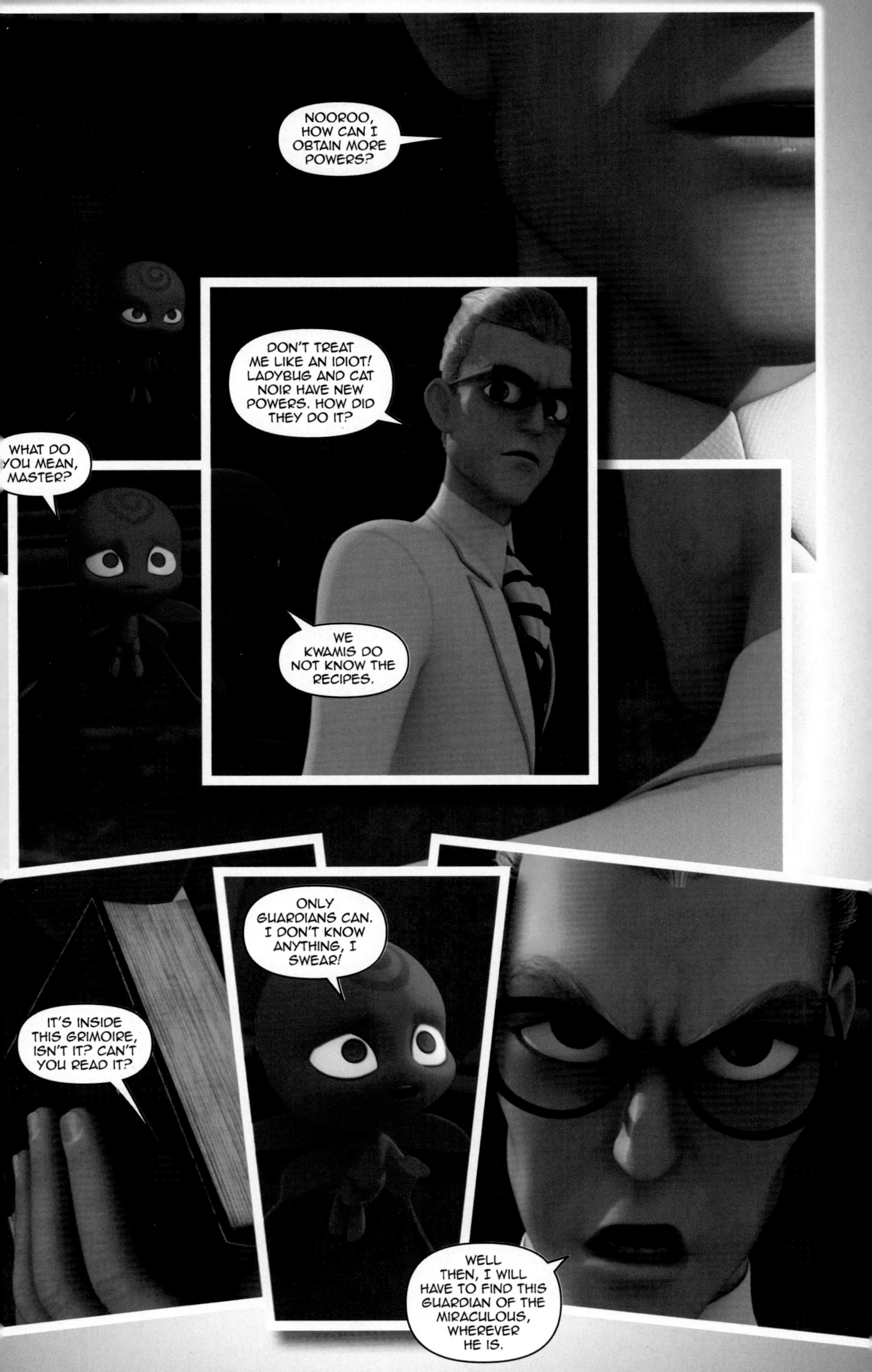
NOOROO, HOW CAN I OBTAIN MORE POWERS?
DON'T TREAT ME LIKE AN IDIOT! LADYBUG AND CAT NOIR HAVE NEW POWERS. HOW DID THEY DO IT?
WHAT DO YOU MEAN, MASTER?
WE KWAMIS DO NOT KNOW THE RECIPES.
IT'S INSIDE THIS GRIMOIRE, ISN'T IT? CAN'T YOU READ IT?
ONLY GUARDIANS CAN. I DON'T KNOW ANYTHING, I SWEAR!
WELL THEN, I WILL HAVE TO FIND THIS GUARDIAN OF THE MIRACULOUS, WHEREVER HE IS.

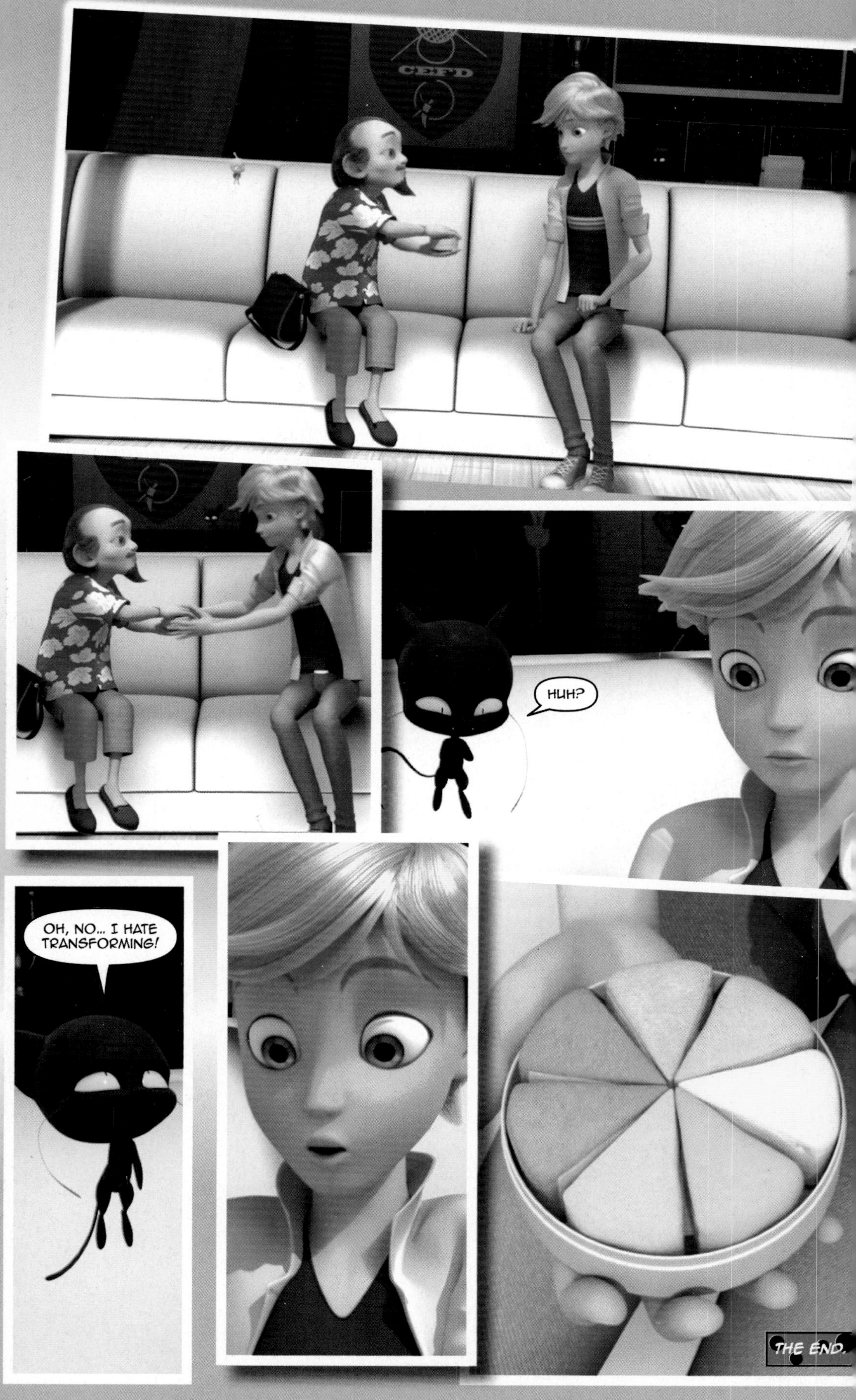
CEFD
HUH?
OH, NO... I HATE TRANSFORMING!
THE END.